Humiliated by my ov
while he quietly remaine(
my hip, where he took my trembling hand in his. He was so close, I could hear his soft breaths, feel them as they blew against my skin. It was as if he was silently asking me to look at him . . . but I couldn't.

I was scared.

"Why?" my tear-filled voice pleaded.

"I'm sorry, Olivia," he replied, misery in his words. "I promise, I'll take you home when I'm confident that the danger —"

"No . . . I mean why me? Why did you save me?"

For a long moment, silence fell over the dark room as I verbally continued to force out the pained thoughts in my head. "I know you couldn't save us both . . . but why me?"

My teary gaze turned to face him, and the vampire's presence was never more real to me than at that moment. His lips lingered just inches above my own, and his sweet, cool breath tingled across my cheek while mine drew in sharply. This was the first time I had seen him out of the shadows—and his human face was stunningly handsome.

Deep-set gray eyes stared back at me with such intensity that my heart began skipping out of its normal rhythm. They were an intricate weave of muted grays and icy silvers that seemed to dance inside his iris, which was rimmed at the edge in a deep charcoal. I felt trapped by the hypnotic color as his dark brows pulled toward each other in—disbelief? It was like he couldn't believe I had asked him the question.

Unthinkingly, I reached up to cup his cheek in my palm, just wanting to touch him. The short bristle on his unshaven cheek scratched at my hand in that good way that reminded a woman that she was touching a man, and his mood seemed to change as a smile began to spread over his lips that I swear could have lit up the darkest sky. Long dimples dug into his cheeks, and that's when it happened—a moment of déjà vu.

Those eyes. I had seen them before! I knew them—knew him.

Book's by Christine Wenrick

Book One: The Charmed
Book Two: The Charmed Souls
Book Three: The Charmed Fates

the
CHARMED

Book One of The Charmed Trilogy

CHRISTINE WENRICK

PRINT - ISBN 13: 978-0-9882069-1-5

E-BOOK - ISBN 13: 978-0-9882069-0-8

For information, please e-mail Red Tree House Publishing, Seattle, Washington
at: christinewenrick@redtreehouse-publishing.com

Cover design by Samantha T. Davis, Mill Creek, Washington
Contact e-mail: Samantha.T.Davis@gmail.com

Editorial and interior design by OPA Author Services, Scottsdale, Arizona
Contact e-mail: Info@OPAAuthorServices.com

Printed in United States of America

June of 2013

Dedication

To my favorite wannebe Dhampirs: Rachel, Felice, Susan, Toni and Becky. Thanks for supporting me, challenging me, and pushing me every step of the way. I couldn't have done this without you.

Prologue

"Ouch!" Too late! The palm of my left hand was erupting blood. I jerked it back from Sarah's tight grasp as the Swiss Army knife that had done the damage fell from her other hand to the forest floor. Sarah's eyes—which had been transfixed momentarily on the bloodletting—met mine. They were filled with the utter panic of someone who realized that at the tender age of fourteen she was going to be grounded for the rest of her life.

"I told you this was a bad idea!" she screeched before her whole expression scrunched in displeasure. "Ewe, gross. Look at all that blood."

Blood was right.

I curled my fingers tight over my palm to try and slow it, but the bright, scarlet liquid continued to seep through the cracks of my fingers and onto Sarah's as she tried to help me.

"You were supposed to cut my thumb, not my palm," I complained. "That's how a BFF blood pact works. Everybody knows that."

"Well, I'm *sorry!*" Her voice was ratcheting higher with every word. "It's not like I've done this before." She reached into her pocket and brought out one of the two little adhesive bandages we had brought with us to cover our blood-pact wounds, but we both realized that the narrow, plastic strip would do little—if anything—to stop this bleeding. Worse yet, the empty campsite clearing in which we were standing offered even fewer options in terms of first aid, and we had only ourselves to blame.

We had hiked up here this morning so we wouldn't be seen, especially by my way over-protective parents. They would absolutely freak out if they saw all this blood, which, at the moment, had me a little freaked myself. And the more the fresh air hit the wound, the more the pain of the rather deep cut began to burn like fire over my skin. "I'm going to clean my hand in the water," I called back over my shoulder as I turned to rush off toward the nearby lake, but after I had gone only about twenty feet some sort of shiny reflection in the tall grass ahead caught my attention.

As I stepped closer I figured it was the sun reflecting off something shiny—like glass or metal. A few more steps and the source became clear—a man's silver watch. The dial cover was cracked—and the watch was wrapped around a plump wrist . . . the wrist of a very dead man's body.

I choked back a scream, managing only to sputter bits of sound as my mind pleaded for my eyes to close, but I just couldn't blink away from the awful sight. I had never seen a dead body before. The man's large, beefy frame seemed unnaturally twisted—maybe even posed—and his brown eyes were frozen in terror. Horse flies clustered around his open mouth. His skin was very white, almost chalky, the exposed area above his collar covered with bluish bruising. And the showy gold rings and three-piece gray suit were definitely all wrong for a man camping in the woods.

"I thought you were going to wash your hand," Sarah said just behind me, but I couldn't speak, couldn't utter a single word of warning in reply.

Then it was too late.

Sarah's ear-piercing scream cut through the forest with the intensity of a hungry newborn, her hard gasps scraping against the back of her throat as she stumbled away from the body. In sharp contrast, I felt chained to that very spot. It was as though my legs were tied to cement blocks, too heavy to let me take even one step back.

Soon, time became lost to me until I heard a voice call out something in the distance. It was the deep voice of a man, not a boy, and as he spoke to Sarah his words were focused and calm.

"Stay right here," he said to her, then I heard his footsteps coming toward me.

Moments later, a long shadow rolled over the corpse in front of me, followed by large shoulders suddenly blocking the hot sun. He knelt before me and I realized how truly tall he was, because my chin was barely tilted downward, but I was staring right into his eyes, though mine were unfocused and blurred.

"I'm not going to hurt you, Olivia," he said gently, and it struck me in my dazed state that Sarah must have told him my name. "I just want to have a look at your hand."

My hand? I had forgotten all about it. The pain wasn't there like before, but I could still feel the warm blood rolling down my palm and trickling to the grass below. When I didn't respond, his much larger hand encircled the uninjured one at my side and squeezed, increasing the pressure steadily until I could no longer ignore it. My mind felt it, and I blinked back hard as my eyes re-adjusted to see clearly for the first time in a long while.

"There you go," he murmured. "Now you're with me."

Just that fast, I went from being focused on nothing to becoming acutely aware of his eyes, a color of gray I had seen before in this world but given little notice to it. On him, however, the color was wondrously unique. A little voice inside my head urged me to explore the other details of his face, but I was locked into the gray, as if it were some sort of vital lifeline at that moment.

"Let's take a look," he said, tilting my palm up towards the sun, and it was strange how I could no longer feel any warmth from it. "This is fairly deep. But if we can slow the bleeding and get you back to your parents and to a doctor, I think you're gonna be OK."

Pulling his shirt tail out of his waistband, he tore a strip of cotton fabric from it and tightly wrapped my palm, applying sharp pressure that sent a shooting wave of pain through the cut and had me yelping twice in one afternoon.

"I'm sorry," he said, now gently easing my hand back towards him. "Sometimes I forget my own strength."

How ridiculous I must have looked, blinking back at him in such wide-eyed amazement. But for the first time in my life I understood what all the fuss was about when it came to a man, and it hit with the subtlety of Timmy Fredricks whacking me in the face with the soccer ball in fourth grade.

"You're a quiet one, aren't you?"

I didn't answer, because every reply that came into my head only made me sound like a dork.

When he squeezed my hand a second time, he paused and a strange expression crossed his face—as if he were trying to understand something. It was gone just as quickly as he said, "Come. Let's get you back."

Sarah, seemingly recovered from the terrifying episode, blathered on endlessly, while I remained at a loss for words as he walked us back to camp. Later, I would live to regret my silence. I couldn't have known it then, but death would touch my life for a second time that day. The lifeless body of the kind man who had helped us was found that night by park rangers in the tall grass . . . near the man in the three-piece suit.

Chapter One

Among the many meaningless decisions we humans make every day, fate likes to step in and wickedly remind us that a single, harmless choice can completely alter the direction of our lives. For me, a train ride to Portland seemed one of those small, insignificant choices.

***

Thump-thump! Thump-thump! Thump-thump!
The thunderous sound stormed into my , launching me out of my floaty little dream world and into this one. With the blare of a horn and the rhythmic clicks of steel rolling over rails, it took me less than a moment to remember that I was on a train—the 5:45 express to Portland, to be exact.

Tonight's trip, however, should have been called the *midnight* line to Portland, because the train had been delayed for hours on the southbound leg from Vancouver, British Columbia; it was nearly three hours behind schedule when it finally left the King Street Station platform just south of downtown Seattle.

Of course, no one offered any kind of sensible explanation for what was wrong or why it had been delayed. They just smiled in that polite way people do—when they're trying to conceal the fact that you're annoying them—and pointed to the station's reader board, which said 'DELAYED' in giant, red capital letters.

That wasn't very helpful, but at least it might explain the unease I had been feeling about this trip.

I had felt it all night, and now there was this strange pressure over my heart, as though someone was holding it in their hands and threatening to squeeze it until the very last beat had been crushed out of it. This had happened a few times over the last couple of weeks, and seemed to be getting stronger, which was slightly terrifying. I knew something was wrong, but it seemed illogical for an active, twenty-six-year-old grad student to keel over and die without any warning, so I convinced myself it was just over-exertion.

Yep, that was it.

"You're awake," my best friend, Sarah Terry, commented from beside me. She was the girl with two generic first names, yet she embodied enough fire and sass to make her icon—and self-proclaimed 'sista' in another life—Tyra Banks, proud. "I was beginning to think you were dead."

I blinked at her in surprise, even though nothing she said should surprise me anymore. Sarah Terry was never boring, and most men saw her as a ball-breaker, which she didn't mind one bit. Tough was just how she rolled. "Nice."

"Hey, I'm just sayin'." She glanced down at the folder and several roughly scribbled pages of sheet music that had scattered at my feet as I was jolted awake. She bent to retrieve them, shaking her head as she piled them on my lap. "I swear, Olivia Ann Greyson, when you're sleepin' it takes trumpets to wake you."

Or really loud thumping noises. "I thought I heard something."

"Heard what?"

"I don't know—a loud pounding sound of some sort."

"Are you sure you're just not hearing noises in your head?" she replied with a snort, reaching into her carry-on pack for her music player.

"Very funny. You didn't hear it?"

Casting a sarcastic facial expression in my direction, she scanned the rows of passengers around us, most of whom had been at the Mariners' baseball game hours earlier and were experiencing the misfortune of sobering up during the long delay. They appeared perfectly busy doing nothing, so she turned back to me, her eyebrows arched in a quirky way. "Yeah, and it looks like I'm not the only one. Girl, you're trippin'—I told you, you should've grabbed a sandwich there at the station."

"I wasn't hungry."

"So you said. But obviously your brain is screaming with

hunger now."

"You're implying," I began dully, "that a loud, thumping noise is just my brain's way of telling me that I'm hungry?"

She shrugged her shoulders. "I'm sayin' that if there had been such a loud noise, then at least one other passenger would have heard it." She was right, of course, though I hated to admit it. The noise had disappeared, and for a moment I was even questioning myself whether I had maybe just dreamed it.

Sarah's gaze slid over to me as her hands worked to untangle her iPod cords. She had always had beautiful hands; long, with slender fingers always neatly polished. Today's choice was a lilac color that worked surprisingly well with her darker skin. "You aren't havin' that strange pulling in your chest thing again, are you?"

"I'm fine," I replied, with more irritation than I should have. "Just a little tired, that's all."

"Hmm," Sarah sounded. "Maybe if you'd stop refusing to see the doctor . . ."

"Don't start, Sarah."

"Whatever," she said, flashing a partially amused smile as she slipped her earbuds in and snuggled deeper into her seat. "Get some rest. You're drivin' once we get to Portland."

"Oh, thanks."

Sarah's breathing soon slowed, and she was asleep.

I lay my head back and closed my eyes, even though sleeping was the last thing on my mind. I couldn't really explain why. I was tired. Classes were ending next week for summer break, and though Sarah was nearly two years younger than me, she was graduating, while I had to go back for another quarter to complete my double master's degree.

Thump! Thump! Thump!

My eyes popped right back open and I swung forward in my seat. There it was again—only this time it was louder! It seemed impossible to me that no one else had heard it. I turned to Sarah, who was still sleeping peacefully with her player going, as if she hadn't heard a thing. Maybe the music concealed the noise.

Then, again, more unsettling noises hammered, clear as day, right above us, its echoed reverberations sounding like someone running across a brittle surface.

My fingers curled around the edges of the chair arms in an effort to stop myself from reaching over and shaking Sarah awake. Instead, I surveyed the faces of the other passengers, but, like Sarah, they were going about their business as if they hadn't heard a thing.

Bang! Bang! Bang!

Several even louder strikes pounded against the car's ceiling, right above us. Hearing them so close had my heart beating at a pace I didn't think was possible.

"Did you hear that?" I asked the man sitting across the aisle from us.

Pulled up short in his reading by the loudness of my voice, his brows creased in annoyance. "Hear what?"

"That banging sound coming from the roof."

The man's expression turned into a dismissive frown. "No, I didn't hear banging on the roof of a moving train." His tone was thick with sarcasm. "You were just asleep. I think you might still be waking up."

He was obviously trying to offer a reasonable explanation, even though I knew I had been awake for a while. I did rub the tiredness from my eyes behind my small, wire-framed glasses, and just when I started to convince myself that he might be right, the sounds thundered away again.

Thump! Thump! Thump! Bang! Bang! Bang!

It was plain as day. Why didn't these people hear it?

An older woman with platinum-blond hair pinned in a high up-do peeked at me over her chair back. She had obviously heard my conversation with the other passenger and needed to get a good look at the woman in the seat behind her, the one who sounded crazy.

Bang! Thump! Thump!

"There," I said, pointing my finger towards the ceiling. "Can't you hear that?"

She continued to stare at me for a moment as if I were daft, then turned to her male companion in whispered panic. "Honey?"

"Calm down," he replied reassuringly. "There's nothing on the roof of this train."

"She must be crazy. We're sitting next to a crazy person on a train," she continued, whispering low—but still easy to hear.

I took offense. I had clearly heard the noises and had never been one inclined to create unnecessary drama. In fact, as a general rule, I always tried to avoid it, preferring not to be the center of attention. But I didn't remember that when I replied in a high-pitched squeak, "I'm not crazy!" Which waked a dazed Sarah out of sound sleep.

"What's goin' on?" she asked in a groggy voice.

The woman turned to her with a disapproving glower. "Your friend here thinks she hears something on the roof of this train. She's getting everyone all worked up."

Actually, it appeared I was only getting *her* worked up.

Sarah squeezed my shoulder with gentle concern. "What is it, Livy?" A true friend, she never doubted for a second that I was telling the truth . . . or at least what I believed was the truth. "Tell me."

All of a sudden I realized that everyone's attention was focused on me. The older attendant, who had taken my ticket when I boarded the train, scurried down the aisle to see what all the commotion was about. "Is everything OK here?"

The agitated woman didn't even hesitate for a breath before declaring, "This girl thinks she's hearing noises on the roof."

"Is there someone on top of the train?" another voice rang out in alarm.

"What?" another voice added.

All right, so maybe I *was* getting people a little worked up.

The attendant raised his arms over his head in an effort to calm things down before they got out of control. "I assure you," he began, "there's no one on the roof of this train. We're outside of Tacoma and traveling at nearly eighty miles per hour."

How had this happened? How had I become the crazy woman hearing noises on the train while Sarah and a whole car full of passengers stared at me? Sensing the frantic whispers rolling through the car, I just wanted all this embarrassing attention to stop. "I'm fine!" I blurted. "I didn't hear anything. I must've been asleep."

With that admission and one last scolding glare from the attendant that said 'no more trouble,' things began to settle down. The onlookers went back about their business, and for that I was grateful. Sarah, however, still looked unconvinced. She had known me practically all my life and knew it was not like me to hear things that weren't there. "What's going on, Livy?"

"I don't know." I whispered so the other passengers wouldn't hear. "It just feels like something's wrong. I've felt it since we left the train station. I can't explain it."

She reached for my hand and squeezed. "I believe you," she said, with absolutely no hesitation in her voice. "But we can't make them stop the train, so just try to relax, OK? We'll deal with it when we get into Portland. I think I should take you to see a doctor in the mornin.'"

I started to object, but she covered my mouth with her hand. "And I don't want to hear any more of your excuses about how you never go to the doctor. You're going to this one."

Frustrated, I dropped my head back against the seat. I knew what I had heard, and I knew it was not my imagination. Staring quietly out the window at the trees racing by under the moonlight, I noticed a flicker of something moving at the edge of my vision. Just before the train was about to arc around a wide bend, about a hundred yards ahead, shadowy objects moved at inhuman speed back and forth across the tracks.

Coyotes or something? But they were too large.

I watched as several shadows gathered in one area just below the next signal light, and a wave of panic flooded me as the sound of another train's horns blared in the distance ahead.

A bright light was barreling towards us.

I knew then what was about to happen.

In those few seconds just before this already rough ride was about to explode, time—instead of ticking forward—seemed almost to float. All my senses heightened as the sounds that previously filled the train vanished.

I turned to Sarah and her now-terrified expression confirmed my fear—that I was incapable of hiding what was about to happen. The blood seemed to freeze in my veins as I threw my arms around her, shielding us both for impact.

In that moment, I didn't remember ever having lived in the world around me with such clarity, such lucidness.

Then the moment was gone.
And the pain hit.

Chapter Two

As I returned to consciousness, my head was pounding and it seemed impossible to open my eyes. I let out a small moan against the pains I was feeling in several places along my body. After a moment, I remembered the crash, but I had no idea how much time had passed. There was a mix of sounds around me, but I didn't seem to hear human screams of suffering, as I expected, just other vivid, terrible sounds, like the screeching of metal before it's about to give-way under a heavy weight, or the high-pitched ping of glass shards crashing against a brittle surface. And even the low, whipping sound heat makes as a flame grows more intense. These were the sounds seared into my mind.

I wished that all of these sounds *would* disappear. But when it became clear that my wish would go unanswered, I finally opened my eyes.

The world around me seemed upside down and out of focus, then I realized—it literally was. The train car had been flipped onto its side, and I was staring upward at the seat I had been in, but the scene was distorted by my cracked and crooked glasses, which were now dangling at the tip of my nose. Smoke permeated the car as flames coming from somewhere nearby billowed up toward the oxygen provided by the shattered windows on the other side of the car. Aside from the hot glow of the fire and a few emergency lights at each end of the car, everything was as dark as the night surrounding us.

Carefully sliding my fingertips over the surfaces beneath me, I realized I was sprawled across two chair arms that were still bolted to the floor. My feet were apparently resting against an unbroken window or one of the pillars between windows. I tried to move just a fraction of an inch, but a white-hot pain shot through my left side like a bullet. With a groan I couldn't contain, I slid my fingers between the summer cardigan and white tee shirt I was wearing. Just below my left breast I could feel the distorted shape and the dull pain of a cracked rib.

"We've got to get out of here," I thought.

"We?" I blinked. "Oh, God—Sarah!"

"Sarah!"

No answer. In fact, the entire car was too quiet, as if I were the only person on it, which I confirmed was definitely not the case as my eyes adjusted to the darkness and I saw all the unmoving bodies around me. Then a small window opened through the smoke, and I recognized the familiar beige top and razor-cut brown hair several rows ahead of me. Panic seemed to set in as I made out the crimson stain seeping through her white pant leg—then my adrenaline began to flow.

"Sarah!" I scrambled over the seat arms, snagging my leggings on several sharp edges as I went, able to ignore the throbbing in my ribs as I imagined the physical force it must have taken to throw Sarah's body nearly the length of the car.

When I reached her, I turned her a bit and put my ear to her heart.

Thank God, it was still beating.

Then I noticed the unnatural direction of her leg and swallowed thickly. There was no question. The leg was broken. It was just a matter of how many times.

I scanned her quickly for any other obvious signs of injury, then took her face in my hands and patted her cheek, absolutely terrified she wouldn't wake up. "Sarah, can you hear me? Sarah!"

A low groan rumbled from her lips as her eyes fluttered open. "Livy, what . . . ?" she began, but then the signs of agony hit her face and she reached for her leg. "Oh, shit, that hurts!"

"I know, I know . . . But I need to get you out of here." I glanced back at the fire that was now steadily moving towards us. "Now."

"I don't think I can walk," she said with a shake of her head. "You'll have to leave me to go get help."

"No way," I replied sternly, and it surprised me that I was the one taking charge between the two of us. That was normally her role. "This car's going to be nothing but fire and smoke in about five minutes. You're coming with me."

Giving her no time to debate the situation, I shifted her body over mine, finding unexpected strength in my muscles even though her weight and my own breaths felt like a meat presser against my ribs. It had to be the adrenaline that kept me going, but as soon as she felt the movement she screeched out in pain just before falling unconscious again.

That would make things more difficult in getting her out of the car, but at least I wouldn't have to bear her cry every time I was hurting her.

The exit vestibule was just ahead of us as smoke and flames continued to billow forward. I bit back screams at seeing so many lifeless bodies crumpled along the way, their eyes wide in shock as if they died at the moment of impact.

"Help us!" I called through the open doorway above me. There was no response, but I soon heard the frantic cries of the other passengers who had made it out of the cars, and it caused an irrational moment of frustration. "What're they screaming about? At least they're out of the damn train!"

My limbs were trembling from either fear or weakness, I couldn't be sure which, and I doubted that I had the strength to lift us both through the opening several feet above me. But there was little choice, the fire was rolling at us more like a wave than a wandering flame, the heat so close that my skin itched.

We were out of time.

Swinging my arms up to the handrails, I held Sarah's body to mine by curling my legs around her. My left side shook violently against the pain, and it was almost impossible to breathe, but hand over hand I climbed, using the first stair riser to support our weight, while the flames reached for Sarah's feet.

"Here—grab hold of this," a man ordered from above me. I glanced up and was never so glad to see someone, even though his face was covered in blood from a deep gash to his forehead. He lowered a piece of metal debris through the threshold. It was hot, but not so hot that you couldn't hold onto it—if the alternative was burning to death.

"My friend," I pleaded. "I need help to get her out."

"Hold my legs," he instructed to someone out of view.

Reaching down through the opening, he grabbed onto Sarah. It took all the strength I had to slide her up my body until he was able to lift her out of the car. I then swung my arms to the bar a second time and pulled my legs up toward my bottom to escape the flames that were attempting to melt the rubber soles of my tennis shoes.

My arms began to shake and I could no longer get my muscles to cooperate. "Please," I begged, realizing what an awful way this would be to die.

"Here! Quickly," the man said as he extended a hand through the opening.

As flames literally licked at my heels, the injured man somehow found enough strength to pull me up through the opening and into the crisp night air. At that moment I was so grateful to be alive that words seemed to be stuck in my throat behind a very real need to cry—or laugh—or both.

The man who pulled me free handed me down to another in a Mariners baseball cap. The scent of beer was still on his breath as he moved me away from the wreckage toward Sarah's unconscious body lying in the grass ahead. As he sat me down the contact jarred my left side, renewing the intense pain I felt when trying to hold on to the railing.

"Are you injured?" he asked.

Mostly coughing my reply, I blinked up at him, "I can wait." God, it hurt to cough. "Thank you for helping us."

He nodded, and I had my first chance to scan the destruction around us. The train had crashed in a rural area near the edges of farmland, a ways from the Interstate 5. Train cars were tossed around like match sticks, and the sky was lit up with powerfully toxic flames, black smoke, and the horrid scent of burning flesh swirling from every car. There was a sickening atmosphere of destruction and death for as far as the eye could see . . . but there were no more screams.

The few survivors there were managed to take refuge under a large cluster of pine trees about a hundred yards away, but there was almost no one at the end cars with us, which was odd considering the front cars appeared as if they had pancaked into the side of a mountain. "Where is everyone?" I asked. " . . . the passengers? I heard them screaming just before your friend pulled me from the car."

The man turned his attention, as if just then realizing the chaotic cries and screams that had been there only moments ago had suddenly stopped. "I don't know. Most of them must be still trapped inside the cars."

Looking back to the car we were just pulled from, it was completely engulfed in flames, and I swallowed hard. "All those people . . ."

"Livy?" Sarah murmured, weakly.

"Here," the man said, offering a small water bottle from his pocket. "Stay here with your friend. The rescue teams should be here soon."

Then he bravely ran back towards the burning cars.

I turned my attention to Sarah, instructing her to take a small sip of water. "Thank you," she whispered, taking my hand in hers as those big brown eyes of hers stared up at me; close to tears she almost never shed. "I wouldn't have made it if—"

"Don't say it," I interjected, not wanting to think about what could have happened. "It doesn't matter now. We're both gonna be fine. How's your leg?"

She groaned. "It feels like it was run over by a fuckin' car."

"That's probably not too far from the truth. Just hang in there. The ambulances should be here soon."

She nodded, but her attention was drawn over my shoulder. "What's goin' on?"

I followed her gaze toward the trees where the passengers had been clustered, but there was something in all the chaos that I had missed before, something my mind wasn't quite able to process. Shadowy figures, like the ones I saw just before the train crashed, seemed to be almost freefalling from high in the trees, crashing down on the survivors, who now seemed to be trying to escape. It appeared that the shadowy figures were attacking them, choking them at their throats.

"What . . . What's happenin'?" Sarah murmured as we sat there motionless, watching bodies being tossed back into the flames of the wreckage as if they were sticks. I then felt her hand patting against my arm several times before finally slapping at it hard. "We have to get out of here—now. *Now, Olivia!*"

There was zero argument from me.

Pushing onto my feet, I spotted a more concealed area of trees and then pulled Sarah up onto her one good leg. If we could get there we could lie low until help arrived. The pain in Sarah's first few steps looked unbearable, but there was no time to console her because we didn't get more than three steps when the air was suddenly blown from my lungs and the next thing I knew I was face down on the ground.

"Owww! What the . . . ?" I turned at Sarah's terrified scream, just in time to see a gaunt male figure looming over her, his bony face pale, his skin matte—like ash—with scraggly, black hair falling several inches below his shoulders. Just looking at him made me physically ill, but then his facial features began to change and my disgust turned to terror.

An already lanky forehead seemed to bulge above his brows as his dark eyes transformed into the most unnatural shade of blue I had ever seen, an icy blue, so pale that was barely distinguishable from the white surrounding them. Long, razor-sharp fangs grew from his incisors, and I couldn't get the heartbeat to quiet in my ears, but the word was loud on my tongue. "Vampire."

This couldn't be happening. Vampires didn't exist. Blinking hard several times, I expected the scene to change, but it didn't.

This has to be a dream. This has to be a dream. This has to be a dream.

Chapter Three

The ugly monster leaned toward Sarah and emitted a terrifying roar that stunned her and me into recognizing the awful, ripe anger in his veins. Seeing that horrified look on her face snapped me out of my own daze. Somehow I found the strength to launch back to my feet, and I challenged him with an unblinking stare (which was by far the stupidest thing I had ever done). That was all it took. Glassy, enraged, ice-colored eyes glared back at me as his thin brows slashed into a harsh line. "Pretty thing," he rasped thickly. "Where do you think you're going?"

Before I could begin to respond he was on me, slamming my spine against the ground, where my side collapsed in agony. Oh, God, it hurt. It really, really hurt.

"Olivia!" Sarah screamed from somewhere behind me.

Why the hell was she not trying to get away, already? My attacker whipped me onto my stomach like a rag doll, then his rough arms snared me around my waist, hauling me to my knees before I had a chance to blink. I knew I had to fight, but I couldn't get past the pain attacking my ribs as he pinned my arms at my sides and then yanked my hair back. His ice-cold breath was right there on my neck, and I was certain his needle-like fangs were about to sink in at any moment. So, I closed my eyes against the pain and braced myself for what I was certain would come next.

. . . And then I braced some more.

Nothing happened, and instead I waited, assaulted only by the absolutely putrid stench of his breath—a stomach-churning mix of rotten eggs, garbage, and charred flesh. The vampire shoved my head forward, his cold thumb pushing my hair aside and rubbing across the base of my skull. He seemed positively infatuated with a small, dime-sized spot, and it was positively creepy. Fear was climbing like a ball to the back of my throat as I tried to fight him with the only thing I had at the moment—anger. "Get off of me, you mangy—"

"Now, now, pretty thing," he taunted, his arm tightening with just the right amount of pressure over exactly the wrong spot on my ribs. Whatever words I had intended to speak were cut off with my own gasping breath. He was hurting me. He knew he was hurting me, but it seemed like some kind of game to him. Why didn't he just kill me and get it over with? It was obvious that he could snap me in half like a twig.

The vampire drew a slow deep breath. "Aaahhh, yes . . . there you are. We've been looking for you. Davin's been looking for you, and now I know why." Long, bony fingers squeezed painfully over my right breast and I choked back a sob as his other hand rubbed along the inside of my thigh. "Oh, yeesss. You're everything he said you'd be. He'll reward Isaac mightily for finding you." His voice then seemed to lower several octaves. "Any guesses as to my prize?"

"Oh, God." I tried to pull away, tried to get this grimy feeling to come clean, but it was no use. He rubbed his cheek against the back of my neck and I was granted a reprieve while his hold on me loosened, but it was only for a moment. When the moment was gone he yanked me back hard against him. "Damn you," he cursed under his breath. "One has to be very careful around you, pretty thing."

I couldn't hold the pain in any longer. I could feel my muscles begin to shake. "Please, let me go."

"How I want to feed from you," he continued, as if he hadn't even heard my plea. "I can smell your scent. It's gloriously salty, with just the right amount of tang. A vampire's milk and honey," he breathed, his frosty tongue licking over the pounding artery in my neck.

Any moment I was going to be sick. Hopefully I could aim and spew as much on him as possible. The way he reeked, it would be like a bath for him.

"Pity," he sighed. "Well, since I can't feed my thirst with you . . . Oh, Sarah . . . ," he called, his tone shrill, like a child playing a game.

Without warning he shoved me to the ground. "No," I gasped. "Run, Sarah! Run!" I could barely get the words out as I turned to her. Isaac was already on top of her, yanking her head back, his fangs placed with quick precision over the thrumming carotid artery in her throat. She didn't fight. Her eyes were full of tears but they held a quiet resolve, as if she were accepting her fate.

I somehow found the strength to stand up just as a wall of wintry air blew over me, sending me firmly back on my butt. A dark blur streaked right by me and straight into Isaac, driving him back from Sarah and into the ground with such violence it tore the earth up beneath them.

It was a second vampire. It had to be.

Effortless in his movements, this new challenger rose to his feet and circled his prey with a quiet intensity, a deliberate calmness of a trained warrior, drawing Isaac further away from us with a 'try it if you dare' taunt in his eyes—his hypnotic blue eyes. Not anything like Isaac's barely-there blue. His were a sharp, piercing blue, almost an electric blue that had the power to cut through someone like a laser.

"What's this?" Isaac spit out incredulously. "Trying to claim my prize?"

"Yes, I am," the vampire replied in a tone so low that I shivered as he said it. Massive, corded muscles in the warrior's neck and shoulders flexed noticeably, even under his shirt. "They're coming with me."

"You can't claim a human that's already mine!"

The blue-eyed warrior's gaze narrowed as a wicked curl lifted the corner of his lips and he replied, "Watch me."

The warrior's first charge was so violent that it sent both combatants flying as the unbelievable power of his long body sent the smaller vampire back twenty feet, stopping only when they both smashed against the base of a tree. On impact, I thought I heard the cracking of bone and wondered if I had just imagined it.

"Olivia!" Sarah cried out behind me, bringing my attention back to her terrified face. This was our chance to escape, and here I was watching two vampires go at it as if I had nothing better to do. In truth, I couldn't get my muscles to stop shaking, and when I tried to stand, my legs gave out under me, forcing me to crawl back to Sarah on my knees. She reached out, grasping my hand in a fierce grip. "I can't move on my leg. You need to go without me."

I blinked at her with disbelief. How could she think I would leave her here, wounded and alone, with two vampires warring over who got to suck her dry first? We had known each other since we met on the playground in first grade. Ironically, Sarah had been the one to step in and help me when some boys were cruelly teasing me, though Sarah to this day swore it was because they liked me. From there, we became inseparable, and because of our friendship our families had grown close and I had made it through some of the darkest days of my life. "I'm not leaving you here!"

Without even waiting for her to object, I grabbed her arm and curled it around my neck, supporting her weight over my shoulders and lifting us to our feet. We had made it a just a few steps when Isaac's body was slammed once again into the earth like the face of a hammer, and this time he appeared to be staying down for the count while the warrior turned to find us.

I froze, my eyes caught in that brilliant blue gaze of his, expecting he would charge at us any second. But instead, he held his ground, his expression no longer conveying steely rage —but interest. The vampire was studying us, scanning our injuries, and, for some strange reason, that made my stomach flip. Something about the way he looked at me held me in place. I swear that for a moment I had completely forgotten how to exhale.

Behind him, Isaac appeared to float back to his feet, and he fixed on me with rabid eyes. "I only need the one," he said, licking his lips. "You can have the other."

The blue-eyed warrior swung back on him without making a sound. "Get used to disappointment."

All hell broke loose then as Isaac hurtled through the air, striking the warrior's chest and sending him crashing back against a nearby fallen tree. With the warrior down, Isaac bounded back through the air and landed in front of us. "We only need her," he murmured. "Take care of the other one. No prizes for this one tonight."

I swung around to discover a third vampire right behind us.

They were literally coming out of nowhere!

The next thing I knew, my legs were swiped out from under me and I fell hard onto my back, smacking my head against the ground. Before I had any chance to recover from the shock of it, Isaac's arms encircled my heels, and he began dragging me toward him. I tried to kick myself free, but his hold was like iron as he flipped me onto my stomach, making me feel as if all of my ribs had cracked inside my chest. Now there would be nothing stopping him from taking me.

"*No!*" It was the only thing I could think to say. "No."

The warrior had returned to his feet, and he looked as if he wanted to break Isaac in half. I had no idea what he would do with Sarah, but somehow I sensed he would not be so cruel. Looking to Sarah with a desperate plea, the warrior's eyes followed mine and then slashed back to me just as Isaac pulled me fully into his grip.

The blue-eyed warrior wouldn't be able to take us both.

He had to make a choice.

He made the wrong one.

With an infuriated roar he lunged at Isaac, tearing him from me by his throat and tossing him like garbage into the torn-up soil. As soon as I was free, I swung around to see the other vampire already driving his sharp fangs into Sarah's throat. Her eyes were full of shock as blood dripped down her collarbone in a long scarlet tear. The life was being taken from her right before my eyes and I was helpless to do anything to stop it.

"Sarah!" I cried in nothing more than a croaky rasp and tears.

I tried to crawl to her with what little strength I had left, even as the vampire continued to feast on her throat. The taste of her blood seemed to excite him into a state of complete frenzy. He was shaking her violently back and forth just before her eyes began to drop . . . and then it was over.

Sarah was gone.

My heart hurt as if it had just been ripped from my chest by bare hands. I had just lost my best friend in the whole world, and I had to watch her die in the most horrible way I could imagine. Collapsing to the ground, sobbing, part of me just wanted to make my death easier for one of these demons.

I had failed.

I promised Sarah I would get her out of here, and I failed.

My shallow breaths were sawing in and out against my battered ribcage as I lay there on the ground, but through all the pain I heard the brutal crunch of bone smacking the base of another tree. By then I didn't care which one of these demons took me or why, I just wanted it to be over with.

When I felt the wave of cool air hit my back, signaling that one of them had come for me, my body stiffened just before a large hand encircled mine. The touch was cold, bone smooth, as he squeezed with controlled pressure, but it wasn't gentle. He was too strong for that. His other arm slid beneath my shoulder to bring me around to face him. His expression wasn't angry or threatening, but showed concern, and it didn't make any sense. "I'm not going to hurt you."

I was sure in my frightened and exhausted state that I hadn't heard him right. He wanted to help me? Vampires didn't help humans.

Isaac barreled right back at us, and the warrior used his own body to shield me from the driving charge. The force of the hit went straight into the warrior's back but never passed through to me. Then he threw his elbow across Isaac's jaw, snapping the vampire's head back before returning to his feet and charging at Isaac once again, the battle continuing.

That was when I sensed the lightest tap on the ground behind me and heard a soft, feminine voice in my ear. "Don't be afraid. I'm here to help."

Tiny arms slid beneath my shaking frame and lifted me from the ground as if I weighed no more than a sheet of paper. I glanced up to see a most beautiful face staring back at me. Even though it was obvious from her ability to lift me like a toy that she must also be one of them, a vampire, there was softness to her. Her eyes weren't electric blue like the warriors but a warm, soft color that I couldn't quite make out. She appeared completely angelic, her heart-shaped face framed with straight hair that blew off her shoulders and shone even in the dark.

She smiled at me and her nose crinkled. There was just enough light to see that her nose was splashed with several light freckles that stretched into her cheeks. "It's time to go," she said.

I took one last look at Sarah's lifeless body lying there in the grass just as another male vampire dropped behind her killer. He was big—really big. Not tall and lean, like the blue-eyed warrior, but thickly muscled like a boxer. With powerful, fluid movements, he fought Sarah's killer, making almost no sound as he worked away at him, appearing to expend even less energy.

I selfishly hoped he would tear the vampire apart.

"Gemma!" the blue-eyed warrior snapped as Isaac still fought like a crazed lunatic to get to me. "Get her out of here. *Now!*"

My head started spinning, and I couldn't stop the sinking sense that I was falling.

Then it was just easier to let go.

Chapter Four

"Olivia," my mother called, and I could see her easy smile and those little crinkles that formed around hers eyes when she was happy—characteristics I really loved. An almost instant warmth seemed to awaken my previously cold limbs. But at the same moment, flashes of light started to interrupt, and sound began to tune in and out like a radio dial, playing sweet, familiar voices, tiny pieces of conversation. "It's not time, sweetheart. Go back."

"Mom? I want to go with you."

She was shaking her head at me. "It's not time," she repeated, and it confused me. Didn't she understand that seeing her again reminded me of times long past, days when we would venture out together, losing the day by exploring the world around us and then coming home to my father to boast about all that we had discovered? It felt comforting, familiar, yet not quite real.

Too soon, her image and voice began to fade, growing more and more distant the harder I tried to reach for her. "Mom! I'm here—right here. Don't leave me!" But she was gone. My heart seemed to collapse inside my chest. "Nooo. Come back." I knew instinctively I had just lost something I wouldn't be able to retrieve.

But then, as if my plea was being answered, I could feel her. She was stroking my cheek with the back of her hand, something she had done frequently when I was a little girl. She was trying to reassure me. But this time her touch somehow different. The knuckles were too wide, the ridges more deeply defined, and the skin . . . cooler, much cooler than I remembered.

"Shhh, it's all right. You're safe now," said a definitely male voice as a large, padded thumb swept the rise of my cheekbone. His tone wasn't much louder than a whisper, yet it still carried with the rough, reverberating depth of a man's voice first thing in the morning. It was a voice of strength, and for some reason I found myself drawn to it.

"Don't leave me," I murmured, and I wasn't sure if I was still talking to my mother or this stranger, whose voice somehow gave me comfort.

"I won't leave," he assured.

I sighed easily, and my shoulders sank back into the mattress just before I slipped back into sleep.

***

Gradually, the flashes of light came more frequently, and I was becoming aware of my body again when the acute sensation of heat began to rise on my skin. Too much heat! Not like on a hot summer day, but as if someone had placed me in a broiling oven. I was sweltering under a fever the likes of which I had never experienced. I was hot, then cold, then hot again, and I began twisting around wildly, trying to ease it somehow before rolling onto my left side, where a knifelike pain shot through my ribs.

Gasping for my next breath, I kept my eyes closed tight and held onto my side, sensing that someone was there beside me—not because I heard even the slightest sound, but because I felt the mattress depress with the weight of someone else.

"Easy," the deep voice said, calmly. "Just take slow, shallow breaths." That was easy for him to say. He was probably breathing just fine, whereas I didn't feel like I had the strength to lift my eyelashes. "Water?" I pleaded.

A cold hand pressed over my forehead and cheek, offering some relief as a glass was tipped to my lips and water spilled over my dry tongue. Simply, it felt like heaven. I reached for the glass with both hands and swallowed several large gulps, my breathing vibrating as a heavy echo inside the container.

"Slow down," he said gently as he pulled the glass away.

"No, please . . . more. I'm so thirsty."

The stranger shifted above me, coolness seeming to radiate over his entire body, and all I could think about was how I wanted to reach out and drag him against me to cool the fire raging inside my own skin. "You can have more. But I need you to take these fever reducers." His thumb grazed the bottom edge of my lip in a silent request for me to open them. "We need to get your temperature down."

I wasn't really sure why I was being so agreeable when I had no idea who this voice belonged to—or, for that matter, where I was—but I did as he asked and was rewarded with the bitter taste of aspirin on my tongue before I could gobble down some more water. "Good," he said. "Now I need to examine your ribs. Just try to stay as still as you can for me. OK?"

It took me a moment to realize he was waiting for my reply. I nodded, and the cotton shirt I was wearing was pushed high on my stomach. Even though he had warned me what he was about to do, I was still caught by surprise. I squirmed underneath his hands, and he patiently waited for me to stop before proceeding over to my left side, directly below my left breast. If it wasn't for the fact that my ribs felt like they were going to collapse under the minimal pressure he was exerting, I would have questioned just what the heck he thought he was doing.

Instead, I froze, holding the very breath I had been inhaling for fear that releasing it would bring the sharp pain back. Strangely, he seemed to freeze at the very same moment and then pulled his hands back. "Breathe," he said. "I'm finished."

"Can I have more water?" I barely got the croaky words out as he tipped the glass to my lips once again. "Where am I?"

"You're someplace safe, Olivia. I promise no one will hurt you here."

"You know my name?"

There was a long silence, and it seemed as though he had no intention of answering my question, but then he simply replied, "Yes."

The hesitation in his voice was strange. It was perfectly reasonable to want to know the identity of the person you were, for the moment, completely dependent on.

"My name is Caleb . . . Caleb Wolfe," he finally said, and it made me smile unexpectedly. I liked the name. It fit his voice, and I could picture in my mind what he looked like, darker hair and a rougher face to fit that voice.

"Thank you, Caleb Wolfe, for helping me."

***

Some hours later, the raging heat that had declared war on my body subsided. My strength returned . . . sort of . . . and I was able to think more clearly. I much preferred this to being so weak I couldn't lift my eyelashes. And although my muscles were still stiff and that fierce squeezing over my heart I had experienced on the train had returned, this was definite progress.

"You can open your eyes now, Olivia," Caleb's now familiar voice spoke from very close by me. "There's nothing here to fear."

Nothing to fear? Was he kidding? The confusion of fever gone, I vividly remembered where I had heard that deep voice before; it was on the night of the train crash, when he'd taken my hand and promised he wouldn't hurt me, that he would get me out of there.

I guess he had succeeded in that. But where had he brought me? I questioned my sanity for even considering opening my eyes and recognizing the situation for what it was. Not good. The vampire had brought me somewhere unfamiliar and unnervingly quiet, especially for me, a woman who, in recent years, had grown used to the blaring noises of the city. But when I finally did open them I was greeted, to my astonishment, by the tranquil sight of thousands of stars twinkling in the night sky above me.

For a moment, I forgot that someone else was in the room as I lay there on a platform bed with no headboard or footboard, sheltered under a high ceiling completely fabricated from plate glass, like a giant skylight, making it seem like we were floating in the midst of the universe.

It was then I realized that the skylight was the only window in the tidy bedroom—the only light source, for that matter, except for a couple of unscented candles flickering on a nearby end table. The absence of light and clutter seemed to be preferred. The bedding, trimmed with lace and tons of fluffy pillows, was decidedly too feminine for a man to have chosen, so I guessed this wasn't his room. It belonged to a woman, unless, of course, he shared this room with a woman.

Hard to believe, though, since I questioned the sanity of any woman who would be with a vampire who roared like a lion and threw other vampires around like sticks.

Either way, it did little to explain why I was here . . . in a strange bedroom . . . with a vampire . . . with lace trimmed bedding.

Didn't they prefer coffins or something?

"How're you feeling?" he asked, with unexpected sincerity, from a low-armed chair in a darkened corner of the room. At first, his long body and features were completely hidden outside the dark edges of the moonlight, but then his chin lifted and his body pressed forward into view. As my eyes adjusted to the darkness I began to recognize the broad outline of his shoulders, the long length of his torso.

Yep, it was definitely the vampire.

His relaxed position—one arm stretched along the back of the oversized chair and his legs crossed, and with a book lying open in his other hand, oozed confidence. It definitely announced his ease with the situation. It was rather annoying, actually, but it didn't stop me from scanning the length of him from head to toe . . . and he noticed. In response, a moonlit, quirky expression, almost but not quite a smile, spread over his lips, like he knew a secret the rest of the world didn't.

Damn.

"I'm fine," I replied in a clipped tone, trying to skip right past that embarrassing little slip.

"Hmph," he grunted, closing his book with a dull thump and setting it on the end table between us. The low candlelight was just powerful enough to flicker over the antique green binding: *The Call of the Wild*, by Jack London.

Appropriate. I had never read the work myself, but the title alone seem to mock the dangerous extent of my situation—so much so that I blurted out the first random thought that popped into my head. "Vampires read?"

His lips thinned, but, surprisingly, not in anger. More like disappointment. "I have always been a reader."

His tone sounded unaffected, his words spoken with such

ease, almost brushing over the senses, and I hated the fact that I had noticed.

"I see," I continued, trying to hold the same unaffected tone but failing miserably. "You're just catching a few chapters in between kills, is that it?"

Considering the situation, it was undoubtedly one of the dumbest things I had ever said. He seemed to relax, though, which was odd, until he said, "You're trying to hide your fear. And not very well, I might add."

OK, so he had me there.

"I'll admit some concern." I nearly choked on that under-exaggeration. "What woman wouldn't be, in my situation? I've been taken, against my will, Lord knows where—"

"You haven't been taken," he interrupted. "I brought you someplace safe."

"Well, isn't that lucky for me! But in most civilizations, unless you have my permission to take me 'someplace safe,' that's called kidnapping."

He sighed deeply. "You were a little busy being unconscious to consult on the matter."

I suppose he had a point, but still, the man was impossible. "Is this something you do often—bring home unconscious women you don't know?"

He didn't answer, and I couldn't really be surprised. It had been a rude question. "OK, so maybe you could tell me where exactly this someplace safe is?"

Again, he didn't answer, just shifted in his chair slightly. This man really was not the best conversationalist.

"Well . . . maybe you could at least tell me how long I've been here."

There was another long stretch of silence before he finally replied, "A while. You've been in and out for just over two days."

"Two days!" I cried, shooting up from my horizontal position and swinging my feet over the edge of the mattress. Immediately, pain and dizziness seemed to grab hold and shake me like I was in some kind of spin cycle. My hands flew to my temples, then to my left side, which was pulsating in sharp waves as my lungs labored against my sore ribcage.

Caleb leaned his long body forward, his arms almost stretching outward as his elbows rested on his knees. He was deciding whether or not to come to me, his face edging forward enough in the moonlight to reveal his incredible eyes. They were no longer the electric blue from the night of the crash but a normal, soft color that he was too far away to identify for sure. "You shouldn't move too much," he said before slipping back into the shadows. "You've fractured two ribs. That's why your breathing's difficult."

"I said I'm fine," I gritted out, deciding to be difficult because I felt completely helpless in the situation, and I hated it. Just then, more pain tore through my side and I turned away to hide the lie about to fall from my lips. "I feel much better."

The vampire just watched me sit there in stubborn silence, focusing on nothing in particular, when the memories I had wanted to forget came crashing back over me. The more vivid they became, the harder it was to exhale.

I clearly remembered the man in front of me. Caleb, the blue-eyed warrior, who had clashed against Isaac with a force I could never have imagined if I hadn't been there to witness it myself. His electric eyes were full of hate . . . Well mostly full of hate. And his fangs—

"Olivia!" he broke in with almost exasperated surprise. "Haven't you figured out yet that I'm not going to hurt you?"

I wasn't sure how to answer that. Logically, my mind told me that if he wanted to kill me he would have done so already, but too many questions were still rolling around in my head. Like why had he brought me here instead of a hospital? Why was he even taking care of me? Was he going to try and touch me—lick me—like Isaac had?

When scared like this, I usually did the stupidest things. And in this instance, inexplicably, I picked a fight with a vampire. "You expect me to believe that you—a *vampire*—don't want to hurt me?" The higher pitch of my voice betrayed the anger in my words. "That's what vampire's do. They kill humans! I saw—"

I stopped myself, cutting the air with abrupt silence, not wanting to go any further inside my head.

At first, he appeared indifferent to my little tirade, but then he muttered something inaudible to himself and said, "I think if I wanted to kill you, Olivia, I could've done so—"

"Stop saying my name!"

"What would you like me to call you? Girl? Child?"

I didn't know! I just wanted this feeling that he was somehow familiar to me to go away. Jumping onto the balls of my feet, I skirted around the bed, not quite sure where I thought I was going, but I got exactly two steps before doubling over in pain. Several odd chirps rose from my throat before I froze the very breath I was inhaling for fear of how it would rip at my body when I exhaled.

The next thing I knew, the vampire was at my heels, leaning over me with a hand under my elbow to help me straighten up, and I realized he hadn't made a sound when he left the chair. "I'm sorry I upset you."

Stubbornly, I yanked my arm away, refusing to look at him and wishing I didn't feel so helpless. He responded with an exasperated sigh and returned to the sofa.

With my chin lowered in a small acknowledgment of defeat, I sat back against the edge of the bed, slowly breathing in and out as I silently pleaded for the pain to stop. "Since you say you don't want to hurt me," I began, " . . . that you're merely helping me . . . then can I go?"

"And where, exactly, would you go?"

The question surprised me. It seemed logical: I would go home and let people know I was alive.

"You seem to have attracted the attention of an awful lot of vampires intent on finding you and who do want to hurt you. And if that's what they want, then they won't stop. So tell me . . . where, exactly, is it safe for you to go?"

Now stunned, all I could do was blink back at him. What could I say to that? I still wasn't convinced this wasn't all some big nightmare. "I'm not safe with you, either."

"I don't want to hurt you. But for some reason, Isaac and his coven do. The question is why? I think you know the answer."

"So you know Isaac?"

"No. I heard him say his own name when he was—"

Caleb suddenly stopped himself, momentarily cursing under his breath before adding, "Tell me why Isaac was so determined to take you?"

I couldn't believe this. He was demanding that I tell him why an obvious madman—or rather mad vampire—wanted to take me? How the heck was I supposed to know? None of it made any sense to me either. "I don't know. Maybe he prefers brunettes," I said roughly. "I didn't even know vampires existed before tonight . . . or, rather, two days ago."

"That's as it should be," he replied calmly. "Humans can't know of this world that exists around them. That's what makes this attack on the train so puzzling. It was too public."

As he spoke those words my mind was drawn back to that frightening night. The memories of Isaac's rancid breath and iron grip were as real as if he were standing beside me at that moment. Just the thought of it sent a shiver snaking up my spine. He had made it very clear he wasn't going to kill me, but instead he was going to take me to this Davin person.

I didn't know if Isaac was still out there looking for me or if Caleb had killed him in their battle. Wrong as it was, I hoped Caleb had destroyed the vampire. The thought of him finding me again, touching me . . . I turned in revulsion, remembering the feel of his cold lick—

"Olivia," Caleb warned—carefully, as if scolding a child for doing something wrong. "You. Are. Safe. Here."

He emphasized each word.

"Is Isaac . . . ?"

"Dead?" Caleb answered for me. "No. He crawled away, like the cockroach that he is."

I blinked back at him in utter amazement, remembering how fiercely they were going at each other. It was incredible to think that no one had died using that much force. That realization only served to emphasize how far in over my head I was.

Tired, frightened, my ribs aching, I climbed back onto the mattress, curling my knees up slightly as I lay on my uninjured side, my back to the vampire. "So your solution's to keep me prisoner here instead of being a prisoner there?" I asked quietly. "What's the difference?"

More exasperated muttering sounded behind me until he finally grumbled, "Gem is here. She'll get you something to eat and find you some fresh clothes."

Gemma? The female vampire who had gotten me out of there? Of course. She had to be the one responsible for the feminine décor, which also meant she lived here with Caleb, and for some reason, that thought bothered me.

An awkward silence stretch between us, and I assumed he was still in the room with me until I heard Gemma's unmistakably tuneful voice call, "Caleb, don't go tonight. Stay here."

His snarling reply faded into the distance. "I'll be back before dawn."

A whooshing sound echoed beyond, like the howling of the wind, and he was gone . . . along with the clutching hold over my heart.

Chapter Five

Gemma entered the room and lit a few more candles, making it easy to see in the brighter light how truly beautiful she was. She couldn't be much older than twenty. Her eyes were a bright olive-green that complemented perfectly her straight, cinnamon hair. Even the long purple streak that ran along her right cheek just seemed to fit her.

She returned from the in-suite bathroom with some folded towels and set them down on the seat of the chair Caleb had just vacated. The room itself was a decent size, everything lovely and meticulously kept. It had to be a guestroom, because there was no way someone lived in such immaculate conditions.

"It's good to see you're feeling better," she said, with a lift to her voice—like hints of an English accent that had been flattened over time. She glanced back through the frame of the open door and added, "Caleb's restless again tonight. If I didn't know him better, I'd say you've put him in a foul mood, Olivia," she teased, with a wink.

I didn't respond, but I felt myself begin to relax, which seemed easy to do around Gemma. She had just been teasing, but it was a ridiculous notion that I could influence the mood of a vampire either way. Unlike Caleb, who made me . . . well, something . . . there was a playfulness about Gemma that instantly put me at ease. Perhaps it was her petite size. One look at Caleb and you knew he had the strength to smack someone into a tree (just not from twenty feet). But with Gemma, no one would guess from looking at her that she possessed a physical strength far superior to mortal men. "Maybe Jax can talk to him," she sighed wistfully. "He usually listens to Jax."Jax?

He must be the other vampire who fought Sarah's—

Nope. No need to go there.

"Are you hungry?" she asked.

I nodded, my stomach almost leaping in approval.

"Why don't you go wash up while I make you something. Can your stomach handle pizza?"

"Yes," I smiled, feeling a bit ridiculous. Five minutes ago I was accusing Caleb of keeping me imprisoned, and now I was taking part in what felt like a slumber party. I knew I had acted childishly and was rude to him, but I didn't care. I had seen his true nature when he battled Isaac on that field. I was right to be cautious.

"Good," Gemma continued. "Here's a fresh set of towels, and I'll grab you something to wear. I assume a tee shirt and set of silk bottoms are OK?"

"Yes, they're more than fine," I replied, glancing at the thin, form-fitting tee shirt I was wearing, "but do you have a bra I could use?"

Gemma laughed in a whimsical little sound. "Yes, you are a bit curvier than me in that department, aren't you? I'm afraid I don't have anything your size."

Her comment about my body didn't bother me. Since I had sprouted as a teenager I always had slender legs and arms and a flat stomach, but my hips and chest were fuller, giving me a traditional hourglass shape. Sometimes it made it difficult to find clothing to fit me just right, but in the last couple of years I had become more comfortable with my curvy shape.

"I can bring you something tomorrow."

"What about the clothes I came in . . . the green cardigan? It's . . . it's sort of special to me."

Her smile faded slowly. "I'm sorry, Olivia. Your clothes were all bloodied and torn. I threw them out."

My eyes lowered to conceal my disappointment. "I understand that they were destroyed," I began in just a murmur, " . . . I do. It's just that the cardigan was a gift from my mother." Gemma gazed at me with utter sincerity in her eyes. "It's all right. I've seen very similar styles currently in the stores. I'm sure she can get you another one."

I nodded to be agreeable, not really wanting to explain how that wasn't possible.

***

While trying to sleep that night, my dreams continued to push toward images I didn't want to remember, and after tossing and turning for several hours, sometimes forgetting and putting painful, added pressure on my sore ribcage, I finally gave up. I opened my eyes for good and scanned the room to make sure I was alone, and, to my relief, I was.

The tightness over my heart had returned, so I rested my hand at my collarbone and inhaled a couple of deep breaths, trying to relax. I wished now I hadn't been so stubborn and gone to the doctor when Sar—

Nope, no need to go there.

Glancing up to the glass ceiling above me, the thick darkness told me that dawn was still hours away. Carefully, I slid from the bed, feeling along the wood plank floor as I headed towards the attached bathroom. As I entered the modest sized room, fresh towels waited for me, along with a clean sleep shirt and bottoms. Soft candlelight flickered on the freestanding vanity, which was topped with a gorgeous, textured-glass sink that resembled a shallow wading pool for your hands. Purely decadent. There was also a walk-in shower area, separated by frameless glass, with a matching tiled bench and rain shower head. Someone certainly knew what they were doing when they designed this home.

Removing my clothes, I stepped into the shower and let the pulsating streams of liquid just soak me in their warmth. The feeling was complete bliss, the idea of washing away dirt and sweat and replacing it with the manufactured scents of shampoo and soap was so simple, yet to me it represented normalcy and hope. These moments of comfort allowed me to think that maybe someday that awful night I was trying so hard not to think about would be forgotten completely, replaced with new memories that would keep the bad ones away.

I poured some exotic, flower-scented oil over my fingertips (thank you, Gemma) and began to massage it over my skin, avoiding the deep scratches and bruise marks covering my limbs. This was the first chance I had to see my body since the crash, and after taking in all the ugliness of my wounds, I closed my eyes so I didn't have to look at it anymore. With each healing cut or bone-deep bruise, I began to remember how it was inflicted and wondered about the scars that might be left behind.

Suddenly, I no longer felt comfort or pleasure from the shower and rushed to finish. Dabbing a dry towel just a few times over my skin, I tossed it to the floor, then tugged the clothing over my battered skin in an effort to cover all proof of that night's existence. But it was still there in my face as I looked in the mirror. There were shadowed bruises along my jaw and throat that after the crash must have looked almost black and purple against my pale skin. And my dark eyes, a perfectly ordinary shade of brown that was neither a rich chocolate nor a brighter hazel, appeared dull and tired.

Within seconds, my shirt became soaked as I combed my fingers through the hair that clung to my back, knowing it would eventually dry to its normal stick-straight style.

I didn't care. I wanted out of here. Out of this room! Out of this place!

But where would I go?

The thought of going back to our apartment at the University and seeing Sarah's things as she left them made my bottom lip start to quiver. I tried to hold back the choking knot that was developing at the back of my throat, but the image of Sarah's shocked eyes as the vampire pierced her throat and the long, scarlet tear of blood that had rolled down her neck would haunt me for the rest of my days . . . as well as the fact that I could do nothing to save her.

But he could have.

Tears spilled from my eyes, and I crumpled to the floor against the wall, igniting the pain in my ribs as fast as gasoline near a flame. Soon, deep sobs exploded from my throat, setting free the knot that had been lodged there. There was no hope of pulling the emotion back in. My uneven, gasping breaths revealed my complete inability to quell the pain. All the death I had seen in my twenty-six years—in the past twelve months alone—was too much. It was as if Death was stalking me, and no matter how fast or far I ran it would always find me.

Caleb was right. I had nowhere to go.

I buried my tear-soaked face in my hands, trying to quiet the racking noise, when I felt strong arms slide underneath me. They lifted me easily against a hard chest. I didn't have to look up to know it was Caleb. He said nothing, which was good, because I was in the middle of a breakdown that I decided just needed to happen. I reached out to him in pure need, burying my face in his shoulder to muffle the violent sounds of my grief, while clutching the material of his shirt in my fists, as if I were afraid to let go—afraid I'd start falling and never quite stop.

He stood there, listening to my cries, pressing his cheek against the top of my head, and it felt so sincere. The security I felt in this vampire's arms terrified me. In this moment, I was not afraid of him; I needed him. What was wrong with me? Why wasn't I thinking about the angry eyes? The fangs?

"Don't cry, Olivia," he said roughly. "It's going to be all right. Please don't cry."

Eventually, my cries and shaking finally began to lose strength against his body, and without ever feeling his strides back into the other room I was suddenly being set back on the mattress. He released my knees and pulled my wet hair away from my shirt, guiding my head gently to the pillow. I was caught off-guard once again as he slid his hand under my shirt towards my ribcage to press lightly against my now re-aggravated ribs. "Easy breaths," he whispered, his voice just above me, still sounding upset.

Humiliated by my own weakness, I couldn't look at him while he quietly remained at my side. His fingers slid down to my hip, where he took my trembling hand in his. He was so close, I could hear his soft breaths, feel them as they blew against my skin. It was as if he was silently asking me to look at him . . . but I couldn't.

I was scared.

"Why?" my tear-filled voice pleaded.

"I'm sorry, Olivia," he replied, misery in his words. "I promise, I'll take you home when I'm confident that the danger —"

"No . . . I mean why me? Why did you save me?"

For a long moment, silence fell over the dark room as I verbally continued to force out the pained thoughts in my head.

"I know you couldn't save us both . . . but why me?"

My teary gaze turned to face him, and the vampire's presence was never more real to me than at that moment. His lips lingered just inches above my own, and his sweet, cool breath tingled across my cheek while mine drew in sharply. This was the first time I had seen him out of the shadows—and his human face was stunningly handsome.

Deep-set gray eyes stared back at me with such intensity that my heart began skipping out of its normal rhythm. They were an intricate weave of muted grays and icy silvers that seemed to dance inside his iris, which was rimmed at the edge in a deep charcoal. I felt trapped by the hypnotic color as his dark brows pulled toward each other in—disbelief? It was like he couldn't believe I had asked him the question.

Unthinkingly, I reached up to cup his cheek in my palm, just wanting to touch him. The short bristle on his unshaven cheek scratched at my hand in that good way that reminded a woman that she was touching a man, and his mood seemed to change as a smile began to spread over his lips that I swear could have lit up the darkest sky. Long dimples dug into his cheeks, and that's when it happened—a moment of déjà vu.

Those eyes. I had seen them before! I knew them—knew him.

He squeezed the hand he held at my side, slowly, gently, till the pressure could no longer be ignored. My breath caught. There was something so familiar in his touch, in that movement, it sent a jolt right through me from head to toe. I blinked hard, then, as if I were standing back there on that sunny day in the tall grass ten years ago, it came to me.

"The lake?" I whispered in wondering amazement.

His thumb scribed small circles over the palm where I had cut my hand as a girl. He nodded, several shuffling emotions seeming to cross his face as he closed his eyes and lowered his head. "I should've saved you both. And for that I'll always be sorry. But I could never have let Isaac take you, Olivia. For me, there never was a choice."

Chapter Six

In stunned disbelief, I continued to be lost in him, lost in the details of his face. The sincere young man who had saved an injured teenage girl all those years ago and again, two nights ago, rescued the woman she had become, was still there. As Gemma put it . . . 'restless in spirit.'

How did I not see it? How did I not see *him?* All I saw that night on the field were the enraged, electric-blue eyes and knife-like fangs, but now that he was right here in front of me I could see him very clearly. In ten years, he hadn't aged a day—but he was changed somehow. His hair was longer, with a natural wave to it that fit with the short beard shadowing his jaw, chin and around his lips. The facial hair made him appear much more dangerous than the clean-cut young man I remembered by the lake, but it fit with the rougher man he had become. His tall body, just as it was back then, was all lean muscle, yet somehow his shoulders appeared even wider, his arms nothing but corded muscle.

In that moment I knew I was quite incapable of putting together a coherent sentence, but if I could, it would be to thank him for helping me. Something I regretted not doing that fateful day ten years ago. But, as they did then under the scorching sun, my words failed me. Instead, incoherent bits of sound sputtered from my throat as an easy smile settled over his lips. "Now, that's the girl I remember," he teased. "The one who was at a loss for words."

After a bit more stuttering I finally managed to get out the one question replaying through my mind over and over again. "How is this possible? They found your body."

For a moment he seemed to reflect on that, as if considering it very carefully, and then brushed the last of the tears from my cheeks. "I think I'll share that story with you another time, when you're feeling better."

Disappointment must have blanketed my face, because his next words immediately tried to convince me of his decision. "Olivia, you need to rest. You've aggravated your ribs. We can talk in the morning."

"But it is morning," I said, glancing up to the sky that wasn't quite as dark. "Or it will be soon. And I'm not tired."

His soft frown said he was unconvinced.

"Please." I pressed. "I . . . I want to understand . . . to know . . ." But I couldn't finish. I didn't know how to ask him for what I wanted because I was unsure myself. My whole world had been turned upside down in the span of two days, and I was just trying to catch up.

"You're not being truthful," he said.

I blinked back, hurt by the accusation because I knew in my heart I was being very truthful.

"About being tired, I mean."

Well, yes, I had been fudging the truth on that. Even though I wanted to bombard him with dozens more questions, my heavy lids were fighting to stay open, blinking slower and slower. "Will you at least stay?"

"Yes," he interjected without hesitation, and my heart responded with a slightly harder thump. "I want you to be comfortable here. You're not a prisoner. But I'd like you to stay here until I know it's safe for you to return to your world." His gaze softened, the gray color almost pleading. "Will you do that?"

Of course, my heart wanted to say yes, but my mind continued to flash on the violent images I had begun to associate with his world. "I . . . I don't know . . ."

His fingertips brushed lightly over my lips to silence them. "I don't want to frighten you," he began, "but once a vampire has your scent, he can track you. Until we understand what Isaac wants from you, it's too dangerous for you to go home. He'll find you."

For a moment I didn't breathe, understanding now why Caleb had brought me here instead of to a hospital. I didn't know where I was, but I knew I was safer with him than out there on my own. "Will he come for me here?"

Shaking his head, he replied, "Vampires have rules. It's a sort of unwritten code. Your being here signals to him that you're under my protection—under the protection of this coven. He'll not come for you as long as you are."

"I can't stay here forever, Caleb. I have to get back to . . ."

"I know," he replied sincerely. "I meant what I said. I will return you safely to your family as soon as I know Isaac's no longer a threat."

I considered that for a long moment. It was summer break, and until the problem with Isaac was resolved I would be a nervous wreck, looking over my shoulder the whole time. "I'll stay . . . for a little while at least. But I have one request."

"Name it," he smiled, exposing the dimples in his cheeks. God, I loved it when he smiled like that.

"Well . . . I'd like to get out of this room. Not that this isn't nice. It's just that . . ."

"You may explore the house freely in the morning—if you feel up to it?"

I nodded, trying to muster a half-hearted smile that soon pulled into a frown.

"What is it?" he asked.

"Isaac," I replied. "I don't understand any of this. He must've wanted other humans on that train—taken other humans—not just me, right?"

Caleb's soft expression faded, replaced with clear concern. "Olivia, there were no other survivors," he responded carefully. "Those who made it out of the train were killed by Isaac's coven."

I sucked in a horrified gasp, my stomach swirling as if I were about to be sick. "That can't be true," I whispered. "Please, it can't be. All those people . . . the men who helped me get out of the train . . . and the children . . ."

Caleb gently stroked his hand over my cheek, his concerned gaze making sure I was still with him. "I feel how upsetting this is to you. I wish somehow I could make this easier. But you should know, your family will believe you died in the wreckage with the other passengers. They won't be looking for you."

"But I . . . I don't understand. Why Isaac . . . ?"

He cupped my face in his hands, his expression so sincere.

"We'll find the truth."

It was amazing to me how this man, who had known me a total of two days and had spent much of that time rescuing me, could want to help so much. Did he have a fondness for taking in strays? Did he have a lot of spare time on his hands? "Why are you helping me?"

He didn't answer, simply gave me a quick smile and squeezed my hand before releasing it. "Get some rest. I'll stay here with you 'til you fall asleep."

I watched him as he returned to the chair. It was the middle of the night, yet his movements were graceful, gliding, as though his feet were barely making contact with the floor, his body showing no signs of fatigue. He reached for his book in the darkness, and it was as if he'd given no consideration to even lighting a candle.

"Is something wrong?" he asked.

I shook my head and closed my eyes, just thinking about what I would have done if he hadn't stepped in on the night of the crash, if he wasn't protecting me from Isaac now. The alternative surely was not appealing, and when I didn't want to think about that any more I let the very human need for sleep overtake me.

***

The next morning, as my eyes started to flutter open, I hoped to find Caleb still there with me, quietly reading in the chair. But it was empty.

Lying back on the pillows, still suffering discomfort and exhaling deep sighs, I wondered what the heck was wrong with me. Was I disappointed? Did I expect that a vampire had nothing better to do than babysit me? But then, he wasn't just any vampire, was he? He was *him*, the man who had helped a terrified teenage girl back to her safe and protected world. He was someone I had never forgotten, someone who still seemed to have the power to render me speechless at the very sight of him, the very sight of those eyes—his shades of gray.

I had so many questions. What had happened to him that day all those years ago? How did he end up here, wherever here was? And how long had he been living with Gemma?

OK, so some questions would just have to remain in my head.

But he had remembered me when he saved me from Isaac. Did that mean he felt the same connection I had, or was I still just that awkward teenage girl fantasizing about something she could never have? Probably the latter, but I couldn't deny that I was drawn to him, which was insane. He wasn't human . . . or maybe only partially human. He certainly appeared human when I watched him reading in his chair, his mind immersed in his book.

Admittedly, though, I had never been very good at seeing the true nature in a man. My abysmal track record with both boys and men proved it. I would meet someone I liked, get to know him, begin dating, and then, within weeks, he would become this controlling and possessive freak.

At first I thought it was just coincidence, but then I realized it had to be me. If there was a controlling, possessive man within a ten-mile radius, I was completely attracted to him. It was ridiculous.

Heaving a few more sighs and taking deep breaths in between, I shook off my thoughts and carefully propped myself up on my elbows, realizing that my ribs were feeling much better.

It was definitely time to venture out.

Once showered and dressed, I returned into the bedroom in a loose-fitting powder-blue blouse and white crop pants that Gemma had left out for me. They were definitely a nice change from the pajamas I had been living in the last couple of days, and a nice change, period. Gemma certainly had good taste, as most of my college wardrobe consisted of jeans and tee shirts. I was still uncomfortable about not having a bra, so I doubled up a sleeveless tank underneath and hoped no one would notice.

The bedroom door was opened to the hallway. "You're not a prisoner," Caleb had said, and I hoped he meant it, because I wanted desperately to leave this room for awhile.

Moving more slowly than usual because of my weakened legs, I opened the pair of pocket doors to my room and crossed the threshold into a small corridor. Across the hall there were two more sliding doors that matched those of my own room, one of which was open and through which I could see a man's study. The dark, rich wood and the worn leather lounge chair with nail-head trim and its accompanying ottoman had given that away, but somehow it didn't seem to fit Caleb.

I walked to the end of the corridor, where it was open to the first floor below, and was surprised to see a makeshift set of narrow, wooden stairs that looked like they had just been built. In fact, the landing I stepped onto covered only about half the width of the corridor, so it was obvious stairs were not the norm in this house. These were hastily built for me, and without a handrail, so coordination was going to be key.

Slowly, I made my way to the bottom and landed on beautiful, planked-walnut floor, soon realizing the house I was staying in wasn't quite like any house I had ever been in before. The space in front of me opened up into a giant, two-story room which featured wide windows that were evenly spaced and soared to the roofline above.

But that wasn't the unusual part.

I walked past what looked to be a few carefully selected furniture pieces, a white three-seat sofa and two matching oversized lounge chairs with a simple coffee table, then I stepped up to one of the windows until my nose was practically touching the glass. After about a three-foot gap from the side of the house, a space that appeared to simply drop to the ground below, there was a large deck with huge pine and fir trees coming up right through it, their limbs stretching toward and arching above the house itself and creating a canopy of green that was so thick it was like being cocooned in a little world of my own.

The house was built above the ground and was definitely far off the beaten path, but if I squinted hard enough I could catch glimpses of familiar mountain peaks through the pockets in the branches. I was somewhere high and remote in the Cascade Mountains . . . but exactly where, I wasn't sure. As my forehead touched the glass I couldn't help but smile. I literally felt "hidden away" from the rest of the world inside a spectacular, modern-day tree house, and it felt so safe, giving me the feeling that Isaac and all the other bad things in the world would never be able to find me here.

Caleb was right. He had brought me to someplace safe.

My attention, however, was soon drawn like a magnet to the large black object resting in the far left corner of the space . . . a grand piano.

"No, it couldn't be," I whispered with amazement as I moved closer along the perimeter. This wasn't just any piano, it was a Fazioli. I had only dreamed of getting to see one in person. The contemporary Italian design—with its wave-inspired form, red soundboard, and sleek Plexiglas center base-instead of the more traditional four-legged base—stole my breath away. I had only seen pictures of it, which had certainly not done it justice.

"Do you play?"

I gasped as Caleb's deep voice startled me from behind. I swung around to face him, unsure why I was so surprised to see him. It was his house, after all, but it was daytime. It seemed logical that a vampire would be sleeping—in a coffin . . . or something.

"I'm sorry. I didn't mean to scare you."

"No, it's not that. I . . . I was just absorbed,"

Nothing about him had changed from the night before. He was still astoundingly good looking. He was dressed now in dark jeans and a charcoal button-down shirt, cut just right to fit those broad shoulders of his. His skin was pale, but not an unhealthy looking pale, and his lips were not quite rosy, just a very kissable color.

Kissable? Good Lord, Olivia . . . Get a grip!

There was an awkward paused while I tried to figure out what I wanted to say. Unfortunately, the 'at a loss for words thing' happened to me a lot, especially when I was nervous. My parents told me it was charming, but I thought it just made me sound illiterate. "The house is . . . well . . . amazing."

He tipped his chin just a fraction and smiled, displaying the large dimples in his cheeks that sent butterflies fluttering through my stomach. What the heck was wrong with me that a simple smile could churn my insides into the consistency of a puddle?

I didn't have time to figure it all out, because he took one smooth step forward and I suddenly realized just how tall he really was—at least several inches over six feet—which made him nearly a foot taller than me. "This was a gift for Gem," he began, " . . . but she doesn't seem to have much interest."

Dumbfounded by what he was implying, I could do nothing more than blink back at him, and then I finally asked, "You bought a grand piano for someone who's never played?"

With a short, self-deprecating laugh, he ignored my rather rude question and repeated his original question. "Do you play?"

I slid my fingers across the smooth, black case and responded with a silent nod.

"Come," he murmured, offering me his hand. There was something so sensual, so seductive, in the way he said the word, it was as if I had no choice but to follow.

He led me around to the duet bench and motioned for me to sit. "I really shouldn't. My playing has been rather poor lately."

"Lately?" he questioned. "That would imply that you've been playing for some time."

I nodded. "Since I was five."

For a moment, he gave me the strangest look. It seemed that he was completely mystified by my words. But his expression warmed immediately and he squeezed my hand, motioning once more for me to sit. "Please. I promise, my expectations are not high."

I found it very difficult to say no to him when he was being so agreeable. With a small amount of reluctance I took my seat. Caleb moved over to the corner windows, appearing to peer straight through the thick branches ahead of him. Only a hint of his profile was visible as he waited patiently for me to begin. "Do you need some sheet music?"

"No," I replied, deciding to play the piece I had composed for my graduate work. I was curious if it would sound better on the Fazioli than the studio piano I was used to at the university.

My, it was a beautiful instrument. As I gingerly began to play some scales, then a few chord combinations, I was thrilled as the first notes traveled through the red soundboard, and for a moment I wasn't sure if I would ever want to stop playing. It felt wonderful, freeing. The tone was so clear and vibrant, it reminded me of how awe-inspired I was the first time I'd heard the unique Fazioli resonance. But the moment didn't last, and soon I began to feel the hesitation in my fingers that had affected the quality of my playing for the last year, and I hated it. It was stripping the joy from something I had loved doing since I was a little girl.

Wondering if Caleb had noticed, I glanced up, fearing I would see a frown of displeasure on his expression, but instead I saw peace. He appeared wholly captured by the music. His eyes closed and a relaxed smile crept onto the visible corner of his lips as he lifted his chin higher.

His enjoyment of the music made me unexpectedly happy. I wanted to try harder, to play more strongly for him. I closed my eyes, revisiting my professor's last words in class on the morning of the train crash. "Truly great musicians don't *play* the music. They *feel* it, *here*," Professor Schuler had said while tapping his hand over his heart.

So that's what I tried to do; relax and feel the music in my heart.

When the last few bars pressed through my fingertips, sending the final notes wafting into the air, quiet once again returned to the room and I opened my eyes. I had nearly forgotten where I was. Caleb was standing there beside me, a smooth grin spreading over his lips. "If that's playing poorly, then I can't wait to hear something good."

Then, in a twist of air, his blurred form wrapped around me like the wind and he was seated right next to me on the bench. He moved so fast that I missed it all with a single blink. "Wow," I replied with an extra breath. "I just need to get used to that."

He placed his much larger hand over the keys and depressed a single note with his index finger, his smile fading into a more thoughtful expression. "Olivia, why would you think you play poorly?"

I sighed, returning my gaze to the keys. "My professor—Professor Schuler—has high hopes for me. But my effort has been disappointing him since . . ."

I stopped myself, realizing I was giving away more information than the question required. "Well . . . just disappointing, I guess."

Caleb's piercing gaze bore into me, and I swore at that moment it appeared he was seeing right through me. "And what do *you* think?" he pressed. "Are *you* disappointed?"

For a long moment I stared at him, unsure how to answer the question. No one had ever asked me how I felt about it before. It had always been about the potential, the instructor's opinion. "I don't know. My fingers have been very hesitant lately. I guess I fear I'm losing my abilities—my gift."

"Hmm," he responded, and it was a very sweet sound, indeed. "Well, my opinion may not be as valuable as Professor Schuler's, but I think you should be playing where all of Seattle can hear you."

I laughed, a truly wonderful and unexpected laugh, and it felt good. "That's just silly. All of Seattle can't hear me at once." I turned back to him, met his gaze, and—oh, my, those beautiful gray eyes of his were so focused on me that my skin felt instantly flushed with heat. My breath seemed to slow and I could feel goose bumps breaking out over my arms. A charged silence filled the air between us as my heart began to thump wildly inside my chest and my gaze slipped lower to those not-quite-rosy lips of his.

The same lips that smiled back at me once they caught on to the direction of my thoughts.

I wanted him to kiss me. And I sensed he wanted to kiss me.

But what if he didn't think I was a good kisser? I mean, certainly I had kissed men before, but never when it seemed to matter as much as this, as if I might only experience his kiss once and it would have to last me a lifetime.

He leaned in closer, his cool breath tingling over my cheek as he tipped my chin up to him with his knuckle. "You're beautiful," he murmured, and I was quite incapable of breathing or blinking at that point. His grasp was gentle, yet inescapable, as he slid his fingers behind my neck and pulled me forward, pressing a soft, lingering kiss into my cheek. His lips were cool, and the contact with his bristled cheek sent shivers down my spine as he passed just over my lips. "So sweet . . . and so beautiful . . ."

Kiss me, just once. I won't be greedy.

My lips parted in invitation, prompting from him a quiet

sigh that caught me off guard, followed by his low chuckle at my ear. "Professor, you said? I bet you're a good student, Olivia. So anxious to learn, aren't you?"

Hello, Yes! Actual tingles trailed behind his fingertips as they slid down my sides and then wrapped the curve of my waist as he drew me closer to him, careful to avoid too much pressure on my ribs. I inched my chin higher, starting to say something in reply when he captured my lips in a full-on kiss that locked me against him.

Oh, my God! I was in heaven.

He tasted fresh, like ice and a breeze, as he moved over me with such confidence, not asking, just taking what he wanted. How could any woman not be a good kisser when she was kissing this man? He kissed me as if I were the special treat, as if my kiss was the key to his happy existence at that moment, and that felt amazing.

He conquered at first, then reduced the pressure and nibbled playfully, coaxing my lips further apart, until I felt myself beginning to sink against him. My entire body was a mass of tingles, and his enjoyment of the kiss seemed just as intense. His breathing was becoming rougher as his hand fisted in the back of my hair and he pulled me so close—it was as if he was trying to inhale me whole. When I heard the sound of his groan against my mouth, I wanted to stand up and cheer.

I was affecting him, and it felt incredibly powerful.

Then I felt a bit dizzy.

I had to clutch at his broad shoulders to steady myself as he began a trail of kisses over my jaw and neck. His mouth continued lower, latching on to the out-of-control pulse hammering against my throat. I thought I might faint when his tongue began teasing over the little thump, thump under my skin, a small whimper slipping out between my hard breaths . . . then it occurred to me where he was!

My eyes popped open as my body went stiff in his arms, waiting for the possible consequence of choosing to kiss a vampire.

He pulled back, sensing my tension, his heated gaze slowly catching up with the situation and changing to concern. "Olivia?"

I glanced away for a moment before meeting his worried eyes again. "I . . . I need to ask you something."

"Anything," he said as his fingertips stroked over my cheek.

"I . . . I . . . no . . . Do you want . . . ?"

When it was really important, I never seemed to fail at making a horrid mess out of a situation.

"What is it?" he pressed.

I inhaled a slow breath and tried to relax. It was just a simple question. "Are you . . . thirsty . . . ? When, you know . . . when you're with me like this?"

Sadness swept into those gray eyes the moment he realized what I was asking. "Are you afraid of me, Olivia?"

"I . . . I guess, a little," I replied honestly. "But it's not about you as much as I just don't understand how it works. Isaac . . ." I paused, unable to stop the shiver of revulsion that ran through me at thinking back to the rough way he had held me in his grasp. "That is, when I thought he was going to kill me . . . said he could smell my scent . . . and it excited him."

Caleb looked away, his expression becoming tight. It was instantly obvious to me that it bothered him to be lumped into the same context as Isaac, but I knew I was being fair by asking.

He was silent for a long while. I feared I had just ruined a perfect moment, the perfect kiss. Finally, I blurted, "I'm sorry, Caleb, never . . ."

Gently but firmly he placed his thumb over my lips to silence me. "Don't ever apologize for asking something you're unsure about, especially when it concerns who and what I am."

Moving his thumb away, he inhaled deeply. "It's true that I'm excited by your blood scent. Just like you, Olivia, your scent is very sweet, very seductive . . ."

As silly as it sounded, I thought I would burst into a smile at that moment. There was a part of me that he found seductive. OK, so it was my blood, but a girl has to start somewhere.

"But I'm in control of my thirst when I'm with you. I've been feeding for a long time now without taking another human life. You become 'adapted'—for lack of a better word." He then paused, as if deciding whether or not he wanted to continue. "I don't want you to be afraid, so I'll be as honest with you as I can. The only time I'm not in control is when I'm feeding. The blood thirst that takes over is too much. I want it too much. It's harder for me to see the moral lines I've set for myself, for my life. Do you understand?"

"Yes," I replied quietly. "But, how'll I know . . . ?"

"There's a room," he interjected, "that's separate from the rest of the house. It's temperature controlled. We'll feed in there while you're staying here."

"Temperature controlled?"

Caleb brushed his lips over the rim of my ear as he murmured, "It would feel cold to your warm-blooded body. But it's comfortable for us. We sleep there, when we need it. Sometimes we can go for days without sleep."

His hand returned to me and began stroking gently over the back of my arm, which should have put an end to my questions. But for some reason it didn't. "Would you be able to stop?" I swallowed hard, my voice just whisper at that point. "I mean . . . if you did lose control, would you be able to stop?"

Without hesitation and with such sincerity he replied, "No."

I inhaled sharply, frankly having no choice in the matter. It was just my luck to meet a man I was starting to believe I could really feel something for and know he could kill me within a matter of seconds.

"I'm a young vampire," he explained. "I don't have as much control as an older vampire like Jax. If I'm too thirsty, then no, I wouldn't be able to stop." His expression then twisted painfully. "But that's not going to happen. Being in control of this thirst—of what I am—it's too important to me."

As I stared at him, I couldn't imagine how difficult it would be to share these parts of himself with a virtual stranger, someone who couldn't possibly understand, and I respected him all the more for trying.

He pulled away from me, rising to his feet at the side of the bench. And I felt as if he'd taken my heart with him. "I'll leave you to explore the rest of the house," he said before gliding away.

I had ruined the moment.

Chapter Seven

"Caleb, wait!" I called, running after him down the back corridor.

Smoothly, he swung on his heels and regarded me with an even expression, appearing to almost distance himself the moment our eyes made contact. He believed I was afraid of him, but that was no longer the truth in any way. I understood that being with him was dangerous, but I also trusted him not to hurt me. He'd shown me that by bringing me here and taking care of me.

"Will you show me the rest of the house?" I smiled up at him warmly, trying not to let my nervousness show. Lord, I felt like a young girl asking out her first boy.

His guarded expression softened and he offered his arm, which I didn't hesitate to accept. "On one condition," he replied. "You must play me some more of your poor music later this evening."

The huge smile that burst over my face at that moment just simply couldn't be contained. He enjoyed my playing, and that felt wonderful. As of late, the only people I had really been playing for had been my professors, so it was nice to be playing for someone just because they enjoyed the music.

"Good," he remarked, taking my smile as my acceptance. "Now, let's see . . . where should we start? Something fun, perhaps," he said. There was such playfulness in his eyes, I swore they lightened a shade. Then he proceeded to swing me off my feet and into his arms, but gently enough not to cause any jarring motion against my ribs as he launched us to the second floor and landed as if he were completely free of the gravity that controlled the rest of us.

And that certainly confirmed who the stairs were for.

"You want to start here? I just got down from this floor."

He laughed. "Actually I wanted you to grab something warmer to wear. You have goose bumps on your arms. It can get chilly up here on the mountain, even in the summer."

Oh, this was embarrassing. How did one explain that the goose bumps had nothing to do with being cold and everything to do with the response to being with him?

Simple . . . one didn't.

Instead, I glanced all around, peeking through the two open doors into Jax's and Caleb's studies and then back to the bedroom I'd been staying in.

"What's with the frown?" Caleb asked, probing into my thoughts.

I blinked up at him. "Nothing. I was just thinking it was . . . interesting, that the three of you live here together? You, Jax, Gemma?"

His smiled reflected his surprise but seemed to follow the direction of my thoughts. "Yes, we live together. We're a coven. But we're not together, together."

"So then you and Gemma aren't . . ."

"Good God, no," he said, as if that fact should be quite obvious to anyone. "Gem's like a sister to me."

Admittedly, that was a huge relief, since I had just let him kiss me senseless at the piano and hadn't stopped to think how it would hurt Gemma. "So, then, she sleeps in the same chilled room as you and Jax, but not with you?"

Another awkward pause before he replied, "Uh . . . no. She has her own room."

It was pretty easy to figure out which room he was talking about then. "Caleb! I don't want to take her room."

"It's all right," he laughed. "She works in Seattle during the week, so she stays at a condo Jax owns downtown."

"Works? Condo?" That all sounded so positively ordinary, so human.

He must have seen the confusion on my face, because he added, "I'll let her explain when she sees you tonight. She said she needed to drop off,"—he raised his eyebrows in curiosity —"some personal items for you?"

Before I could think better of it, I crossed my arms over my silk shirt, answering his question without ever uttering a single syllable. And there was no possible way I wasn't flushing with embarrassment from the neck up.

"I see," he smiled.

"Is Jax with her?" I asked, then added as a sidebar, "I don't need anything," and turned back towards the stairs before my face turned the color of a tomato. "I've not seen him since I've been here."

"You must be feeling better," he teased. "You're just full of questions today, aren't you? Yes, he's with her. He likes to watch over her while she's in the city. He can be a bit of an 'over-protective sod,' as Gem puts it, and it drives her crazy."

"This . . . ," I replied pointedly, "coming from the man who bought her a grand piano?"

Next thing I knew I was being lifted once again into his arms. "Careful," he said with an amused glint, "you're going to hurt my feelings." He then calmly stepped from the edge and dropped us back to the first floor. I held him tighter in preparation for a hard landing and a hard jolt to my side but was amazed when we touched down as lightly as a feather.

"Can we do that again?" I asked, a bit short of breath, as he set me to my feet.

His light laugh filled me with warmth as he directed me towards the open kitchen, though I had to admit I was confused as to why vampires would need a kitchen in the first place. The space was very modern, finished with pine countertops and stainless appliances, but I was a little fixated on the really large Sub-Zero refrigerator. Compared to the rest of the house, this stainless steel titan was completely oversized, almost dominating in an otherwise efficient floor plan for three people.

Caleb seemed to take note of my fixation but just continued to push us forward to the only actual closed-door room on the first floor, where I froze in speechlessness. Books of every imaginable size, color, and condition lined the walls of the high ceilinged library. Grounded by a leather sofa that was tucked between shelves, it was a warm, quiet getaway that was obviously well used. There were several books on naturopathic medicine splayed over a small glass coffee table.

I moved through the room, touching the worn bindings with

my fingertips as I searched through the titles, and spotted a very old copy of one of my father's favorite novels, *Great Expectations*. I couldn't resist pulling the hardbound classic from the shelf, then, almost as suddenly, pushed it back to its rightful place.

Suddenly, a wall of cold air whipped around me and Caleb was standing there, reaching for the book. He lifted it to me with a smile. "Ah, Dickens . . . one of his best. You can borrow any of these you'd like while you're here."

"Thank you," I replied in nearly a whisper, realizing all of the sudden just how very aware I was of him. How could one not be; he seemed to fill the room. And I had made such a fool of myself the night before, breaking down like that in his arms.

"Is something wrong?" he asked.

"No," I responded quickly. Probably a little too quickly. Returning my attention to the book, I touched my finger over a small piece of torn notebook paper being used like a bookmark. "Is someone already reading this?"

Shaking his head, he pulled the scrap out of its resting place, silently reading the rather effeminate handwriting on the page. "Jax refers to these as 'little gifts' from Gemma."

"I'm not sure I understand?"

He handed me the scrap of paper. "See for yourself."

> *Shake me! Shake me! Shake me!*
> *You can't rattle me enough.*
> *Sometimes you make it hard to breathe.*
> *But always, you make my heart light up.*

"It's beautiful. Gemma writes poetry?"

"She doesn't think so," he replied. "She says these are just her random thoughts. Once she's written them down, she leaves them around the house, and then forgets about them. May I?" he asked, motioning towards the paper in my hand.

"Of course."

I handed him back the scrap which he preceded to tuck in his pocket. "She doesn't know it, but Jax keeps all of these as we find them."

I was having trouble imagining the tough, brawny vampire

—the one that appeared as if he could knock anyone silly—collecting a woman's short poems. "That's very sweet."

"What can I say?" he laughed. "Jax is a sensitive brute." He then reached into his shirt pocket. "Oh, by the way . . . I almost forgot." He pulled out a very familiar pair of wire-framed glasses. "Gem asked me to give these back to you. She had the broken lenses fixed. I'm assuming you might need them if you're going to be reading."

Glasses? My free hand flew up to my face, trying to find the frames that normally sat on the bridge of my nose, but I had already known they weren't there. Had I not had them on at all since I woke? My gaze seemed to dart around the room, focusing on objects both near and far, large and small. Everything was crystal clear, no blurriness whatsoever.

What was going on?

Pressing my fingertips to my temples, I tried to rationally comprehend how, after wearing glasses since I was five years old, I suddenly didn't need them. It didn't make any sense. I considered the possibility that when I hit my head in the crash it might have altered my vision somehow. But that seemed ridiculous. Even if that were true, it would more likely make my vision worse, not better, right?

Caleb was trying to be patient while watching about ten different emotions cross over my face. But his patience soon ran out. "What is it?"

"It's nothing," I replied quickly—too quickly.

"Olivia?" His gaze narrowed, letting me know that he was hoping for a better answer than that.

"It's just that I've needed these glasses to see anything since I was a young girl. But since I woke, I can see fine without them. I'm trying to understand how that's possible."

He remained calm, even though his expression showed clear concern. Pressing his open hand across my low back, he pulled me closer to him. When I felt the coolness of his body touching mine the pleasant shock of it made me drop the novel in my hands to the floor, nearly hitting my left foot, his right. When I tried to bend to retrieve it, he held me in place, wrapping his arm around my waist as he raised my chin with his thumb to meet his eyes. "Have you had any headaches . . . any dizziness?

Any other symptoms at all since the accident, that aren't related to your ribs?"

I hesitated to bring another thing up, because I could see the unease it was causing him, but his concern seemed to deepen, as if he knew there was something else. "One," I murmured. "I've had this tightness in my chest. It was infrequent at first . . . but now it seems to be constant."

He stood stiffly, that thorough gray gaze of his studying me as if somehow he could find all the answers he needed just by looking at me. "It's not painful," I added quickly, trying to reassure him. "It's sort of like having the breath knocked out of you."

That didn't seem to help much.

"It could be that you're having trouble breathing against your fractured ribs."

"I'm sure you're . . ."

I was cut off by a large, loud gurgle from my stomach. Mortified, I covered it with my hands, hoping that he had not noticed, but that was just wasted wishing.

"You're hungry!" he exclaimed, his worried expression vanishing. "I'm sorry. I should've offered you some breakfast." He tapped his finger against the end of my nose. "Wait right here. I'll bring you something, and then we'll figure out what's going on, OK?"

I nodded, and in an instant he was gone.

Picking up the book from the floor, I set it on one of the end tables for later and then wandered from the library into a wide area that contained no furniture, like an open atrium or entry hall, minimal, with several most incredible pieces of art hanging along the walls.

The wall in front of me had five large glass windows that looked out to where the tree limbs were sparse and the sun was brighter against the glass. I walked forward to check out the amazing view—without the aid of glasses (that part was cool) —and one item caught my attention. It was a stainless steel, cantilevered arm that was bolted directly to the floor just to the right of the glass.

I had never seen anything like it before. A rectangular glass panel was mounted at the top with a long stainless handle, but there were no markings or descriptions to give me a clue about what it was for. I told myself to wait until Caleb returned to ask, but I decided I was being silly. It was probably just some sort of control panel for heating, or shades for the windows, although I didn't see any shades.

Slowly, I turned the handle in a clockwise direction. The five large panes of glass opened ninety degrees in one sweeping motion across the front of the house, and a powerful wave of warm air spilled inside. My breath caught as I stepped forward into the sunlight that was now bathing the hardwood floors all around me. The wonderful, fragrant scent of fresh evergreen and wildflowers seemed to mix with the sun, creating the perfect cure for someone who had been stuck in bed for several days.

"Olivia," Caleb's deep, and clearly unsettled voice, spoke from behind me. "Move away from the glass."

"But Caleb, this is amazing," I proclaimed, just before making the mistake of peering over the sharp edge. I had no idea how right I'd been when I had referred to this place as a tree house. The stunning drop to the forest floor below had to be at least twenty-five feet. Not prepared for such a distance, the ground started to sway in a rhythm that didn't seem to match my head and stomach at that moment. Then a gust of wind twisted in around me. I closed my eyes and tried to make the spinning stop as I slammed my open palm against the glass panel.

"Olivia!" Caleb called, just as my knees began to buckle and I slipped forward towards the long drop.

Without warning, I felt Caleb's rough arm snag around my waist, and he yanked me back to the floor. In that one motion, all the air was squeezed from of my lungs as he continued to drag me across the wood. A pungent, burning odor drew my attention to the arm that was pulling me. I was shocked to see it blackening, right before my eyes, ignited by the sun's blistering rays.

Caleb's skin was literally on fire!

Releasing me from his grip, he left me lying on the floor, stunned and motionless, in the middle of a bright pool of sunlight. My heart slammed almost painfully against my chest while I tried to process what had just happened. I swung around to see Caleb on his knees, his back to me, against the shaded threshold of the library. He was doubled over in terrible pain, his breathing threaded and hard. Then I caught a glimpse of blackened skin extending down his face and throat, and my heart dropped inside my chest.

Oh, my God! What've I done?

Chapter Eight

"Caleb!" I scurried across the floor on my knees, feeling like the room was somehow getting wider with each step. "I'm so sorry, I . . ."

"Get back!" His voice was sharp, sternly warning me in that heavy bellow of the warrior from the night of the train crash. Normal people would have halted in their tracks once they heard that tone, but for some reason with this man, I could do nothing normal. I couldn't stop myself from continuing to push towards him. This was all my fault!

If I had just waited to ask him . . .

"I said *get back!*" This time his tone was so commanding, I stopped. I realized that he wasn't going to let me anywhere near him when I saw his straining, rigid fingers crack the frame of the sliding door he had been holding onto. "God, Olivia," he began, a thick, almost desperate quality resonating in his voice, "I need you to get away from me—*right now!*"

He had no idea how much those words hurt me. It was as if I were causing him physical pain at that moment with my own hands, which was the last thing I wanted.

I wanted to help!

Jumping to my feet, I raced over to the window panel and quickly spun the metal handle counterclockwise, back to its original position. A few thundering heartbeats later the glass panes practically slammed into their closed position, the sun's rays safely dimmed once again behind what I now stupidly realized must be some sort of filtered glass.

I swung back to see Caleb still doubled over on the floor at the entry of the library, his breaths sawing in and out, working against the tensed muscles of his back.

"Tell me how I can help. Please, there must be . . ."

"Refrigerator," he gritted out. "Right side."

The Sub-Zero monster? That answer didn't make a lot of sense to me, but I didn't question it, racing back through the short corridor to the kitchen and putting away any thought of the pain in my ribs.

The right-side door swung open easily for me, and I gasped when I saw what he was asking for, what he needed—human blood. There were several dozen bags, just like you would see in a hospital or clinic, each labeled with a specific blood type.

Good Lord, what if I chose the wrong type to bring him? Were vampires picky about that sort of thing?

Deciding that he was in so much pain that it probably wouldn't matter, I scooped up as many bags as my arms could carry—a selection of several different types—and ran back around the corner towards the library. Caleb had not moved, but his breathing was still labored and he deliberately kept his back to me.

He knew I was there, though, and his hand shot up and slammed against the splintered door frame in a sort of wordless plea. "Don't come any closer!" he growled. I stopped a few feet from him, noticing how his chin lifted and his head turned ever so slightly toward me as he seemed to whiff the scents that must be coming from the bags in my arms. As he made this tiny motion, for just a moment I clearly saw the charred black skin all along the side of his face and throat, and it was clear to me that his whole body was still rigid from his effort to hold in the pain.

"Oh, God," I said in a choked whisper that told him I could see the damage to his face, causing him to turn away again the moment he realized how much he had revealed to me.

"Set the bags on the floor and go to your room," he commanded me, roughly. "Shut the door and do not come out until someone comes for you."

I dropped to my knees and slid the bags across the floor, one at a time, pausing to make sure he could reach each one. "*Olivia —now!* You can't be here for this!"

That snapped me to attention, and I scrambled up from the floor and sprinted toward the makeshift staircase. I headed for Gemma's room, slamming the door behind me, and rushed to the bathroom, slamming that door, as well, knowing that Caleb could hear and know I was following his orders. I headed straight into the open shower, where I huddled on the tiled bench at the far end. I couldn't seem to stop shaking as I pulled my knees in and tucked my head away. I was terrified—not because of his angry voice, not because of the bags of blood in the refrigerator, and not because I couldn't be anywhere near him when he fed, but because I didn't know how much I had hurt him.

What had I done?

"Stupid girl," I muttered to myself. "You should set *yourself* on fire and see how it feels." How ironic would it be if the death that seemed to stalk my life managed to kill a vampire! A vampire?

Ridiculously, I sat there in the shower for what seemed like hours, re-playing over and over the moment when Caleb had yet again saved my life; but this time I knew I didn't deserve it. The memories of his skin burning haunted me, and the worst of it was seeing the damage to his face, his wonderful face. "I didn't mean to," I murmured miserably. " . . . I didn't . . ."

I was unsure of how much time had passed when a light knock sounded at the bathroom door. "Olivia, it's me. Can I come in?"

I recognized Gemma's soft voice, but I said nothing in reply, instead choosing to keep my head tucked in my arms. How angry would she be with me for hurting Caleb?

After a few moments the door clicked and slid quietly open. I lifted my head just as Gemma poked her head around the edge of the door before stepping inside. Her cinnamon-colored hair was elegantly clipped back from her face, a couple of strands falling loose against her cheeks as she gave me a sympathetic smile that seemed to point out how a shower bench was certainly not the most comfortable place to have a conversation. "Oh, my . . . you do look a fright," she half-teased, her faint accent a bit stronger as she moved to enter the shower space.

I was stunned by the notion that she was concerned for me. It didn't matter how I felt. I was the one who caused this whole mess. "Gemma . . . I'm so sorry. I didn't mean to hurt him."

"Oh, hush. Of course you didn't mean for this to happen. He's going to be fine." My shoulders literally slumped in relief at hearing the words. Thank God. "He'd have to be in the sun longer than a few seconds to kill him. His body's just going to need some time to regenerate."

"Regenerate?"

She nodded, stepping fully into the shower stall and then kneeling in front of me. "Regenerating to a vampire is sort of like sleeping to a human. It helps the body repair itself, usually after battle or something like this."

"So I could've killed him . . . ?"

The hesitation in her eyes told me that she was being careful in choosing her words. "The sun could've killed him, Olivia, not you. That fact is part of his life—something that he must deal with every day. Not just today. Do you understand?"

I nodded, though I didn't really feel much better. The fact was, if I hadn't been so careless, none of this would've happened.

She gently patted my knee. "Stop worrying, all right? You're scaring him."

I blinked up at her, not understanding what she meant.

"He's heard how upset you've been up here all afternoon. It's worrying him. I promise he really will be all right."

"Why are you being so nice to me? I've only been here a few days, and look at all the trouble I've caused!"

Gemma just responded with a dismissive wave of her hand and a very unladylike snort. "Join the club. You couldn't possibly cause as much trouble as I have—not in three days, not in three years." She lifted her chin and sighed deeply, a rather broad grin spreading across her face. "I'm starting to think Jax and Caleb find it one of my more endearing qualities, actually."

I made a miserable attempt at a laugh as Gemma straightened up and unceremoniously offered her hand, beckoning with her other hand in a signal for me to get off the bench.

When I rose and came forward she stopped me, reaching for the shirt at my stomach. "Looks like you got some of the brunt of it."

Clueless as to what she was talking about, I glanced down, surprised to see a long burn mark across my midriff where Caleb had wrapped his arm around me. Gemma barely touched the angry, red slash and I flinched immediately. When I thought about it, I realized that I had felt some pain in that area all afternoon, but I had assumed it was because I had re-injured my ribs.

"Here, take that shirt off," Gemma instructed, grabbing a towel from the rack and motioning for me to follow her back into the bedroom. "Lie down on the bed. I'll be right back." And she literally meant it. Not five seconds passed before she was back at my side placing an ice-wrapped towel over my stomach. "Caleb won't be happy that he injured you like this."

"Then don't tell him," I whispered as she gently spread the soothing coldness over the ribs that had been re-aggravated. "There's no reason he needs to know."

She stared back at me with a sarcastically scolding smile, the olive color of her eyes appearing to twinkle with much more gold in the daylight. "You know that I can't keep this from him. He'll know. Probably already does."

"How can he know? He's not even here."

"Well," she laughed, "there's the fact that he can hear you, for one. But even if he couldn't, he would still *know*. He and Jax both have powerful senses. They can feel any heightened emotional state in a human . . . like pleasure, anger, fear—even pain. I can't hide this from him because if you feel physical pain from this injury and he's tuned into you—which, in your case, he definitely is—he'll feel it, too."

I lay there in stunned silence for a long moment. That explained a lot. Like how he always seemed to know what I was thinking. And why he looked at me as if he could see right through me. And how he'd been able to tell when I was not truthful with him by tuning in to the very feelings I was trying to conceal. "He must think I'm a habitual liar."

Gemma offered me a sympathetic smile. "More than likely he thinks as I do . . . that you're just scared. You've had a lot to process in a very short time."

She ever-so-gently lifted the ice off my stomach and rose to her feet. "Caleb mentioned that you haven't eaten today. I can bring you up something. Then, you should get some rest."

I couldn't deny that I was both hungry and tired. "Sure," I said agreeably. I wanted to be alone for a while, anyway, so I could take in everything I had learned.

***

The next day, Gemma surprised me with a beautifully prepared brunch on the tree house deck just beyond the kitchen. It was the perfect, private mountain getaway, although Gemma had to jump me over the three-foot gap between the house and the deck with the same twenty-five-foot drop to the ground below. I asked her why the deck was separated from the house like that, and she replied that it was to make sure there was enough room for the trees to move in the wind. That was really comforting—but then, what did I expect from a tree house?

For the first time I was able to get a sense of just how spectacular this little tree house was. It seemed we were standing at almost the highest point on the mountain, surrounded by numerous, sharp peaks and thick forests in every direction. The sound of swift-moving water came to me, though seeming to be somewhat in the distance, while lush evergreens closely rimmed the tree house on every side, forming a shaded canopy over the edges of the deck. And in some places the tree trunks came right up through the deck itself.

Gemma had set up a small bistro table, complete with bright yellow plates and sparking glasses. "Gemma, it's amazing out here. Where is the sound of water coming from?"

"There's a large spring and a waterfall just up the mountain, near the top. It's one of Caleb's favorite spots. He set up one of those funny-looking water wheels so we could get power and water to the house."

"That's smart, but it doesn't seem to me you use any power at all, except for the kitchen appliances."

"We use it," she replied coyly, then changed the subject. "Actually, this is my favorite part of the house. It's a great place to get some time alone and think—especially when Jax and Caleb get on my nerves, which can be pretty often." Then she mumbled, to herself, "The turds."

"Are you sure you're feeling up to this?" she asked as we sat down. "I have some ice here, so—"

I cut her off with a finger to my lips and a sharp, "Shhh."

Gemma just rolled her eyes and shook her head with disapproval, knowing exactly who I didn't want to overhear us. "Oh, all right," she added dryly. "Then, I brought you some ice for your juice this morning."

I scowled at her, determined not to have Caleb find out anything about my burn. "That's not necessary," I replied evenly. "No need for juice."

"Caleb was right," Gemma laughed. "You can be a handful, Olivia."

I blinked back at her. "A handful?"

"Yep. That's what he said."

I had never considered myself a 'handful.' In fact, I was usually very agreeable. "The turd," I found myself saying—in agreement with Gemma—which had her laughing even harder.

"Have you seen him this morning?" I just couldn't stop myself from asking.

Her gaze slid to meet mine with a lift to her brows. "Yes."

OK . . . so she wasn't going to make anything easy for me.

"Can I see him? Just long enough to tell him how sorry I am."

She shook her head gently. "That's not a good idea right now."

I decided that was the worst answer in the world. When she noted my disappointment, however, she added, "He knows you never meant to hurt him."

That made me feel a little bit better, at least.

"So, your ribs seem much better today. You barely even flinched when I checked them this morning."

That was certainly true, and it surprised me how little pain I felt after re-injuring them yesterday. "They do."

"That's odd . . . ," she replied. "It's only been four days."

I shrugged. "Maybe they weren't broken, just bruised."

Gemma's perplexed expression indicated that she didn't buy that for a moment, and I really couldn't understand it either, but I was grateful to have the pain gone.

"Why can't I see him?" I asked, really needing to know the answer.

"He doesn't want you to. Not right now."

"Oh," I replied flatly, her answer stinging with the effectiveness of a whip. He didn't want to see me. Could I really blame him, after I had practically burned him to death?

I scanned the food in front of me and became aware of the enormous amount she had prepared. In a glass covered dish there were scrambled eggs stirred with ham and vegetables and topped with melted cheese. That alone would've been enough, but the two plates beside it were arranged with rolls, both sticky and plain, and assorted fruits and cheeses. It all looked delicious, but how in the world did she expect me to eat all of it?

She answered that question by serving a plate for herself. "What's the funny look for?" she laughed.

"You're . . . you're eating."

She nearly choked on the bite she was taking before answering, "Yes, I do it every day."

"But that would mean you're not . . ."

"A vampire?" she finished for me. "No. I'm a Dhampir. Or technically a Dhampiresa, but that's just too long to say, isn't it?" She relaxed back into her chair, swinging her crossed leg easily over one knee as the light breeze drew in the scent of fir and blue lupine around us. "I'm a hybrid. My mother was human . . . my father a vampire."

Suddenly, it clicked why she had her own bedroom and didn't share the chilled room with Caleb and Jax. And why she would even be outside on a sunny day like this. It was silly—I should have put together sooner that if she were a vampire she wouldn't be able to come out here. "Your father was a vampire?" I asked curiously. "Vampires can have children?"

She nodded with a negligible shrug. "Male vampires can— females can't."

"That hardly seems fair."

"No, it's not. Actually it's very similar to humans."

"How so?"

"When a female becomes a vampire she can no longer produce any eggs, like a woman after menopause. But men, of course, just keep right on procreating until they're dead." She rolled her eyes. "I swear, you'd think the male species as a whole was about to die off any second, the way they rut around."

I smiled, taking a couple bites of eggs and ham that my stomach didn't seem to appreciate as much as I thought it would. Evidently, it was in a fickle mood this morning. "So it's common for the male vampires to . . . ?"

Gemma's eyes narrowed. "Hey, don't get any ideas. Human women almost always die if they become pregnant and give birth to a vampire's child—just like my mother. The birth is just too much for their bodies to handle."

I swallowed hard. "I'm sorry about your mother."

"It was a long time ago." Gemma said the words evenly, as if she had a lot of practice saying them, but there was probably a lot more to how she really felt underneath. Certainly, there must have been times when she wished she had a mother. I couldn't imagine how my life would have been different if I had never known mine. Clearly, she had found a way to deal with it, because she appeared to be a genuinely happy person.

"Can you have a vampire's baby? I mean, being that you're half vampire yourself?"

She nodded. "It's still difficult for a Dhampir, but we're much stronger."

"You've strength like Caleb and Jax then?"

Gemma took a bite of her cinnamon roll and pointed to my plate. "Eat," she ordered, noticing I wasn't touching my food. It had nothing to do with Gemma's cooking; the food all tasted fantastic. I just wasn't hungry. But to satisfy her I took another bite I really didn't want.

"I'm strong," she continued, " . . . though not nearly as strong as Jax or Caleb. But I'm fast, have pitch-perfect hearing, and can see just as well at night as I can during daylight. I also have their extra senses, but I can't sense the emotions in humans as they can—and particularly Caleb. His ability to feel is very strong."

My heart beat a little faster, and I wasn't sure whether I was excited by the fact that he could so easily feel my emotions—or fearful of it. Could he feel the pain tearing through my heart in that moment when I saw the vampire kill Sarah? Could he feel my fear when I woke several days later in an unfamiliar place?

Or how about when my stomach flittered the moment he walked into a room? Did I even want him to?

"I know what you're thinking, Olivia," Gemma said, cutting into my thoughts, "but you shouldn't bother to try and hide your feelings from him. He'll feel that, too."

How strange, how wonderful, how painful it must be to feel another person's emotions. All of it seemed to add up to one very large burden that would somehow have to be managed. Gemma's comment about 'being tuned in' made a lot more sense now.

"So," I began in a clumsy effort to change the subject. "You can obviously be out here in the sun?"

"For a little while," she shrugged, "but I burn as easily as a newborn. Which is why we're sitting in the shade. I have vampire blood running through my veins, so I also have their weaknesses . . . human ones, as well . . . just not to the same degree."

"I'm not sure I understand?"

She set down her fork, resting her slight weight back in her chair, her tone even, as if she was simply stating plain facts. "I'm pretty durable. I can take a pounding almost as well as they can, but if I'm cut, I'll bleed, just like you, but the vampire side allows me to heal faster."

"Oh." My voice faded, imagining Gemma's small form hurt and bleeding. "No wonder Jax is so protective."

She arched a brow. "Why do you say that?"

"Caleb mentioned that Jax could be a . . . What term did he use . . . ?"

"Over-protective sod," Gemma offered with a tiny smirk on her lips.

"Yes! That was it—over-protective sod."

"Ha!" she spouted loudly into the mountain air. "They're both over-protective sods! Neither of them ever allows me to even lift a finger at the first sign of trouble." She glanced back through the house and continued to speak as if Caleb were standing right next to us. "Yes, you heard me right. And you know it's true."

I laughed, imagining Caleb's grumbling protest at that moment. "I'm sure they mean well."

"Caleb I can excuse because he's a young vampire who just needs to be set straight by the right woman," she began—and had me blinking back at her in my chair. "Jax, though, is just an old, stubborn, illogical . . . ,"—she waved a hand—"Well, you get what I mean."

"He doesn't look that old," I offered. "I would guess he's only five or six years older than Caleb." I paused for a moment, considering that statement. "Not that I really know how old Caleb is."

"Caleb's thirty-nine in human years," she replied, "just like me."

"You're thirty-nine?" I blurted, rudely, believing it impossible for her to be any older than her early twenties. Caleb I understood. He didn't look a day older than the day I met him ten years ago, though his longer hair made him appear more . . . more . . . something. But Gemma?

"Dhampirs age very slowly, so we always look younger than we are."

"I guess," I snorted. "How old is Jax, then?"

Gemma's lips pulled into a soft smile. "He was thirty-one when he was turned, though he looks a few years older, but I think it fits him well, don't you?" I couldn't really answer her question because I had only seen Jax once, and that time only for a few seconds. I just remembered that he was very, very . . . big. "Life was shorter," she continued, "harder, two hundred years ago."

"*Two hundred?*" I blurted. I had assumed Jax was older than Caleb because he appeared to be the head of their coven—but two hundred?

"Yeah, I know. He's two hundred and twenty-three, actually. And as stubborn as two hundred and twenty-four," she grumbled. "But he's lived a long, often hard life. He has the heart of a gentle giant, though. He saved Caleb from being doomed to a life of killing humans that I'm sure would have eventually destroyed him. And gave me a home, a place where I could fit in even though I'm neither vampire nor human, just somewhere in between."

"What do you mean, he saved Caleb?"

"Jax taught Caleb how to live—how to feed his vampire

thirst without killing humans."

I dropped the fork I had been swirling around my plate and pointed at her as I put it all together. "That's what the blood in the refrigerator is for?"

Gemma nodded. "About seventy years ago, Jax fell in love with a human named Isabeau. Meeting her changed him. He had more respect for human life and wanted to become a better man for her. But to be with her meant that he would have to succeed at something he had failed at for over a hundred years . . . changing the nature of the vampire within him."

My food completely forgotten, I found myself hanging on every word of Gemma's story.

"You see, not long after he was living in England he'd heard rumors of a northerly coven who fed without killing humans. He didn't know whether to believe it, at first, because no one had ever seen a vampire who didn't kill humans. But he sought them out, and when he finally found them, asked them to teach him their ways. The transition is never easy, though. Jax tried and failed almost continuously over the course of his life. But after meeting Isabeau, he found something more powerful than his thirst. He was able to change, for her."

"Whatever happened to Isabeau?"

Gemma's lips thinned into a sad smile. "She died a few years later."

As she said those words I felt an overwhelming ache in my heart for Jax, a vampire who I had never even spoken to. It was the strangest thing. I understood losing someone you loved, but I could only image the pain of losing someone like Isabeau who he must have considered a soul mate. "That must've been hard; to lose the person you changed your life for."

"An immortal life, at that," she replied quietly. "Jax was angry for many years following her death, but he maintained control of his blood thirst to honor her. And once he firmly had that control, he began to change."

"Change? Change how?"

"His skin wasn't as ghostly pale, and his senses grew stronger, like his ability to feel human emotions. He became more civilized than other vampires, his skin more tolerant of the sun. That's why he and Caleb can walk like humans during the day under clouds or rain."

"But not in direct sunlight?" I murmured, remembering once again my stupid mistake.

"That's right," she answered, reaching for my hand and squeezing it. "They are rare and they are enchanted. That's how I see them, anyway. Their heart has stopped beating and their soul is gone, but their extra-sensory gifts are extraordinary. And over time they've been freed from some of the burdens of a life they had no choice about."

"So, the vampires like Isaac, who continued to kill humans, are different? They can't come out during the day?"

Gemma nodded. "They live like the traditional vampires you read about in stories—living only in darkness, sleeping during the day . . . and their thirst is relentless."

My mind recalled images of the vampire's frenzied thirst as he took Sarah's life. A thirst that was so powerful it seemed completely out of his control. Even just the memory of it was absolutely terrifying. "Yes, I remember," I said almost absently. "So Caleb and Jax are these good vampires?"

"Yes," she smiled. "They call themselves Daywalkers."

Chapter Nine

Later that afternoon, my fingers glided over the last few bars of Carl Orff's *O Fortuna* from my parents' favorite ballet, Carmina Burana. It was truly a beautiful and somewhat haunting piece of music, and every time I played it the composer inside me just wanted to soar.

It felt good to be playing music that I loved again and not just the music I was supposed to master. Actually, it had been Gemma's idea to play something for Caleb. She had told me on the previous day that he had loved hearing me play and that it would help him with his recovery. I wasn't quite sure if she was just trying to give me something to do so I wouldn't worry, but I jumped at the chance to play on the Fazioli again, especially if it would also help Caleb.

My retreat into music also gave me a chance to let this whole idea of Caleb being a Daywalker sink in. The pieces seemed to fit, though. The night of the crash, in his battle with Isaac, Caleb had seemed every bit as dangerous as Isaac had been, maybe even more so. But everything I knew about him since that night fit more with the man trying to control what he had become. The Caleb I knew, both as a teenager and as a woman, would never hurt me, and I just wished I could see him again to tell him that.

"Caleb was right, Olivia. You play wonderfully . . . and with no sheet music."

Turning back to thank her, I was startled to discover Jax Walker lounging on the sofa beside her. I hadn't even heard him come in, which wasn't really a surprise, since I never seemed to hear Caleb, either. The dark, coffee-colored hair that I remembered from the night of the crash was pulled back at his nape, and he was dressed all in black, his large, muscled frame fully relaxed in his seat. I had little doubt, though, after having witnessed his strength as a fighter, that he could cross the room in the blink of an eye.

"Play some more," Gemma urged as Jax stood to his full height. He wasn't as tall as Caleb, but he more than made up for it in muscled bulk.

"She will not," he announced, in what sounded like more formal English. "She is uneasy about my presence."

Swallowing hard, it was so strange to have someone just announce how I was feeling as if they were reading a sentence out of a book. No doubt, he would have already picked up on my accelerated pulse and the nervous rubbing of my hands against my shorts. He struck me as someone who picked up on details most people would miss. Almost as though he searched for them like clues, so they would aid him in protecting those he cared for.

"Oh stop it, you big bully," Gemma scolded as she slapped her hand against his leg playfully. "You're just trying to intimidate her."

Frowning, he turned to look down at her as she sat on the other side of the sofa with her legs crossed and her head focused on the open notebook in her lap. "What are you about? I am merely stating a fact."

"You know as well as I do that you don't merely *do* anything." She looked up briefly from her notebook to give him a cheeky grin, then returned to it. "Besides, you should be grateful to have a musician in the house. I know how much you both adore feeling the music."

"Feeling the music?" I asked.

Gemma glanced up from her notebook once again. "Jax and Caleb can feel the music—feel the vibrations in the sound." She tapped her pen against her head a few times as she narrowed her eyes in thought. "Sort of like the strings on that piano. When the hammers pound against them they vibrate, right? Music vibrates through their bodies in much the same way."

"I think that is enough music discussion for today," Jax said, clearing his throat.

"Is that true?" I asked. I was really curious. Despite being intimidated by the man, I couldn't really stop myself. I found this idea fascinating. "Because if it is, it would be an amazing gift to hear music in that way."

"It is," he replied simply. "And Gemma is right, Olivia. You do play most beautifully."

He appeared a bit uncomfortable just then, while I thought I was about to burst. I had no idea why it meant so much to me that Jax liked my music, but it did. Perhaps it was the fact that I knew how long he had lived and how many opportunities he must have had to hear the truly great works of many composers over the course of two hundred years. If he had stayed close to the music, seeing live performances at a time when there was no such thing as TV, video games, or movies, he would have heard the music in its original form, not while listening to someone else's interpretation. That would be amazing.

Jax turned back to Gemma, who was already smiling at him as if she found the whole exchange between him and me amusing. "How is he doing?"

No need to clarify who *he* was.

"Good," she replied. "He should be up and about soon."

"He will need to feed. I will take him out tomorrow." Jax spoke without contractions in his language, but it sounded completely natural coming from him. It fit.

"If you're worried about feeding here because of me," I interjected, "I could go outside tomorrow. Gemma could take me. Wouldn't that be easier while he's recovering?"

Gemma nodded, immediately approving of the idea. "That would be fun."

Jax didn't respond and turned his head slightly, as if focusing his attention towards another part of the house. It didn't last long, and a few seconds later he returned his attention to me. "That is not the reason. Caleb could feed here, but we must get him outside to work his muscles. He cannot be immobile for very long." Jax then paused, as if considering something additional. "Besides, with Isaac still unaccounted for, Caleb would never approve of the two of you out there by yourselves. And frankly, neither do I."

Why did I get the feeling that he a Caleb just had a conversation the rest of us were not privy to? "I don't understand. Can't Isaac only come after me at night?"

The slightest spark of surprise flickered through Jax's amber eyes just before he turned back to Gemma. "You have been explaining quite a lot to her, no?"

She sighed, as if the answer to that question should be quite obvious. "If she's going to be staying here with us, then she needs to know these things."

Jax hesitated for a moment, and I wondered if Caleb had even had a chance to talk to Jax about the idea of me staying. It wouldn't matter, though. I decided I would only stay until I knew Caleb was all right. Then I would think of a way to deal with the Isaac situation on my own. I refused to be the cause of any more accidents that would hurt any of them. It seemed so strange to say because I hadn't known any of them that long, but I already cared deeply about all of them.

"Isaac may have Dhampirs within his coven, and they can and will do his bidding during the day," Jax explained. "We cannot take the risk."

"Over-protective sods," Gemma muttered under her breath, her accent slipping a bit as she dropped her 'o.'

"Gemma!" Jax warned. "It is not safe and you know it."

"All right, all right," she quickly resigned, tossing her hand through the air. But Jax continued to watch her as she returned to writing a few lines in the corner of the notebook. His chin lifted, a smile spreading across his lips. The pleased smile of a man who knew he couldn't stay upset with the woman because there would be a new 'little gift' for him to find later.

"I will be in my study," he announced but then turned back at the last moment. "By the way, Olivia . . . It is nice to have music in the house," he said just before springing, light as a feather, to the second floor ledge.

My mouth proceeded to drop to the floor.

"I told you," Gemma whispered. "Gentle giant."

"I heard that," Jax growled from upstairs.

She rolled her eyes and returned to me. "Are you tired?"

"No. But I think I'll go into the library and read for a bit . . . if that's all right?"

"Read away. I'm sure you'll find something in there of interest."

I nodded and started towards the library before swinging back on my heels. "Oh, and Gemma . . . ? I want to sleep in the library tonight. You've been much too generous with your room."

"Olivia, I really don't—"

"I *do* mind," I insisted.

She seemed to consider that for a moment and then shrugged her shoulders. "OK, but Caleb isn't going to like it."

"Well it's not his decision." And to make my point clear, I announced in a raised voice, "Do you hear that, Caleb Wolfe? I'm sleeping in the library tonight."

Jax's deep throated chuckle floated down from the second floor.

"Oh, I think he heard that," Gemma snickered. "And no, he doesn't like it. In fact, he's grumbling as we speak."

"Too bad," I said as I marched towards the library.

***

The book binding to *Great Expectations* had been splayed open over my stomach for quite a while as I lay on the sofa just staring up at the ceiling, my fingers tapping away against the hard cover. I wasn't sure what was wrong with me, but my thoughts kept circling back to the fact that Caleb had refused to let me see him today. And tomorrow he would be gone all day with Jax. If he wasn't trying to avoid me, he was doing a fine job of looking like it.

A light rapping at the library door broke into my thoughts. Gemma poked her head in and, with a concerned smile, asked, "Are you going to eat something for dinner?"

Shaking my head, I replied, "I'm not hungry."

That brought a frown to her face. "You really should eat something. You haven't had much at all today." She stepped inside the room, her arms full of clothing, blankets and a pillow.

I got why she was concerned. I had felt a little off today. "I promise I'll eat more tomorrow."

She nodded but didn't look convinced. "I brought you some clothes to sleep in tonight and some items to make up the sofa."

I smiled. "Thank you. And thank you for respecting my wishes to sleep here."

"You're welcome." She set the items on the end table just over my head before kneeling in front of me and placing her hand over my forehead and cheeks. "Are you sure you're feeling OK? You feel warm to me. You're fever isn't coming back, is it?"

She was trying to keep the worry out of her voice but was failing miserably.

"I'm fine," I assured her. "Just distracted, I guess."

She seemed to accept that and left the room, shutting the door behind her. Strangely, though, I lay there like that for a few more hours, feeling just too restless to sleep. When I finally did try to sleep, I stirred on the unfamiliar leather cushions beneath me, my mind shifting in and out of consciousness. For most of the night I wasn't sure I had gotten anything that would actually qualify as meaningful sleep, and yet there were pieces of time I couldn't remember, so I must have gotten some.

There were moments when I felt chilled to the bone, my limbs shaking with goose bumps, and others when I was too hot, burning, as if internal flames were trying to burn away all of my worries from the day. At one point, the uncomfortable heat seemed to take hold and I found myself twisting and pulling, trying to get free, but it just kept getting stronger and stronger until finally, mercifully, I felt some relief. It spread over me like a cool cotton sheet, easing me until I was relaxed enough to sleep.

That's when I must have started dreaming. In my dreams, Caleb was there with me, somehow lying beside me as he pulled me against his cool body and stroked his hand over my back. "Hold onto me," he said. "Just hold on. We're going to cool you down, sweet girl. I promise."

Untucking my head, I laid my cheek against his throat, my breaths now relaxed and even. His palm pressed against my other cheek, and it was like I could tell how hot I was by how cold his skin felt against mine. It wasn't cool, it was cold like ice. "Stay with me," I murmured.

***

The next morning, I woke to my own soft moan, stretching like a lazy cat after a nap as I rolled over on the soft mattress . . .

Wait, mattress?

My head popped up and dizziness hit me, so I plunked it right back down into the pillows and then opened my eyes slowly. The huge glass ceiling to the stars was above me, only this time it was daylight. Thick, gray clouds loomed overhead, and I was completely at a loss as to how the heck I ended up back in Gemma's room. Surely, I would've felt if someone moved me during the night. I wasn't normally a very heavy sleeper.

I lay there for a moment trying to recall any details and came up with very little, but I did remember feeling too warm at one point, and then cooler. I decided that must have been when I was moved.

Sometime during the night, Caleb had carried me from the library to here. It was the only explanation. How he had managed to do it without waking me was a mystery. And why hadn't he stayed? Why hadn't he let me see he was OK—or, at least, healing?

Despite the fact that he had completely disregarded my wishes to stay in the library, and now a bit self-conscious because I had no idea what I might have done or said in my sleep, a beaming smile pulled across my face.

He was all right!

That realization let me forgive him anything and allowed my mind to focus on other things, like how all of a sudden I was very, very hungry. Not quite springing from the bed—it seemed my head wasn't quite ready for that this morning—I grabbed the three-quarter length robe from the bathroom hook and made my way downstairs to the kitchen.

Gemma was already waiting at the center island, perched on a stool with her finger tapping against her cheek, obviously amused by my noisy footfalls through the house. Fresh eggs, hash browns, and sizzling sausage deliciously stimulated my senses as I propped myself on an empty stool and dug into the plate she pushed in front of me. With each bite, my head felt better and my appetite seemed to grow.

"My gosh, you're hungry," she laughed. "It's good to see that your appetite has returned. Does that mean you're not upset about waking in my room?"

I drank some juice to wash down the food and shook my head. "No, I'm furious with him." My easy tone, however, did not match my words. "Why did you let him do that?"

"I was up talking to Jax last night," she shrugged. "I wasn't using the room." Then she leaned closer and whispered, "I don't need much sleep, either." She winked and then shuffled her expression quickly back into concern that looked as if she was about to break into laughter at any moment. "But you're furious, Olivia. This sounds serious."

"Very funny. I'll make it clear tonight. I'm sleeping in the library, and you're sleeping in your room."

"OK, sure, whatever you say."

Now halfway through scarfing down the feast on my plate, I noticed that Gemma was not joining me. "Did you already eat this morning?"

"Yes, but I was more thirsty this morning, if you know what I mean."

I nearly bit my tongue on that last bite. "You mean blood?"

She shrugged. "Some days my body needs it. It's a good thing, too 'cause today I think you'll be able to finish all the food on your own."

Suddenly feeling a little embarrassed at my uncontrolled appetite, I slowed down my feeding frenzy long enough to consider what she was saying. "Does it taste funny?"

"The blood? What—like sour milk or something?"

"No. I mean is it hard for you to drink?"

She laughed. "If it was, then I probably wouldn't drink it."

"I suppose that's true," I conceded. "But where do you get all this blood? It looks as though it comes from a hospital."

"Jax," she replied simply, as if that should answer everything, which it totally didn't. "The Walker Foundation,"—she added with quote marks in the air—"owns the blood donation clinic where I work during the week. I manage the clinic, hiring part-time nursing students from the University to draw blood. It gives them some experience, some extra cash for school. And the blood techs come and go, so no one's really around long enough to notice that I'm not aging."

"So you bring the blood here from the clinic."

"Yes," she replied carefully. "What's with your frown?"

I hadn't even realized that I was frowning. "It's just that . . . I don't understand. How's it different to feed your thirst by drinking donated blood? Isn't it all human blood?"

"Ah, very good question," she smiled. "You are catching on fast. It has to do with adrenaline."

"Adrenaline?"

"Yep. It's released into a prey's bloodstream as an automatic response to fear. Adrenaline is like a drug to vampires, as powerful and addictive as anything we can imagine. That's why they frenzy when they're feeding. They need it. They need to kill for it. And that need makes it nearly impossible to make the change."

Once again, that image of the vampire frenzying as he drank from Sarah ran through my head. That wild look in his eyes was something I'd never forget. I couldn't help but wonder if Caleb went through the same wildness when he needed to drink. He had been honest about how he had less control when he was thirsty. Did he really have any more control than a vampire like Isaac?

"Donated blood," she continued, "blood that is given freely, is much purer than feeding on someone who is responding to an attack. That's why vampires intentionally frighten their prey before they feed. They want the blood stream to be overloaded —they can smell it. Daywalkers are different. They control the amount they take in . . . similar to diabetics controlling their blood sugar levels. In essence, *that* control helps them gain *more* control."

Suddenly, not feeling as hungry, I cleared my plate and went to wash it off in the sink. I thought about what Caleb had said to me that day at the piano—how being in control of what he was, his thirst, was the most important thing to him. I decided that he was truly a warrior in spirit, but not because he fought bad men like Isaac; rather because he fought to hold onto to those things that were most important to him—respect for himself being at the top of the list. How could someone not admire that? "When did they leave?"

"Early. Before dawn. But Caleb was with you most of the night."

Drying my hands off on a towel, I turned back to her a little confused. "He was?"

She nodded. "You were running a fever last night. He was worried."

"I didn't know. I mean, I thought I was just having trouble sleeping . . ." Then it hit me that my dream of lying there with Caleb must have been real.

"I knew you were warm," Gemma said with a narrowed gaze. "Caleb wasn't going to leave you this morning, but Jax convinced him it was in your best interest."

I placed my clean dish in the cupboard and returned to my seat at the island. "My interest? Him feeding today is somehow in my interest?"

Gemma let out an unladylike snort. "Surely, you realize that it doesn't take them an entire day to feed. They're tracking Isaac today."

"Isaac!" I cried, jumping back off the stool. "That's too dangerous for Caleb to be doing after he just—"

"How many times do I have to tell you? Caleb's fine. In fact, he's feeling so normal he was downright surly this morning about having to leave you."

I still thought it was too dangerous.

All day I tried to find things to distract myself from the fact that I was praying he wouldn't find Isaac. If he couldn't find him, he wouldn't fight him. I hated thinking about the two of them going at it again like they did on the night of the train crash, especially with Caleb just recovering from his burns.

Once again, as night began to fall, I found myself lying in the familiar position on the sofa in the library, with my ankles crossed and my fingers tapping away against my book's hard cover. In the span of a few shorts days, it seemed, I had become incapable of focusing on anything other than Caleb Wolfe. It was ridiculous. He was a vampire, for Pete's sake, one that I hadn't even seen in two days. What the heck was wrong with me?

The hours continued to tick slowly by as I waited for him to return. I just needed to see that he was all right. These feelings growing inside me were so unfamiliar, so out of character for me, that I felt sure Caleb Wolfe had cast some sort of spell over my heart.

Turning onto my good side, my heavy lids now warned me that I wouldn't see him again tonight. A chill began spreading over my bare legs and feet, but I was too sleepy to even cross the room to grab the blanket and pillow Gemma had left for me. Instead, I decided to let a few hours of darkness come for me and deal with the cold later.

I was curled up in a ball against the leather cushions, my legs and feet tucked in tight to try and keep myself warm when I heard the light sound of a book thumping shut just before a warm blanket was wrapped around me. The chill in my legs seemed to disappear almost right away as I tucked myself against something solid, something familiar—something safe.

"Caleb?" I murmured as I felt myself being lifted and then carried, but tonight I was so tired I could barely hold my head up, let alone open my eyes. Moments later, I felt myself being set atop a soft cushion and warm blankets being pulled over me. "I'm sorry I hurt you."

Cool lips pressed tenderly against the corner of my mouth, and then another on my cheek just before his deep voice whispered over my ear, "Shhh, everything's fine. I promise you, everything's OK. Just sleep, my sweet girl. Sleep for me."

I rolled on the mattress towards the sound of his beautiful voice, wanting to reach for him, but my arms felt like lead and I sensed that my mind was drifting off again. "I miss you," I heard myself say. "Please don't go."

Then, in a wonderfully euphoric end to the dream, several more tender kisses were showered over my face and throat. I raised my chin higher to receive every single one of them. "I'll be right here when you wake, Olivia," he said.

Chapter Ten

The next morning, I was kicking my legs around in an effort to free myself from the bed covers I had somehow got tangled up in when I rolled into a hard wall that didn't want to move. I stopped my squirming long enough to consider several things that had just occurred to me. One, I remembered that I shouldn't be able to roll around much at all on the narrow sofa I had fallen asleep on the night before. Two, it shouldn't be this comfortable or this warm because I didn't have a blanket. And three, most importantly, there shouldn't be a wall.

A large hand came to rest over the curve my waist and I knew . . .

Caleb.

My eyes popped open to see him sitting there beside me with an amused quirky little smile on his lips, probably from witnessing my ridiculous battle with the covers only moments before. I clamped my bottom lip between my teeth to hold back the smile that wanted to burst over my cheeks. After all the dread and fear of the last two days that I had somehow scarred him forever, he appeared even more handsome than I remembered. Unruly strands of dark, chestnut hair were tucked behind one ear, and his eyes, those wonderful shades of gray, matched the blue-slate shirt he wore with the sleeves rolled up to his elbows. Gone was any trace of the blackened burns over his skin, which had returned to its normal, perfect, pale color.

Without warning him, I sprung from my horizontal position and threw my arms around his broad shoulders and hugged him so fiercely that it was like a choice to let him go at that moment would be the difference between life and death.

He was healed and he was safe, and that was all that mattered to me. Caleb didn't budge at my enthusiastic launch into his arms, but a surprised, guttural gasp escaped him as he caught me, followed by a quiet chuckle over my ear. "Well, good morning to you, too."

"You're all right," I said, my breathing quickening as I encircled him in a virtual chokehold around his neck and rested my cheek against his rough, bristly one.

"Of course, I'm all right," he replied in an incredulous tone, as if the state of his wellbeing should have never been in question, but my grip only tightened around him. I felt relief, but also terrible guilt as I remembered seeing his burned and blackened face. I just couldn't believe I had been so careless.

"Hey, you're trembling," he said, pulling his arms tighter across my back, "Olivia, I really am perfectly OK."

"I'm so sorry, Caleb," I began miserably. "I didn't mean—"

"Shhh, easy," he murmured as his fingers threaded through my hair. Sometimes he was so gentle when he touched me, it was hard to reconcile that fact with the warrior I knew storming within him. "What happened was not your fault. It was mine."

Confused, I pulled back to meet his sincere gray gaze. How could he think my carelessness was his fault? "I've kept you in a place that's new to you. Told you to explore the house, but I didn't bother explaining anything that might be unfamiliar." He sighed heavily. "I just didn't think."

I continued my hold on him, burying my face in his neck. We stayed like that for a long while, his quiet words continuing to reassure me as I pressed myself so close I was sure my thundering heartbeats were bouncing right from my chest into his. He responded to my closeness, his breaths roughening as he shifted his hands beneath me, sliding them behind my thighs to curl my legs around his hips, like a wrench. I could feel myself growing more excited against him, a tingling sensation swelling low in my belly. A wonderful warmth seemed to invade my entire being, and at the same moment my breaths quickened, rising and falling in unison with his.

"Olivia," his husky voice murmured just before he drew back.

"No, don't pull away," I replied with soft protest, but soon it became clear he wasn't pulling away. His lips came over mine in a rough, heated breath that stole the oxygen from my lungs in an instant. His kiss was so powerful, I felt as if I were being crushed by the force of it, sinking into a pleasure so deep that it began to take over everything else. The desire in these kisses was very different from the tender ones he gave me at the piano. They were passionate, hungry, consuming, feeling more like the familiar caress of a well-established lover than a mere second kiss.

"Olivia," he rasped as his fingers dug into my hair and pulled my head back, angling me exactly as he wanted, then he slid his tongue inside my mouth and pushed his kisses deeper. I had never in my life felt anything close to this. His taste seemed to explode into my mouth, and I prayed I was affecting him even a fraction as much as he was affecting me.

Then, as if he had heard my thoughts, his deep moan reverberated over my lips, his nostrils flaring to take in more air as he twisted me beneath him. "My sweet Olivia. I promise you everything's OK—everything."

The sound of my name was never more beautiful than when spoken from his lips, expressed with such reverence that I began to tremble again in his arms. I worried he would think my trembling was a sign that I was afraid, but he must have been able to feel the truth in my heart, because his kisses only deepened, forcing me to grab onto his shoulders to steady myself because my heart was now pounding in my ears and my head was swimming in a sea of wooziness.

Mercy! Don't ever let this end.

But end it did—too quickly. He pushed himself from me without any warning, a little roughly even, his gaze hot and his breaths sawing in and out of his chest.

I blinked back at him, too stunned to do anything more than to glide my fingertips over my swollen lips, realizing suddenly where those kisses would have taken us if he had not stopped. "Caleb . . . ?" I moved toward him, but he pushed back, his extended hand keeping distance between us while he worked to bring his breathing back to normal.

"You just might be the death of me some day, Olivia. But it's going to take a lot more than a little sun."

I was startled that he could even joke about such a thing. "That's not funny."

But then he became playful again. He reached for me, but I was able to dart away. It was almost a given, though, that if he was really trying he would have caught me. "Olivia," he began with a sigh, "this isn't good for your ribs. Now, lie back down so I can check them."

Quite simply, I didn't want to.

Whether it was my stubbornness or my insecurities, I wasn't sure—probably both. But he *had* pushed me away from him, and fast. Men weren't usually the ones pushing away from a woman. Might it be just my luck that I was the only one who felt this crazy attraction between us? Maybe he still saw me as the awkward teenage girl who had been tongue-tied at the first sight of him? That was an embarrassing thought, and it only got worse when I remembered how he hadn't seemed to want to see me for the last two days, and I suddenly felt foolish. "My ribs are fine!" I snapped. "Ask Gemma."

His dark brows pulled together, but it wasn't in anger, more from concern. "Yes, she mentioned that. I'd like to see for myself, though. Now, lie down . . . please."

"No."

Admittedly, I was behaving like a spoiled child as I tried to scramble off the bed. But in an instant, I found myself swung into his arms and then gently splayed flat on my back, his long body coming over me with a devilish glint in his eyes as he held both of my wrists together, above my head, in a single, large, strong hand. "My sweet girl is stubbornly feisty this morning, isn't she?"

Oh, I was about to give him feisty alright, but he cut me off with another kiss—and it shocked me still. These kisses were playful, tender, and slow. After only a few moments, I stopped fighting him and simply sank back into the deliciousness of them. He gently released my wrists and nibbled just a bit at the corner of my mouth before pulling back with a smile, his eyes showing just a touch more blue in them than before.

Now I was even more confused. I reached for him, my hands sliding behind his neck and pulling him down to me once more. He allowed it, allowed his body to sink more fully against mine, allowed his kisses to go deeper. But before long we were both breathing hard, and again he pulled away from me for a second time. "Christ, Olivia!" he practically growled.

This time I smiled because his eyes were sparking with even more blue.

Oh yeah. He felt it, too.

Shaking his head as if he were trying to regain focus, he began working on the buttons of my shirt. Which, I was rather excited about until I remembered the burn that was still healing on my stomach. A jolt of panic whipped through me and I slammed my hands down over his, keeping the shirt pinned to my stomach. "I promise, my ribs are fine. There's no need to check them."

He had a strange look on his face that I couldn't quite read. "Are you uncomfortable with me opening your shirt? It's sort of a requirement to see the bruising."

Once I followed his train of thought my eyes widened. "No!" I replied in a rather thin, high voice, and then cleared my throat and repeated the word more normally.

His eyes narrowed with suspicion, and I could tell he was trying to feel my emotions. I tried to clear my mind, but it was too late. His brows tugged a bit as he moved my hands, returning to splay one hand directly over the burn. My breathing was all nerves as his hand just rested there over my shirt for a long moment. Then a flicker of sadness passed through his eyes. "You've been doing a good job of hiding this from me."

He moved his hand and opened the shirt, then froze. In trying to conceal the pain over the last couple of days, I hadn't been taking care of the burn as I should have, but, to my surprise, it didn't look that bad. Still, it wasn't acceptable to Caleb. The playfulness and joy vanished from his expression, replaced by a painful grimace as he gently rested his cool palm over the burn to try and offer some relief. "I'm sorry," he said quietly. "I never meant to hurt you."

"It doesn't hurt anymore. And the burn is healing. Soon, it'll be completely—"

"That's not the point!" he snapped, but I knew he wasn't angry at me. He was angry at himself.

Crossing the two ends of my shirt over each other, he didn't bother to close the buttons as he got up and left the room without another word. I scrambled from the bed to follow him. "Caleb! Don't go."

He swung around and came to a stop, still visibly upset. As I approached him, his right hand reached tentatively for my left side, and I stepped right to his hand. Gently, he pressed his fingertips over my side, his eyes watching me carefully as he moved along each rib. When I didn't wince or try to pull away he slid his hand over a larger area, sure he had not been in the right place. But I remained quiet and still, even when his knuckle grazed my breast, which sent a thrilling jolt to my heart. "Your ribs do seem much better," he began. "But it doesn't make any sense. It's been less than a week."

I shrugged. "They must've been bruised, not broken."

"No. I heard them crack when Isaac—"

He cut off his own words, probably not wanting to scare me at mention of Isaac's name.

"Can we go outside today?" I asked, hoping for a quick change of subject.

He looked to the overcast but dry skies and paused, as if considering his options. "Do you feel up for a walk today?"

I nodded eagerly, hoping my enthusiasm would be enough to convince him.

A slow grin spread over his lips as he brushed them over my cheek, and I noticed his eyes were completely gray again, no blue. He just had the most amazing and surprising eyes. They always seemed to be changing.

"After you've showered and had something to eat, put on some warm clothes. I'm going to show you the proper way to use the front door."

Exactly one hour later I was standing in front of the glass doors, practically bouncing on my feet at the thought of getting to explore the woods around us with Caleb. I was all prepared for cold weather in a pair of warm, corded pants, a thick red sweater with a white tee peaking underneath, and some hiking boots I borrowed from Gemma, even though they pinched my feet a little.

When the wave of cool air hit me I smiled. The next

moment, he was standing there beside me, his button-up shirt and jeans unchanged, the obviously chilly temperatures having no affect on him.

He assessed me from head to toe, his gray gaze not a bold sweep like mine had been that first day, but more like a slow, almost wicked inventory of every detail. It was then I started to worry, after feeling the whole of my skin flush under his stare, that the sweater I chose would be too warm, even though I was sure it was plenty chilly outside.

"I like you in red," his deep voice murmured before he helped me into the white ski jacket I carried over my arm.

All I could do was smile. I just couldn't stop smiling.

He then took my hand and stepped us back from the windows before turning the lever. Once again, five of the southern facing glass panes moved uniformly to a ninety degree position. I stepped forward to check out the view, knowing what to expect this time, but Caleb's firm squeeze of my hand pulled me back. "That's how you got yourself into trouble the first time, remember?"

He curled his arm under my knees to lift me into his arms as a small smile pursed his lips. "Are you sure you're up for this?"

I took a deep breath and glanced over the edge one more time before nodding, "Yes."

"Good. Hold on tight," he smiled, "and don't look down."

I nodded and he stepped forward until the bottom fell out from under us. Air rushed so fast over my cheeks that I couldn't contain my excited squeal. I closed my eyes in a long blink and then popped them back open again to see the world blurring by me. Stretching out my hand, I reached towards the sky against the heavy force of the air. When I sensed that the ground was getting closer, I locked gazes with Caleb and tightened my grip around his neck, instinctively curling in towards his body. "I've gotcha," he responded to my stranglehold.

Even on such a steep drop, it felt like we began to slow just before the connection with the ground, as if somehow Caleb was defying gravity for just those few precious seconds. His feet met the ground with slight thump, and I was pretty sure my eyes were round with amazement.

"There, see? Easy."

He released my knees, letting my feet fall lightly to the ground, his arm remaining secure across my back for support while I tested out my admittedly shaky steps.

The magnificence of the home I had been staying in for the past week became clear to me when I looked up at the structure from the ground. It really did look like a fantastic tree house. I had never seen anything like it before. The wood and glass structure was hidden amongst a cluster of giant evergreens, almost as if the rectangular box had been cut right into the middle of them. But as I looked closer I could see that the house itself was supported by what looked like several existing trees. Those trees pushed up through the deck in several places while also appearing to support the house underneath.

One could walk right by this place and never notice there was a home overhead—which, I was sure, was very intentional. "How did you do this?" I asked in slow amazement. "How did you build this?"

"You like it?" he replied, sounding relaxed as he circled his arms around me and tucked his chin on my shoulder.

Like it? I liked it so much, words escaped me. For a moment, only bits of sound tried to pass for words. Tapping my fingers against my pant leg, I inhaled a slow breath. "It's like . . . something out of a story. Like . . . it can't possibly be real."

"I like structures that don't interfere with the nature around them," he said. "This idea was inspired from some Japanese architecture I had been reading about."

I turned in his arms and blinked up at him. "Caleb?"

He smiled and squeezed his arms around me. "In my human life, I was a hungry and inspired architect. I had big plans to become the next generation Frank Lloyd Wright. But I never really got the chance, so this project was sort of my labor of love." He pointed to a center cluster of trunks. "See those trunks? I stamped and stained them to look like aged bark, but they're actually concrete. They blend nicely with the real trees, though."

"I think it's perfect," I said with wonder. "The most perfect home I could ever imagine. But how? How did you build this?"

He inhaled a deep, heavy breath, a contented sound. "It

wasn't easy, that's for sure. Jax nearly killed me himself about a dozen times, especially when I told him I wanted to add a piano." He laughed, and it was such a beautiful sound. "But it was worth it. I think Jax agrees." He leaned in and kissed the end of my nose. "Let's just say, when you're immortal you have a lot of time on your hands."

This time I laughed. "I suppose that's true."

Caleb tugged at my hand. "Come," he said. "This way."

He motioned me forward on what appeared to be a natural elk trail. I inhaled the clean air and natural beauty around us. The scent of pine and fir trees mixed wildflowers and earth to transport my mind back to that first day I had met Caleb as a sixteen-year-old girl. On that day, Caleb had been very human, and I could still see him, the human man. He had brought the soul of who he was with him into this immortal life, and to me it seemed an amazing feat, considering the burden of having blood thirst and anger driving your existence.

"The day I met you . . . ," I began. "That day, by the lake?"

"Yes," he replied, his attention focused on my backwards steps over the uneven terrain.

"You remembered me?"

"I should think that was pretty obvious when I brought you to my home."

I smiled, swinging back around to continue forward. "Do I look the same to you?"

I knew this was one of those questions men hated. They probably saw them as a trap with no right answer. But Caleb actually seemed relaxed, like he didn't have to search for any answer. "You were a pretty girl then, Olivia. But I much prefer the beautiful woman you've become."

Heat shot to my cheeks and threatened to swallow my face whole. At that moment, I was just thankful to be leading us so he couldn't see how those words turned me to Silly Putty. That was the reaction of a teenage girl, not a grown, confident woman. But still, my heart had skipped at least three or four beats. I had never considered myself beautiful. Maybe attractive, but I certainly had flaws. I had always wished I had a more unique eye color than bland brown, or that my brown hair was naturally a little shinier, not quite so stick straight.

And I had never exactly been thin, always curvy. But Caleb seemed to like my blah brown and my curvy shape, and suddenly I felt like the most beautiful woman in the world.

"You liked me saying that, didn't you?" he asked. "Your heart is fluttering."

Damn! My body's responses were so traitorous. That was when I decided his ability to hear every sound, feel every emotion bursting through me, was darn inconvenient. Yet I still couldn't seem to hold back the huge smile on my face.

He laughed softly behind me. "Still fluttering . . ."

Trying to get the attention off my embarrassing lack of bodily control, I asked, "That was your last day? Your last day as human, I mean?"

"Yes," he answered simply, not making anything easy for me.

"Am I prying too much?"

"No. You can ask me whatever you want."

"Will you tell me about that day, then? What happened?"

There followed a long silence, and for a moment I was afraid he wasn't going to answer. "After I left you with your parents," he began, "I believe I contacted park rangers to meet me at the location of the body you found. I arrived before them and must've been gathering my tackle and lure from the rock when she came for me."

I turned back to him. "She?" I questioned. "A female vampire?"

He nodded, motioning for me to continue on the path, nudging me forward when I didn't fall right into step. "*She* is Celeste, actually."

My heart seemed to drop to my stomach as I tried to focus on putting one foot in front of the other in a straight line. He called her by her first name. And it wasn't past tense. Suddenly, I wasn't so sure I wanted to know the answer.

"Celeste had seen me the night before and decided I would make a good mate. She waited for the right opportunity, a moment when I was alone and the sun was behind the mountains . . ."

Mate! The word rang in my head till I thought my stomach was going to heave. Heat began to sweep from my face into my neck, and I could tell I was angry—or worse, jealous. I hated the fact that I already felt so possessive of him. That was something I resented about my own past boyfriends. Everything would always start out great, but after a few weeks they all became needy and controlling. I seemed to have a knack for picking out that type of man, maybe because on the inside I was that type of woman. God, I hoped not. But right now, with the jealously I felt towards this Celeste, I couldn't make a good case to defend myself.

"So when you say she 'came for you,'" I asked, carefully, "you mean she bit you . . . she changed you?"

Just then, the path opened up through the trees. A huge rock shelf appeared to our right and floated proudly, like a stage over the expansive tree-lined valley below, revealing a breath-stealing view of Mt. Rainier in the distance. At this altitude the air was crisp and thin, and I literally felt as if I were standing at the highest point of all the terrain around me.

Caleb scooped me into his arms, springing us up about fifteen feet to the rock's surface. For the second time in a day I was flying in the vampire's arms, and it felt as if I were right where I was supposed to be.

He set me to my feet, then moved to stand right on the jagged edge that dropped several hundred feet to the valley floor below. He had no fear. In fact, he barely seemed to be aware of the steep drop, though there was no doubt he knew it was there.

"The term we use is turning," he answered, finally, his stare remaining unmoving from the valley beyond. "And yes, she turned me."

I swallowed hard. "Is that all it takes to turn someone . . . one bite?"

He was silent for a long while, seeming to consider if he wanted to continue this discussion, but ultimately he must have decided he did. "Vampires carry a toxin in their saliva . . . a catalyst, so to speak. When combined with the victim's blood it works like a virus, paralyzing the prey while the vampire feeds. If the victim is not drained, the virus continues to spread through their system until they are turned."

Caleb then turned back to me, seeming instantly to understand the fears running through my head. "You don't need to be afraid, Olivia. My saliva or blood alone can't hurt you. It's only when the two are combined—as in a bite—that it's dangerous."

He watched me closely for a moment while I tried to comprehend what he was telling me. "Sarah never had a chance, did she? Once the vampire bit her?"

"No, she didn't. But as hard as it is to accept, she did have a more merciful end."

"Unlike you?" I questioned.

He inhaled a large breath and gazed back over the valley. "I feel that I'm upsetting you. No more questions today."

"No Caleb, please. I want to hear this. The fear you feel inside me is because I'm realizing what you went through, not because you're frightening me."

He responded with a frown, but I pressed on, hoping he wouldn't stop me. "Was it painful? Being bitten I mean."

He nodded. "Once the toxins invade your system you're incapacitated until the transformation's complete. Your heart and lungs stop . . . you appear dead, but you're only frozen. You can still feel and sense everything around you."

"So . . . how was she able to stop? To not . . . ?" I couldn't finish the words. They were too awful. Luckily, he understood what I was asking so I didn't have to.

"The night before, she had fed on the body you found in the grass. That gave her the control she needed to stop before she drained me."

Celeste fed on humans. She wasn't a Daywalker, or at least she wasn't, back then. And if she turned him, did that mean she mated him? As what he told me began to sink in, I suddenly felt suffocated in my own clothes. I didn't understand what was wrong with me. It wasn't like me to have such a reaction to another woman, but with Caleb I couldn't seem to help myself.

Caleb turned to catch me fidgeting against the rock, his concern was visible as his brows pulled together and he watched me tear off my coat and shove it on the rock beside my hip. "What're you doing?" he questioned. "You're not cold?"

I blinked up at him. "No."

He came to me, his gaze watching me carefully. "Why are you so restless today?"

I swallowed hard, not wanting to admit how much his story was bothering me. "I'm fine, really. Please go on."

Caleb continued to study me, or rather feel me. I could tell now when he was doing it. I inhaled a slow breath and cleared all the thoughts in my head. It must have worked; he scowled at me, able to tell when I was hiding my feelings from him. But I really didn't want him to feel my jealously of his past mate.

He came to sit beside me, his arm curling around my back as he pulled me to his shoulder. "After the rangers came and took my body away, I could already sense Celeste watching, following. When the virus was finished with me, the next day, she was waiting for me. At the time I went with her because, essentially, I was alone and I didn't understand how to survive in my new world, how to feed the painful thirst that stripped every other thought or desire I had."

Mentally, I scolded myself for making him remember such a horrible day. I doubted I would ever truly be able to understand what he went through.

"She brought me to this side of the mountains to live with her and her coven. Through them I could see the monster I'd become . . . and what I'd have to do to survive."

"You're not a monster!" I defended sharply.

A humorless smile died on his lips and my heart ached for him, understanding that he saw himself that way, as a monster. I could see he hated himself for killing humans to quench his thirst when he was first changed, but how could he stop the need, the very nature of what he had become, when he barely understood what had happened to him?

I remembered what Gemma had said about Jax saving Caleb from his previous life: " . . . which I think would have eventually destroyed him."

Now I understood. Knowing that by asking him to talk about his past I was causing him pain, I wanted to tell him that he could stop, but somehow it seemed better to just let him talk about it however he wanted. So I just curled my arms around his waist and rest my head against his shoulder.

He kissed the top of it, seeming pleased by my closeness, his voice more relaxed and peaceful as he continued. "I met Jax about a month later. He was defending the territory Celeste and her coven were trying to cross into. I could see right away that he was different from other vampires, and it didn't take him long to figure out that I was a new vampire struggling with this life. So he took me under his wing and taught me how to live as a Daywalker. And eventually I returned here with him. He's been like a brother to me ever since."

"What about Gemma," I asked.

"Gem . . . ?" He laughed, a deep, rich sound, full of joy that I could hear a thousand times over and never grow tired of. "Well, she's just been a lot of trouble. But there isn't a single thing I would change about her."

"And Celeste?"

His smile began to fade. "She wasn't too happy about my decision to leave with Jax. When you're mated in this world, it's to be for life."

"Mated?" I echoed with a dry mouth. My heart seemed to clench violently as if the steadiness of its beats were no longer in my control. "You're . . . you're still mated to her?"

His head snapped around. He must have seen how his words had upset me. "No," he said, placing another kiss atop my head. "I haven't seen Celeste in ten years."

That answer should have made me feel better, but it didn't. And I was ashamed to admit that jealousy seemed to be swallowing me whole, growing more powerful by the second. My skin felt flushed and hot, and I wasn't quite sure how I was supposed to look him in the eye again without revealing the depth of the feelings for him that had come on so fast. "But you agreed to be mated with her?" I questioned. "Some part of you must've loved her?"

He didn't answer for the longest time, and I worried what that might actually mean. "It wasn't like that," he finally said, pulling my chin up to look directly into his eyes. "At the time, I needed her to show me how to survive in a world I didn't understand. But I'll never forgive her for taking my human life away from me. Never."

I drew back the hands I was wringing in my lap and silently wondered if Caleb was being completely honest with himself about his feelings for Celeste. He must have felt something for her to agree to be tied to her for life—an immortal life at that, no less.

Frustrated by the direction of my thoughts, and full of nervous energy, I wrestled with the coat at my side before crossing its arms in towards the middle and neatly folding the jacket in half. Caleb grabbed the coat and moved it to his other side. When I blinked up at him, his brows were pulled together in concern. "You're too restless today, Olivia. Do you want me to take you back to the house?"

I shook my head quickly. "No. I want to stay. I like being here with you, talking to you."

I smiled gently, hoping he would let us stay. "What about your human family? My father had once told me 'The Wolfe's moved back to Denver.'"

"Did they?" He gazed out over the valley for a long moment, as if trying to think back. "The memories of my human life aren't complete. They're fragmented—the timeline is all jumbled up. I don't have clear memories of them."

"I'm sorry, Caleb. I'm sorry made you talk about your past."

"Don't be. Since I've been with Jax and Gem I've been content with my immortal life." But then he looked away and muttered, almost inaudibly, "That is, until you came back into it."

I wasn't sure what he meant. I had disrupted his life—really, all of their lives—since my arrival. In fact, Jax and Gemma, the two people who had been his family for the last ten years, had hardly been home.

I sat up, erect, beside him, tapping my fingers on the rock's cold surface while sensing his questioning gaze. Slowly, he pulled his arm from my back. "You're playing for me again." I looked up at him, confused as to what he was talking about. "The tapping of your fingers . . . You do it a lot. It sounds rhythmical, almost like you're composing music in your head."

"You can hear sound in my tapping?"

He gave me a dry look, as if that had been a stupid question —which it was.

"The other day, when you played for me, you mentioned your music professor. You're a student, then, at the University?"

I nodded, trying to stay still but feeling like I had ants crawling all over my skin. "U-Dub. Sarah was my roommate . . .

and my best friend since grade school."

"I'm sorry," he said sincerely, offering his hand to me, and I took it. He pulled me over his outstretched legs until I straddled his hips and settled close. "Are you sure you're not cold?" I nodded while he traced a finger across my collarbone, sending tingles under my skin. It seemed that in whatever ways he touched me, my body simply responded to him. "I've something I want to ask you," he began, speaking slowly and carefully. "You haven't mentioned your family much since you've been here. Are your parents here in Seattle?"

"My parents' home is downtown, but I live with Sarah on campus. Or, rather . . . lived . . . I guess."

He seemed to frown slightly at that answer, realizing I didn't answer his question exactly. "Are you returning to school next fall?"

I nodded with a smile. "To finish, hopefully. I feel like I've been in school forever. Although, I did take a year off. I received bachelor's degrees in Musical Performing Arts and Music Composition about three years ago. I've one more quarter left before receiving my Master's in both."

"I'm impressed. You're my accomplished little sweet."

I laughed. "I don't know about that. Sarah was two years younger and was graduating with her master's . . ." I paused for a moment to count up the days I had been here. "What day is it?"

"Thursday," he replied.

"Oh. Tomorrow, then," I said in a barely-there voice. "She would've been graduating tomorrow.

Caleb stroked his fingers over my back to bring my attention back to his concerned face. "Even though I still had a quarter left in the fall, she was going to come live . . ." I stopped, realizing I was starting to babble. "Is this what you wanted to ask me?"

"Not exactly," he replied, the strain returning to his brows. "Your family's been under the assumption that you've been dead now for nearly a week. I was wondering why you haven't pushed me to contact them, or somehow let them know you're alive."

I let my head drop onto his shoulder and stared up at him.

"Isn't it safer this way?"

"I guess," he replied, sounding almost disappointed by my answer. But I wasn't sure what else to say. The love and security of my family that I took for granted as a sixteen-year-old was now gone, and it wasn't Caleb's responsibility to try and fix that for me.

"Caleb?" I asked, changing the subject.

"Yeah?"

"How come you remembered me the night of the crash? If your memories are fragmented, I mean."

He blinked, as if my question had either surprised him or he had never considered it before. Taking my hand, he thumbed over the palm I had cut that day so many summers ago as he seemed to consider something. "Actually . . . when I saw you I flashed back to the moment I squeezed your hand. I can't explain it, I just remembered. When I saw you again on the night of the crash—saw how Isaac was hurting you . . ."—he turned his head, his lips tight with anger—"I knew I had to get you out of there. Honestly, there wasn't much forethought about it."

He had seen Isaac hurting me and moved to stop him. I was so grateful that he didn't leave me there with him and I had no idea how I would ever repay him. "I should've said this to you a while ago, but thank you for not letting Isaac take me." I then lowered my head, shaking it as if sweeping out bad thoughts. "At the time, I was in so much pain, I didn't care which one of you took me, or why. But I hate to think how . . ." I paused, trying to get my bottom lip to stop quivering, " . . . how things would be different for me right now if I were with him instead of you."

Caleb folded me into his arms, his parted lips only a hairsbreadth from my own as he gazed at me and said, with such sincerity, "I would never let that happen."

His unwavering need to protect me, like his earthy scent, a wonderful mix of fir, sage, and something worn like leather, was nothing short of addictive. All I wanted was to stay here with him, be close to him, be touched by him, and let the rest of the world fall away.

My head fell back as Caleb slowly traced his lips over my

collarbone, his tongue sweeping out in a playful little lick that seemed to suddenly heat me from the inside out. I was pretty sure that was me moaning beneath him as he stretched my sweater lower and drew his kisses so close to my breast that I held my breath for the moment he would take it into his mouth. "I like kissing you, Olivia—tasting your skin. In fact, I'd say you're rapidly becoming my favorite treat."

Honestly, how could the man talk at a moment like this? I couldn't even seem to keep my wits about me, let alone put together a coherent sentence. Holding on to him for dear life, I curled my fingers against the tough, corded muscles of his arms while a slow burn began to spread over me like the hot summer sun, and it was strange considering how cold and gray it was outside today. "Tell me what you like," he said.

I swore I would get even with him for teasing me like this. "I . . . I like this," I murmured back. It was all I could think of . . . and I did like it.

His wide smile pulled across my skin as he chuckled low. "Yes, I know. I can feel how much you like this. And this," he added, his thumbs stroking over my nipples right through my sweater. I squealed and then squirmed on his lap. One of his hands slid down to my hip and gripped firmly, pulling me back into place. "Just relax," he whispered. "We're just going to let you enjoy a little bit more."

Mercy, if he gave me much more I would soon be begging him to rip my clothes off right here on this rock! "Caleb, please." I pulled tight within his embrace, my breath hot against his throat as I tried to control a desire raging inside me I couldn't fully understand. It was as if this vampire's touch offered some sort of vital life force essential to my continued existence.

He groaned against the corner of my mouth. "Tell me what you want," he murmured, but he really didn't want to know, or else he wouldn't have me tongue-tied beneath another kiss. He pulled my hips forward until I was wrenched against his body, my neck straining as his mouth seemed to want to devour me and his hands kneaded into my thighs. "Caleb, it's too much," I whispered feeling sure I was about to implode.

Then suddenly, the bottom dropped out from under me as my swollen lips fell away from him. Raising my chin to the sky,

I tried desperately to find relief from the cool air, but I couldn't.

"Olivia, what's wrong?" Caleb's hands swept over my cheeks and forehead just before I felt myself beginning to fall away.

"Oh, God! You're burning up again!"

Chapter Eleven

Caleb was on his feet, racing through the trees before I even had time to process what was happening. "It's going to be all right, Olivia." His voice sounded so far away, and then everything was a blur until the whooshing sound of the glass doors opening above us signaled that we were back at the tree house.

I felt the sensation of weightlessness for several seconds as we flew upward before Caleb landed with light tap. "What's wrong?" Gemma worried voice asked, trailing behind Caleb as he sprung up to the ledge and continued straight into her room.

"Her fever's back," he snapped. "Damn it! I should've never taken her outside today."

"Caleb, you couldn't have known."

He stretched me out on my back on Gemma's bed, his hand sliding once again over my cheeks, feeling the warmth that was turning into real heat. "God, she's getting warmer. This is happening too fast."

Actually, it felt as if I were a chicken being broiled from the inside out. I started losing track of what was happening around me and pushed away from the hands that gripped me, pulling at the sweater that was keeping the fire inside.

"Change her into some light clothing. I'm going to get some fever reducers, ice and cold cloths."

I didn't even hear Gemma's answer before all the hot clothing was gone, replaced with just an oversized cotton shirt. "Gemma, please," I rasped with a dry throat, "it's too hot."

"I know, sweetie. We're going to get you cooled down here. Caleb, hurry! She's getting warmer."

Next thing I knew, cold cloths were being pressed over my forehead. It was heaven, but the coolness lasted for just a few seconds before the cloths felt as warm as my skin. I was lifted, supported behind the shoulders, and raised higher. "Olivia, I need you to take these," he said, dropping two pills on my tongue before bringing a glass of water to my lips. I grabbed the glass with both hands, gulping every drop as if I hadn't tasted water in weeks. "Good girl."

He lay me back down gently, and at first I tried to cling to him, wanting to soak in some of the coolness from his body. But then I felt exhausted, my lids so heavy I didn't know if I could keep them open. "No, stay with me," he whispered urgently, stroking his palm over my face to push the damp hair out of my eyes. I blinked them back open to his worried face. "Tell me what's happening. Are you in pain?"

"Hot . . ." That one word was all I could manage to describe the fire raging inside me, and I only hoped it was coherent.

"Goddamnit!" he cursed fiercely under his breath.

"Caleb, it's too late for this," Gemma said. "You need to cool her down. Now!"

Moments later, the sound of clothing being ripped seemed to be the only sound in the room as I fell limply against the mattress. The heat seemed to be winning this time, invading every cell while my limbs became very heavy.

"Hold on, Olivia," Caleb's hard voice said as his long, cool body wrapped around me and he pulled me to him.

"Find Jax, now! I need his help."

Then the world fell to blackness.

***

Sometime later I opened my heavy lids to discover that I was lying quite comfortably in a quiet, candlelit room. Thankfully, the unbearable heat that felt as if it had zapped every bit of my strength was gone, replaced by a more tolerable warmth. I could hear Caleb's low voice in the distance, speaking to Jax. Their conversation, though hushed, was tense. So tense, in fact, neither he nor Jax were tuned into the fact that I was awake.

"I have indulged this behavior of yours long enough," Jax growled. "This is forbidden—and you know it. There are consequences for the choices you are making. How could I ever face Gemma if you were gone and I knew I could have prevented it?"

"Jax—"

"No. You need to return this woman unless you plan to—"

"Never!" Caleb snapped. "I won't do that to her."

There was a long silence then before Jax asked, "What is this about, Caleb?" There was no answer, and I was afraid to even breathe for fear they would hear me. "Look, I understand. Of all people, you know I understand this. Her humanness is part of what draws you to her. But these rules are in place for a reason. You cannot just break them because it suits your purpose."

Hearing both of their voices so tense with each other was upsetting. These were the voices of the family I was breaking apart, and I hated it. Caleb had already told me how Jax was like a brother to him. I didn't want to come between them at that level—ever.

"The vampire men who break these rules are selfish," Jax continued. "Do you think claiming a human woman has ever been about her?"

Caleb continued to say nothing, and that silence revealed everything.

"No," Jax answered for him. "They saw something they wanted, and because we are strong and seductive to our prey, they claimed them. Most of these women die painful deaths from a vampire's uncontrolled lust or childbirth. You know this."

"It's not like that," Caleb defended. "I'd never hurt her."

"No, you do not *want* to hurt her," Jax pressed. "There is a difference."

Caleb's emphatic response was quick. "No. I would never hurt her!"

"And what do you call this? You are hurting her now. There is something going on with this woman that we do not understand. And instead of returning her to her own world where she can be cared for by her own kind, you have her locked away up here."

"It's to protect her! She's not safe out there with Isaac tracking her."

There was another tense silence between them, but, thankfully, when Caleb spoke again his voice was much calmer.

"Surely, Jax, you know how I feel. You were with a human yourself."

"Yes. I was one of those selfish creatures. And I have told you how it nearly destroyed me to see Isabeau die in the world I brought her into."

Just then I fought to hold in a gasp. Gemma had not told me how Isabeau had died, but from the devastating pain in Jax's voice, just then, I knew it wasn't good.

"I speak to you now as a man with many regrets. I would have rather been away from her and watched her live a long, healthy life with another than see her die as I did. I wish I would have considered her more than I considered myself."

"I *am* considering her," Caleb said with a loud, frustrated growl. It was the sound of someone being torn in half by the division between what he wanted and what he knew was right.

"Easy, Caleb," Jax replied calmly. "You are letting your anger cloud your thinking on this matter."

"I'm keeping her safe from Isaac and his coven. How can you expect me to return her when we know they might still be tracking her?"

"That does not make any sense. Why would an entire coven of vampires want to capture a specific human woman? More than likely Isaac just wants her for himself—"

"And that makes it OK? What the hell's wrong with you, Jax?"

"I am sorry. You know I wish the woman no harm. And I do see what this is doing to you."

There was a break in Jax's voice, and I knew the gentle giant Gemma described was emerging, and he obviously cared for Caleb very much. "We can help her. Return her to her human world, where she can get the medical attention she needs, and you and I will continue to track Isaac. We just need to make it clear to him that she is under your protection. He will stay away from her if that is made clear."

Caleb was silent, and my heart broke listening to that silence, knowing he was doing more than just considering what Jax was proposing. Soon he would take me back to my world, where I might never see him again. But as much as I hated the idea, I didn't want him to fight with Jax anymore over me. It was hurting him. So I needed to be selfless and go back to my world, as he would ask of me, as I promised myself that I would if my being here hurt him.

Sitting up slowly, I swung my legs over the side of the bed, knowing the voices would hear I was awake. Instantly, a blast of cold air blew the sheets around me, and at the same moment several candles blew out from the force of it. The few remaining lit candles glowed over Caleb's bended form as he appeared on his knees before me, his hands stroking strands of my messy brown hair back from my face. "You scared the hell out of me."

"I'm sorry," I murmured, meaning it for so much more than just scaring him.

"How are you feeling?" His palm moved over my forehead and cheek.

"I feel better. Just a bit tired."

He dropped his head to my shoulder and I wrapped my arms around him in return, trying to reassure him everything would be OK, though there was no way for me to know that myself.

I glanced up to see Jax in the candlelit shadows behind us. His stiff frame stood there, just inside the door, with an intensity to his expression I had not seen before. Yet his amber eyes displayed something entirely different. Empathy. He watched Caleb hold me as if it was for the last time, and great sadness crossed his eyes. He felt the pain he was causing the younger vampire with his insistence that I be returned. I sensed Jax was the kind of person who would gladly take that pain himself to spare it from someone he cared about, so I couldn't even be angry at him. He was protecting his coven—his family —from what he perceived as a threat, a break in these vampire rules. But my heart was breaking, breaking for this man, this vampire, who had somehow made my heart completely his in less than a week.

"Leave us, Jax," Caleb commanded without turning around to acknowledge him.

Jax simply turned and left the room, sliding the door closed behind him without making a sound.

Caleb pulled back, his voice soft with concern as he saw the involuntary quiver in my bottom lip. It felt silly that I couldn't seem to contain my emotions over a man I had known for less than a week. And yet the pain was very real.

"Hey, what's this?" he asked, his thumb tracing my bottom lip.

"It's time for me to go, isn't it?" My breathing felt unsteady as I waited for a confirmation that didn't come. He couldn't have known I had overheard him and Jax's conversation, but still it hurt that he was holding back from me. I tried to slip my arms from his embrace but Caleb wouldn't allow it. "Don't pull away from me," he said, bringing me back to him. Before I even had a chance to respond he hooked one hand under my knees, the other behind my shoulders, swinging me up into his arms and placing me at the center of the bed. His long body rolled over me like a shadow, his fingers weaving into my hair until they were rooted within the long strands.

He placed soft kisses all along my cheek and jaw, taking his time. "You're still warm," he breathed.

"Caleb, I need to wash off," I said, trying to squirm away from him. "I'm dirty from the sweat of my fever." He ignored me, continuing to cover my face with kisses, until I stopped making even the slightest effort to fight him. God, I didn't want to fight him. I didn't want this world to ever end with him . . . but it would. I knew that.

I tried to turn my head from him, but he followed, taking my lips in a gentle sweep as soon as he had the chance. The kiss held me to him and somehow managed to tickle me at the same time. His tongue flicked out, his teeth grazed my skin, and I realized at that moment that I would do whatever he asked of me.

"Olivia," he whispered, my name sounding like a prayer on his lips, causing the last of my resistance to fade. I began to sink into the mattress, bearing the weight of his body between my legs. He was heavy, but it was the perfect weight, exciting me, driving me higher as I stroked my hands over his back. He growled approvingly, his breathing rough as he forced my mouth open wider for his exploration. Something powerful was now driving the urges of his body, and, realizing that something was me, I felt incredibly seductive.

I was floating.

It was like desire, ache and confusion were all swirled into one, and suddenly I didn't care what rules I was breaking. I just needed him. If I had to let him go, then just once I wanted to experience what it would be like to be with him completely, to feel his body inside mine, to feel him taking me.

Caleb must have been thinking the same thing, because he tore his mouth from mine, his lids sliding low over his eyes as he rasped, "Olivia, we can't do this."

Was he crazy? We were consenting adults. Of course we could do this.

As long as Jax didn't catch us.

I curled my hands behind his neck and drew him back down to me. "Don't stop, Caleb. Please, don't stop."

That seemed to be all the encouragement he needed. His mouth came crashing down over mine as he shifted his body. I was hot, pinned beneath him firmly while his fingertips brushed small circles over my outer thighs. He then flicked his wrist behind my knees and hooked my leg around his waist, opening me further to him as he pressed upward with demand. His eyes closed, his teeth clenched, and he dropped his head into the crook of my neck. A deep, guttural groan rumbled against my throat as the hard bulge in his jeans notched against me.

Mercy, he felt good . . . and thick! Caleb was growing more and more excited, his lungs pumping so hard it was as if he were no longer able to contain the giant volumes of air being swept in and out.

"Caleb, please," I begged, but I could feel him begin to push away from me. I was confused and instinctively fought to hold onto him.

He suddenly froze, pinning my head against his chest as a wave of energy seemed to ripple through his entire frame. Something was wrong, but I couldn't move even an inch to try and help him, he had me held to him so tight. A low, dangerous growl rolled above me like the snarl of a large feline. Then, without warning, he shoved me against the mattress and rolled over to the edge of the bed. He was breathing incredibly hard, his back rigid and unyielding.

I was stunned, unsure what I had done wrong. Certainly, I didn't have a lot of experience with men, but I knew it wasn't normal for them to pull away like that. Then, this well of dread rose inside me. Was it something about me? I didn't want to believe it.

Gently, I reached for him. "Caleb, what is it?"

As soon as my fingers touched his back he pushed away and was gone in an instant, leaving only chilled air in his wake.

I was stunned, the pain of rejection stinging like a thousand little needles pricking into my skin at the same time. He had hurt me. He had pushed me away. He didn't want me in the same way I wanted him, and it seemed so unfair.

Rolling over on the bed, I curled my knees up as the threat of tears pushed at my eyes.

What was wrong with me? I was acting like some sniveling idiot over a guy I had known for less than a week! There had to be a logical explanation for his behavior. Putting my nose to my skin, I sniffed. I didn't smell anything, but he was a vampire. He could probably smell about a hundred times better than I could with a stiff breeze blowing at me.

That had to be it. He was repulsed by my post-fevered body.

I sprang to my feet, jumping into the shower before I even remembered to grab a towel. As liquid warmth splashed over me, I glanced down my body and could see that all of the cuts and bruises from the night of the train crash were gone and I looked nearly normal again. Even the burn on my stomach was almost healed.

When I finished, I threw on the ivory colored robe hanging behind the door and quickly rubbed a hand towel through my hair. I stared at my reflection in the mirror and wanted to crawl right back into the shower. My soppy, unfinished state stared back at me. There was zero color in my cheeks and tired circles under my eyes. I looked a complete mess. How could I possibly expect him to see me as the slightest bit seductive when I looked like this?

Bursting through the door to Gemma's bedroom, I was startled to see Caleb sitting at the foot of her bed. His expression was pained, and his hands rubbed nervously over his jean-clad knees. I pretended to ignore him, moving through the cabinets and removing clothes mindlessly from the hangers. That's when I felt his fingertips skim along my thigh. "Caleb, just go. I'll gather my things and you can take me down the mountain. Or you can have Jax take me. Either way, I don't care. I can get home myself from—"

"Jax is not taking you!" he growled. "I will take you home to the city."

I began shaking my head at the cabinet full of clothes as I realized there was nothing to pack because nothing there was mine. "What am I doing?" I murmured, continuing to try and ignore him.

"Please, Olivia, let me explain."

That didn't help.

"No!" I whipped back, sounding more like a spoiled child rather than the twenty-six-year-old woman I was. "I get it, all right. You don't want me in that way. That's fine. I'll—"

The next thing I knew, I was being snared around the waist and twisted around till I was flat on my back against the mattress. Caleb's long frame leaned over me while his arm bracketed my other side, leaving no escape. Startled, I blinked back into his gray eyes until I could no longer stand it and had to turn away. His rejection of me was just too painful.

"No. Look at me," he ordered, pulling my chin back to face him, and the sincerity I saw in his expression kept me there. "Of course I want you. God, Olivia! I want to bury myself between those beautiful thighs of yours and claim you till you can't scream. I want you so much, it's driving me insane!"

I swallowed hard, stunned, surprised and mostly confused. "But then why . . . ?"

He sighed heavily, his expression almost sad. "Because I'm not human. I'll hurt you. And that's not something I can live with. We . . . can't be together in that way!"

"But why? It is possible. Gemma's parents were a vampire and—"

"And like most human women who are with vampires, her mother is dead. She died giving birth to her. I don't want that for you."

"But that doesn't mean—" I blurted, but he cut me off by placing his thumb over my lips.

"Yes, it does," he said softly, letting his hand fall away. "Women's bodies . . . human bodies, are not able to handle the strength of a vampire. If I were with you—as I desire to be—I would hurt you, physically. Being with a human woman takes control. I'm a young vampire. I don't have that kind of control yet. And even if I did, I wouldn't take the chance of impregnating you."

"Caleb, this is the twenty-first century. I use protection. And it's not like you're going to give me a disease or something. You don't get sick."

After a quiet moment, the smallest smile twitched his lips. "Fair enough . . . But we still can't be together that way. I won't risk hurting you."

I hated that answer, but I couldn't say I didn't understand his reasoning, especially after overhearing his conversation with Jax. Jax had sounded absolutely devastated by whatever had happened to Isabeau, which, as wrong as it was, only made me more curious. "Why did you push me away?"

Caleb shook his head as if he were completely confused by what I just asked him. "I just told you why."

"I know. And I believe you. But I think there might be another reason. When you were with me, I could feel your body . . ."—I fought for the right word—" . . . struggling with itself. Your voice, your sounds . . . your breathing changed."

His gaze slid away from me, almost as if he knew what I was about to say. I could see the anguish in his face, his gray eyes pleading with me not to say the words. But I cared for him too deeply. I needed to know the truth. "Do you change when your body desires someone?" He remained silent, but I knew it was the truth by the shamed look in his eyes. He could only keep the dark side of himself at bay for so long once he became aroused. When we both had hit a point of such desperate need, the warrior emerged to claim what it wanted. I reached my hands to his face, smoothing them down over his sides. "Let me see you."

He shook his head once, his answer resound. "No."

"Please."

"No, Olivia! I don't ever want you to see that side of me again —and that's final."

"Again? Are you talking about the night of the crash?"

"I saw the fear in your eyes. How you looked at me."

I stared back at him completely stunned. "That's not fair. I thought I was going to die. That you both were there to kill me."

He threw his hand up, turning away from me. "Well that makes things much better."

I pulled his chin back to me. "My point is, I didn't see you then. But I see you now."

Like a stubborn bull, he shook his head again. "No. That's the one thing I can't give you."

"No . . . that's two things. You won't be with me, either."

His face instantly changed and every muscle of it tensed up, following what I meant.

I turned on my side, away from him. I wasn't angry at him and I knew he would be able to feel that. But I was hurt and sad that he didn't trust me enough to give me what I was asking. He slipped his hand under the curve of my waist and pulled me up on the mattress until my head rested comfortably on the pillow. Molding himself against my backside, he draped his arm over my stomach.

"I want to stay with you," he began, "be with you like this— tonight. Is that all right?"

I nodded. "I'm going home in the morning, aren't I?"

"Yes."

***

When I sensed the morning had arrived, I didn't want to open my eyes. If I opened them, I would have to accept that this would be the last time I would wake with Caleb at my side. I was lying over his chest, my face turned away from his, with my arm splayed over his stomach. He was propped up on several pillows and curling a strand of my hair around his finger.

"I can tell you're awake," he said, reaching his hand to my forehead and then to my cheek. "And your fever's gone. That's good."

I didn't respond, which he didn't like. "Olivia, please say something."

"I'm not angry," I assured him.

"Yes, I can feel that."

"I'm resolved . . . I need to go," I replied. "I've been selfish, too."

"Why would you say that?"

"Because I know you're breaking the rules by keeping me here. And if I continue to stay, that puts all of you in danger. Even knowing this, I still want to stay. It's selfish."

"How do you know about the rules?"

I turned my head over on his chest so we were now face to face again. "I overheard you and Jax talking yesterday."

He was stunned. "We were downstairs in the library. How did you hear that?"

"It doesn't matter. The point is that I know what I heard, but I'd still like you to explain it to me. What rules are we breaking?"

"You're not breaking anything. I am," he declared. "It's forbidden for us to tell a human of our existence—our world—unless we plan to turn them. It's the only way to keep this world separate from yours."

I was silent while processing this new information, but he already knew why I was pausing. "And no . . . I'm not going to turn you," he added, almost angry that I was even considering it.

"But why? If it meant we could be together . . . if it could help my fevers—why not?" I asked with frustration, moving off his chest.

He caught me at my waist and rolled me until I was flat on my back, lingering over me quietly for long moments before he spoke. "You are so beautiful."

My breath drew in sharply at the unexpected compliment. No one had ever told me I was beautiful. Pretty, maybe, but never beautiful. It made my stomach ache all that much more that I couldn't be with him.

"Your humanness is part of that beauty. The heart that beats inside you, the soul that surrounds your goodness, the sweet wine that runs in your veins—all of these things are part of you, and they're as precious as any diamond, any gem. I could never take that away, especially not for my own selfish reasons."

He then cupped my face in his hands, his eyes pleading with me. "You must see the value in your own human life. Do you understand?"

I was flabbergasted. To him, I was beautiful, and I realized I would miss those things, my heart, my soul, even my sweet wine. Would he even find me as attractive without them?

He snuggled closer and pressed his lips gently against mine, parting them slowly, sweetly; his kisses patient as he moved downward over my throat. "Do you have any idea how much I want to stay here with you?" I asked him.

"Yes," he breathed. "About as much as I want to tear that robe from your body."

***

By mid-day I was showered, changed, and ready to go. Gemma helped me select a comfortable pair of khakis, a white silk camisole and some gold beaded slip-ons for the trip home. Since I had been here, my wardrobe taste had definitely improved from the simple tee shirts and jeans that were a staple of my college wardrobe. These clothes made me feel pretty, feminine. I knew Gemma's influence would stay with me long after I left.

"Here," she said, handing me a pink box, topped with an intricate hand-wrapped ribbon.

"What's this?" I asked.

"Open it," she replied giddily.

I did, and inside was a cypress-green cardigan with the same ruffled trim as the one destroyed in the train crash. In fact, it looked exact to the one my mother had bought me. I moved my fingers over the soft fabric, my eyes welling with happy tears.

"I know it doesn't replace the one you lost," she began, "but maybe it helps."

Gazing up at her, I felt the full weight of just how much I would miss her. She was truly a friend to me. Her infectious laugh and her always smiling face made being around her so easy. "Thank you," I sniffed, "I love it."

"Why don't you put it on for the trip home?"

I nodded, pulling the cardigan through my arms. When finished, she helped me cut the tags and adjusted it across my shoulders. "You look perfect."

Caleb and Jax were both standing near the glass door exits waiting for us to come down. I noticed Jax's big tough exterior seemed slightly eroded today. He was watching Caleb constantly, probably wondering if he would ever truly forgive him. I empathized with Jax, though. He was the head of their coven, and he was just doing what he needed to protect them, as I saw it, to protect his family.

Just before I reached them, I slipped my hand inside my pocket and walked right up to Jax, curling my fingers around the hand at his side and squeezing lightly, transferring a small, folded piece of paper from my hand to his. A smile curved his lips, understanding I had found one of Gemma's 'small thoughts.' "I swear to you," I told him, "I'll not tell anyone of your coven, or this place."

I then reached up and kissed his hard jaw. The bewildered look on both Caleb and Jax's face was almost comical, but I wanted Caleb to forgive Jax, for them to be a happy family again after I left.

"Thank you, Olivia," he said with an emotion that surprised me, and then studied the details of my face again, as if seeing me for the first time. He returned my squeeze just before he let my hand go, taking the precious scrap of paper with him.

I then moved to take my place beside Caleb. "You look beautiful, my sweet," he whispered. Gemma squealed and clapped her small hands together. I smiled weakly. The painful reality of what I was about to lose was setting in.

He lifted towards me a man's wool coat, a deep, charcoal gray—almost black—color, with wood buttons. "Here," he said. "It will be cold until we get farther down the mountain. I want you to wear something longer and warmer for the trip." He held up the coat for me to put my arms through, then reached around me to button up the front. "Sorry, it's a little big on you."

I didn't care. I knew this was his coat. His earthy scent of fir, sage and leather was all over it. I wanted to hold on to it for dear life. "No, that's OK. I love it. Thank you."

He gave me a quick peck on the cheek, and then turned the lever on the control panel and scooped me into his arms. He dropped us over the edge without hesitation, and as air crashed against us, I stared into his face, aware that this would be the last time I would get to experience the weightlessness of freefall with him.

***

About a half-hour later we reached a lower plateau, where several vehicles were parked. He walked me to the passenger door of a silver and black X-Terra. The windows were tinted and the doors already unlocked. He opened my passenger door, lifting me easily up into the high seat. I glanced through the back and saw a thin sleeping cushion and large ice cooler. If I had to guess, I thought there would be several bags of blood inside the cooler. I realized this vehicle had been prepared to shelter him in case he was unexpectedly caught in the sun.

He jumped in on the driver's side, a forced smile crossing his lips as he started the engine. I remained quiet, mirroring a tight smile back, and then turned my unfocused gaze out the window.

With traffic, it took about two and a half hours to drive into the city from the steep mountain pass. As we neared downtown, he spoke some of the precious few words exchanged between us. "Which exit should I take?"

I didn't answer him right away, and he could see I was thinking.

I thought about the room Sarah and I had on campus, but realized what was left had probably been cleared out by the university once it was reported that Sarah and I both died on the train. That left only the second option, my parent's condo.

"Uh, get off on the Mercer exit—towards Lake Union."

His eyes watched me, confused by my hesitation in answering such a simple question as where I lived.

After he parked, he insisted on walking me up. Once in the elevator, I hit the button for the top floor. "So that's where you get your fascination with tall heights," he teased, trying to lighten the tense mood. But I didn't respond.

What was there to say? He was leaving soon and my heart was breaking.

Once we arrived at my door, I opened it with the hidden key above the door frame and walked in, assuming he was right behind me. But after taking off his coat and setting the key on the counter, I looked back to see him still standing in the hall.

"You have to invite me in," he said.

"What?" I laughed; my first laugh all day. "Of all the silly vampire rules, this one is true?"

"Very true. Now, are you going to be rude and make me stand out here in the hall all day or are you going to invite me in?"

I dropped my hand out to him playfully. "Caleb, would you like to come inside?" I mocked as I batted my eyelashes.

"Yes," he answered, shutting the door behind him.

It was dark in the room until I opened the drapes and blinds, but Caleb's brows were already drawn tightly together as he scanned the room. The space looked like a typical, modern Seattle condo. There was a small kitchen at the front entry, centered with a large counter-height island, tastefully done in cherry wood and topped with dark brown granite. The kitchen was open to the rest of the space. Hardwood floors and simple, ivory-tinted walls filled with framed photos and memorabilia made the simple space feel lived in and homey.

In front of us, giant floor-to-ceiling glass doors faced towards the east. I drew back the lined drapes to the large stone terrace outside that showcased a hundred-and-eighty-degree view of the inner city lake and downtown Seattle to the south. It was spectacular and had been the reason my parents bought the condo.

None of this however, was causing Caleb's concerned expression. It was the fact that he couldn't tell what any of the rest of the furniture was in the room because every piece was covered in white linen cloths. And in between the covered furniture pieces were the packed boxes that Sarah and I had started bringing over from our university dorm room the morning of the crash. It quickly became apparent to him that someone had not been here for quite a while.

"You live here?" he questioned.

I began pulling the linens off the furniture and tossed them into a pile on the floor. "I lived on campus with Sarah at the university, remember? We were planning to move here together once school was out for the summer. This was my parent's home."

"Was . . . ?" he questioned slowly.

I nodded. "They died about six months ago. A car accident."

Suddenly, the linens I was carrying were lifted from my arms. Caleb tossed them to the pile and turned back to me to take both of my hands in his own. "Olivia, why didn't you say anything to me when I asked you about them?"

His voice was filled with surprise.

I shrugged my shoulders. "I didn't want you to feel sorry for me that I don't have any family. With my parents and Sarah gone, there'd be nobody looking for me."

"No extended family?"

I shook my head. "No."

He released a deep sigh and pulled me gently into his chest, kissing the top of my head. "I'm sorry about your parents," he said sincerely. "I'm just grateful you weren't with them in that car."

I pulled back from him, taken aback by his assumption. "I was with them. We were driving over Stevens Pass last winter in icy conditions when our car went over the ravine. They were both killed instantly, but I survived."

After seeing Caleb's horrified expression, I regretted not choosing my words more carefully. His normally lively shades of gray were suddenly flat; his body was standing rigid before me. "How badly were you injured?" he nearly demanded.

I ran my fingertips over the slope of his jaw. "It's OK. I only had cuts and bruises—some stitches."

I was surprised when this didn't seem to calm him in any way.

"Olivia, you've survived a car crash, a train wreck, and an attack by vampires all in six months. And your injuries have been relatively minor."

I hadn't thought about it before, but, when he put it like that, it did seem rather remarkable.

Stepping back from him, I moved to open the sliding doors to the terrace. Knowing the last of our time together was near, I suddenly felt suffocated and in desperate need of some fresh air. Once I crossed the threshold into the gentle breeze, I inhaled several deep breaths, sensing Caleb right behind me. I couldn't do this. I just couldn't continue to stand here and talk with him as if life would go on normally.

"Did you have any fevers after the car accident?" I started shaking my head. I wasn't going to invest any more of my life with this man, this vampire, knowing he wouldn't be there tomorrow. The hole over my heart would be large enough without adding one more minute of precious time to my memories.

I spun on him quickly, clear that I needed to do this before I lost my nerve. "You know, it doesn't really matter, does it? None of this really matters."

"Olivia?" he blinked back in surprise.

"No! I can't do this anymore. You need to leave."

"Don't do this," he pleaded. "I'll be back to check on you after you've seen the doctor—"

"No! I don't want to see you at all. You brought me back to this world. Now leave me be so I can move on with my life. I don't want to see you again."

And just like that, I ripped a hole in both of our hearts.

The pain on his face mirrored how I felt inside. I couldn't believe I was saying these things to him, especially after feeling so close to him the previous night. But this was self preservation. I needed him to leave. I was about to shatter into a thousand tiny little pieces right in front of him . . . and he could feel it.

"I'm sorry I've hurt you. I never wanted to hurt you," he said, taking a long step towards me, but I stepped away, throwing my arm out as a barrier. I didn't even want him to touch me again—only to pull away for the last time.

"Just go!" I cried, my voice beginning to crack, my chin quivering.

I could only watch as he lowered his head and walked towards the front door, just like a normal human man, when he could have easily jumped from the terrace. In this world, he had to blend in, appear normal, something very hard for me to imagine.

I held my breath, waiting for every painful second to pass until the door finally closed behind him, and I then crumbled to my knees, covering my face with trembling hands. Tears erupted; there was no way for me to hold them back. I was sure the entire city of Seattle would hear.

Losing him now, this vampire I had only known for a little over a week, hurt as deeply as losing my parents and Sarah. I didn't understand it, but somehow I felt connected to him in a way I had never felt with another human being. And now it was gone.

I stayed there, crying on the terrace, until there was nothing left inside.

Then the most peculiar thing happened. The tightness that had been lodged like a fortress over my heart for the past week was gone.

And for some reason, I just felt even more empty.

Chapter Twelve

In the hours before dawn it always amazed me how quiet a city of six hundred thousand souls could be. It was the best and worst time of day. The best because it was incredibly peaceful watching the urban landscape renew itself for another day. The worst because I knew I was never truly enjoying it alone.

Feeling the familiar comfort of a warm coffee mug cupped in my hand, I stood on the terrace and stared across Lake Union. The water's surface rippled with reflections of city lights and the remnants of the fading moon as a mild summer breeze brushed the lacy edges of my night shirt over my thighs.

Nearly every day at this time I would wake, feeling a rawness in the pit of my stomach that reminded me of a loss I could not shake. One long and painful month had passed since that awful day on the terrace, and despite my best efforts to move on, the vampire was still somehow with me, simmering under my skin.

The terrace surrounding me felt as lonely and empty as the day he had walked out of my life. A small bistro table and chairs were the only items I had purchased to try and fill the huge space, though they took up barely a fraction of it. But they were pieces I selected, an attempt to quell sad memories of those I'd lost, an attempt to make this place my home.

While sighing inwardly at the sad state of a garden terrace that lacked any kind of garden, I began to feel pressure pull through my heart as a cool gust of wind curled around me. Inhaling a deep breath, I sensed the same prying eyes on me from the night of the train crash. Searching the darkness, the warning inside my head heightened just before my heart began to race. I forced myself to walk a slow and deliberate pace back to the covered safety of the living room in an effort to convince myself that my anxiousness was nothing more than the deluded workings of a mind and body that had gotten far too little sleep the past few weeks. And sure enough, as soon as I stepped beneath cover, the eyes disappeared—but the firm grip over my heart remained.

Standing before the upright piano my parents bought for me when I was a child, I pressed several keys, random notes in a minor key. Though this compact instrument was not nearly as elegant or resonant as Gemma's Fazioli or the university's studio grand piano, the gift had worked as I learned my craft. Since returning to the city, however, this was the first attempt I had made to play. Most times, I would just sit in my chair, yards away from the piano itself, and stare at the keyboard, waiting for an urge—that never came—to run my fingers over the keys.

I feared my gift was lost to me.

It felt as though so many things I used to identify myself with were gone. So much so, I wasn't quite sure of the person that was left. Nestling in the large chair-and-a-half before the gas fireplace, I dangled my legs over the round, padded arm, aimlessly watching as the sun cracked over the horizon. The tightness in my heart was beginning to fade, replaced instead with an empty ache, a longing to see the man and the family I still missed dearly. I wrapped a strand of hair several times around my finger, the same curled playing the vampire loved so much, and wondered if he ever thought of me.

Stop it, Olivia! Let him go.

He would be upset if he knew I had not been to see the doctor since I had returned. I wasn't even sure why I hadn't gone, but my stubbornness seemed to be in high gear. The incidents of fevers had mostly passed. Since I'd been back, I only had a few episodes, and now, knowing what to look for, I was able to catch them sooner, taking fever reducers and preparing ice cold baths.

Caleb would not like it . . . but then, it wasn't his concern anymore.

For the first couple of weeks after I was back, my life had been nothing short of uninspired. I remained close to home, venturing out only when the refrigerator was bare or the craving for a latté was too great. Each day since the day he left, though, I did wake up every morning, pry myself out of bed, and face the world, and that was at least something.

After the initial numbness, I knew I had to stop wallowing in self pity and return to some sort of normal existence. I finished uncovering the furniture and unpacked all of the boxes Sarah and I had brought over from the university. I made a few attempts at applying for a summer job, and even filled out the paperwork to submit for my last quarter of graduate school, but I seemed unmoved to actually turn it in.

That concerned me.

Music had defined my life for the past twenty-one years and was always the remedy for whatever ailed me—but not this time.

The summer sun now rose fully above the horizon, and blinding, early-morning rays burst into the room. I glanced away to cover my eyes, looking down at the hair twisted around my finger, and then froze. What . . . ?

I had been so lost in my random thoughts, I didn't even notice that the curl I was playing with was much longer than it should be, spilling over my shoulder another several inches. I stared more closely at the strands, which were not only longer but also a visibly different color, a beautiful color. Not just brown, but a shiny, rich mahogany, with wine accents that filtered through in the sunlight. It was amazing!

Startled, I popped up in the chair and scrambled for the bathroom mirror and gasped at the person reflecting back to me. It was me . . . but somehow I was changed. Blinking several times, my silver rings tapped wildly against the edges of the porcelain sink as I tried to re-capture the image that was normally there. No good. The alarming change was still there, and it included way more than just my hair. My skin, which had always appeared fairly youthful, now almost glowed, radiating a smooth, flawless complexion, even in my tired, sleep-deprived state. I touched my fingers over my lips, which were now a soft pink, like the rosy flush of a girl's cheeks. But the biggest change was my eyes. Where wireframe glasses once set over the bridge of my nose, now two brighter, hazel-green colored irises looked back at me, their vivid clarity and remarkably lighter color startling me.

It was as if the face in the mirror had emerged in grace and beauty overnight. No longer the simple woman I knew, this new "me" left me anxious, confused, terrified!

For the next several hours I cleaned and organized every corner of the condo, and then I spent a few more hours going back through the process again, and again. Before I knew it, the day had slipped away, and when it became clear that the change in my appearance wasn't just some bad dream, I sat in my big chair trying to think of a logical explanation for how and why this could all be happening. Eventually, I had to ask myself if it could be connected in some way to the fevers.

Perhaps Caleb had been right to suspect a link between the accidents. Maybe some sort of trauma from one of them was affecting me. But who ever heard of an accident causing someone to become more attractive?

My feet were tapping wildly against the wood floor, about to take off without me, when I snatched a pair of sunglasses from the side table, raced out the door, hoping that movement would help me expend some of my restless energy. Once through the entry gardens, I was deciding whether to head north or south when a man in his mid to late forties stepped into my direct path, and I nearly smashed right into him.

"Miss Greyson?" he asked.

I wondered how this stranger knew my name, because I was quite sure I had never met him before in my life. Good grief, this was all I needed right now.

"Who's asking?"

"Oh, sorry . . . my name is Gideon, Gideon Janes," he spoke in a very thick and mannered English accent. The name definitely fit with his scholarly façade, which seemed harmless enough, since his small glasses cast him as a perfect university professor character. What didn't match, though, was his clothing. Possibly current a few decades ago, the oversized corduroy pants, wrinkled collared shirt, and definitely questionable "coordinating" plaid jacket were a disaster. Swallowed under so many layers on a summer evening, it was obvious he preferred the indoors to outside—perhaps a library or quiet corner of a coffee shop.

"Miss Greyson—"

"Olivia," I prompted.

"Yes, yes, of course. Might I speak with you in private? It's really rather urgent, I'm afraid. I'm . . . an old friend of the family."

OK . . . so he wasn't a college professor.

I studied his polite but tense expression, trying hard to remember him from the past, but there was nothing. "You knew my parents?"

He hesitated before answering. "Yes, a very long time ago. I'm sorry for your loss, Miss Greyson. The accident was about six months ago, was it not?"

I nodded, my attention distracted for a moment by a rather bored-looking young man leaning against the base of the flowering cherry tree in front of my building. He appeared about my age, maybe a few years older, and certainly handsome, with messy, textured blond hair and golden summer skin. He drew my notice, though, not for his attractive features but because his gaze had been unmoving. He was definitely staring at me. More surprising was his complete indifference to the fact that I had outright caught him staring. He just kept doing it. His tall frame, though a few inches shorter than Caleb, relaxed against the tree in jeans, a tee shirt, and vest that hugged his fit, athletic body.

Did no one realize it was the middle of the summer?

He stood there with complete confidence, almost arrogance. He darn well knew how attractive he was.

Gideon turned to see what had caught my attention. He made some kind of gesture toward the young man that I couldn't see. The leaning figure just threw up his arms impatiently, then crossed them in front of his broad chest.

"Who's that?"

"Oh, he's my . . ." he started then paused as if searching for the answer, ". . . my nephew, Alec."

Alec lifted one of his folded arms and waved half-heartily with an irritating smirk, causing the prominent dimple on his chin to widen. I could feel my face scrunching into a scowl at his utter lack of sincerity. I hadn't even heard this man speak, but I already disliked him very much.

"Miss Greyson," Gideon interjected again. "Can we go

somewhere where we may talk in private? It's really rather urgent."

I wanted to shout, "Oh, for Pete's sake. I just want to be left alone!" But instead chose, "Really, it's not a good time. Can this wait till—?"

"Oh come on, Gideon . . . ," Alec suddenly piped up, in a curiously very American west coast accent. "There has to be some mistake. There's no way she—" he began, but Gideon silenced him, slicing his hand through the air as if conducting the final note to a symphony.

I stared with fury at him. Just what was his problem? Lifting my oversized sunglasses from my eyes, I made sure that he could see the full expression of my dislike of him. But then, without warning, he straightened from the tree and within three long strides was suddenly standing directly in front of me. "Gideon?" his low tone questioned just before he tore my sunglasses off my face and out of my hand.

"Hey—stop it!" They both gawked at me while I took a step back.

"It has begun," Alec said.

What the devil? These two strange men were making me more than a little uncomfortable. There was no way I was going anywhere with either of them. Caleb would totally agree . . . or at least I think he would, if he were here. "What's begun?" I snapped, jerking the glasses back from Alec's hand.

"Olivia, I can see that you're upset," Gideon said calmly. "May I assume it has something to do with the changes to your appearance?"

I stood there dumbfounded. "How did you . . . ? Do you know why this is happening to me?"

"We can explain everything. But we need to go someplace safe—"

"Safe?" I echoed. "Why—?"

"We can't talk openly here," Alec replied. "It's not safe for you."

"What do you mean it's not safe? I live here!"

"Miss, are these men bothering you?" I hadn't realized how loud my voice was getting when a man and his very tall teenage son stopped as they were passing on the sidewalk. I glanced back to see Gideon's nervous expression, but Alec never flinched. He was not intimidated by the pair in the least. That's when I noticed in more detail the lightweight vest he wore over his shirt, like a hunter's or hiker's vest, with a small assortment of items pushing from behind his pockets.

Alec turned his gaze to me, waiting to see if I would cause a scene.

I wasn't sure what to do. If Caleb were here there would be no way he would let me leave with these men. But if they knew what was happening to me how could I not find out?

Besides, Caleb wasn't here. I had to remember that.

I shook my head. "No, they're not bothering me. I'm sorry for making a scene." The man's eyes narrowed, questioningly. "Really, I'm fine," I added, and the two finally moved on.

Surprise flickered in Alec's eyes. He was expecting me to run, which had crossed my mind, but understanding what was happening to me outweighed my need to flee. "Where do you want to talk?"

"There's a church not far from here. That'll be safe," Gideon replied. "Our car is just over there. You can ride with us."

Ride with them? "I don't think that's a good idea," I said, taking a step back.

Alec glanced towards the darkening skies, then back to Gideon. "We don't have much time."

"Please, Miss Greyson," Gideon began, "we need to go. You're going to have to trust that we mean you no harm."

I sighed; quite sure this would prove to be one of my dumbest moves. "All right, lead the way." After saying the words, I couldn't help but think that Caleb wouldn't like this one bit, not one bit.

But it wasn't his concern anymore.

As we approached St. Mark's Catholic Church and the sun was beginning to set over the horizon, a familiar feeling started to make my head swim. I ran my hand over my forehead, my fingers collecting beads of perspiration as I fidgeted uncomfortably on the leather seat. If I could just get the car to stop spinning for a second, then everything would be fine. At least, that's what I tried to tell myself.

Alec was watching me carefully in the rearview mirror when

his gaze shifted to the man beside me. "Gideon . . ."

"I know," Gideon replied quietly.

Suddenly, it felt as if my head couldn't stay on my shoulders. I fell back against the headrest as a giant wave of heat swept through my body, the burning rage this time coming so fast that I had no time to react. "No. Not again."

"Alec, quickly," Gideon called out. Alec weaved the car in and out of traffic while Gideon tried to hold me steady against the seat. I tried to pull free from his grip as another wave crashed over me, the red-hot flames licking over my skin like fire.

"Do you have her, Gideon?"

"I've got her," he replied then turned back to me. "Olivia, I've some medicine here to help you, but you need to try and stay calm till we get to the church."

"What's happening?" I gasped. "Please make it stop."

"We're almost there," Alec added roughly.

This time, it felt like the heat would destroy me. The pain was so consuming, I felt weak as a newborn, and my breathing became terrifyingly thready as I snatched Gideon's hand and squeezed.

When the SUV stopped, Alec was at my passenger door in seconds, swinging it open and dragging my overheated body into his arms. "Gideon!" his said with alarm. "She's on fire."

"I know. We need to get her inside quickly."

Alec wasted no time rushing me up the stairs and into the enormous, high-ceilinged church, where every sound echoed off the stone floor around us.

"Gideon, so good to see you," a man's jovial voice called in the distance just before another wave of heat tore through me. I screamed, my body now trembling violently in Alec's arms as he held his firm grip and forced my head to his shoulder. "Oh, my," the man said.

"Father Karras, we need the room."

"Yes, of course—this way."

Brief glimpses of dark wood accents and stained glass flashed in my mind as I pulled my body tight in the strong arms holding me, preparing for the next assaulting wave I sensed was about to hit. "We're almost there, Olivia," Alec tried to reassure.

"Please, Alec," my pained voice whispered against his throat. "Please . . . it hurts."

The heat then attacked with such violence my breath hitched on a hard gasp. For a moment it was as though my voice was trapped and unable to cry out against the pain that racked me. My hand fisted in his shirt, the strained muscles of my fingers curling around the cotton at his neck, eventually tearing part of it away.

"Gideon, damn it!" Alec barked. "Get the shot ready, now."

When my voice finally returned to me, it was barely recognizable. "Alec, I'm sorry," I murmured, not even remembering what I was apologizing for.

"It's all right, Olivia. We're here to help you. I swear we'll make the pain stop," he said, just before kicking open the door to a small, dark, windowless space, where he set me on a cot in the corner.

I struggled to get free of Alec's arms that had me pinned when the heat returned, this one more powerful than any I had experienced before. God, I knew I wouldn't be able to take much more. I clutched inwardly, the foreign, shrill sound clawing from my throat scraping at my own ears like fingernails on a chalkboard.

"Gideon, *now!*" Alec ordered as his impossibly strong arms held me down.

Gideon's voice hovered somewhere above me. "Olivia, I'm going to give you something so that you can sleep," he said, just before a sharp needle pinched my arm.

Another wave was beginning to hit when everything fell to blackness.

Chapter Thirteen

When I returned to consciousness I called out for the one person I really needed to see at that moment. "Caleb?"

No answer.

He wasn't here. He would never be here. Loneliness squeezed over my heart at having to wake up and face another day without him, but this day seemed more punishing than the ones before it.

The sound of water splashing against itself had me swallowing against my own dry throat. I opened my eyes and tried to focus on the shapes and movement above me, shapes outlined only by the low light of a candle that crackled against its wick, while the scent of vanilla bean drifted through. After a few seconds my eyes began to adjust and I could see that the figure above me was Alec, carefully wiping my cheeks and forehead with a cool, damp cloth. His concern was clear in the sharp lines that furrowed his brows and the deep dent in the dimple of his chin. I blinked up at him slowly, seeing a man far different from the arrogant one I had met earlier that day . . . if it was even the same day.

"How are you feeling?" he asked as he reached for a fresh cloth and began soaking it in a cold water basin, twisting the rag tight till it was free of all its excess, and then dragged it over my throat, bringing almost instant relief.

"Better," I croaked. "But where are we?"

"Do you remember coming to the church?" I nodded slowly, barely recalling much more than the incredible pain that had cut through me like a knife. "Father Karras offered us a couple of rooms to stay in until you're feeling better." He seemed to pause for a moment as if considering something and then added, "Well, actually, they're sort of available to us whenever we need them."

I felt my brows pinch. Why would anyone need standing room reservations at a church?

"I'm sorry you've been in so much pain," he continued. "This is the first time I've seen this process. I didn't realize how violent it would be."

"Seen this process?" What the heck? My mind began to run wild with several exotic illnesses. God, why didn't I go to the doctor as Caleb had asked? "Am I dying?"

He smiled, though it was a strained smile, and then shook his head. "You're not dying."

"Then what's happening to me?"

He paused again, and I was sure he had no idea how my heartbeat hung on that silence. "You're transitioning," he replied, and the current breath I was inhaling stopped in my lungs.

What had he just said? Surely, I hadn't heard him right.

"The fevers are your body's response to the physical changes happening inside you."

I opened my mouth to speak but only strange, stuttered sounds spilled out. I needed to start this conversation over again because what Alec was saying was nothing short of insane. "T-Transitioning? What're you talking about?"

Just then Gideon stepped inside the room's open doorway, crossing to stand beside Alec, who was seated just at my hip on the small cot. He placed his hand over Alec's shoulder and gave a light squeeze, as if to signal he would take it from there. "Olivia, you may not know this, but you're a very special woman, and we've been looking for you for a very long time."

"Looking for me? You make it sound as if I've been in hiding. I've been right here."

Gideon offered a humorless smile, one that displayed sadness and some hesitancy. "Yes, that's true . . . hiding in plain sight, so to speak. But the parents you knew, the Greysons, have been hiding you since you were five years old."

"Wha—what?" I stuttered in disbelief. "I'm sorry, but you've got the wrong woman."

He pressed his hands into the air, as if trying to hold off an invisible force. "You are the right woman. Let me try to explain."

Alec set the rag down and secured my hand, his hold like the reassurance of a close friend. "Slowly, Gideon," he said.

Gideon began pacing the small room, his gazed fixed away from us as he spoke. "The Greysons were members of the same organization Alec and I belong to, a group known as The Brethren."

"I'm telling you, you have the wrong girl. My parents never belonged to any Brethren."

Alec squeezed my hand. "Olivia, please, just listen."

There was something in Alec's voice. Concern? Empathy? Whatever it was, it felt sincere. At this point I had very few people left to trust. I would have to go with my instincts, and my instincts, for whatever reason, told me I could trust Alec.

"The Brethren was formed nearly two centuries ago when a British Lord of some social and political influence discovered the truth about the existence of vampires. His young wife had just died at the hands of one."

Vampires? I inhaled slowly, unsure where he was going with this—and suddenly concerned for the family I left behind on the mountain.

"In retaliation for her death, the man enlisted the help of eleven other men he trusted. We refer to them today as The Twelve Elders. All men of great wealth, power, and influence, they became committed to hunting and destroying the Immortals before they stole anymore of their family."

As I listened, my stomach felt like it was balling into a tight coil. Where were they going with this? I could hear the tap, tap, tap of my nails as they clicked against the cot frame. The simple sound was so blaring, so grating to my nerves, I thought my head might explode.

"Over time, The Brethren has grown in members and purpose, with sites all around the world. Each generation of male descendants following the original twelve pass down their seat at the table to the next. They are aided by Guides such as myself, Vampire Hunters, and Guardians such as Alec here."

Tap. Tap. Tap. My only thought was protecting Caleb and his coven. "Gideon, vampires don't exist," I said in a dismissive tone.

Alec glared into me with the unbending stare of a hawk on

its prey. "You're a terrible liar, Olivia. You know they exist."

How dare he? Even if he was right, and I had just been caught in a bold faced lie.

"Alec, please," Gideon replied.

"How does this have anything to do with my parents?" I cried with impatience.

Gideon' stopped pacing the small room, now gesturing wildly with his hands as he spoke, his eyes never holding full contact with either Alec or me, clearly showing he was nervous. "Your parents, the parents who raised you . . . weren't your birth parents. The Hendrickses—or rather Greysons, as you knew them—were assigned by The Brethren to raise you in Boston after your true mother and father had passed. With the promise that they would return you to us when you reached your fourteenth—"

"Wait! Stop!" I shot up to a seated position on the cot, having to steady myself against the side rails so my queasy head would stop swimming. "That's not true."

Alec reached to still my legs under the blanket to ensure I wasn't going any farther. "It's true. Let him explain."

But I didn't want to listen. I could literally feel the air leaving my lungs, the void now weighted down with heavy sadness. Was this man really telling me that the mother and father I mourned were not related to me? That they were surrogates?

I didn't want to hear any more, but Gideon, in his clumsy indifference, pressed on, unconcerned how much his words were hurting me. "In time, the Greysons loved you like their own daughter and feared for the responsibilities ahead of you. So they took you away in secret."

I was shaking my head wildly back and forth, refusing to accept any of it.

"Slower, Gideon," Alec warned.

"The Brethren have been looking for you ever since. It wasn't till a few months ago, when they heard of a young woman in Seattle who miraculous survived a car crash over a ravine that we were put on the path to finding you again."

I pushed farther up on the cot until my back was stopped by the cold, plaster wall behind me. Pulling my knees to my chest and wrapping my arms around them, I just needed him to stop talking so I could process something.

Alec watched every move with a careful gaze, touching gently over my arm. "I know this is hard, but hear him out. It's important."

"This can't be . . . this isn't true . . . I'd know—"

I cut off my own words, remembering my mother's beautiful face, who I so longed to resemble, but didn't. I didn't look anything like her, and now, as if being struck over the head by a light bulb, I understood why.

How could I have not seen it?

Gideon moved a chair alongside the cot, taking a seat beside my curled up legs, his unrelenting words continuing to hammer into my head. "Your real mother was a Dhampir named Eve."

The hammering suddenly stopped, and numbness took its place. A Dhampir? Like Gemma? That would mean I was also a hybrid, part human, part vampire? This was crazy!

"Beautiful and gracious, Eve was the daughter of a human mother and vampire father, though she never knew her mother. Your grandmother died giving birth to Eve."

"Easy, just breathe." I heard Caleb's deep, calming voice in my head, trying to reassure me and overwrite the blaring noise and confusion.

"Gideon, please. Stop! You're saying I'm part vampire?"

"Gideon," Alec warned in a clipped voice, the eyes of the hawk never moving from me.

"Yes, you're a Dhampir like your mother, and have vampire in you by birth. But your father was human, so you're mostly human. But you've inherited some very special gifts from your mother."

I felt dizzy. This just couldn't be true. How could I not know that part of me, even a small part, was a vampire? How could it be possible that Caleb, Gemma, or Jax couldn't sense it in me? "This is insane," I cried, " . . . I'd know if part of me was a vampire. I don't thirst for blood."

Alec's brows instantly pulled tight in question at my choice of words, while Gideon tried to calm me. "Yes, you would know and be much more prepared for this life had you begun your training when you were supposed to. But after the Greysons stole you away they raised you as a normal human girl, suppressing your gifts and abilities. You had no reason to believe you were anything different."

"I *am* a normal, human girl," I cried. "I don't have any vampire—"

"Yes you do," Alec cut in. "Think about it, Olivia! Your hearing is far superior to that of any human. You have an intuitive sense when vampires are near, an inner signal that warns you. And your body is strong, able to survive a car crash over a ravine with only minor cuts and bruises, able to repair itself quickly when you've been injured."

I inhaled sharply. My brain shuffled back through a lifetime of memories, some as recent as the tension in my chest before I boarded the train, memories of overhearing Caleb and Jax's hushed argument in the first floor library, an argument I shouldn't have been able to hear. And my ribs . . . How did they heal in four days?

I recognized myself in everything Alec had just described. I didn't want to believe it, but the truth was staring me in the face. "What about my eyes? If I'm part vampire, I would never have needed glasses, but I've worn them since I was five?"

"You don't need them now, do you?" Alec asked. "Remember, you're mostly human. Your father had poor eyesight. You probably inherited that from him. But now that you are transitioning, your vision is correcting itself."

Unbelievable. I wanted to run out of the room and not hear another word, but I knew the time for blissful ignorance had passed. As much as I didn't want to accept it, it all fit.

Gideon continued, "You received your vampire traits from your grandfather, but it's your mother that makes you truly special, Olivia. I knew Eve and your human father James while they lived with The Brethren. Dhampir's like your mother often develop special gifts in addition to their vampire traits—characteristics they can pass on to their children. But in your mother's case, she was rare, even for a Dhampir. She had the unique gift of being able to charm vampires with just her presence and touch. Her scent, beauty, and grace would draw them in like bees to honey. Once she had contact with their skin, they were unable to resist her, and the illusion surrounding her would trap the vampires' mind. All they knew was they wanted to stay with her, be near her, possess her."

Possess her? Like a man becoming controlling and possessive of a woman? At that point, I really wasn't sure how to breathe, how else to explain all of these pieces of a puzzle fitting together.

"Over time, Eve discovered that she could channel her touch, focus it in on her target. To a vampire she became a mirror, a reflection of the evil they had become. They didn't like what was reflected back and were temporarily stunned in a sort of pain-filled hell. That precious time allowed the Hunters, such as your father, James, to destroy them."

The hammering finally smashed my heart wide open inside my chest. My mother and father both hunted and killed vampires? All I could think of was Caleb. If my mother were alive today, would she lure and trap him so my father could kill him?

"My father was a Vampire Hunter?" I asked, my voice now sounding lost, even to me.

Alec nodded proudly. "It's said for being human he was an exceptionally strong fighter . . . and a good man."

"Very true," Gideon agreed, pushing his glasses higher on the bridge of his nose. Then he looked directly into my eyes for the first time since he walked in the room, and that terrified me even more. "From the moment you were conceived, Olivia, The Brethren knew that you'd be a very special second generation Dhampir. One who would inherit all the beauty, charms and gifts from your mother."

"The Brethren refer to you as a Charmer," Alec said. "Just as your mother Eve was before you, and you are indeed unique and special."

I held my sad gaze on Alec. "You . . . you're saying that I have the same abilities as my mother? That I'm capable of these horrible things?"

The hammer and the hawk now stared at me with a stunned expression. It hadn't occurred to either one of them that I would find my mother's gifts anything less than special, but I only saw them as a curse. I wanted to curl myself into a ball, a shelter within which I could touch no one, do no damage. My heart broke when I realized that Alec's declaration meant I had trapped Caleb in some sort of illusion, just as my mother had before me. Obviously, that meant nothing he felt for me was ever real! His thoughts and feelings weren't genuine. He was merely reacting to something I was inflicting upon him.

Bile retched from deep within me into the back of my throat, and I was certain I would be sick right there. I desperately wanted to deny that any of this was possible. "I don't have vampire strength or my mother's charm," I said, in a tiny whisper. "I'm just plain Olivia."

Being mostly human," Alec replied, "you won't have the strength of a vampire. But with time and training, you will become stronger. You'll learn how to defend yourself, use your extraordinary gifts. We'll teach you—help you. That's why we're here."

I looked at Alec with nothing but a lost stare. The idea of me defending myself against a vampire was ridiculous. I witnessed their inhuman strength when Caleb fought Isaac the night of the train crash. Either one of them could have killed me as easily as breaking a toothpick.

"Your allure, charm, and ethereal voice have always been a part of who you are," Gideon continued. "But your body now senses your exposure to the Immortal Ones. This transition wouldn't have started unless you had made contact. It's a signal to your body that it has to adapt, strengthening your defenses of touch and physical beauty. It's merely protecting itself, protecting you. The fevers you've been experiencing are evidence of that."

"You can't be serious," I said. "Charm? Ethereal voice?"

Alec sighed. "You don't see yourself as others do. You really *are* quite beautiful."

I blinked back at him dumbly while Gideon leaned in closer. I was uncomfortable with being cornered like this, but there was nowhere for me to go. I just wished Caleb were here so he could wrap his arms around me and whisper assurances that everything would be all right. But it wouldn't be all right, and I wondered if it ever would be again.

"Judging by how quickly you're changing, I'd say you've had a lot of contact."

"Yes," Alec nodded. "You need to tell us what's been happening, so we can help protect you."

I felt trapped. They knew I had been with vampires. How could I protect Caleb and his family when I wasn't prepared to answer these questions?

Think, Olivia, think!

"I'm not ready to talk about it," I said, truthfully, moving my eyes away from their stunned stares.

"Olivia, please . . . ," Alec replied. "We can't help you if you don't talk to us."

"Help me? I don't even know you! I just met you and you tell me that . . . that my entire life has been a lie, but I should trust you? I'm not that stupid."

I couldn't hear anymore. I was hoping this was all a bad dream and that I was still somehow in the mad heat of fever. I pinched my arm hard, trying to wake myself, but nothing happened, except that Alec noticed what I was doing and a worried frown crossed his expression. "That's enough for today," he told Gideon softly.

"Enough?" I questioned sharply. "You mean there's more?"

All I could think of was how I was to be used as a weapon to lure vampires like Caleb and his coven, forcing them to battle for their lives. With every second that went by I felt as though I was crumbling under the truth of what I was—that I was his enemy—and that everything he felt for me was not real.

Oh God, none of it was real to him.

The day he walked out my door and I fell to my knees sobbing on the terrace floor was still so painful to me it felt as if it happened yesterday. I didn't think the heartbreak could get any worse, but now it had. Knowing that his feelings for me were never real broke my spirit in a way I didn't think possible.

That pain quickly turned into anger. "I don't want any of this! I don't want to be a Charmer or a lure—or whatever the hell you call it! This isn't my battle." Tears were beginning to build at the corners of my eyes, and not wanting to break down in front of them, I dropped my head onto my knees.

"That's enough, Gideon," Alec bit out. "She's had enough for today."

But incredibly, Gideon ignored him and continued on, his

chair screeching closer across the stone floor. "No, Olivia! You need to understand you can't stop this transition. This is who you are. You are a Charmer. You can't run from this. You can't hide from it. Vampires can now sense you, and if they're close enough they'll seek you out wherever you are. They won't even understand why they're doing it."

Every word Gideon said terrified me, realizing if what he was saying was true, I would know very little peace in my life to come. I was shaking my head over my knees, praying for a way to start this day over and to never leave with these men.

"Gideon!" Alec stormed.

"Olivia, I'm not trying to hurt you. But you must accept this. You must understand who you are and what you're capable of. This is your calling."

"Enough!" Alec commanded, grabbing Gideon by the arm and forcing him outside the room, mercifully closing the door behind them.

***

Two days later, I was sitting inside the nave of the church, watching as the sun rose through the stained glass windows and shone in a kaleidoscope of color all across the wooden pews. I was feeling better and had been given a little more time to gain some perspective, though I still wasn't quite sure what I was going to do. The Brethren wanted a decision from me about leaving to begin my training, but I didn't want to think about it. Seattle was my home, even if I had no family left.

I had spent the last two days walking the church grounds, finding comfort in the quiet and examining my own beliefs about God, destiny, and higher callings. If I had never met Caleb, Gemma, or Jax, I still doubted I would have ever chosen my newly discovered parents' path. Taking another life, human or immortal, just seemed wrong. And I refused to believe that this was what God wanted from me or my life.

Despite what Alec and Gideon said, I saw only a plain girl with no strength and no charm whatsoever. Why couldn't I just go back to the predictable life I had, the one that mirrored who I was? Of course, if I had been asked a month ago what I wanted for my life, without question I would have chosen to stay with Caleb on the mountaintop. But now, I didn't seem to want for anything. Not school, not music, and definitely not to charm bloodthirsty vampires.

I wasn't sure how long I had been sitting there thinking when Alec quietly sat down next to me. For awhile he said nothing, which was good, because I had no idea what to tell him. Finally, he got tired of watching me wring my hands in my lap and said, "I know this has been hard for you to take in, and I'm sure you have questions. You can ask me anything."

I glanced up into his warm expression and saw a man who had the glow of a California beach lover, the scent drifting off of him reminding me of sun and sand. Except it was clear he had far greater responsibilities on his shoulders than surfing. Who wouldn't, after learning of this supernatural world around us?

"I don't have any decisions for you."

"That's OK. You don't have to decide anything today."

I could see he meant that. I appreciated that he didn't push me so hard, unlike Gideon, who seemed almost obsessed with wanting me to just accept things and return with them. "Why did you bring me here? To a church, I mean."

Alec's expression showed relief. He seemed happy that I had asked him the question. "Sacred ground," he answered. "Vampires can't sense you here, and they can't cross over consecrated ground. You'll learn that there are safe places for you to be, like a church, or your home, because vampires must be invited in—or in daylight."

Daylight? Didn't Alec and The Brethren know about Daywalkers? That seemed important information if you were smack in the middle of war with vampires. "There's something I don't understand . . . well, actually, several things. But won't vampires immediately sense that I'm a Dhampir?"

"Usually, yes—but in your case, no. Once you made contact with the vampires, your body began adapting its defenses, developing a protective shell around you. Vampires are drawn to you, but they can't sense who you are at your core."

With those words I felt another crack form over my heart. Nothing with Caleb had been real. Nothing. "Do these defenses block a vampire's extra-sensory perceptions?" I was curious whether, after my transition was complete, Caleb would no longer feel my emotions.

He smiled. "That's a very good question, Olivia. I'm not sure. Some vampires do possess specific abilities, just like your mother's touch. My guess would be if it's a special gift to them, then probably not. Special gifts like that, as you'll soon see with your own, are very powerful."

I knew that Alec was answering all of my questions as truthfully as he could. It seemed a big part of who he was. He didn't want things hidden, preferring them to be out in the open, even if it was difficult. Truth was very important to him.

Gazing at the light streaming through the beautiful stained glass, I could feel my resistance starting to weaken, replaced with reluctant acceptance that this was to be my life, a life of running from vampires who were drawn to me. How ironic and cruel it was that I had fallen in love with one. And even more ironic that the fevers he was trying so hard to spare me from had been caused by contact with him.

"What is it?" Alec asked.

"I was just wondering how much longer the fevers will last?"

He reached for the hand in my lap and squeezed it gently. "Your change has been very rapid. No doubt a direct correlation to your exposure. Gideon knows about this from your mother. The fevers were hard on her, too. He believes that since your last one was so quick, so violent, that the transformation is nearly complete. But there's no way to know for sure."

That certainly wasn't the answer wanted to hear. That last attack had me convinced I was dying. "Can I ask you something?" he asked.

I nodded in reply.

"Will you tell me what happened the night of the train crash?"

I thought about my answer before I spoke. I was beginning to like Alec and didn't want to lie to him, but I also wasn't about to betray the promise I had made to Jax—to all of them. "You know I was on the train that crashed?"

He nodded. "Your name was released as one of the passengers. Even though it was reported that there were no survivors, we knew there was a good chance you were still alive."

I stared past him now, remembering that awful night. "Alec, even before I boarded that train, I sensed something was wrong. It felt like—"

"Like someone was watching you?"

"Yes . . . exactly."

"As a Dhampir you sense when vampires are near. That's very helpful in being able to defend yourself. Over time you can learn to recognize specific vampire energies and how to track their location, just as they do you."

"So that night, when I kept feeling like something was wrong, the tightness in my chest . . . it was because I could sense vampires were watching the train?"

"Yes," he said, but his expression was cautious. "But are you saying that vampires were following the train?"

I nodded quickly. "I heard them on the roof of the car that night, and saw them crossing the tracks just ahead of the train before we crashed."

Alec's brows pulled tight together again. He was clearly concerned by this new information. "Wait a minute. You're saying the vampires caused the train to crash? But why would they do that? That seems like a lot of trouble to go to if they were simply hunting for food."

I closed my eyes, thinking in more detail about that night. "After Sarah and I were able to get safely onto the grass, we saw the vampires attacking and killing the other survivors."

"Out in the open like that?" he questioned with disbelief. "How were you able to escape?"

I decided to give him the abbreviated version, since I wasn't about to launch into the whole battle between Isaac and Caleb. "A couple of vampires were fighting each other to take me. I got away while they were battling."

His face grimaced. "I'm sorry, Olivia," he began. "You must have been so scared. But if you were able to get away, why were you missing for so long?"

"I was injured in the crash and attack. It took me awhile to recover and get back home."

"And your friend Sarah?"

I lowered my head. "The vampires killed her."

Alec, still holding my hand, rubbed his thumb gently and

sympathetically over the back of it. "This explains a lot. But everything is going to be better now, I promise. Now that you know, you can learn how to protect yourself. You've an incredibly powerful gift—you just have to understand it better. Then you won't have to be afraid like that anymore."

"How long do I have to stay here?"

His brows lifted in surprise. "We were just keeping you someplace safe until you recovered. But Olivia, Gideon is right. Now that the transformation is almost complete, it's not safe for you to be out there alone. You must decide soon if you're going to begin your training."

"I told you, this isn't my war. It may've been my mother's, but it's not mine."

"It doesn't matter that it's not your war. Whether you've known it or not, you've been hiding from this your whole life. Now your destiny has found you, and you have to face it." He then shook his head, as if frustrated. "Why are you so unwilling to see the evil in them? To believe that this cause—saving human lives—is worth the sacrifice?"

"Of course, saving human lives is worthy. I just don't believe that all vampires are inherently evil. I believe that in all creatures there are shades of gray." My heart pinged as I said the words. "Deciding to exterminate an entire species based on the actions of some—or even the majority—just makes us murderers, no matter what cause you're doing it in the name of."

Alec stiffened in his seat, clearly disagreeing with my point. "Is that what you were thinking when you watched them kill Sarah?"

My breath drew in sharply, feeling as though he had just struck a fresh blow across my cheek. He did remind me, though, that no matter how much I cared for Caleb and the others, it couldn't erase all the evil I witnessed the night Sarah was killed.

"I'm sorry," Alec reacted quickly, sighing, "I shouldn't have said that."

"Is that why you're part of this Brethren . . . a Guardian? You believe this cause is worth the sacrifice?"

"Yes," he answered without hesitation, his voice rising. "I

believe my calling for The Brethren is worth the sacrifice. I'd give my life to protect you. You're too important."

"Give your life for me? What are you talking about?"

His lips pressed into a thin line, his expression now one of complete resolve. "I'm to be *your* Guardian, Olivia. I'm responsible for protecting you. And that's exactly what I'm going to do—even if, as I suspect, you give me nothing but grief along the way."

Chapter Fourteen

"What?" I cried, bolting up from the bench and blinking to counter the bright sunlight streaming through the windows.

He rose slowly to his feet, just inches from me, practically daring me to challenge him on the subject, and hitched his hands confidently on his hips. "You heard me. I'm your Guardian. It's my responsibility to keep you safe."

And challenge him I did. "I didn't ask for a Guardian!"

He splayed his arms out in welcome. "Well, look at that—now you've got one. In fact, you've got a whole team of us, all solely devoted to keeping your ass out of danger."

"That's ridiculous! I don't want you, or anyone, risking their lives trying to save me." My rebuttal sounded so loud through the open hall that it echoed off the walls. Then I swung on my heels and headed towards the exit doors, sweeping past the empty rows of pews at a brisk pace, acutely aware of his loud footsteps right behind me. "If my fate is to be hunted and eventually killed by vampires, I'll be damned if I let you throw your life away trying to stop—"

My words were abruptly cut off when Alec seized my upper arm and swung me back around to face him, anger darkening his narrowed eyes. "That's *not* your fate, you stubborn woman! Don't ever say that!"

"Why shouldn't I say it—it's the truth, right?" I knew that using the word 'truth' with Alec would hit home. "Isn't that what Gideon said? That they'll find me wherever I am?"

A heavy sigh escaped him as he began shaking his head, his hold still tight on my arm to keep me from leaving. "Yes, but your gifts are much more powerful in some ways than their brute strength. You just need time to learn how to use them."

"I hate to break it to you, but I've seen firsthand the strength of a vampire, and I'm telling you, there's no way I'd last two seconds in a battle against them—let alone long enough for them to touch my skin."

"I do!" Alec snapped. "And I'm one hundred percent human, with none of your gifts. But I've been trained and have weapons to defeat them."

I stared at him blankly, imagining him fighting against Caleb —or, rather, the blue-eyed warrior I'd witnessed on the night of the crash tossing other vampires around like a matchsticks . It was obvious from Alec's hard, athletic build and the 'minimal effort' grip he had firmly cinched around my arm that he was, indeed, strong. But how could he—or any human, for that matter—defeat a vampire with ten times the strength? Even with an arsenal of weapons. Why would he willingly choose this violent path for himself?

Yanking my arm from his grip, I continued forward, but before I could reach the door Alec's arm came across my neck and collarbone, pulling me back and virtually lifting me off my feet. His grip was so tight, I felt strangled. Gasping for breath, I instinctively reached my hands for the steel vice around my throat as he held me against his body. "Defend yourself, Olivia," he spoke low in my ear. "Someone has just grabbed you from behind and is cutting off your air. What're you going to do?"

My throat ached from trying to bring oxygen in my lungs. I knew I didn't have much time before I passed out. Desperate, I tugged his arm with both hands with all the strength I could muster and pulled it across my body. Before I realized what was happening, Alec flew over my shoulder, his muscled form slamming against the floor as he hit square on his backside, momentarily stunning him.

"Oh, God, Alec!" I gasped between choking breaths, my lungs frantically trying to take in more air as I dropped to my knees in front of him. "Are you all right?"

He didn't move, but a wide grin spread across his lips, followed by a momentary cringe that reflected the discomfort from his shoulder hitting the stone floor of the church. "Now, that's more like it."

"What?" I said with disbelief, slapping him across his arm. "How could you do that to me? You were hurting me!"

He moved to his knees, facing me, mimicking my position on

the floor. I swung to strike him again, but he blocked my hand before I could make contact. "I'm sorry. I just needed you to see that you're much stronger than you believe."

Just then Gideon came rushing in, his crooked glasses and messy clothing showing obvious signs of having been rudely awakened from a sound sleep. No doubt, he had heard our loud argument. "Alec? What's going on here?"

Alec stood up, extending his hand to help me up from the floor. Refusing to accept it, I stood up on my own. A rather sarcastic smirk crossed his lips as he shook his head, saying to Gideon, "Just a bit of training."

Gideon's expression quickly changed to one of surprise. "Oh. Well . . . good, then. Does this mean you've decided to return with us?" He asked that directly of me.

"No. I still need time to think. This is all happening too fast."

Alec watched me as I continued to back towards the door. "Olivia, don't go. I'm sorry I frightened you. We'll give you time to come to terms with this, but let us protect you in the meantime."

"I—I need a few days. Then I promise I'll be back to give you my answer." I could feel the sweat on my palms, unsure if they would actually let me leave.

"This isn't a good idea," Gideon intoned, with raised brows, but Alec held up his arm to stop the Englishmen as he tried to move towards me.

"Let her go," he said, appearing somewhat calmer now. "We can't force her. It has to be her choice." He turned back to me as I reached the doors. "Remember the places I said you'd be safe. Stick to them. We'll be waiting for you here."

I nodded once, then bolted through the door and raced back the dozen or so blocks to the condo under the hot morning sun. I had no idea what I was going to do or where I would go, but as I navigated through the streets in my neighborhood I realized that I had left my bag, which contained my wallet and keys, back at the church. There was no way I was going back for them.

Remembering the spare key above the door frame, I decided that once in the condo I could get the keys to my father's car, which was parked in the garage. That's it, I thought. I would

drive to clear my head, sort everything out somewhere—
somewhere I could think—anywhere but here.

So that was the plan. That's all I had for now. Get the car
and drive . . . somewhere.

After throwing on some hiking shorts and an armless white
tank from my dresser, I tied a light windbreaker around my
waist and was lacing up some running shoes when my mind
suddenly became set on where I was going.

I wanted to see him.

No, I wanted desperately to see him.

I had no right to think he would even consider seeing me
after how I had behaved on that last day on the terrace, but I
had to try. I was scared, confused, and all I wanted was to feel
his strong arms around me as he whispered that everything
would be all right. My motives were purely selfish; I wasn't
considering at all how my return would affect Caleb, Gemma or
Jax—but I couldn't stop myself. Caleb was the only person left
alive in this world with whom I felt such a strong connection,
and if that made me weak, then so be it.

I needed him.

Before I knew it, I was on the road in my father's black Buick
sedan. The immaculately kept interior reminded me of him as I
drove southeast, towards the mountains. The trip would take a
couple of hours, which would give me time to reflect about the
absurdity of my situation. I thought about my human family,
the Greysons, who had raised and sheltered me from The
Brethren. When Gideon first told me they had stolen me away,
I was angry that they had lied to me all these years about who I
really was. But now I understood. They gave me the gift of time.
Time to be a normal, human girl, time I wished I would've
appreciated more now that there was no going back.

I also thought about my birth parents, Eve and James.
Would they be disappointed to see how their daughter was
running, like a coward, from her obligations, her "calling," as
Gideon put it? What a disappointment I would be to them!

Curious in a strange, new way, I wondered if I looked like
either of them. It was weird to not have even a picture in your
mind of what your parents looked like. It sort of felt like I
didn't belong anywhere, but I remembered how Gemma talked

about being "somewhere in between, in between human and vampire." She could easily have lived her life as an outsider, yet she had managed to find a place for herself, a home with Caleb and Jax.

The truly cruel part in all of this was the realization that I could now be with Caleb and his family, since I was a hybrid, like Gemma. But because of my mother's gift—no, curse was more like it, I would attract constant danger from other vampires if they tried to shelter me. Not to mention that I would be trapping them inside an illusion.

I couldn't do that to them.

So why was I running to Caleb? In my heart I knew I wanted to see him one last time, to tell him the truth. If he would see me, I promised myself I would treasure every minute before he'd most certainly send me away again. It was absolutely wrong of me, but I didn't care.

I needed him.

Before I knew it, a couple of hours had passed and I was close to the trailhead turnoff. After the final, long stretch over a rough and dusty dirt road, I could see the other cars parked ahead of me, but Caleb's silver and black X-Terra was gone. Was he not here? He had to be. It was too hot and sunny out for him to be away from the protection of the tree house.

Standing at the trailhead, I stared up at the high terrain before me. I swung my sling over my back and wrapped my long hair in a high ponytail under a baseball cap before starting the long climb toward "home" and the man I desperately missed. Feeling the hot sun already blaring on my fair skin, I knew Caleb couldn't come get me, even if he sensed me here. It would kill him.

Judging by the location of the sun, I would have five or six hours of summer daylight left to reach the house before the sun fell behind the mountain. A daunting task, considering I had to hike about nine miles of rough terrain, all uphill and rising about thirty-five hundred feet to exactly where, I wasn't sure. When Caleb had brought me down the mountain, he hadn't followed any particular path. I had to be careful to stay on trails that would lead me in the right general direction without getting side-tracked onto another trail. As I was growing up I had hiked enough with my father to understand if that happened, it would be easy to get lost up here in the thick wilderness.

After walking for a bit, I remembered how Gemma, a hybrid like me, could race over the ground like a nimble cheetah. If there was any truth to the idea that I was also a Dhampir, then I wanted to test the limits of my abilities. Starting at a tentative trot, then revving up to faster and faster speeds, I was soon racing up the steep hillside as if it were merely a flat plain. I was surprised that my breathing was not strained. It was even and steady, my legs surefooted and stronger than ever. A euphoric rush came over me as I climbed at a pace that would ensure I reached the top before nightfall—if I was headed the right direction.

Half way up the mountain, I stopped at a point where the trail split off into two diverging paths, but I remembered the house being straight ahead. I was worried that either—or both —of the trails would take me away from the direction of the house, so I decided to continue ahead, following a much more difficult elk trail rather than to take either of the easier, man-made ones.

That forced me to slow down and walk again.

At first, I trekked slower through the heavy overgrowth, but soon each obstacle I faced was a new challenge. I hurtled over fallen logs, bounded over mountain streams, and stretched high for limbs to dangle from, like a spry monkey. My newfound endurance and agility was thrilling me. Right now and right here in the forest, life was like a giant playground where I could be unguarded, adventurous—even a bit reckless.

Maybe having these gifts wouldn't be such a bad thing.

Eventually, I had to remind myself that I was still nowhere near the top and that this was no time for play. But as I climbed higher up, darkness made a fast approach, the sun setting behind the hillside in mere minutes. Once the light dimmed, the temperature cooled in no time. My thin clothing, appropriate earlier when hiking in the direct sun, was now doing little to warm my body in the chilly evening air. It seemed that maybe one of the traits I didn't inherit from my vampire grandfather was the ability to withstand the cold.

Right now, I craved warmth.

Pulling the windbreaker from my waist, I zipped it up tight. Though the waterproof material did offer some shelter from the chill, my bare legs were freezing below my shorts.

Worse than that was realizing, after having been swallowed for most of the day under a canopy of trees, I hadn't noticed the rain clouds that were moving in rapidly from the south. I had prepared mentally for the possibility that the weather could shift in a blink at this altitude, but experiencing it was something altogether different. A white firebolt shot across the sky in warning just before each loud crack of thunder echoed against the high terrain. At this altitude, the lightening appeared to snap and dance right at the ground, threatening to spark a flame in whatever it touched.

Soon, rain was falling in buckets, and my thin clothing became soaked in minutes. I glanced around through the darkness in search of the home I felt sure was near, but I couldn't see it. Finally, I took shelter from the rain under a tall fir tree to try and keep warm, realizing it was quite possible I would be stuck here all night in the cold. Feeling tired from my pre-dawn start and the hours of hiking, the need for sleep re-emphasized another one of my very average human traits.

Raising my face to the sky above me, with every limb in my body trembling, I felt fear. I didn't want to freeze to death out here, not before I had accomplished what I set out to do. "Please, just once. Let me see him—just once. I promise I'll cherish every minute. Please, just a little more time," I begged the power in stormy skies above me.

Huddled underneath the tree, my impassioned pleas were interrupted by the sharp cracking of a branch straight ahead. Peering through the darkness, I saw nothing, but then I heard a low, fierce-throated growl coming from the thicket directly ahead. My heart pounded and every muscle froze as I stared again into the brush and caught the large glowing eyes of a cougar, eyes that seemed very surprised I found them.

Cougars were traditionally ambush predators, sly and usually hidden. But as I locked onto the big cat's eyes, I was shocked at how their intensity reminded me of the electric blue of the warrior I saw on the night of the train crash. Primal, clear and focused, I knew that if the predator chose to continue with its attack, there would be nowhere to run or hide.

A low, almost inaudible growl rumbled ominously from its throat as the animal's ears lowered and its jaw pulled back to reveal those deadly, canine teeth. The large-bodied cat was crouched low to the ground and absolutely still—whether in warning or ready to attack, I wasn't sure.

Right now I didn't feel so gifted. There was no way to charm a cougar. My best defense was the strength which, until this morning with Alec, I didn't even know I had. Obviously, this was not the time to figure it out. I could only act, if needed. Slowly, carefully, I dropped back on my rear, preparing to kick my legs against the body of my attacker when it came for me. The next seconds that passed felt like the longest of my lifetime, and the slamming of my heart was so completely out of control, it thundered in my ears.

The cougar took one slow step forward, then froze in place when another deep-throated growl sounded from the bushes right beside it. The cat's ears snapped back, lying close to its head, and it swiftly turned to spit a fierce hiss into the night. Believing I was now in a food war between two large cats, breathing seemed unimportant.

Then, without warning, a blazing-fast shadow hurtled like a torpedo against the cougar's body, driving the animal cripplingly to the ground. I blinked hard, swinging my head around the tree trunk, and there was Jax, rolling the animal over. He had one arm around the beast's abdomen and front paws, while the other pulled the big cat's fierce jaw back, exposing its tender throat.

Jax raised his head, his piercing blue eyes filled with wild abandon as his mouth opened to reveal the sharp vampire incisors growing in length right before my eyes. In this state, Jax was not in control. It was clear that he intended to drive his fangs into the cougar's throat. His nostrils flared wide, inhaling the addictive scent of blood and adrenaline. His breathing threaded, his muscles straining, he fought the monster inside him. *Jax, no!*

As if hearing my silent plea, he paused, but his body began to shake with uncontrolled violence. A loud roar erupted from his throat, his mind fighting the baser thirst of his body.

Then, without warning, he snapped the cougar's neck and threw the carcass to the ground behind him. Still in a state of incredible need, he crouched on his hands and knees and inhaled fierce uneven breaths as every muscle in his back and shoulders seemed to flex and curl under the strain.

He was trying to regain control.

I swung back around the tree, hiding again, still holding my knees with one arm and bringing my other hand up to cover my mouth tightly to mute any fearful cries that might escape. My body was shaking uncontrollably, and I could still hear Jax's strangled sounds behind me. Caleb had warned me not to be close when he or Jax was thirsty, and now I understood why. Normally a very restrained man, Jax's blood thirst had consumed him within seconds once he locked his fix on the cougar.

The urge to scream passed immediately, and again I folded both arms over my knees and dropped my head until I was in a sort of sitting-up fetal position. I knew I couldn't run from him, so I tried to be still and as small as possible, not making a sound except for the shaking of my body and the frantic pounding of my heart, which, unfortunately, would be easy for him to hear. I sat like that for several agonizing moments while I listened to Jax's fierce growls and hard breathing. But soon it began to become quiet behind me. I hoped that meant the transition from vampire back to man had begun.

Of all the stupid situations to get yourself into, Olivia!

I dreaded Jax's reaction to seeing me back here, especially after he had been the one to insist Caleb take me back to the city. I might not even get to see Caleb before Jax demanded that I leave again because I wasn't supposed to be here. Worst of all, I was there solely for my own selfish reasons. Jax would always protect his coven first. And, ironically, that was what I admired most about him.

"Are you all right, Olivia?" His rough voice was close above me. Slowly, I raised my eyes, blinking against the rain to see him crouched there, his movements small, tentative, his expression uneasy. With a jerky nod of my head I gave him a wordless reply, then wrapped my arms tighter around my legs.

He grimaced, clearly upset with himself, then reached out his hand until it brushed my arm. "Are you hurt?"

For the life of me, I couldn't understand why he wasn't furious. "Th—Thank you for helping me." Until now I hadn't really noticed that behind his brutish shell there was a terribly conflicted soul. Not in the literal sense, because, according to Gemma, vampires no longer had souls, but it was there—regret, a long lifetime of it. "I don't understand, Jax. Aren't you furious that I came back?"

A wry grin distorted his expression. "I am furious that you would risk yourself climbing this mountain alone. As will Caleb be when he senses you are here."

"Then don't tell him," I replied simply.

"I cannot—"

"—'keep this from him,' I know," I finished, with a roll of my eyes.

There was a long silence between us, while he exhaled heavily, virtually emptying his lungs. Then, drawing a deep, slow breath, he said, "He has not been the same since you left." I was literally holding my own breath, hoping the 'he' that Jax was referring to was Caleb and the 'you' was me. "Even Gemma has been sullen and moody," he sighed. "I ordered Caleb to take you home because I thought it would be best for him, best for all of us."

"I never meant to hurt any of you, Jax. You have to believe that."

"I do. Your intentions have always seemed good."

Suddenly, I felt queasy, knowing I was deceiving all of them. Coming back here once again, knowing what I knew, was the ultimate selfishness. I would disturb their world in some immeasurable way. I wanted to confess all my sins right there, but Jax's next words stopped me.

"The only thing that has kept Caleb moving forward these last few weeks was being able to sense that you were all right. That all changed three days ago, when he felt your fever violently return. Then you vanished from his senses completely."

I blinked back, stunned. I hadn't even considered how staying in that church, on consecrated ground, would affect him. Or that he could detect my feelings of pain from so far away, which meant he was still attuned to me. It seemed almost reckless to hope that he still might care for me in some way.

"He has been making himself crazy trying to find you," he continued, lifting his face to the sky, the rain pelting against his skin and clothing. "As I did earlier today, he will be able to track you here now. I sensed you at the bottom of the hill but could not come for you until the sun disappeared behind the clouds for good at the top of the mountain."

"Where is he?" My voice was fraught with worry.

"He has been searching for you in the city for the last three days. He will be home as soon as he can be. Of that I am sure." He offered his hand and pulled my shivering frame to my feet. "You are freezing! Why did you not say anything?"

"I'll be all right," I replied between the vibrations of my chattering teeth.

Scowling harshly, he said, "Caleb mentioned that you always say that. It frustrates him to no end." Then he glanced down at his own soaked tee shirt and pants. "I am afraid I cannot do much about that here." It will be a cold trip back for you, but I will get you there as quickly as I can."

He was right. Within minutes, we were back at the tree house. I noted that I had been a considerable distance away when the rain stopped me, but I was relieved, and a bit pleased, to see I had been going the right direction and would have eventually found it.

The glass doors were already open above us, and Gemma was standing there, anxiously waiting our arrival, when Jax's feet hit the tree house floor. "Are you both OK?"

"Of course I am," Jax replied, as if insulted that she had even asked. I couldn't help but smile—albeit a chattering teeth kind of smile—at how he sounded a lot like Caleb. "We need to get her out of these wet clothes right away."

She nodded as he passed me into her arms. "I—I missed you G—Gemma," I stuttered through my teeth.

"I missed you, too, sweetie." She walked us towards her room, her voice trailing back to Jax as he closed the glass doors. "I don't know why I couldn't just go with you," she grumbled, and he didn't allow her to get away with it.

"Because, then, you would be wet and freezing like her, and I will not have that."

The over-protective sod was back in full force.

Gemma muttered something under her breath.

"D—Don't," I pleaded. "He me—means well."

She winked, her voice sweet as an angel as she replied, "I know."

About an hour later I was feeling much better. A chill would race through me now and then, but the constant shivering had stopped, and at least I was in some dry clothes. Now I could focus on sleep, which I desperately needed, because I felt like every limb in my body was slack from exhaustion. Though I wanted to stay awake, my heart aching to see him, my eyes just wouldn't cooperate. They were growing heavier by the second.

"Are you hungry?" Gemma asked in the dim light of the bedroom.

"Yes, but more sleepy."

"Here," she motioned towards her bed. Lie down and get some rest."

I shook my head and grabbed an extra pillow from the bed. "No, this is your room. I'll be fine on the sofa in the library."

A frown crossed her face. "Not this again. I don't mind."

"I do," I answered firmly. "Honestly, I think I'll be out as soon as my head hits the pillow. Can I just grab a blanket?"

"Of course," she replied, disappearing for just a second before returning with the item.

"Thanks," I smiled, then headed towards the library, hoping soon I would see the vampire I had missed so much.

***

Startled out of a deep sleep, I heard the glass doors open to the house and knew it was him. Although I hadn't seen Caleb in over a month, I was able to sense him. The tightness pulled harder in my chest, a clear signal that he was near. It was as Alec and Gideon had said, I could recognize certain energies. Caleb's presence was clearer and more distinct to me than anyone else's.

My heart thundered away in anticipation of finally getting to see him. It was as if the huge hole that had taken refuge within my heart over the last month was a little less deep. Then I heard his first, furious words as his usually silent feet thudded against the wood floor. "*Where is she?*"

That certainly didn't sound good.

He was warning me that he was upset, because he knew perfectly well where I was.

"Easy, Caleb. She is resting," Jax answered, unruffled by the younger vampire's temper.

But Caleb was not about to let it go. "Don't tell me to relax right now, Jax. What the hell happened?"

"She hiked up here today to see you and got caught in the weather after dark, but she is fine," Jax answered, as if he were in a casual conversation.

"She really is OK, Caleb. I got her out of her wet clothes and warmed her up. She's sleeping," Gemma added, and then corrected, " . . . was sleeping."

"If she's so fine, then why did I feel complete terror in her earlier?"

This was not good. I was hoping Jax would leave out the small detail about the cougar.

"Well, that one is a little tougher," Jax began, and I knew it was all over with. "I sort of had to take care of a cougar that decided she was going to be his next meal."

"What?"

Suddenly, without warning, the doors blew open in front of me and a jolt of fear—fear of him—ran through me for the first time since the battle in the field on the night of the train crash. He was literally towering over me, his face contorted by a furious expression, as he yelled, "*Are you insane? Are you out of your freaking mind? Do you have a death wish, Olivia?*"

A bit unsettled, I sat up on the sofa, tossing the blanket that was covering me to the side. "I understand you're upset—"

"Upset?" he snapped. "Upset doesn't begin to cover it!"

He paced the room, his hands gesturing wildly through the air as his long strides crossed back and forth. I could see the tension gripping his shoulders, and when his eyes turned back to me they appeared worn, dull, like a man who needed sleep. But that didn't make sense. He was a Daywalker, and Daywalkers didn't need a lot of sleep.

"Hiking up here by yourself . . . almost being mauled by a cougar . . . nearly freezing to death. What the hell is the matter with you? Are you trying to punish me?"

If it was possible for a vampire's pale complexion to flush with anger, this would have been the time it happened. I was so thrown by how upset he was that I was at a loss for words. Right now he seemed too angry to reason with, so I chose to sit there, quiet and still, on the sofa and wait patiently for him to calm down enough for me to speak with him.

Thankfully, it worked.

After a few more minutes of pacing a permanent trail into the area rug, he finally stopped. Standing in the middle of the room, he pinched the bridge of his nose, his head shaking back and forth, until his breathing began to slow. When he looked up again I could clearly see all of the fear that was behind the rage. He knew he had lost control, the vampire inside him trying to take control. And, true to his word, he was fighting to take it back.

I blinked wide as he dropped to his knees in front of me, his arms hanging loose at his sides, his head slumped in defeat. It was as if all the strength inside his powerful body had been drained away in an instant, leaving only the man. "Olivia, I thought . . ."

"Caleb," I whispered, reaching out to cup his wretched face in my palms. My heart ached from seeing how much pain he was in. "I. Am. All. Right," I spoke softly, emphasizing each word, certain of what he really needed to hear at that moment.

He set his hands atop both my knees, his fingers pushing my legs wide so he could slide his hips in between. Wrapping his arms around my low back, he slowly let his body come to rest against mine, his chin lying over my shoulder. "You don't understand." He sounded tormented as he spoke. "When I felt the pain of your last fever, worse than any before . . . and then nothing for three days . . ." He paused for a long moment, too upset to continue. "I thought the fever had killed you."

I was shocked. I had no idea of the worry I had caused him by having been hidden in that church. I didn't think. Reaching my arms over his broad shoulders, I curled into his body, my lips placing soft kisses on the cool skin of his neck. To finally feel him pressed against me once again was the answer to my prayers. I let go a breathy sigh, wishing I could live in this moment with him forever.

This was why I needed him.

"I'm so sorry," I breathed against his throat. "I didn't mean to worry you like this. I'd never want to hurt you like this."

Encircling me even more tightly, he pulled me closer until there was no part of my body that wasn't holding onto him.

"Why have you come back?" he asked, his low, velvety voice sounding broken as he spoke.

I drew back from him, staring sincerely into the beautiful shades of gray that I had missed so much. "I needed to tell you I was sorry about what I said to you that last day, on the terrace. I didn't mean it . . . honestly, I didn't."

He shifted his body ever so slightly, surrounding me completely with his strength, a strength that was filled with great tenderness. "If there was any way I could take that day back, I would," he whispered with feeling. "You have to know I would. I felt the pain I caused you, and it was unforgivable."

Grazing my fingers across his back, I tried to reassure him. "It's OK. I . . . I . . . discovered some things about myself while I was away."

"Tell me," he breathed.

Suddenly, I couldn't speak. Panic struck me in that very moment, for all too soon I would lose him all over again. How could I possibly explain to him about being this awful Charmer? About what I was meant to do? How could I ask him to understand that?

At my silence, his body went rigid against me. "Olivia, why are you afraid?"

"I did . . . I—I mean I have . . . I've come here to tell you these things. But I need more time. Time to find the right words to explain everything."

He pushed back from me with a dazed, confused expression in his eyes. "Does this have to do with the fevers?"

Slowly, I nodded.

He threw up his hands and slapped them back against his sides. "You can't ask this of me! I've worried about you every single day for a month. I need answers and I need to understand what's going on."

I reached for his hands, squeezing them gently. "Caleb, it's more complicated than that. But I believe the fevers are gone. I'm not dying or anything."

He studied me carefully, sensing I was telling him the truth. I wanted to be as truthful with him as I could, even though I knew that eventually my fears would betray me. "What did the doctor say?"

A jolt shot right through me. His question had caught me off guard, which I was sure showed on my face. "You haven't been to the doctor, have you?" Growling, he twisted away until his back was to me and lowered his head over hunched shoulders. I dropped to my knees on the floor behind him and leaned against his back, my cheek resting against his shoulder blade.

"You can't ask this of me," he repeated. "You can't keep me in the dark like this."

"But I *am* asking," I said, my voice finding more strength. "Caleb, I've not even had time to process things myself. You have to trust me. Trust that I will tell you when I'm able—when I have the right words. I wouldn't have climbed up this giant mountain today, nearly getting mauled by a cougar and freezing to death, if I didn't want to tell you."

The muscles in his back flexed visibly. "That's not funny."

"It's a little funny," I teased, kissing his shoulder through his shirt, hoping he would not press any more right now and would give me the time I was asking for.

He inhaled a deep, slow breath, then pitched around on me so fast I nearly choked out my own. Scooping me up in his arms as he stood up, he stormed right out of the library and past Gemma and Jax, as if he knew exactly where he was going.

"Caleb! Where are . . . ?" My breath caught as he jumped us up to the second floor ledge. "No," I cried, "its Gemma's room." The sound of Gemma's giggle carried upstairs behind us.

The next thing I knew I was dizzily being dropped on my back onto Gemma's bed, my body bouncing against the mattress as Caleb plopped down beside me. The full length of his long frame molded against mine as he pulled me close and nestled his head into the crook of my neck. "You don't deserve it," he began, "but I want to lie with you—here tonight—as you sleep. And I can't do that on that damned couch!"

I smiled, inhaling deeply and curling against him. He would give me time.

Chapter Fifteen

"Mmm," I moaned into my pillow with a contented sigh the next morning as I rolled over beneath the silky sheets. The space beside me was empty now, and despite my initial disappointment at that, I could sense that the man who had held me there through the night was close by. The pressure pulling in my chest confirmed as much and, strangely, I was starting to get used to the sensation. I loved that my body had a way of recognizing when Caleb was near—and how that made me feel more connected to him.

I could sense him directly now. He was downstairs in the kitchen with Gemma and Jax, engaged in a lively banter that brought a smile to my lips. Just to know that things appeared back to normal with them again meant so much to me because they meant everything to him. They were his family. Hopefully, the balance had been reset and wouldn't change while I was here.

"Gem, I agree with Jax on this. It's not safe for you to be in the city alone. Let him stay there with you tonight."

"You would agree with him," she complained. "You guys' know I love you, but—"

A smooth hum over Caleb's lips interrupted what she was about to say. "What is it?"

"My sweet girl is awake, and she's filled with joy this morning."

"You're happy to have her back here, aren't you?" she asked, but he didn't respond.

I rolled onto my back and slapped my hands against the mattress. Dang it! Why didn't he respond? He could feel my happiness, but none of them had any idea my Dhampir half could hear their conversation in the kitchen. "Why don't you go to her?"

He exhaled a quiet breath that sounded almost like a contented sigh. "I want to give her some space. I don't want to smother her."

Smother? Was he crazy? All I wanted was for him to smother me!

"Besides . . ." he continued, "I'm working on my apology for last night."

"That is good," Jax replied, in all seriousness. "You were thirsty from pushing yourself the last few days. I know you were scared for her, but that fear allowed your blood thirst to get the better of you. You must be more aware of the triggers so you can always maintain a level of control. You cannot expect a human to understand what is behind displays of anger such as you showed her last night."

Thanks to Jax, I now understood it perfectly. Caleb's anger was tied to the thirst of his vampire half. He had mentioned more than once that he was considered a young vampire and that Jax was teaching him how to maintain the control he so desperately wanted. This was just another part of it.

"Yeah, no kidding," Gemma said, underlining her sarcasm with a loud snort. "After that angry rant you're lucky she let you—"

"Gemma," Jax warned, "show him some leniency. This is all very new for him."

"Yes, you're right," she replied, with sugary sweetness in her tone. "What I meant to say was . . . an apology would be good."

"Now I *am* worried," Jax teased.

Caleb laughed lightly, but there was an undertone of clear concern. "Do you think she'll forgive me? The last thing I want to do is frighten her any more than I already have."

Jax replied with a low chuckle and a one-word reply. "Listen." I wasn't sure what he meant by that, but then he added, "I think she already has."

"Yes, I hear it," Caleb replied, and I realized, just as he had done before, when we were walking, he was listening to the rapid rhythm of my heart. "I love hearing her heart flutter like that. She's irresistible when she's happy and free."

With a joyous squeal I sprung from the bed and bolted straight for the shower, wanting to look my absolute best for him this morning. I may have been too quick in judging the idea of having extra vampire senses. In some cases—like the occasional, necessary eavesdropping—it was very convenient.

After drying my hair and applying some minimal makeup, I practically bounded over to the closet, all prepared to rifle through Gemma's clothes to find something special to wear, when I noticed she had already set out a few items.

It was as though she could read my mind.

My fingers touched the delicate pearl buttons of an ivory tuxedo blouse that she had paired with a red-floral print skirt. Holding the skirt up to my waist, I saw it would fall just right, a few inches above my knees. They were feminine, pretty, and perfect clothes, and I couldn't wait to wear them for him.

A few minutes later, I descended to the first floor in bare feet. Happy smiles were there to greet me as I entered the kitchen. I couldn't remember another time, ever, when I had felt so happy just to be someplace. It was like I was home, which was remarkable for a woman who felt like she'd had no home for a long while. "Good morning," I said cheerfully as I swept my eyes over the French toast with blueberries Gemma had prepared.

But in an instant the mood seemed to change as I stood there watching a roomful of smiles disappear. I stopped smiling, too, suddenly confused about what was going on. The three of them were staring at me in stunned silence. Then the two men's brows pulled uniformly together and Gemma's mouth gaped open in surprise. Heat flooded my face and neck and I was uncomfortable with the attention being focused on me. I glanced down at my clothing, wondering if perhaps it didn't fit me well, as I fussed with the thin material of my skirt. "I know this isn't something I'd usually wear, but . . ."

"Olivia?" Gemma began with a sharp exhale. "Your eyes? Your hair? What's going on?"

My hands flew to my cheeks as I finally, stupidly, remembered the changes in my appearance. Last night, with my tired red eyes, rain-soaked face, and hair pulled back in a ponytail and hidden by a cap, my changes had not been as noticeable, but in the full light of morning the difference was now obvious.

Jax turned to Caleb, the concern in his eyes commanding that the younger vampire explain what was going on, but it was obvious from the look on Caleb's face that he was just as surprised as the others.

I slid my gaze to meet Caleb's. There was worry, confusion, and a hint of frustration there, perhaps because he was feeling duped at agreeing to my request for more time to explain. He wanted to know what was going on—now!

Leaving his stool, he came to stand just inches from me, his brows still drawn tightly with concern. All evidence of the smile that had been lighting him up only moments ago was gone. I lowered my head, trying to hide from his disapproving gaze, but his knuckle caught the tip of my chin and lifted it back up until our eyes met again. "Tell me what's happening?" he ordered, stretching out each word in a quiet demand, as my heart began to race faster and faster. Thump!Thump!Thump! There were no breaks in between.

I hadn't anticipated they would react to my changes like this. Actually, I hadn't thought about it at all. Alec and Gideon said vampires would be attracted to my changed features, that I would become what they found desirable. But right now, as I glanced into Caleb's eyes, I wanted to run away. He looked at me as if I were sick.

Tell him the truth, Olivia! That's what you came up here to do.

In my head I knew what was right but, standing there in that horrid moment, terrified of losing him once again, I couldn't find any words. What words could possibly explain all of this?

What words?

"I—I . . . I'm—"

Caleb's eyes widened in alarm, seeming to take in all of my panic, my fear, my anxiety, and every inch of his tall form became rigid. "Olivia, you can't keep this from me any longer. You know why this is happening to you! Don't you?"

He would not let this go. He would give me no more time.

"Yes," I whispered back, almost inaudibly.

He released his hold on my chin, his frustration building, and my one word answer didn't help matters much. "Tell me."

Words were stuck in a ball at the back of my throat and I just couldn't seem to speak. Shaking my head at him, I began to back away, nearly tripping over my own feet.

Caleb was startled, a flash of injured surprise crossing through his gray eyes as he watched me step back from him.

"It's OK, Olivia," Gemma tried to reassure me, but it was too late. There was nothing that could fix the awkwardness of that moment.

My gaze went to the others, their faces still just as stunned as Caleb's. They all deserved to hear the truth from me, but I was a coward. I was afraid of forever losing this family I had grown to love and my invitation to stay in this home, the only home where I felt I belonged.

Caleb remained silent as he continued to watch me back away. I had hurt him, cut him deeply, just as sure as if I had plunged a dagger straight through his un-beating heart. Seeing the pain I was causing him, I tried once again to speak, to explain. "Caleb, I . . ." But it was no use. The words wouldn't come. "I'm sorry," I murmured before turning and racing upstairs.

***

Over the next few hours, I remained in Gemma's room, bunched up in the chair near the bed, staring at the door, expecting at any moment that Caleb would enter and demand the answers he deserved.

But he never came.

Then my stomach tied up in tighter knots as I heard the sound of the glass doors opening, and wondered who was leaving. What if it was Caleb? What if he finally had enough of me keeping the truth from him? The knot pulled even more tightly. I didn't want to believe that after a second chance to be with him I was just going to let him walk away from me without even a fight. But then I inhaled a couple of deep breaths, and that's when I could sense it—sense him. He was still here, and relief washed over me with the strength of a storm. I knew that he hadn't given up—yet.

That was when I knew I had to make things right. I couldn't continue to hide in this room. Slowly, I slipped from the chair and went out into the hallway. The door to Caleb's study was closed, and I sensed he was in there. I didn't know if he was angry, hurt or disappointed—or perhaps all the above—but he clearly didn't want to speak right now. Even though I had hardly made a sound, he had to know I was there and was still choosing not to come out. I decided to wait for him downstairs for as long as necessary.

This time it was my turn to wait until he was ready to talk.

Returning to the kitchen, I found a sandwich and some bottled water that Gemma had clearly left out for me on the counter. I perched on a stool and quietly inhaled the turkey on rye. The unnerving silence in the house told me that both Jax and Gemma had left. Once again, my antics had driven them from their own home.

I sighed, getting up to clean my plate, then I walked over to the beautiful piano.

Taking a seat on the soft-cushioned duet bench, the eighty-eight keys of the Fazioli spread out before me, I realized that I wanted to play—really play—for the first time in a month. I had all this pent-up confusion inside me from trying to understand who I really was now. Was I a gifted pianist who was always falling short of her potential, or was I a Dhampir who possessed the gift to trap vampires and lure them to their deaths? Or was I simply a woman who had fallen on love with an amazing man and didn't know how to express it?

I hoped, somehow, to release all of this pent up emotion and confusion through the smooth, ivory-surfaced keys, but instead, I only sat there, staring at them as if they were some great mystery to me.

"Will you play something for me?" It was Caleb's velvety voice. My breath caught with hope as I swung around to see him standing there, all the tension and doubt seeming to have evaporated from him. "I'm sorry. I startled you again, didn't I?"

"No, it's not that. It's just that I haven't played since I left here. I worry my gift is lost."

He moved to stand just behind me, then smoothly straddled his leg over the bench seat and lowered himself right beside me. His long thighs stretched out on both sides of me, and suddenly I was very aware of his presence. My heart skipped several beats at feeling his body separated from mine by only a paper thin veil of air. He sat there with such strength, such confidence, completely at ease with himself, while I felt as though I could crumble. His hand brushed over my shoulder and pushed my longer hair back as he leaned in to whisper at my ear. "You play beautifully, Olivia. A gift like yours doesn't just vanish."

His steady breathing remained at my ear and I felt as though I would melt against him right there. I didn't understand how I was capable of hurting him as I had. "I'm sorry about this morning," I offered, still staring at the keys. "I—I didn't mean . . . ," I began, but was again at a loss for words.

Then, I was just at a loss.

Cool lips pressed softly just under my ear, then slid lower over my throat, creating a tingling path as he searched for that one point where my pulse beat the strongest through my skin. Once there, he locked me beneath his lips, drawing my sharp hiss of reply as he cupped my face in his hand to hold me in place while he licked and nibbled against the thrumming skin. His touch was so light, yet, so inescapable, and incredibly intimate, as if the whole world had just stopped for us in that moment.

"Caleb," I swallowed hard.

"Talk to me, my sweet girl," he whispered over my skin. "Tell me what's in that anxious little head of yours." I tried to keep my balance as I held on to his hard, corded arms. "Come here," he breathed, his kisses now low on my collarbone as he pulled me to him. His fingers glided down my back, over the thin chiffon material of my blouse, their cool tips seeming to memorize every detail, every curve.

Everywhere he touched me, my skin sizzled underneath as he slid me towards him, his hand reaching beneath my knees and hooking them over one of his hard, straddled thighs. "Caleb?" I cried softly again, my body now angled back slightly while his arm supported me at my shoulders.

"Yes, my sweet," he answered just before taking my lips in a soul-searing kiss I felt all the way down to my toes, striking from my memory everything I had wanted to say. Sliding his hand behind my neck, he angled me further, his lips pressing, demanding more, his nostrils flaring as his rough facial bristles dragged over my skin.

He had such control over me, making me feel open, exotic, special, like I possessed that one thing he was unable to resist. It relaxed me to the point I couldn't stifle the not-so-small moan that escaped my lips. It was embarrassing, almost, but his approving low chuckle vibrated over the sound just before his tongue pushed past my lips, gaining entry, teasing, inhaling my hot breath until I felt weak from the state of it.

My skin came alive with tingles as he released several of the delicate pearl buttons of my blouse, his palms opening the thin fabric over my breast, sending a sweet shock to my heart as his thumb caressed over the tips of my nipples through the delicate lace of my bra. The friction of it drew another desperate sound from me as I buried my fingers in his thick chestnut hair, tightened my grip on it, and pulled his head lower until his tongue was right over the lacy edges of my bra.

Mercy! I thought I was about to go up in flames, and this time it wasn't from any fever, just pure excited response.

His arms squeezed around me as he groaned, breathing hard over my kiss-moistened skin. It sounded as if he was trying to slow his own desire, control his own need, which I totally wasn't going to help him with. "I want you to trust me," he breathed. "To tell me what has you so frightened. I promise I will protect you. I want to protect you."

"I . . . I want to tell you, Caleb . . . but I'm afraid."

He brushed back up my neck until his lips were at the shell of my ear. "Don't be afraid, sweet girl. It's all right." As he continued to support me behind my shoulders, his free hand began a slow caress over my hips and thighs, then gently pried my knees apart. "What do you want, Olivia? I'll give you whatever you want."

Gazing into his beautiful eyes, I could see they were heated, but sincere, as his cool fingertips continued to skim along my inner thighs under my skirt, stopping to tease for a moment with small circular motions of his fingers over my panties.

I gasped, arching my back towards him as I bit into my bottom lip.

He smiled in response, a playful, knowing smile that only

invited sin. "Do you like this?" he asked, tapping his fingers and then massaging in the same slow circles until I was gasping for breath, grabbing a fistful of his shirt, any reply that had come to mind lost within those hard breaths. "I can't be with you how we both want," he continued, "but I can satisfy this beautiful body of yours in other ways—without hurting you. Would that please you?"

When I didn't answer him, since I was too busy trying to hold back the passionate murmurs that were struggling at the back of my throat, he moved his hand beneath the silk, taking my silence to mean that I wanted him to continue.

But I had to stop him!

I wanted desperately to enjoy pleasure *with* him, not *from* him. There was a difference. The only problem was convincing him of that when he seemed so determined for this not to happen. I had an advantage, though, trusting that my newly discovered Dhampir body would be able to handle the strength of him inside me, and that was what I wanted more than anything, for him to make love to me.

At least, I wanted to think of it as making love.

I grabbed his hand to stop him, and his slanted brows questioned me while I tried to regain my breath. "This would please me. But there's something I want even more from you."

His breath drew in deep, his gray eyes now blazing. "Tell me."

I reached my hand up to his face, tracing the line of his jaw with my fingertips. He smiled so brightly, his long dimples dug deep into the edges of his cheeks. "Show me," I said, tucking a loose strand of his hair behind his ear. "Show me your other side."

The brilliant smile disappeared almost instantly. He exhaled a heavy sigh and pushed me back from him, returning my legs to the bench while his arm straightened my back up before releasing me fully.

"No! Please, Caleb," I cried, my breathing still heavy from our exchange. "Please don't push away from me." I tried to pull closer to him again, but he wouldn't allow it.

"You know I can't give you that," he grumbled, getting up from the bench, until soon I was watching his tall form, rigid with a tight control, walking away from me.

Angry and hurt that he would reject my request so easily, I rather awkwardly sprang to my feet and charged after him. "You want me to trust you, but you don't trust me," I cried to his retreating back. "You don't trust me enough to let me see you—all of you."

He stopped, whirling smoothly around on his heels and halting me in my tracks just short of him. His eyes were still glazed from our heated exchange, but his expression was torn. "It's not that simple, and you know it."

"Yes, it is that simple. Please. Please just trust me."

Frustrated, and perhaps feeling a bit cornered, though, that really had not been my intent, he threw up his hands then slapped them back against his legs. "Why's this so important to you?"

I blurted out the next words before I thought about how they might confuse him. "Because I want something real! Something, that isn't an illusion."

When I saw his bewildered response, I felt guilty. I knew it didn't make any sense to him, and he was trying so hard to understand. It certainly wasn't his fault I was who I was.

Quickly, I turned from him to retreat back towards the piano, but he touched my shoulder, and then reached forward a bit more and curled his hand more securely around my arm to hold me there. "You think what we feel for each other is an illusion?"

"In a way . . . yes." I took another step back from him, and he didn't like it, his hand reaching out for me before he stopped short. "You only want to show me the parts of yourself that you choose—that you deem acceptable. You won't let me be with all of you, so I can want all of you. That's not real."

My heart ached watching the anguish twist his expression. "Olivia . . . ," he said, shaking his head with frustration, his mind and heart appearing to grapple with the two sides of himself. I knew what I was asking him to do was the one thing he feared most, but I hadn't prepared myself for the swift change in his response. "For the last time, I can't! I said *NO* and I meant it."

He disappeared in the blink of an eye, and it felt like a slap in the face, the open room falling to silence as his last words slammed against me with the force of the air he left behind, crushing what was left of my hope.

I just stood there for a moment, before returning to the piano's bench seat, my back turned away from the instrument I loved. His refusal to give me what I knew we both wanted hurt me in a way I hadn't prepared myself for. Feeling the sting of tears pressing against my eyes, I propped my elbows on my knees and dropped my face into my palms.

I had failed. He didn't trust me, not in the way I wanted him to.

He couldn't trust me to always see the good and real man behind the vampire he had become. But what could I really expect? I hadn't been honest with him, either. I just wanted to pretend that I could stay here with him, hiding myself from the rest of the world and refusing to face what I was destined to do. That refusal was catching up with me, and it was obvious I could no longer stay and wait for . . . what? I didn't even know for sure.

No, it was time for me to return to where I belonged and try to figure out where to go from here. "Thank you for the time," I whispered as I sniffed and wiped away a tear I couldn't stop from falling.

Then suddenly, a stream of wintry air blew around me and long, cool fingers encircled my hands, prying them away from my face. I glanced up to see Caleb's pained expression. He was on his knees in front of me, squeezing my hands gently as he brought them to rest on my lap. "I'm sorry," he said. "I didn't mean to hurt you."

I blinked back at him, surprised and worried to see so much conflict there, his heart obviously struggling with whatever it was he was about to say. "If I do this . . . If I give you what you want? Will you tell me what's happening to you—what you know? I won't force you, but I need to know you will tell me. That you trust me enough to talk to me without this . . . this fear hanging over you."

"Yes," I answered without hesitation, surprised how easily the word fell from my lips. But in that moment I knew I was hopelessly in love with him. I would give him whatever he asked and I would risk the heartbreak of never knowing happiness like this again to just truly be with him for one exquisite day.

In my excitement, I tried to reach for him, but he held my hands secure, covering them with his own as he pressed my palms flat to the bench at each side of my hips, and then leaned forward until he was so close that the puff of his breath was right there on my lips. "I need you to hear me, Olivia," he began, and I could see the conflicting emotions rolling though him, everything from tension and desire, to worry. "We will do this slowly—carefully. Like when I'm feeding, I don't have as much control once I've changed. I don't want to hurt you. Do you understand?"

"You won't hurt me, Caleb."

He appeared truly struck by my complete confidence in that fact. After staring at me for what seemed an endless moment, his gaze dropped to my lips as he licked over his own. "I want you to stay very still. Just relax and let yourself enjoy what you feel. I will feel that. Trust me, it will be enough to bring about my change."

I nodded quickly, feeling completely at his mercy as my breathing already started to quicken and he hung there at my shoulder, his long, powerful body hovering just above mine. He kissed me under my ear, just once, as if to quietly draw my attention, but all my mind could process was how I wanted to grab him and pull him against me, but I couldn't. His hands still held mine in his grasp as he inflicted a sort of sweet torture over me, one that meant the denial of his touch. He wanted me wanting, holding very still and never quite letting his body make contact with mine, perfectly controlled as he absorbed my desire at a distance.

This was not fair! My breaths were getting faster and I started squirming uncomfortably beneath him. "Relax, Olivia," he said with a touch more struggle to his voice. "Just stay with me."

At first I was confused by what he meant, but with each steadfast rise and fall of his powerful lungs it became clear that he wanted me to follow the rhythm of his breathing. My own excited lungs were already working much harder than his, so I raised my chin high and relaxed completely, dropping my head back on my shoulders as I tried to slow everything down. Caleb was right there with me, adjusting his body with mine so that his lips remained at my ear. "That's it, follow me," he breathed, squeezing my hands in tempered praise once my rhythm began to mimic his.

"Caleb, please . . ."

"Shhh, stay very still. Trust me, sweet girl."

"I trust you."

He released the hands that he had pinned to the bench and moved them to my knees. Tingles rose on my skin as his hands moved to pull my thighs apart, stretching my red printed skirt high and flat over my thighs. He filled the empty space with his body, the fabric crushing between us as his hands gripped the swells of my bottom and yanked my hips forward until I was firmly pressed against him. The excitement coursing through my veins at the contact made me feel out of control, and all I wanted to do was to scream at the madness of it.

"Easy, my sweet. Just concentrate on me. I will bring you deeper."

But I could hear it in his voice, he was fighting just the same to keep the need he was feeling under his control, and somehow it made me feel better that I wasn't the only one who felt this blistering attraction between us.

He rolled his hips and pressed his aroused body forward, his breathing rough as he tested how we fit together. I moaned softly at his ear, wrapping my legs around his hips and holding on by a thread at his shoulders as I teetered over the edge of the bench. Caleb sensed how I was surrendering completely, and that unquestioning trust began to shred the last of his control. He grabbed the edge of the bench, his arms bracketing me as his fingers squeezed over the bench frame. "My God, Olivia," he rasped. "Your body is amazingly responsive. You'll never understand how much I want this body. How much I want you."

"Please, Caleb. Please."

At my desperate pleading, he groaned thickly, his breath seeming to catch in his throat as he moved his head over my shoulder so I could no longer see his face. His fingers continued to strain against the bench beside my hips. Now completely rigid, a remarkably powerful current of energy swept through his body just like before, the vibrations of it rolling over my skin where we touched. Low growls, like the primal sound of the cougar, rippled over my shoulder, and I knew there was a battle raging within him. Always a warrior, the man was fighting to not give in to the other half that was now taking over.

Caleb's fierce panting, frozen frame, and low groans all signaled that the transformation behind my shoulder was complete. "Can I see you?" I asked gently.

"Olivia, I—"

"Please."

Slowly, he returned us to a vertical position and then pulled back his head to meet my gaze. It was the first time I had been face to face with the vampire since the night of the crash, and the contempt he felt towards this side of himself was there in his eyes. To know he saw himself that way, as a monster, ripped at my heart.

I took my time to absorb every detail of his changed face. Just as on the night of the train crash, the vampire displayed an unyielding shell of strength. His sharp incisors protruded just behind his lips, and the startling, electric blue of his eyes shone forth like the most vivid sapphire. Yet, as I stared deeper, I could still see him—the man, my Caleb—inside the brilliant blue. All the reluctance, fear, and anxiety he showed when I asked him to do this was still there in his uneasy eyes.

Seeing him clearly like this never caused me to be afraid, not even for a moment. The man, the vampire, and the warrior were all there with me as one . . . and he was breathtakingly beautiful.

Tears of emotion I had no way of stopping fell over my cheeks, causing terror to reflect from his sapphire blue. He believed I was somehow repulsed or frightened by this side of him, but that was far from the truth. Seeing him, every part of him, only made me feel closer. Though I feared he would push away any second, so I pulled myself close, as close as the bench would allow. "No," I murmured. It was my turn now to say, "Stay with me."

He stilled, seeming unsure of what was happening.

My fingertips traced the line of his lips, passing dangerously close to his cutting fangs. I wanted him to know, without doubt, that I was not frightened. I cherished this man and I didn't want to share him with the outside world, preferring to remain hidden with him here in the trees.

A wide smile broke across my cheeks as I smoothed the worry lines at his brow with my thumbs. Caleb remained rigid, and I wasn't sure if he was fighting for control inside. If he was, he never let me see it, so I pressed my lips to the tense bone at his jaw, silently pleading for him to relax.

All the feelings I had for him, ever felt for him, even on that day so long ago by the lake, were welling in my heart, and I desperately wanted him to know the joy he brought to my life. "I love you, Caleb," I said. "I love the creative mind that built this home. I love the giving man who gave the gift of a grand piano. And I love the protective warrior who saved me. I love all of you. I just need you to know that."

Relief seemed to roll through him in one lengthy exhale as he dropped his head forward against mine. I knew then I was so much in love with him that I wanted more than anything to be with him—just once, right now—before he would send me away.

The warrior, as always, would fight me, so I would have to persuade him.

Blanketing his face with kisses, the dampness from my lashes transferred to his skin. For a second he appeared completely stunned, unable to move, and I used that to my advantage. "Thank you for trusting me, for giving me this gift," I whispered while drowning him in more soft kisses. And though my words relieved him, he continued to hold his body tight, his breathing once again becoming strained.

"Olivia, no," he said roughly, his voice low, frustrated at me for tempting him this way. "I don't have complete control." He fought with every muscle, every ounce of resistance he had not to lose control with me, but I pushed him because I knew exactly what I wanted.

"I'm counting on that."

He appeared stunned by my reply. "This is a dangerous game you're playing. Stop this—now!" he demanded, his chin high, like a man straining to keep his drowning face above water. "I will hurt you."

I nibbled not so playfully at his earlobe as my eager hands began pulling at his shirt. He responded by slamming his open palms against the bench, his eyes closed, his teeth clenched, a low groan rolling in his throat. "Olivia!"

Pushing the crisp cotton fabric slack over his shoulders, I ran my palms over the light dusting of hair on his chest, memorizing every detail of his skin, every plane of muscle that flexed beneath my fingers as I kissed my way down his neck. His low moan signaled that his resistance was weakening as he slipped forward, offering no more objection. I smiled against his skin, flicking my tongue out over his nipple as a sharp hiss escaped between his teeth.

"Olivia," he repeated in a hoarse, almost desperate voice while I bunched his shirt in my fist, tugging the material down his back and pulling his arms from the bench—which meant he was allowing it. If he had wanted to stop me, he could have. "If I take you, I won't be able to stop. I can't stop. God!—I don't want to hurt you."

"You won't hurt me." I spoke it with confidence because I truly believed it. There was no way fate had brought me back to this man after all of this time and not wanted it to stick somehow.

Little by little I dealt with his button-flys, opening him to me with a smile, while—in stark contrast—he braced himself against the bench with clenched teeth. He looked as if he were holding on by a thin thread as I slid his clothing down the well-defined hollows of his hips until the long, thick length of him sprung free. Blinking several times, I took in the size of him, wondering now if he really could hurt me. He slipped forward with a loud groan, his imposing frame coming over mine as he swallowed me inside a dark, fiery gaze. It was there in his eyes, in the husky lull of his voice. There was no turning back.

And I didn't want to.

Caleb Wolfe was beautiful. The defined muscles of his abdomen, arms, and legs were long and lean, like a swimmer's, and I ached to slide my hands over each one. "Please, Caleb. Tell me you can feel me. Tell me you can feel how you excite my body?"

He remained unmoving, locked, his breathing hard, and for a moment I didn't think he would answer, but then he rasped, "I feel you, my sweet."

"Then you can feel how much I want to hold you inside me?"

He cursed under his breath. "Yes!"

I leaned forward, whispering tenderly at his ear. "Then just let go. "Let go for me."

Those words broke through the last shred of his control. His thunderous roar came just before his hands slid under my knees and pulled them high off the bench. My upper body fell back until my palms and forearms braced over the piano keys behind me, the sounds transmitted to the strings random and awkward, yet somehow beautiful.

Skimming his hands over my thin, red skirt, he pushed the sheer fabric to my waist, giving him access to the thin strip of silk blocking him from what he wanted. Both hands intertwined under the simple strings and ripped the garment apart as if it were tissue. Then, in one swift motion, he tore open my blouse. I gasped as the delicate pearl buttons cracked and rolled against the wood floor below us.

Even though he was excited, he caressed with a tender touch, his hands moving like a bird's feather over my skin. He was driving me so high, I almost couldn't breathe. Then he reached for me, one arm pulling me up from the keys in a secure hold with that hand as he curled my leg around him with the other, and I braced myself at his shoulders, staring into the most amazingly vivid blue eyes I'd ever seen. "I need you to give me a sign, Olivia . . . if I'm hurting you."

Understanding what he wanted from me, I bit—not so gently—into his neck, letting him know that was my promise to signal if he hurt me. His response to my bite was another sharp hiss through his teeth as he raised his head and stretched his neck out, trying to calm the overwhelming need coursing through his veins—but it was of no use.

He couldn't wait any longer.

Caleb lined his hips up with mine and held one of my legs firm in his hand just before he pushed deep inside me with a low, guttural groan. The instant shock of such fullness had my head falling back with a sharp gasp as I inhaled the sweetest breath of air in my human existence. Never had I felt such a powerful collision of emotions and sensations.

He was beautiful. The way he held me to him, the way he fought to control the physical needs of his own body. How he held still for a moment so my inner muscles could adjust around him. "Damn," he breathed. "You're so warm."

Caleb smoothed both of his hands down my thighs, curling my legs behind his back as I continued to struggle for breath within his embrace. "Hold on," he said, then gripped the edges of bench, canted his hips back and thrust forward, pushing himself so deep that my breath again hitched under the pressure as I realized only then that he hadn't been fully seated inside me.

I couldn't believe it. Never had I experienced a man filling me to the absolute limits of what my body would accept. It was a pleasure that was indescribable.

"Caleb," I replied with a rush of breath, floating, moaning in almost desperate response to the exquisite pressure continuing to build and build in every fiber of me.

He reared back and thrust forward, this time with a force akin to being ransacked. My breath caught while I was crushed beneath his body, and it surprised me when I heard my own voice plead, "Again."

He didn't hesitate, delivering two more hard, penetrating thrusts. "Goddamnit, Olivia," he cursed, the strain in his voice conveying the effort to hold back, to not hurt me, even though it was evident his body screamed at him for more. "I don't want to hurt you."

My fingers dug at his shoulders. "Again."

His voice cracked and his breathing was thick as he scraped his bristled cheek against mine. "God help me, I do want more. I need more."

"Please Caleb, just let go. You're not hurting me."

He replied with three more deep thrusts, then his hips fell into a smooth rhythm that had me moaning as he finally began to let go, locking the piano bench in an iron grip to keep it from continuing to scrape over the wood floor beneath us.

Risking a look at his face—even though I longed just to keep my eyes shut tight and sink into the feeling—I saw that he was absolutely beautiful when receiving pleasure, his expression lost in a sort of hazy rapture as his steady thrusts began churning up a kind of tingling low in my stomach that I'd never, ever felt before, and I was almost desperate to see it to the end.

As if hearing my thoughts, he lowered his head and watched me while continuing to drive into my body with deep, penetrating thrusts. I could see in his expressions the wonder that must have been exploding over my face as I got closer to a sharp edge that he was about to shove me right over. "Caleb!"

"Yes," came his rough whisper. "You're there. I feel it."

Until this night, I had been intimate with only two men in my life, and each of them had taken a small piece of my heart with them when they left. But as I lay here now, feeling this vampire's perfect body move with rhythm and force inside mine, his need as acute as my own, I knew that he would not take a piece; he'd take my whole heart. Everything I had to give was now his to take freely. I would not ask for anything in return, and I would have no regrets. I just wanted to give him pleasure and for him to know how much joy he lavished upon my soul. I loved him! Even if it meant that this special love was only real for me.

I had enough love for the both of us.

Every muscle tightened like a coil around the man who in such a short time had become the center of my private universe. My hips began to rise beneath him as I screamed his name with absolutely no desire to hold back the high-pitched noise, my constricted body springing free in intense waves that ripped through me.

"Oh, God . . . yes . . . perfect . . . perfect," Caleb groaned just before he pushed deep in one final drive, throwing his arms over my head to brace himself against the piano.

Behind me, I could hear the destructive grinding of the piano's heavy center base against the wood floor as Caleb's arms shoved the enormous piano from its resting place. His body was stretched so far over me I was sure he only touched the piano with his fingertips as my inner walls clamped down on him repeatedly with my release. His hips flexed, growling out in a long, exquisite roar as he shuddered and came inside me.

Shaking and exhausted, I collapsed away from him.

His arm caught me so I would not crash to the floor and he pulled me back with such gentleness, his broad chest curling around me, that I felt shielded and safe. But his voice sounded terrified. "Did I hurt you?" he croaked, almost unable to speak through his heavy breathing.

I was confused by the question. He had to know, to feel, that I was in a state of complete bliss, and yet he still agonized that he might have somehow hurt me. My breathing was too erratic to allow me to answer him verbally, so I pulled back and shook my head, watching his visible relief.

After a few moments of quiet splendor, each of us gazing deeply into the other's eyes, his head gradually dropped to my shoulder and the man was back with me, pressing kisses along my throat as his breathing began to return to normal.

"Again, Caleb," I said, and he laughed against my skin.

"Yes, my sweet girl. I will satisfy this hungry body of yours again. But I'm afraid this time it'll be slow torture for you. I'm going to enjoy every minute of it . . . starting right here."

He tore away the tattered remains of my shirt and dispensed my bra to the floor in quick fashion. Cupping one of my bare breasts in his hand, he smiled. "I've wanted to do this since that first time these nipples hardened for me under your shirt." His head lowered, his tongue flicking over the small peaks that had been denied to him while his fangs were present before taking the mound more fully into his mouth.

I cried out, arching into him. "Oh, my."

We continued this dance between man and blue-eyed warrior, back and forth, back and forth, into the searing darkness of night, all the time with me not knowing whether, once I told him the truth, I would ever again know this much pure joy in my life.

I convinced myself it would be bearable.

As long as I had tonight.

Chapter Sixteen

The next morning, I woke to the brisk scent of the mountains mixed with a hint of sage and man, bringing a smile to my lips that was, quite simply, unavoidable. Unavoidable because any fear I had that I would wake to discover the night before had been nothing more than a vivid dream were gone the moment I recognized that scent—his scent.

That fragrance made my belly want to flip with a squeal of joy and my toes curl. I tucked an oversized pillow beneath me and stretched myself into consciousness, sensing the man—the vampire—responsible for drowning me in such happiness, was still there, lying quietly behind me.

He kissed my shoulder and brushed his fingertips along my back. Strangely, his fingers were not callus-tipped, as I remembered them from that long-ago day by the lake, but refined and bone-smooth, as if he had never done manual work in his life. The irony of a Daywalker's skin being so indestructible, yet so touchable, was not lost on me. It was only one of a growing list of things that fascinated me about him.

In a bit of a 'good morning' declaration, I wriggled a little closer to him under the sheets, enjoying his low chuckle at my ear. "If you don't stop that, things are going to start off this morning with a bang."

"Promises, promises," I teased, which only prompted him to squeeze around me tighter, his chin right there in the crook of my neck. "Did you sleep at all?"

"No," he answered. "Don't need any. But you've only been asleep a couple of hours. You're still tired."

He said it as a statement of fact, not a question. So what was I supposed to say to that, other than the truth—which he already knew? "Mmm, yes, but I don't want to sleep the day away."

Slipping his hand under the covers, he stroked along the inside of my thigh. "How're you feeling this morning?"

After a momentary pause to actually think about how I did feel, I answered, "I'm all right." And I did feel 'all right,' I supposed. My Dhampir body had held up just as I thought it would . . . though I was definitely tender.

His smooth caress over my leg stopped the moment I answered, and he exhaled a heavy sigh. "You're downplaying, Olivia. I feel your soreness. Your body needs rest. We'll wait until you're ready."

Waiting would probably be the smart thing to do, but try telling that to my well-sated body. We'd gone at it three times throughout the night, until I thought I could no longer even squeal my happiness, and still my heart jumped at the thought of him taking me again. Every minute I wasted not being with him, as time marched closer to the truth, I knew I would regret later, when he would surely send me away. "But I'm ready now."

He tucked in tighter behind me and spoke over my cheek. "Olivia, it's an amazing gift that your body can accept mine— that I've not hurt you more than I have. I don't understand how it's possible, but I'm not going to take it for granted, and I won't take any chances."

Not turning to look at him, I continued to stare straight ahead. "It is for that reason, and not that I didn't please you?"

Without warning, I was suddenly rolled from the pillow until my back lay against the mattress. My naked form was displayed to his full view. For a few seconds there was an instant tension in him just before he tossed the covers back over me and reset his hot gaze on mine. "How can you ask me that? Did you not hear, see, and feel my body's every response to you? You made me crazy!"

Oh, there was something, along with about twenty other toe-tingling sensations; I just didn't have a word for it. Altogether it had been so fantastic that I thought I might have imagined the whole thing. "It's just that . . . I can't feel your body's responses in the same way you feel mine. It's unfair. You know exactly how I feel and what I want almost before I do."

A low, predatory laugh escaped him as he snuggled against

me. "It is a bit of an advantage, isn't it?"

I answered him with a single, frustrated breath.

"Hey," he scolded in a tone that implied I should've known better. "Look at me." I lifted my gaze, and he was there waiting for me, his expression so sincere. "It sounds like such a bullshit line to say, but I mean it. I've never wanted any woman as I want you—and that's even more true today after being with you last night."

Biting my bottom lip, I tried to suppress the giant grin that wanted to crack over my face but had the feeling I was failing miserably. With a long blink I leaned in closer. "Then 'want' me again, Caleb. Right now."

Those beautiful gray eyes of his glimmered; pleased that I wanted him so much. His palm held my cheek as his thumb grazed my bottom lip. "I will have you again, my sweet,"—and my heart leapt—"when your body's ready and not a minute before"—then crashed again.

Bothered by my failure to persuade him, I decided to play a little less fair and tossed the sheet back until even my toes felt the quick breeze. Caleb froze as his gaze feasted hungrily over every inch of me. It was so amazing and empowering to see how I affected him.

"You're a wicked little sprite this morning, aren't you?" he said as he drew the sheet back over me. "You'll pay for that later."

"I hope you mean that."

Caleb brought his lips within a hairsbreadth. "Oh, I mean that."

He returned his fingers to caress along the inside of my thigh. "You've worn me down, sweet girl. I'll need to feed soon."

"Probably a good idea," I began with a wriggle of my brows. "Because you'll need the warrior's strength later."

His expression quirked with a playful smile. "I assure you, my strength will be just fine."

I kissed him then, quite simply because I had to. There was nothing I didn't find completely fascinating about this man, this vampire. He relaxed into the moment, pulling me closer while at the same time wrapping me up in the sheet. That seemed to defeat the purpose, so I glanced back up at him, ready to further challenge him if I could. "I'm afraid your little seduction will have to wait. Jax and Gem are close."

"What?" I said with a shriek, yanking away from him. "They're almost here? We have to clean up or Jax is going to freak when he finds out you were with me."

"Relax," he said, curling an arm around my waist and drawing me back against him. It was amazing how safe I felt there, like I could stay in that one spot for the rest of my life, right here, with him holding me in his arms. "There's no way to hide last night from him—especially after the damage to the piano—but I don't care. I don't regret what happened, and I'm going to tell him that. I just hope you don't regret it, either."

"I don't," I blinked back at him. "I just don't want this—us . . . I mean, whatever this is, to come between you and Jax."

"It won't," he replied with confidence, and it amazed me the absolute trust he had in where he stood with both Gemma and Jax. They were his family. He wasn't afraid that if he did something they disapproved of he would lose them. I was envious of that, considering how terrified I was of losing Caleb at any moment once he discovered the truth about who I really was.

Caleb kissed me on the forehead and slid from the bed, grabbing a pair of jeans that were tossed over the nearby chair, and slipped them over his narrow hips. "Jax always listens to reason," he began, though I was having trouble focusing on anything other than the man right in front of me. "I just need to talk with him. We have something we need to take care of today, so I'll be leaving with him shortly after they arrive. That'll be a good time."

"Something to take care of?" I asked, following him up and walking over to the cabinet.

He turned and relaxed into the chair, his shirtless body exposing the toned, corded lines of his abdomen above the low-rise beltline of his jeans. I tried to observe him with discreet interest as he lowered his head and several renegade strands of chestnut hair dropped over his cheek. Licking at my lips, my breath caught when his gaze shot back up and caught mine, a knowing smile curling his lips before I could return to rummaging the cabinets for something to wear. "A project," he replied. "Nothing you need concern yourself with. But I'll be gone for the next couple of days . . . returning here in the evenings."

I stared at the clothes on the hanger in front of me, trying to disguise the sense of unease I could feel blooming within me. I couldn't just stay here and continue to play house with him as if everything were normal. I had to tell him the truth: *Hey, Caleb, turns out my mother was a Charmer and used to hunt and trap your kind with my father. I'm a Charmer, too, and nothing between us is real . . . but don't worry, you can trust me.*

Right.

"Gem will look after you," he added. "And please try to stay out of trouble while I'm gone."

"I will," I answered without hesitation, wanting to please him.

Caleb was quiet for a long while, his fingers brushing over the arm of the chair, and he seemed distracted for a moment. "You're thinking about how you're going to tell Jax about us, aren't you?"

He glanced up with an even gaze. "Yes," he answered, honestly. "But he means well, Olivia. He just needs me to assure him that I'll find a way to make this work."

My eyes drifted away from him, trying not to show the sadness welling inside. I loved Jax's commitment to their coven, but I could only imagine how upset he would be when he discovered I'd been with Caleb, and even more so when he learned how I had been lying to them since I had returned.

"Hey," Caleb broke into my thoughts, searching my face and asking for me to find his eyes again. I did. I could not resist his wonderful shades of gray. "Come."

He extended his hand and I took it. Pulling me into his lap, he brushed the hair back from my face and palmed my cheek, the stiffness in my legs a gentle reminder of the previous night's passion and everything I had to lose. "I will find a way," he whispered with feeling. "Because I can't let you go this time. I won't let you go. I want you to stay with me—here in this house. I want this to be your home, too . . . if you want it to be."

"I . . . I," I began; terrified I would say something to ruin this incredible moment. He wanted me to be with him! It was as if every dream I never realized I had wanted had come true, all within those few words. "Caleb, are you sure? I mean, we haven't known each other—"

"I've never been more sure of anything in my life. I feel it here," he said, resting his hand over his heart. "I want you here with me. I want to be with you—protect you from Isaac, or whoever else threatens you."

A whirlwind of emotions raced through my head. I wanted desperately to believe every word he was saying was true, but I remembered Alec and Gideon's warnings about vampires being drawn to me and not knowing why, wanting to possess me. I didn't feel possessed, but I couldn't know for sure if what he felt, what he was declaring, was real or part of the illusion. It was frustrating because I was elated and confused and sad, and I was also praying that he wasn't feeling me at this particular moment. I didn't want my doubt to hurt him.

So I wouldn't.

I threw my arms around his neck so tightly it appeared my very life depended on it. His words did fill my soul with joy, with hope. I was beginning to convince myself that I could hide out here with him and let the rest of the world fade away, to believe that the dream was possible.

When I finally relaxed my grip, he brushed my hair behind my shoulder and blew a tickling breath over the shell of my ear. I squirmed in his arms as he chuckled, drawing me closer to stop my wriggling. "I love you, Olivia."

For a moment I wasn't sure he had really said it.

"Somehow I knew I loved you the moment I saw you again the night of the train crash. Nothing else mattered to me except getting you out of there."

"Oh, Caleb," I squealed, squeezing my arms around him in a virtual stranglehold this time. "I love you, too."

"So, does that mean you'll stay?"

I smiled at him with a joy and contentment I'm not sure I had ever felt in my life until just then. "Yes, I'll stay."

We sat like that for several minutes, and I didn't care if Jax and Gem walked in on us. I just wanted to stay right like that with him until someone forced the moment to end. As I nestled my head into the curve between his shoulder and his neck his deep voice purred at my ear, "Hmmm, that's it, my sweet. Let me hear your heart flutter."

***

Caleb left with a very tense Jax soon after he and Gemma arrived home. I didn't envy Caleb the task ahead of him, trying to explain how the wood floor under the piano ended up ripped from the substrate but still assuring the coven leader that everything was going to be fine. Jax, in his wealth of life experience, didn't seem an easy man to convince of something if he didn't want to be convinced, but it was clear how important Caleb's happiness was to him. He had said as much after saving me from the cougar. I could only hope those feelings would be enough to cause him to see reason.

It was then I mentally sort of checked myself. What was I thinking? I was acting as if there was a place for me here, with this coven, and that was just plain silly. I didn't belong here. No matter how much it felt right. No matter how much I wanted it to be true. A Charmer existed to draw vampires in to meet their deaths. At least, that was the case with my mother. Had there even been another Charmer besides her? Gideon sure made it sound as if there hadn't.

"Well, it looks like someone finally caused more trouble around here than me," Gemma laughed as she sauntered into the bedroom. "An impressive feat, considering the previous benchmarks I had set."

I sighed at her, worriedly, and sagged into the chair behind me. "That's not really helpful, Gemma."

"Oh, you poor girl," she mocked. "You worry too much."

"It's just that . . . Why are you and Jax so nice to me? All I've done since I've arrived is force you from your own home."

An unladylike snort escaped her. "Don't be ridiculous. You've done no such thing! I'm in town a lot for my job. And Jax, as my designated overbearing protector for the month, is there with me. We're nice to you because we like you."

"I can't believe Jax feels that way. Especially after—"

"What happened between you and Caleb is private," she interjected soundly. "And quite frankly none of Jax's damn business. He knows that."

My shoulders sank in relief. It seemed almost too good to be true that Gemma was being so practical about the whole thing, and it was. Glancing over her shoulder quickly, as if worried someone might be eavesdropping, she returned her bright expression to me and said, "But oh, my God," she squealed, "you have to give me all the juicy details. How was—"

"Gemma!" I blinked back at her in disbelief.

"What?"

When I refused to lighten my frown she just waved her hand dismissively. "Oh, all right. But you can't really blame a girl for trying. The piano? I mean come on, there's got to be some juicy stuff in there somewhere."

My frown deepened, but she brushed it off with a simple shake of her head. "We're getting off track here. My point is that Jax knows Caleb is a grown man and can make his own decisions. But Jax's concerns are legitimate, and Caleb understands that."

I sighed. "So there's no easy solution."

"True. Jax will probably want him to turn you to keep the coven safe—even though he doesn't want you to be turned. Does that make sense?" She didn't even wait for me to process what she was saying before she was off to the next one. "And there's no way Caleb will ever agree to turn you, so they'll end at a stalemate. That could go on for months—years, even—in vampire time . . . and by then you'll be one of the family. Jax will have to let you stay."

I rolled my eyes, wondering if any of this even made sense to her. "I want to stay. I'm just not sure I can."

"Why?" she asked with a simple shrug of her small shoulders.

"There are some people I'm sort of obligated to. They won't let me stay here."

The joyful smile left Gemma's face, replaced by one that showed instant concern. "Have you told Caleb this?"

"No," I answered in defeat. "He wouldn't understand."

"Wouldn't understand?" she blinked back. "It's plain to see he's in love with you, Olivia. He'd do anything for you. Don't you think he deserves the truth?"

I nodded, trying not to remember that The Brethren's proprietary nature over me was only one part that Caleb would not understand. "You're right. I'll try to tell him tonight."

"Good. There has to be a way to sort through these . . . obligations." But her expression remained unconvinced. "Why are these people deciding how you live your life, anyway?"

"It's a long story."

"We have two days."

After a soundless minute in which it appeared she was trying to read my mind, she added, "Don't go, Olivia. I've never seen Caleb so at peace with himself as when he's with you." She then seemed to check herself, bringing her finger to her chin. "At least, that's when he's not furious at you for hiking alone up some mountain . . . or almost getting mauled by a cougar . . . or nearly freezing to death," she laughed, obviously overhearing the rather loud argument in the library.

Who was I kidding? All of Seattle probably heard that argument.

"What do you mean by 'at peace with himself'?"

She bounced onto the bed and rolled onto her side. "Even though he's a Daywalker—a good vampire—Caleb's never forgiven himself for the human lives he took when he was first changed. As long as I've known him, he's been . . . restless, always searching for that one thing that's eluded him."

"What's that?"

She replied with just one word: "Redemption."

Redemption. The one thing he wanted more than anything was something he could only find for himself.

"You see, darkness takes over a vampire's soul, but they can bring the essence of who they were into this life. Blood-thirst and anger control them, but just as with humans, there are levels of good and evil, right and wrong, in every vampire."

"Shades of gray?" I whispered, remembering the shame I witnessed when I looked into Caleb's sapphire eyes after he had changed. I now realized that's what I saw, his need for forgiveness.

"Yes. As with Jax, Caleb is the very best example of a good and right man, no matter the thirst driving his body. And he's fighting hard to hold onto the goodness, the rightness."

I knew what she was saying was true. There couldn't be more contrast between Caleb and a vampire like Isaac. And the same chasm existed between my two choices—between accepting who I was and what was being expected of me, the battle between my feelings for the man I wanted and what I was destined to do, luring vampires to battle for their immortal lives. I couldn't become the avenging angel The Brethren wanted me to be. I couldn't follow the path of my mother.

"Gemma, were you angry with your vampire father about your mother's death?"

Gemma seemed to reflect for a moment before she answered. "I wish I'd known my mother. I struggled with her death when I was young . . . and, at first, maybe I did. But I no longer blame my father. From what I understand, they loved each other very much. Sometimes that's enough reason to forgive."

"Where's your father now?"

"I'm not sure. I know he was in Europe a few years ago. When my mother died, he was nearly destroyed by it—that darkness, that evil I was referring to, took him over completely. He was never the same after."

"Then, he isn't a Daywalker? He doesn't see you?"

She shook her head. "He left me when I was a teenager. That's when Jax found me. He was furious that Michael had abandoned me. That was my father's . . ."

As she spoke, I couldn't help but think about Jax. His overprotective nature toward the teenage girl he had found alone was just, of course. But his constant nurturing of the grown woman she had become hinted that his feelings ran much deeper. He collected her poems and rarely left her side, refusing to let her put herself in even the slightest danger. There seemed to be more there, and I doubted that Gemma was oblivious to it.

" . . . and, to this day, Jax doesn't even like me to mention his name. But as I got older, I understood. Seeing me was too hard for my father. I was becoming the spitting image of my mother."

All at once I realized this woman could understand better than anyone the sense of loneliness I felt after losing my family. But I couldn't help agreeing with Jax. A true father should care for his daughter, perhaps even more so if she was such a reflection of her mother. "I'm sorry, Gemma."

"No need to be sorry. Everything worked out OK. That path led me here to Jax and Caleb. I've always loved them as if they were my real family. I wouldn't want to be anywhere else."

She paused then exhaled a heavy sigh. "I worry for Caleb, though . . ."

Dread hit my stomach like a ton of bricks. "Why?"

"The night of the train crash . . . when he found you? Has he told you why he was there?"

"No. I guess I assumed it was a coincidence."

Her eyes drifted away. "No. It was one of those restless nights," she began. "He'd search, finding humans who needed his help, as if somehow it would make up for the lives he took. That constant drive for redemption was the reason he made the transformation to Daywalker so quickly, but he had no regard for the risk to his own life. Just because he's immortal doesn't mean he can't die. Jax and I feared he was trying to get himself killed. So we stayed close, just in case he needed us."

My heart was pounding in my throat. Surely, she was exaggerating when she said he was trying to get himself killed, because it didn't make any sense. He fought so hard for other people, for life.

"That night, he heard the train crash and sensed the vampires were near. He knew then that something was very wrong. When he rushed to help he found you, recognized you, and once he brought you back here, he began to change. When he's with you, his priority remains solely with you. There's no longer a need for him to be out chasing death."

Gemma then grabbed my hands, holding them in hers. "Don't you see, Olivia? He's finding the redemption he needs in you. You give him a reason to accept who he is . . . to be happy and at peace with this life. If you go away again, I worry he will return to his restless ways."

What had I ever done in my life to earn the love of a man like Caleb Wolfe? I didn't deserve him. And now I hated even more that I had been lying to him. I couldn't do it any longer. No matter what it cost me, even if I lost him forever, I had to tell him the truth. "Gemma, how can a vampire be killed?"

Her brows arched in surprise. "We'll certainly not by a

cougar, or freezing—"

I put my fingers over her lips, stopping her words, letting her know how real the fear was behind my question. "Please. I need to know."

She frowned. "What're you planning to do . . . save him in battle or something?"

"I'd give my life for his."

"Don't say that!" she returned quickly. "There's never going to be a need for you to trade your life for his. He's too strong. So stop worry—"

"How?"

Her forehead wrinkled as she realized just how worried I was about this. "All right," she sighed. "I already told you about the big three . . . heat, sun, and fire. Obviously, if he isn't able to feed his thirst for a long period of time, he could die of thirst—but that's not likely to happen."

"What about stakes through the heart? Garlic? Silver—"

"Olivia, stop! I'm sorry I said anything. You're getting yourself worked up to a frantic state over this."

"Gemma!" I cried, sounding much like Jax when he was frustrated with her.

"Calm down," she ordered, straightening herself on the bed. "Garlic and Holy Water are irritants. Silver only weakens them, and stakes through the heart incapacitate, but they don't kill."

Her worried gaze refused to leave me as she must have watched a thousand different emotions roll through my head. It seemed complete panic was starting to take over inside me. I couldn't lose him—not after we had just connected in such a profound way.

"Listen to me. Nothing's going to happen to him. He's unbelievably strong when he's fighting for something he really cares about. Sometimes, even stronger than Jax, even though he's still a young vampire. His body kicks into a whole other gear when he feels the most threatened."

That did make me feel a better, but not completely.

"Do you want him to feel your panic right now?" she asked. "You'll have him flying back here in a second."

She was right. That wouldn't be fair to him, but I couldn't shake the feeling that this project was something very dangerous, and only one idea popped into my head. "Gemma? Are Caleb and Jax hunting for Isaac again?"

Gemma's brows knitted together. "I don't know. They didn't tell me."

I dropped my head back against the chair with a sigh. It would be a long day waiting for them to come home safe.

After breakfast I kept myself busy cleaning Gemma's room. I washed all of the towels in the bathroom and changed all of the bed sheets, inhaling their wonderful lavender scent. It stirred memories of the night before, the feel of Caleb's body over mine, how we moved together as one.

"What're you doing?" Gemma asked.

I whirled around with a start, hoping my cheeks were not flushed, like cherries, from my sensational thoughts. "I'm giving you back your room."

With that, Gemma's lips formed into the cutest little frown. "And where do you plan to sleep?

"I don't know," I answered with a deep exhale. "But I don't want to take your room from you anymore. Not if Caleb will let me stay."

"If? It should be quite obvious there's no 'if' on his part." She couldn't realize that I meant *if, after I told him the truth, he would let me stay.*

Then a thought seemed to strike her as powerfully as the sun's rays. "I've an idea," she squealed, clapping her hands together in glee before grabbing my hand and pulling me downstairs.

She released my hand as we came into the kitchen. I was more than a bit confused. "You want me to sleep in the kitchen?"

Gemma smiled and reached for the area rug on the floor between the sink and the island. I thought it was there to keep feet warm on cold winter nights but soon it became clear it had a much more important purpose. It concealed the outline of a door with a recessed handle she grabbed to lift up. Beneath was a pitch black hole that she jumped right into.

"Gemma?" I called after her, unable to see much of anything.

"Hold on," she replied, and within moments a small flicker of light illuminated the space below. "This is one of Jax's old lanterns," she called up. "You should be able to see down here now. Are you OK to jump?"

I seated myself on the edge and looked down into the concrete room below. It was about seven or eight feet to the floor below, but it was the only way down. "Yes," I said and then hopped down, landing much more lightly than I thought I would.

The small space was still dim, but as I looked around I noticed the floor, walls, and ceiling were all sealed concrete. It was very clean and definitely cold, but not freezing. There was a chest-style refrigeration unit in the corner, which I assumed contained more blood, and two stainless steel tables, each with a thin white leather pad and small bolster pillow. The bolsters were dented slightly in at the center and I realized this was where Jax and Caleb slept when they needed to, where Caleb had recovered from his burns.

I grazed my fingers over one of the cushioned tops, imagining Caleb recuperating here in this small, dark room, all alone.

"Here," Gemma said, breaking into my thoughts, standing at the threshold of a thick metal door that looked like the entry to a fortress, the size and weight of it very different from anything else in the house. Inside were a few boxes of collectable items, such as vinyl records, a '50s style juke box, and an antique writing desk with quill pen set. All memories of Jax's past life, I guessed.

Gemma slapped her hand against a luxurious, queen-sized mattress that was tipped on its side against the wall. "Jax bought this for me, but it ended up being too firm. I bet Caleb doesn't even remember it's down here."

It was amazing how both Jax and Caleb spoiled this woman with gifts like mattresses and grand pianos yet were not even bothered when her interest waned. They would just find something else to shower her with affection. "This is perfect, Gemma. Will you help me bring it upstairs?"

She laughed as if that were a silly question. "Well, duh. You can hardly get it up without a Dhampir's help. Now the only question is where do we put it? I supposed we can make a room for you out of the library."

"No," I replied instantly. "I love that room how it is. It would be sad to see it become a bedroom." Then I thought for a moment. "Do you think Caleb would mind if we put it in his study?"

"I think as long as you were there, he wouldn't care where you put it. It's a good choice though. There's enough room, I think, if we shuffle some things around."

"Are you sure he won't mind?"

She nodded, waving her hand through the air. "He'll be fine. We just can't touch anything on his desk or his drawings. It may not look like very organized to us, but he sees things three-dimensionally. Everything has to be in a certain order for the whole picture to come into focus."

***

A few hours later, standing in front of those drawings in Caleb's study, I saw firsthand what Gemma was talking about. It was almost like a wall of art, with dozens of hand-drawn sketches posted in what seemed a random order. There were detail drawings for the tree house, as well as some other sketches of a small glass atrium. His talent just made me smile. I immediately wished I could see it finished, but I knew I probably never would.

"He's pretty gifted, isn't he?" Gemma asked into my thoughts. "This is his contribution." I turned back to her with a puzzled look. "His gift to our coven," she clarified. "Each of us has our part. Mine is working at the clinic to bring home food. Caleb designed and built this home for us. Pretty cool, huh?"

I nodded quickly. "And what about Jax?"

Gemma laughed. "Well, he paid for the whole thing. And of course he helped Caleb build it."

"I know this might be rude to ask, but how does Jax afford all of this? Does he have a job like you?"

Shaking her head, she answered, "No. A job doesn't really work for a vampire—or a Daywalker for that matter. Especially, if you consider all of the limitations to their life . . . no sun, blood for food . . . Jax had his own family wealth before he was turned, and now—two centuries later, with interest and investing—he has a lot more money. He'll never have to worry about it, and he shares what he has with us."

I turned back to admire the sketches one last time. "You know, you are more like a family than most families I've known in my life. What you have here is special. I hope you know that."

Gemma wrapped her arm around mine, squeezing it slightly. "I do. But we should get back to work if we're going to finish before dinner. Now that we've found a spot in the corner that'll work for the bed, we still have to figure out how we're going to fit Caleb's desk in here."

It was early evening when we finished dressing the bed with silky, gold and ivory bedding, a feather down comforter, and several soft pillows. It looked absolutely perfect, and it felt absolutely right as I stretched out my tired body on the mattress. Unlike Gemma, I didn't mind at all the extra firmness of my new bed.

Finally, I had someplace I could be with Caleb and not have to evict one of my gracious hosts in the process. It just felt right.

After dinner, I talked easily with Gemma until it grew very late. Caleb was still not home, and I started to worry. He had promised he would come back in the evening, so I began to think once again that this project might have something to do with Isaac.

Too exhausted to keep my eyes open any longer, I prepared for bed in a narrow half-bath between Jax's and Caleb's studies and nestled under the warm covers, soon falling fast asleep.

It was sometime later I was tickled awake.

Chapter Seventeen

Swatting the air as if batting at a gnat, I wriggled around on the mattress, whipping the hot covers off me as I tried to restore my right to sleep. But the tickling didn't stop; then something cool brushed across my collarbone from shoulder to shoulder. I wasn't sure if I was dreaming or half awake when I spoke the name in my thoughts. "Caleb?" I whispered, rolling over to feel the length of him beside me.

My palms found the lightly hair-dusted brawn of his chest as I slid them up to two very wide shoulders. This sure didn't feel like a dream. Soft lips trailed their way up to my throat, pausing just over the thick artery that was furiously pumping blood from my heart. He kissed his way along it, slowly, licking at it as if the vein was precious. I never doubted for a moment that he wouldn't hurt me before he continued his path upward. "Am I dreaming?"

He offered no reply but instead captured my lips in a hard, searing kiss that brought me back to a lucid state in seconds. Rolling me beneath him, his lips moved with fervor against mine, nibbling, licking, coaxing me to part them more fully for him. And once I did, he took full advantage, teasing my tongue with his until I felt dizzy and weak. "You smell of oranges," he breathed just above my lips, his hand moving under the hem of my nightgown just above my knee, and sensuously sliding the thin fabric upward, his breath growing rougher as he did. "Vanilla and oranges. God, I love that scent."

"I'm glad you approve."

"Yes, but I don't like this nightgown," he said as he raised my upper body with a strong hand and peeled the lacy, purple confection over my head. "No more clothing when under these covers . . . unless it's silk. I like your skin next to silk."

His eyes sparkled as he stared down at me, his long dimples bracketing his smile. Freshly showered and changed, he was dressed deliciously in a pair of silk lounging pants which were tented at the moment over a very large bulge. "So, I see my little temptress has been busy today."

"You're not upset, then, that I've invaded your room?"

His hands moved to the swells of my bottom, curling my legs around him until I cradled his hips. "Not as long as you're part of the package," he replied, huskily, his lips lingering just over mine.

Closing my eyes, I tilted my head and parted my lips, expecting him to take me back into his embrace, but when his lips remained suspiciously absent I peeked through my lashes to see him grinning back at me. "Ah, Olivia . . . you're such a tempting creature. I've thought of little else today but being here with you tonight and teaching you all the ways I can excite this beautifully responsive body of yours."

Without warning or explanation, my thoughts focused on how he was saying he was distracted—by me no less—and my worries from earlier in the day picked that moment to come flooding back. I wrapped my arms around him with a fierce grip, hiding my head in his neck as my warm breath quickened against his skin. He was shocked by my swift change in mood and, I was sure, could now detect the almost desperate fear lodged in my heart. "Olivia, what is this? Why are you afraid?"

My voice sounded high and anxious as I spoke. "Caleb, you must not get distracted. You must keep yourself safe. I didn't climb back up this mountain to watch you get yourself hurt or worse—"

He pushed back from me, his eyes wide with disbelief. "What the devil is the matter with you? I told you, we are working on a project." His voice was loud with his surprise but he was not angry . . . more like befuddled.

I was upset that he was not taking this more seriously. I squirmed out from under him, which wasn't easy, considering he was all lean muscle—and he was so surprised that he offered no help at all. But at least he didn't resist. Once I was freed from the full weight of him, I pushed back, only then remembering that I was completely naked. But still I shot him a fierce look.

"You're tracking Isaac, aren't you?"

"No," he defended, but then took a long pause, as if he was considering what I just asked for a moment. "But if that's what you mean by being distracted, then you're right. I haven't searched for Isaac as I should have. I'll take care of it, I promise. He won't threaten you again."

My eyes must have flashed into sheer panic, judging by the startling change in his expression. I sprung to my knees, throwing the covers over the end of the mattress and swinging my arms wildly in the air, my heart beating in a rapid thump against my ears. "No! That's not what I mean."

Caleb reached up, wrapped one arm around my waist, and almost roughly snatched me back under him, pinning my body between his firm muscles and our new firm mattress. His smoky gaze bore into mine with an intensity that told me he was searching for answers. He was trying to feel my fear, to understand it, but I wasn't sure how that was possible, since it wasn't entirely clear to me. "What do you mean?" he asked, sincerely wanting to understand what was happening.

"I don't want you to find Isaac—to battle with him again. I know you're stronger. I saw that the night of the crash. But there are other ways he can hurt you—trick you." Then I started rattling off every horrible thought I had entertained during the day, horrible foreshadowing of how Caleb could be killed. "He could trap you somehow in the sun, or burn you with fire, or—"

Caleb swiftly brought his hand over my mouth to stop the frantic words that were spilling out. His face grimaced as he shook his head. "Gemma!" he mumbled, then returned his concerned gaze to me.

My lips were silent below his hand until he finally released his hold. "It's not her fault, Caleb. I pushed her to tell me. I needed to know—to understand how I could lose you."

"Unbelievable, Olivia. I'm a vampire! I'm a hundred times stronger than you—than any human—and you're worried about me getting hurt."

"Yes," I replied simply, as if that fact should be obvious.

There was a long silence between us before Caleb slid down on the mattress and curled his arms around my waist in a protective hold, pressing his ear between my breasts to listen to the erratic beats in my chest, monitoring the thumps until the pounding eventually began to slow. "I do understand that you want me to be safe. But this is who I am, Olivia. This is who you've fallen in love with."

"But—"

"No," he interjected. "I'll always fight to protect the things that are important to me—that I love. And I love *you*. I'll fight anything that threatens that love. And that includes, Isaac."

With sadness, I stared vacantly up and through a small skylight in the corner of the ceiling while he tried to re-assure me with gentle strokes of his fingers on my side. I knew that what he was saying was true. I was being selfish by asking him to change who he was at his core. That was not fair. But what *was* fair was trying to be clear with him about where my fear came from.

"Caleb?" I said softly, smoothing my hands over his back.

He squeezed his arms around me, and I knew he was trying to persuade me by his strong presence that everything was going to be all right. "I know you think I'm being silly . . . but you don't understand. Death follows me. My parents? Sarah? Even you, that last day you were human. I just need you to understand why I'm afraid."

He pulled me down on the mattress until my lips were even with his, the scent of sage and oranges hanging over us as his body wrapped around mine, creating what seemed an impenetrable barrier. "My sweet, sweet Olivia, please don't be afraid. I'm meant to be here with you."

His answer was beautiful and perfect, yet it did not ease my fears.

So I just let him hold me, nurture me, and love me in his arms until my heavy eyes grew sleepy again, the blue-eyed warrior staying at bay, the man knowing that this was what I needed from him tonight.

***

When I woke the next morning, the space beside me was cold and empty. I rolled toward my edge of the mattress, hating the thought of being away from Caleb for a second day when I really just wanted to spend time with him. I was trying to not be too needy, but I wanted every minute that I had left with him before I had to leave.

Alec probably had half of The Brethren already out searching for me.

As I stretched back on the mattress, my hand touched a piece of paper lying next to me. I raised up onto my elbows and saw several blank sheets of composition paper and a single, long-stemmed white rose lying where his body had been, along with and a short note, almost a scribble, from him.

Think of sweet sounds for me today.

Caleb

I pulled the note to my chest, rolling over slightly so I could inhale the fragrant scent of the flawless white petals.

I love him.

I would have happily sat and played on the grand piano today, thinking of sweet music Caleb would want to hear, but he was having the broken piano base repaired after already having replaced the mangled wood planks on the floor.

Once showered and presentable, I slipped on a casual, knee-length gray skirt with a contrasting hem, topped with a long-sleeved blouse. I knew Caleb would be pleased. He had loved the red skirt I wore the night we made love, and I blushed, remembering how he had caressed the light fabric under his hands.

All day I carried the fragile rose with me while Gemma and I rattled on about nothing in particular. But as the night came and it grew darker and Caleb still had not returned, my mood became more somber. I waited by the glass doors, staring out into the pitch black of the forest, my bare feet and legs cold from the night air. Brushing the wilting petals against my collarbone, I hoped he would return soon.

"You miss him, don't you?" Gemma asked, already knowing the answer as she came to stand beside me.

I nodded. "I'm sorry I'm not better company this evening. It's just that it's getting so late," I sighed, thinking about how he would not even get to see the skirt I wore for him today.

She curled her arm in mine and smiled. "Let me go make you some tea. It'll help you sleep."

"OK," I nodded.

Minutes later, still staring out into the dark, a familiar tightening began to stretch over my heart. Gasping in short breaths, I squealed with excitement, realizing they were close. I could tell it wasn't Caleb, who by now I could easily sense, so it must be Jax.

"Gemma," I cheered, "they're coming."

"Olivia, wait!" she cried from the kitchen as the tea pot whistled at full steam.

I started to look towards her voice when my head was pulled back around by a large, shadowy figure that came through the night and plowed straight through the plate glass, reaching for me. I closed my eyes just as shards of glass whipped all around me, pelting my arms and legs in hot little strikes against my skin.

"It's a Rogue!" Gemma yelled in the distance.

Suddenly, I found myself face to face with icy eyes of a vampire. Pale and gaunt, every muscle inside me clenched with fear as the creature's stare burned into me, his sharp fangs displayed like the warning hiss of a snake just before it's about to strike, his long tongue flicking between his fangs to serve notice that my sweet blood would satisfy his raging thirst just fine.

In that moment, I realized this was what Alec and Gideon warned me about.

His hands tightened over my arms, which were still covered by my blouse, and tumbled me to the hardwood floor as the oxygen was sucked from my lungs in an instant. Searing pain shot up my back as glass shards cut through my blouse where he had me pinned against the wood planks. Blood began flowing rapidly, the scent only making him more frenzied as he blurred above me.

All I could think of was the defenseless cougar locked in Jax's arms.

Oh, God, was this it?

Evidently the answer was no, because his weight was lifted from me as Gemma drove into him, sending him flying across the hall. I cried out, rolling onto my side as I watched her leap to her feet, her posture ready to strike him again. I couldn't believe what I was seeing. This small woman was taking on this huge killing machine.

When the vampire returned to his feet, his mad eyes locked on me. Gemma inserted herself between us and he flew at her, driving her to the floor. Somehow she emerged from beneath him, springing, light as air, to her feet, and then higher, holding herself effortlessly against the force of gravity as he charged her a second time.

She responded with a brutal kick across his jaw, sending the vampire spiraling backwards while her feet returned weightlessly to the floor.

"Olivia! Go to the storage room. Lock the door," she commanded in a voice I did not recognize. "Now!" she yelled again. Clumsily, I scrambled to my bare feet, moving slowly to avoid all the glass. The vampire's eyes followed me like a rabid dog across the room, then he suddenly charged Gemma, driving her back and down, onto hundreds of glass shards spread over the floor.

"Gemma!"

She didn't make a sound as the vampire flew from her to me, launching both of us though the air like a cannonball. He smashed me against the wall so hard my mind was stunned, the force driving the glass shards deeper into my back. I tried to focus, but couldn't, as lots of twinkling white lights danced like lightening bugs in front of my eyes.

The vampire was about to tear into my throat. Then I remembered that day in the church with Alec. "Defend yourself, Olivia!" his voice bellowed in my head.

With all the strength I could muster, I shoved against his chest, sending the vampire backward only a couple of steps, but that was all I needed to raise the long sleeves of my blouse. He roared back and was quickly on top of me again, his fangs aiming straight for my neck as he grabbed my upper arms, which were still covered with fabric. I wasn't touching him yet.

Great gift this was going to be—if I didn't even have the strength to touch him on his skin.

He lunged towards my neck. A shrill scream ripped from my throat as he stopped just short. He hesitated, and I took advantage of the moment by reaching up around his arms.

Instantly, he stumbled backwards, shaking his head as if trying to get rid of some awfully painful thought. I saw Gemma's stunned face for only a fraction of a second before she drove a jagged piece of glass straight through his heart, while at the same time the edges she held it with sliced deeply into her own hand.

The glass did not kill him, but it incapacitated him. In what I was guessing was unimaginable pain, Gemma lifted him like a toy as blood flowed freely through her shirt and the glass continued to grind into her soft skin. She tossed him like garbage out the open window to the long drop below. Then she flew over to the control switch in front of the windows, moving her hand to the back side of the panel to press another button I had never noticed before.

Without warning, ultraviolet lasers dropped in front of each glass pane, surrounding the tree house in a bright green light.

I glanced back just in time to see Gemma crumble to her knees.

"Gemma!"

Chapter Eighteen

I started towards Gemma but she halted me immediately with an extended hand. "Stop! Stay right there. You've no shoes. You'll cut your feet."

I was stunned. This small woman had just had hundreds of shards of glass driven into her back—and she was worried about my feet? As she rose and came toward me I could see she was favoring her right hand. I hooked her other arm over my shoulder and helped her up the stairs to her bedroom. "Don't worry. Everything's going to be OK."

"I'll be fine," she tried to reassure, but her speech sounded slow and slurred.

I threw back the bed covers and top sheet so she could lie on her stomach. After carefully removing the scraps that were left of her shirt, I could see the full extent of the damage. There must have been at least a hundred shards embedded in her skin looking like they had been shot into her back by a giant blow gun!

She had to be in great pain, but she didn't make a sound. "I'll be right back," I said.

Rifling through the drawers and cabinets in her bathroom, I found some alcohol, a pair of long-nosed tweezers, and some mesh bandages. Grabbing some towels, I thoroughly wet half of them and then rushed back to Gemma's side to immediately began cleaning and wrapping the bleeding hand she had sliced open when driving the glass into the vampire's heart.

"Olivia, are you hurt?" she asked, and I just stared back at her in disbelief. How could she be thinking about me right now?

"I'm fine. We need to focus on getting this glass out of your back." Saying the words, though, sounded strange to me. My voice resonated as stiff and unfamiliar. I shook the wooziness from my head and focused back on her.

"Are you sure?" she pressed. "The way he threw you against that wall . . . it should have broken your back."

"What?" I questioned, the whole sequence of events registering in my brain as just a blur. "I don't think so. I'm OK," I repeated, sounding like a stuck recording. I definitely was not handling the pressure of this situation well, especially considering I had been warned by Alec and Gideon that something like this might happen. The vampire had been drawn to me from out of nowhere and appeared almost in a trance as he pushed at me. "I'm so sorry," I said, realizing just then that what had happened to Gemma was all my fault. "Please tell me you're not in too much pain."

Gemma appeared to be distraught now. "Sweetie, I know you're upset, but I need you to focus. Can you do that for me?" She tried to keep projecting her normal melodic voice, but was unconvincing.

"Yes. Just tell me what you need."

"This is important," she began, reaching for my hand and giving it a slight squeeze. "We need to get the blood cleaned up before Caleb and Jax get back."

I ignored her and with the tweezers pulled out the first shard in her back.

"Olivia, listen to me," she said, louder this time, and more firmly. "They'll have already sensed something is very wrong, and I know they're on their way back here. They can't be around this much blood when they're upset. They won't be able to control their thirst. Do you understand?"

"Yes, but Gemma—"

"Listen to me. I'll be fine," she interrupted, seeming now more than a little bothered. "I need you to go to the kitchen, grab some bleach, and get rid of the blood on the floors as best you can. Then burn the towels. Clean and wrap yourself where you've been cut. Use plenty of alcohol, Olivia. It can sometimes help mask the scent of blood, if the wounds aren't too deep. Then you can help me—*but not now!* Just do as I ask."

Confused and scared, I just sat there for a moment. I'd had no time to process anything, and now Gemma preferred I clean the floors over helping to repair her small, cut body.

"I need you to focus, sweetie. I need you to do this *for them.* Please."

"Okay," I answered shakily, and then tried to concentrate on what needed to be done. After retrieving some slip-on shoes from Gemma's closet, I made my way to the first floor to get the towels and bleach, then returned to the areas where the vampire had crashed through the glass. Blood and glass littered the floor, and couldn't help but be a little skittish at the idea the vampire was still somewhere outside.

Don't think about it, Olivia!

Neon-green lasers glowed sharp against the black night outside as cold air whistled in through the broken pane of glass. As I cleaned the spot where Gemma had been driven into the glass shards, my heart hurt thinking about the pain she must be suffering as I did my work. There was so much blood! I felt queasy—and tried again to replay the night's events, but my mind seemed to be muddled in a thick fog, and I was having trouble remembering the simplest detail.

The bleach I was currently soaking the wood floors with was not helping. The offensive smell nearly overwhelmed me to the point that all I wanted to do was sneeze. I used almost every bath towel I could find, creating a bloody pile that I then ran with and dumped into Gemma's tiled shower, the best place I could think of to safely burn a pile of towels. I squeezed a whole lot of lighter fluid onto the gory pile. Flames billowed high as cotton, blood and bleach burned, and once the towels were well on their way to being destroyed I began to appraise the damage to my own back in the bathroom mirror. Though my wounds were not nearly as bad as Gemma's, I was surprised at how many shards were stuck into my skin, some pretty deep —but I couldn't quite remember how they got there, which seemed strange.

What was even stranger was the fact that I couldn't feel any pain. I was sure I should be feeling something by now, but perhaps my Dhampir side was stronger than I thought. Even though I had been wearing a skirt, I was amazed to find only a dozen or so small shards in my legs, which I removed and bandaged myself quickly. The damage, by far, was to my mid-back, which I couldn't reach. I decided to cover it for now with lots of gauze and have Gemma help me remove the glass later.

Remembering what Gemma had told me, I poured the entire contents of one bottle of alcohol over my back and bit back loud cries of pain, feeling as though fire was devouring my skin. It took a couple of minutes for my arms and legs to stop shaking, but once they did I used a damp towel to collect as much of the blood as I could, then wrapped my midsection with layer after layer of gauze, trying to cover the scent.

Then I remembered the acid scent of the bleach. That would help.

Racing back to the kitchen, I stumbled around in circles for a bit. Think, Olivia! What the hell is wrong with . . . bleach, yes that's it. I grabbed the jug of bleach and search the drawers for a plastic sandwich bag. After using a fork to poke several small holes on one side of the bag, I saturated a white hand towel in the bleach and placed it inside the bag, sealing it in securely.

Back in Gemma's room, I glanced briefly toward Gemma, who was still lying motionless behind me. Her lids were closed, hiding what I was sure was an unimaginable amount of pain. Working faster, I placed the plastic bag between my back and the ribbed tee shirt I had changed into, facing the holes outward so the bleach wouldn't have direct contact with my cut skin. I used a belt to cinch the bag tight around my waist, then added another shirt as a second layer.

"Ok, Gemma," I said, dropping to my knees at her side, my arms bracing against the mattress in an attempt to make the room stop spinning, "I did everything you asked."

Her voice was weak in reply. "Thank you."

Worried I was running out of time, I worked on her wounds with a wild mix of efficiency, haste—and, I hoped, some gentleness. About forty-five minutes later I had all of the glass removed and placed onto a bloodied towel over my knees. Taking the glass into the bathroom, I set the glass on the counter and ran warm water over a fresh towel.

Moving back to Gemma's side, I began washing away the rapidly drying blood, carefully looking for any shards I may have missed. "You did great, Olivia," she said through still-clenched teeth."

"Are you going to be all right?" I asked worriedly, my hands shaking now that they had nothing to do.

She turned her head and gave me a forced smile. "Yes, but I need to know you are, too." I nodded in reply but her scrunched expression appeared unconvinced. "Olivia, the Rogue slammed you into the floor as hard as he did me, and then into the wall—denting the sheetrock. Aren't you in pain?"

"I think you're confused, Gemma. He slammed you against the floor and wall. Not me."

"Olivia . . . ? What're you talking about?"

Before I could answer, a familiar tightening sensation pulled inside my chest, and this time I knew, without doubt, that Caleb was near. Our connection was growing stronger by the day. As crazy as it seemed, I could sense him—and even see him in my mind when I closed my eyes, which I did now. His breathing was light and steady as he practically flew up the steep mountainside toward the house, but his eyes appeared menacing, gripped with both anger and fear. I sensed another was with him—no doubt it was Jax. I tried to familiarize myself with Jax's body's energy so I would recognize it better in the future. "They're here."

"I know," Gemma replied in a frustrated tone. "The question is, *how do you?*"

I ignored her pointed question. "How do I let them in?"

"They know where the outside switch is hidden. They'll be up shortly. I want you to stay here with me until they have a chance to regain control of themselves. It's the safest way."

I nodded. My stomach was turning over as I prepared for the approaching storm. "Did I do enough to clean the scent?"

"I'd say so. You reek of bleach! But the bleach and alcohol will help minimize the scent. They should be able to maintain control now."

Just then, the light buzzing sound of the lasers disappeared and a wave of air blew in soon after the glass panels swung open. Glass shards pinged against the floor from the one broken panel as it returned to its locked position.

I didn't hear their feet hit the floor, but I could tell they were there. Low, vicious snarls of rage erupted from both of them as they sniffed the remnants of blood, bleach and alcohol. It was clear that the men were not here—the blue-eyed warriors were.

"What the hell happened?" Jax snapped. "It looks like a war zone."

A split second later I jumped back when the door to Gemma's room crashed against the wall. The warriors' electric blue eyes were wide in rage as their noses lifted high, inhaling the scents in the room. In unison, their gaze swept over our wounds in quick assessment.

Caleb zoomed in on the dozen or so bandages on my legs below my skirt. His hands balled into angry fist at his sides as he remained at the door.

He was waiting until he was in complete control before he came to me.

Jax focused on Gemma, who was still lying face down on the bed, the towel on her back now freshly covered in blood as the older, more controlled vampire flew to her side. He spoke no words at first, only lifted the towel to examine the damage underneath, then cursed furiously under his breath. "Oh, Gemma," he finally spoke, his voice raspy. "Look at you. I am going to need to stitch some of these up."

"I'll be fine, Jax," she murmured quietly. "I'm just tired."

Jax took several deep breaths, his body still as his face transformed into his human form right in front of me. The electric-blue was replaced with a soft amber that reflected his worry for Gemma. He was controlling his need for blood, but his emotional pain was blooming as he continued to touch with light fingers over her back.

Just then, I felt a cool hand reach for the one at my side. I turned and saw that Caleb, the man, was also back with me, but he, too, showed the same unease in his expression. I was so glad to see him, I wanted to just wrap my arms around him and collapse against his strength, but he didn't seem to want to co-operate at the moment. Instead, he pulled me away from Jax and brought me to stand in front of him. "I can see the cuts on your legs. Are you hurt anywhere else?"

Holding myself perfectly erect, I crossed my arms in front of my skirt, shaking my head in silent reply. Immediately he reached out to cup my face in both his hands, his gentle fingers brushing back some of the strands at my temple. "Hey," he said softly, making sure he had my full attention, "Are you all right?"

I knew he needed to hear me say the words. My body and mind were so numb, I knew he couldn't possibly be able to feel how I was. "Yes, I am. But Gemma is hurt."

There went the broken record again. This time it seemed to almost skip, over and over again, repeating and repeating in my head. It was then I had to admit to myself that I was indeed unsure of how my own body really felt. Caleb studied me, his nostrils flaring as he took in the powerful scents around us. Overwhelmed by the bleach and alcohol, his eyes wandered, and his face puckered up before he returned his questioning gaze to me.

I was fuzzy myself on where all the bleach was coming from.

"How much pain are you in?" Jax asked Gemma in a quiet voice.

Caleb, obviously satisfied enough with my answer, moved over to the bed to see Gemma. Once he saw close up all the cuts in her back, he hissed in anger. It was taking every ounce of strength inside both of them to hold their vampire tempers in check. "Gem, answer Jax. Are you all right?"

Gemma finally turned to face them. She looked as if she was in absolute agony; her bloodshot eyes appeared drugged. "You both know I'll be healed in a day. I'll be fine," she grumbled, trying very hard to seem irritated by all of their attention.

"Do not make light of this, Gemma," Jax growled in short reply. "These are deep cuts. You could have been killed."

"Easy, Jax, she'll be OK," Caleb reassured.

Jax raised his head and sniffed into the air, then disappeared into the bathroom, returning with the cloth full of bloodied glass shards from the counter. I brought my hand to my mouth to cover my gasp, realizing that I had forgotten all about disposing of the glass I had left in the sink.

Caleb seemed to be holding his body rigid in silent fury as he dropped to one knee beside the bed and began wiping the fresh blood from Gemma's back with the wet cloth. "It's going to be all right, Gem. We'll make sure this never happens again."

Jax's gaze fixed on me. "Did you remove these from her back?"

I nodded.

Caleb glanced back at me, flashing a look questioning my

still unspoken answers.

"Thank you," Jax replied, with feeling.

As both men turned their full attention to Gemma, I stepped silently out of the room. Gemma was once again grumbling at the attention, so I knew everyone was too distracted to notice that I had left. I tried to use the moment to close my eyes and replay everything that had happened tonight, but it was all jumbled up. Caleb would ask me later what had happened, and my current muddled state wasn't going to help him get rational answers.

Quietly, I descended back down the stairs to where the attack had happened, hoping I could replay everything in my mind once I was there again. Looking once more at the damage, I was amazed to see how large an area it covered. I massaged my fingers over my temples because my head was starting to ache the more I slowed down.

Why can't I remember?

My gaze lowered to my skirt, which I had worn to welcome Caleb home, and I was somehow shocked to see that it had now become a frightful mess, torn and cut. I twisted it around on my waist to straighten it, but it still hung in abysmal disarray. Returning my fingers to my temples, I shook my head in an effort to clear my mind. Think, Olivia, think! It was Gemma who went into the wall, right?

I could still hear everything being said upstairs in Gemma's room. Now that Jax and Caleb were finished asking Gemma about all her specific injuries, Caleb asked the questions foremost on their minds. "What happened tonight, Gem?"

"It was a Rogue," she began in a croaky voice. "He broke through the glass before I had a chance to get to the lasers."

She then gasped, apparently startled as Caleb hit a tender spot on her back while cleaning her up. "Sorry, Gem."

"Why was a Rogue trying to break in here so badly?" Jax growled.

Gemma responded with a sharp exhale. "You wouldn't have believed it. He was like a mad dog trying to get to Olivia. You should check her carefully. The Rogue slammed her about as hard as me. I think she might be in shock."

In an instant, a wave of cold air blasted against my body,

sending the light skirt blowing about my legs—and there was Caleb. He now stood within inches of me, his expression one of worry and frustration, then it changed to all worry when he saw the confused look in my eyes and my hands held to my temples. "Where are you injured?" he asked again, his hands also coming to my temples. "Did you hit your head? Is that why you're rubbing at your temples?"

It was too many questions. I didn't know where to start.

His eyes bore into mine and his breathing halted, his voice too upset to speak. He was trying to feel my pain, but he couldn't. My mind and body were still numb. When I said nothing and slid my gaze away from him, he folded the hands at my temples into his own. "Olivia, don't do this. Don't close down on me. I need to know where you're injured."

I pushed away from him in a sudden jerk, unsteady on my wobbly feet. "I said I'm fine," I snapped, very angry now, but I had no idea why. I knew he was trying to help, but I didn't quite feel myself.

Caleb was having none of it. His arms wrapped around my back and legs and he swung me off my feet into his arms, preparing to jump me back to the second floor, but didn't even get that far when I yelped out in pain.

Where he held me my skin burned like fire, the glass shards now crashing back into my memory.

"Olivia?" he questioned with clear worry, setting me back down on my feet.

In an instant, Jax was there in front of us. "What's wrong?"

"Nothing!" I yelled; then started to stumble away towards the stairs, but Caleb's arm shot out like an iron bar, halting me in place. He dropped to his knees behind me, clamping his large hands on my hips, letting me know I wasn't going anywhere. Sniffing at my back, he cursed as he passed over the bleach then moved straight to my mid-back.

"Olivia," he scolded, clearly smelling the blood in my cuts, "why are you trying to hide this from us? We need to know that you're injured."

Caleb reached in front of me with quick efficiency and began to unbutton my outer shirt. Once he pulled it free from my arms he saw the plastic bag I had cinched around my waist with a belt. Muttering more curses under his breath, he removed the items, his frustration with me increasing. "Why did you do this?" he growled.

I didn't answer him. Instead, my lost gaze seemed to fix on Jax, who was studying me carefully. Caleb pushed up the ribbed tee and saw the massive amounts of gauze wrapped around my mid section. "Olivia!" More curses sounded under his breath as he began removing the gauze, even more annoyed that he had to get through yet another layer to see the damage beneath.

Knowing I was making him angry, I wanted to help. "Caleb, I can do this. I know the blood is hard—"

"Don't start. I'm fine with the scent. You have yourself so covered in bleach and alcohol; it's giving me a headache."

"Olivia, look at me," Jax commanded. When I met his gaze, he scanned my eyes, asking me to follow the finger he held in front of my nose.

When Caleb finally finished removing the gauze and reached the cut skin, he sighed as if he himself were in pain. "Olivia . . . you haven't even removed the shards from your back." He ran gentle fingertips right to the edges of my cuts. "And they're so deep."

Jax stepped beside Caleb to inspect the wounds. "She is in shock, Caleb. She cannot feel the pain yet."

I turned to both men. "I couldn't reach the glass. I was going to have Gemma help me remove it later."

"It is all right, Olivia," Jax replied gently. "I will help you get them out."

"I can get them," Caleb argued.

"They are too deep, Caleb. They will bleed heavily once removed. My resistance to blood scent is stronger than yours. You would need to have complete control of your thirst."

"I can handle it Jax. We just fed!"

Jax took a long look at the younger vampire and could see his impatience. Even though it was clear Jax was the leader, he always seemed to support Caleb's efforts to challenge himself. "Very well, you can assist me. Take her to your room, and I will be there shortly. I want to check one more time on Gemma."

"Yes, please help Gemma," I pleaded. "She was injured."

Both men stared at me in silent bewilderment. "Jax, why is she so confused?"

Jax looked equally as baffled. "Take her to your study. Let me talk with Gemma," he replied then disappeared to the bedroom.

Caleb lifted me gently into his arms, this time knowing exactly where to hold me so he missed all of the glass. As he carried me towards the stairs, moving at a purposely slow pace, I noticed he was taking in all of the destruction. That's when I saw the white rose he had left for me this morning lying on the floor, blood on its once perfect petals. "My rose! I must have dropped it"

Caleb glanced at the bloody flower, his teeth grinding in anger at seeing where the Rogue had thrown me to the floor. Noisily drawing in a deep breath, he tried to calm the emotion brewing within him. "It's all right. I'll get you another rose."

"I'm sorry, Caleb. I should've hidden it someplace safe."

He stopped and stared at me with furrowed brows. "Olivia, you're not making any sense."

"Ok," I replied simply. His expression twisted, his worry now increasing.

Then he noticed the profound hole and smeared blood in the sheetrock wall directly in front of him. Another incensed snarl rolled in his throat as he glanced up, toward Gemma's room. "Jax," he began, speaking at a volume appropriate only if the man were to be standing right beside him. I laid my head on his shoulder, feeling so tired now I was sure I could fall asleep right there. "The Rogue threw Gem pretty hard into the wall. Check her well."

When I listened closely I could hear Jax whispering at Gemma's side. His whispering was inaudible, though, and I was too exhausted to try and focus in. Caleb took a step toward the wall, sniffing at the blood left behind.

Without warning, Jax was in front of us, blocking Caleb from moving any closer to the wall. Caleb stared at him in surprise as Jax put out his arms and began removing me from his arms. "What're you doing?" he demanded.

"I need you to go talk with Gemma. I will take Olivia to your study. I would like to check her one more time, just to be safe," he said, his calm, deep voice soothing to me.

"Jax?" Caleb questioned hard.

"*Now*, Caleb!" Jax ordered.

Caleb was gone in an instant, while Jax had me just as quickly in the study. He set me down easy on my feet and pulled the covers back, having me lie on my stomach so he could begin removing the shards from my back.

I turned to look at him. "What's going on?"

"Wait for it," he replied, motioning with his finger into the air.

A few seconds later Caleb's voice erupted in anger from Gemma's room. "*What?*" he shouted. "That's impossible! What the—" and then his voice broke off.

"That is him learning that you were the one thrown into the wall by the Rogue, not Gemma. I did not want him carrying you when he sniffed your blood scent on that sheetrock. It is going to take him a few minutes to calm down."

Shaking my head, I tried to once again remember the details of the night. "Was it me who hit the wall?" I asked. "I thought I remembered it was Gemma."

"It is OK, Olivia. You hit your head pretty hard. You memories will be a little confused for a while."

"I didn't mean to make Caleb so angry with me. I'm just having a hard time remembering."

"Trust me; I think he knows that now. Do not worry about him. Let us just focus on getting this glass out of you, all right?" Jax's voice was so peaceful, I felt completely relaxed, even though I was now beginning to feel the pain in my back.

A couple of minutes later, a wave of cool air hit the room and Caleb was there, standing over me, his breathing so hard it startled me. I could see the worry in his eyes, and I wished there was something I could do to make it go away.

Jax was already on his feet, his forearm braced on the taller man's chest, warning him. "Are you calm?"

"*Calm?* No, Jax, I'm not calm. A Rogue came after her tonight . . . in our home! Crashing through glass to get to her while she was under my protection. It doesn't make any sense."

"I agree. Something is not right, but we need to focus on her injuries right now. You cannot be here unless you are in complete control."

He nodded, his fingers pinching the bridge of his nose. "I understand. I'm in control. I need to be here, Jax. I need to help." But I could hear in his voice that he was not in control, he was scared. "Is she going to be OK?"

"I have not had a chance to look at her yet. You can stay, Caleb. I can use your help, but I need you to be focused right now."

"What can I do?"

Jax turned back to kneel beside me on the bed. "Olivia, I am going to have Caleb remove your shirt. It will be easier for both of us to work on you. Is that all right?"

"Yes," I replied, and then in one efficient motion I felt my shirt being ripped in half across my back. "Caleb!"

"I'll buy you a new shirt," he grumbled. I sensed he wasn't in the mood to argue about it at the moment.

"Caleb, find us a second set of tweezers, some ice, warm towels. Oh, and more gauze . . . if we have any left." Caleb did as he was instructed and was back before I even realized he had left the room.

"Olivia, this is going to be painful, but I need you to stay as still as you can, all right?" Caleb muttered more curses beneath his breath and Jax was quick to respond. "Caleb, focus."

"Ok," I replied lightly.

"I know you are a bit disoriented. Your memories will probably clear up by tomorrow. But tell us what you do remember," Jax asked, trying to distract me as they began digging deep into my back.

"I'm not sure. It happened so fast. I remember standing by the window when he came out of nowhere and crashed through the glass. The pieces went flying everywhere."

I returned my gaze to Caleb as he continued to pull glass from my back. His expression was wretched, and I worried I had caused all this by not telling him that I was hurt. "I'm sorry, Caleb. I didn't remember that the Rogue threw me against the wall. I really didn't."

More pain twisted his features before he lowered his lips to my cheek, pressing a soft kiss against my skin. "Shhh. Don't worry about a thing, my sweet. It's going to be fine."

"Olivia, what else do you remember?" Jax asked.

"I—I . . . I remember him pushing me into the wall. I hit my head and things were dizzy for a minute. I saw flickering lights —"

Metal tweezers dug hard into my back, and I felt as if a raw nerve had been pierced. I turned my face into the mattress, trying to muffle cries of pain, and my body went rigid.

"I'm so sorry," Caleb said, his voice barely recognizable. He laid a gentle hand on my shoulder. "Try to relax, my sweet. It won't happen again. I promise."

In a quiet voice Jax asked, "Do you want me to finish?"

"No," Caleb replied simply then addressed me. "Go ahead, Olivia."

Relaxing, I rest my right cheek against the mattress. A wave of weariness came over me that was so strong I had to close my eyes. I started to float off into a hazy, muted dream, then jerked my eyes open, remembering I hadn't finished.

"I tried to push him off of me," I began, in a tired voice, but my eyes were closing again and my words began to be all mixed up. "I tried to defend myself, Alec, like you showed me, but he was too strong. I'm not as strong as you think I am, Alec. There's no way I can fight against a vampire. I did try though. I did try."

There were no more questions, only silence as they continued to pull glass from my back.

"Can I sleep now?" I asked.

"Yes, go ahead and sleep. But I am going to have Caleb wake you every couple of hours to check on you though."

Then I heard his amazing voice whispering in my ear. "Just sleep, my sweet. Just sleep."

Chapter Nineteen

That night I was standing in the middle of a grassy field. Thick smoke and flames billowed from the train's wreckage and filled the sky. Doomed cries from lost souls trapped on the train echoed all around me just before Isaac's brutal grip on my arms slammed me back against the wall, driving shards of glass deep into my back.

I knew somehow this scene was wrong, and all I wanted was to escape and return home to the mountain where I belonged. I fought and pushed and scratched to get away, but Isaac's inhuman strength refused to let me go.

"Olivia! Wake up. Olivia!" My eyes popped open as I was shaken from my horrible nightmare, trying to remember where I was. Caleb was there, holding me, his whispered tone gentle and coaxing as he stroked my temples with a light touch. "It's OK. I swear it is. You're just having a nightmare. Isaac's not here. He won't hurt you. I won't let him."

I clutched at Caleb's strong shoulders and rest my head against his chest, wanting to just absorb some of his strength, his fearlessness, because somehow it made me stronger, too.

"Tell me how you are," he murmured into my ear. "Are your thoughts clearer?"

I raised my head and gazed into his worried face, wanting to assure him. "My thoughts are clear. You don't need to worry. My back isn't hurting too much, either."

A frown knit across his brow as he ran his fingertips across my bare back. "Yes, I can see that. You seem to be healing as quickly as Gemma. Why do you suppose that is, Olivia?"

I could tell by his tone that he already knew the answer. He just wanted to hear me say it.

I was running out of time.

***

After the confusion of the previous night, the absolute quiet the next day was sort of unnerving. I had expected more hurried and chaotic movement, but there was a stillness to it. Judging from the cloudy daylight peeking through the skylight above us, I was guessing it was sometime that next afternoon. I was resting on my side, with my right cheek pressed against the pillow. Caleb quietly watched me from across the mattress as my eyes fluttered open for good. He was relaxed, handsome in his dark jeans and navy button down shirt which, as always, had the top three buttons open. But his expression was one of quiet pain, and his eyes, those beautiful shades of gray had no light dancing inside them.

Something had changed. I could see it there in his arched brows. He needed answers, and he needed me to give them to him.

I had run out of time. I had run out of time and I didn't want this to be the way I spent the last of it—just lying there, staring at each other, waiting for the truth to break everything apart.

Pushing the warm covers to the edge of the mattress, I noticed that I still wore the cotton skirt from the previous night and was naked from my waist up. As a swirl of chilled air passed through the room, I shivered, causing the cherry peaks of my breast to harden and goose bumps to surface over my arms. Caleb's eyes darkened as he watched me, but he made no move towards me—even though it was obvious he wanted to touch me.

He moistened his lips as I scooted closer to the loving man who had stayed at my side all night and well into the next day. Tenderly I thanked him with gentle and slow kisses along his neck, my senses seeming to come to life as I tasted the slightly salty extract of his skin and inhaled the infused scent of fir and sage that was such a part of him. He teased me, lifting his chin away, but I followed and ascended over his bristled jaw 'til I found his waiting, parted lips.

Caleb didn't wait for me to take them. Instead, he pushed forward, capturing mine in one swift motion as he came over me, his hand going behind my neck to hold me in place and making sure my back was lifted away from the mattress. He nibbled playfully in a heady mix of softness and strength that ignited a need I was helpless to ignore. I craved to feel him inside me again, claiming, stretching—overwhelming my body with shivery, tingling pleasure.

His tongue plunged hungrily into the recesses of my mouth as his breathing began to change, his nostrils flaring to suck in more air as his lips locked over mine. I could feel in each kiss, each velvety exchange, how much he wanted me and rejoiced in knowing that he wasn't stopping or pushing away after the chaos of last night . . . so I pushed further.

My prying fingers began slipping the buttons from his shirt. He felt it, but still he didn't try to stop me, instead moaning against my lips and grasping the sides of my face to slant my head further back, taking more.

Once I had freed all of his beautiful skin from behind the buttons, I stopped and patiently stoked my hand low over his firm stomach, back and forth, back and forth, waiting with quiet patience for that moment when his breathing would cross a point of no return. He was almost there when his mouth finally tore from mine, his breaths shallow now—and fast—as he lifted himself above me, his eyes shining with complete understanding of where things were headed. And in spite of his obvious excitement, his expression remained serious . . . and now he pushed away and protested. "We're not doing this." His raspy voice came out as a hoarse whisper. "You're injured and not in the right frame of mind."

I smiled at him, sliding up his body until my breasts were presented to his mouth like a banquet for the taking. "I think my frame of mind is right where it should be." The need was there in his eyes, and I could feel the cool rush of excitement within his breath as it crashed against my nipples. "Please, Caleb. I need you."

"Olivia . . ." he said with a frustrated sigh, but he couldn't stop himself from flicking his tongue several times over one nipple before taking it more fully into his mouth, drawing on it so tightly I felt the pleasure down to my tingling toes. I drew in a short, sharp breath and scraped my fingers through his hair as he rolled onto his back, bringing me with him, his cool tongue whipping back and forth until I felt as if I was being sweetly tortured with an ice cube.

I was lost in a blissful daze by the time his mouth finally released me with a soft pop and his head dropped back, his heavy lungs filling to capacity now with each vital intake of air. I stared down at him and could tell he was trying to regain control of his desire, trying to stop his change from happening, and it bothered me . . . at a time when all I really wanted was for him to be bothered.

Refusing to be detoured, I shuffled down quickly to the rippled lines of his stomach, my mischievous tongue licking just over the ridge of his low-rise jeans. "Olivia," his rough voice warned, but I ignored him, practically tearing open his button-flys. I knew he would not give me much time, and his low, rolling growl told me his body was being pushed to a place where he was losing control. I tugged his clothing down on his hips until the long length of him sprang free. "Damn it, Olivia! I'm not a—

. . . Oh, God," he groaned as I took him in hand and dragged my tongue over the swollen head, then along the sensitive ridge underneath. In response, his thighs bunched and his hips tightened. "Son of a—"

Grabbing my upper arms, he hauled me back up till my cheek was resting at his throat. His panting breaths were completely out of his control.

"Don't refuse me, Caleb," I whispered, nestling my face into the crook of his neck, my tone like that of a high-pitched angel as I slipped my hand back down and began stroking over his flesh from base to tip, needing to feel at that moment how much my touch affected him, how easily I could dissolve the warrior's control. "Let me have what my body needs. I need you."

He groaned, his hips jerking, involuntarily, the man now long gone. The blue-eyed warrior was here.

"There he is," I murmured into his ear sweetly, "I love my blue-eyed warrior, Caleb. I love him."

Choked sounds rolled from his throat that I hadn't heard from him before. Almost like cries of relief, pure happiness. Acceptance. "I won't refuse you, Olivia," he breathed. "I need you, too. I need to be inside you."

Suddenly, his strong hands clamped at my waist, raising me high into the air above him. I smiled as he fit the center of me over his hips. His glazed, sapphire eyes stared into mine while his hands slid along my skin and under my skirt. Long dimples formed at the corners of his smiling mouth as he ripped away the silk fabric beneath. I watched as he kicked his clothing from his legs and stroked his long shaft several more times before bringing the head to press at my entry.

I lowered onto him slowly, and when I felt him penetrate inside the softness, I clenched around him, wanting so desperately to hold onto the moment, to the incredible sensation. The pressure was perfect as my inner walls accepted him, molded to him exactly, as if knowing this was *the* man, the *only* man, the perfect counterpoint to me.

I began to move, and he gasped as he slid his hands around to firmly grasp my hips while staring straight into me with those piercing blue eyes of his. They were inescapable as his hips lifted and he met me with strong thrusts upward, his strokes so smooth, so high into my body, I felt completely possessed. The pleasure licked up my spine until I thought I would scream and shatter into millions of pieces, like glass.

I never wanted it to end, but it would end . . . soon.

At the very highest moment of all this joy, a terrible, paralyzing fear and sadness came crashing down on me. "Caleb, please don't . . ."

I left the rest unspoken because he wouldn't understand it, couldn't understand it . . . *please don't send me away.*

Thinking he had done something wrong, he stopped his thrusting, and I cried out as if I were in pain from the absence of his movement inside me. "Olivia?" his low voice questioned.

Staring down into the warrior's glazed blue eyes I saw all the love and passion he felt for me, and my heart cracked. Why do I have to be an illusion? Why can't this be real?

I placed my palms flat over the corded muscles of his chest, moving my hips, riding him even faster, grinding down with all the force I could muster. With each thrust I involuntarily gasped, shocked at the depth to which he possessed me. I was one with him, I belonged to him. For the rest of my days I was his and his alone, even if we were apart.

A hard, guttural groan ripped from his chest just before he lurched upward to a seated position. Using one big hand as leverage against the mattress, he continued to pump inside me —faster and faster. "Hold on to me, sweet," he said, his lips right there against my throat. "You're mine. All mine."

Oh, God, the pleasure he gave was almost too much, and it was killing me inside to know it wasn't real. He didn't— couldn't—really love me. He didn't see the real woman under the illusion. In this moment, as my trembling body was receiving the greatest pleasure I had ever known, my heart was being ripped in half by the knowledge that it would all end.

I tilted my head back as far as it would go and stared through the skylight above us as he continued to push my body closer to the edge. Storm clouds were rolling in, surely a dark sign of things to come.

My eyes reached higher, looking now to the heavens beyond those horrible clouds, as tears began to fall over my cheeks. On the long climb up here I had promised God that if I could just have one more chance with this man, this vampire, I would enjoy every precious minute, and I had.

Time is so fleeting.

My heart breaking now, I could feel my body plunging toward a blissful place of no return, signaling that the end was near. I let my tears speak to God, telling him how thankful I was for the sacred time he gave me. I would demand nothing else and live for the rest of my days on these cherished memories and the sound of Caleb's voice calling for me—his sweet.

I was now ready to let go—to let him go.

My nails clawed at his skin as my tears turned to squealing cries, my inner muscles clamping around him, massaging him furiously, trying to draw him in and hold him as deep as I possibly could.

In one final thrust, Caleb buried himself to the hilt with a groan and his hips jerked as he came hard inside me. "That's it . . . Oh, God, yes—take me with you." His eyes blinked hard, as if he was gripped in a release so blinding he hadn't fully expected it.

I collapsed onto his shoulder, my tears wetting his skin as he held me there, and I shook against him.

We stayed like that for several minutes, the only sound that of our out-of-control panting. As we slowly returned to earth, still in unison, I was struck by the irrational fear that I would never again know this kind of happiness, this kind of love, this kind of easy peace.

"Olivia," he finally said, wrapping his arms around my shoulders so I couldn't move from him, "I love you. Tell me what's happening."

My time was up.

"Caleb," I said simply, "I've found the words."

Chapter Twenty

Caleb rolled us back onto our sides, one arm protectively lifting me while the other held one of my thighs as he pulled himself from me. "Stay right here."

He returned seconds later with a warm, damp cloth and began cleaning me. His sultry, satisfied gaze engulfed me the whole time as I held onto him, the color of his eyes still heated from our lovemaking but sparked with an understanding of how difficult this was for me. When he was finished, his thumb wandered across my cheek, lightly brushing away the last of the salty tears of joy that had been replaced with the underlying dread in the pit of my stomach. I remained quiet for a long moment while he waited patiently for me to give him what he now needed—the truth.

So I took a deep breath and began.

"The three days when you couldn't sense me—when my last fever broke? I was speaking with two men when it started. They took me to a nearby church . . . helped me get well. That's why you couldn't sense me."

His brows furrowed into a questioning expression, already challenging. "Why did these men take you to a church instead of a hospital?"

I sighed. "So I would be protected within sacred ground . . . from vampires."

His face became even more tense, and his eyes lost their luster. I so wished I knew what he was thinking. "Vampires like Isaac," I added, trying to make sure he understood that I didn't see him the same way.

"Who are these men, Olivia? These humans know about vampires?"

"Their names are Alec and Gideon," I replied, at the same moment detecting a flicker of recognition happening behind his now cold and suspicious eyes. "I met them for the first time that morning. Gideon said he had known my parents and that he needed to speak with me in private." Shaking my head, I continued describing the strange encounter. "I didn't recognize Gideon, and I didn't remember my parents ever mentioning him. Both men seemed kind of odd, but they insisted we needed to go someplace private to talk."

Caleb stiffened. "I don't like this, Olivia. Were these men tracking you?"

I nodded slowly. "In a way."

"Then why would you go with them?"

"I didn't want to, but my appearance had already begun to change, and I was scared. I didn't understand what was happening, but they implied that they knew what was occurring and why—so I had to go. I—I had to know."

Caleb pulled himself closer, his hand brushing my hair from my cheek as his concerned gaze held me fixed. "Did they hurt you?"

"No. They didn't *physically* hurt me." With one small exception, when Alec grabbed me around the throat.

"Olivia," Caleb bit out. "Don't play word games with me. Did they hurt you in any way at all?"

I stared directly into his eyes, letting him know I wasn't hiding from him. I wanted to be as honest as I could; that was the very least he deserved from me. "Their words hurt me. They told me that the parents who'd raised me . . . who died in the car accident . . . weren't my biological family. My real father was a man named James, and my mother was—"

"A Dhampir?" Caleb finished for me.

I involuntarily blinked at him, then my eyes widened in surprise. Did he already know?

Caleb's expression crumbled, as if he was scolding himself. "Since you've been back I've had my suspicions. But after last night . . ."—his face turned away from me a moment—"seeing the evidence of how brutally you were thrown against that wall, then watching your wounds heal so quickly, Jax and I knew the truth." then, shaking his head, his eyes now looking deeply pained, he asked, "But why couldn't we sense this about you? I should've felt it the night of the train crash."

My gaze slid away from him as I tried to reassure myself that I actually had the courage to face him and do this. Here was the hard part. "That's more difficult to explain."

Caleb brought his knuckle under my chin and forced my eyes to meet his. "Tell me. You're doing fine."

I choose my next words carefully as I took a deep, slow breath. "As a Dhampir, my mother had . . . special gifts. Like Gemma."

"Yes, it's common for Dhampirs to have gifts."

"Well, these gifts make it very difficult for you—a vampire —to see who I really am." I closed my eyes in another slow blink, actually a squeeze, because the words were almost physically painful to say.

"I know who you are," Caleb answered without hesitation. "I feel every heightened emotion you have as if it were my own. I know what every look—every expression on that beautiful face—means. And I know how your body feels at every moment when I'm making love to you."

God, I loved him.

"I think that's because it's your special gift. Gemma says you can feel even more than Jax. It does allow you to see more of me than other vampires, but you must know what I'm saying is true. You couldn't sense that I was a Dhampir."

"But what about Gemma? Why couldn't she sense it?"

"She's half vampire. My guess is, it's the same for her as for you."

Caleb was quiet, taking everything in. I could see he had more questions for me but was hesitant to ask. Maybe he wanted to let me finish first. I began nervously fussing, rolling my skirt between my fingers, wishing I didn't have to go any further. Caleb noticed my restlessness, and a crease appeared between his brows. "What are these gifts?" he asked. "And why are they changing your appearance?"

I now understood why he didn't want to ask his questions, and the sadness that pricked at my heart must have shown on my face. "Did you prefer how I looked before?"

For a moment he appeared stunned. Then he held my face in his hands, his sincere expression so loving it made my heart beat faster. "Olivia, you were—and are—amazingly beautiful.

I'd desire you either way. When I first saw the change that day in the kitchen I was concerned because I feared something was wrong with you. It had nothing to do with my attraction."

He sealed his words with a slow, tender kiss. This was more than I ever expected from him at this point, and it gave me hope that we could somehow find a way. I opened to him, wanting the moment to last as his long arms wrapped me in strength and love. I wanted to believe that my time with him wouldn't have to end. But I had to get the words out. I had to tell him the truth. I wanted no more secrets between us—no matter how much I stood to lose.

His breathing was deeper now. He released his hands and his kisses began to slow as he pulled his lips away from mine. "Now will you please answer the question?"

"Just give me a minute," I replied, quite breathless and needing my focus back because it was only going to get harder to explain from here on.

"Alec and Gideon said that my physical changes are part of a . . . a transition that's happening as my mother's gifts develop inside me. The fevers were a physical response to the changes."

He studied me carefully. "So this transition is now over—your changes are complete—and your fevers are gone?"

I nodded. "Yes, I think so."

Caleb starting shaking his head and I feared he was upset, but instead, relief seemed to fill his voice. "Olivia? Why have you been so afraid to tell me this? Don't you understand what this means? You're a Dhampir. We aren't breaking any rules. You can stay here with me. We can be together."

For a moment my heart leaped. His desire and happiness almost had me convinced that I could stop my confession right here and stay with him in this house as long as he would let me. But that wouldn't be fair to him. "I can't stay, Caleb. It's just not that simple."

Suddenly frustrated, he replied, "Why the devil not?" He pulled back but kept his thigh in a possessive lock over my hip, as if putting me on notice that I wasn't going anywhere.

"What happened here last night will happen again if I stay."

"Olivia . . ." he scolded, "it's not your fault if a Rogue comes after you in our home. He crossed a line that he knew he shouldn't. The Rogue will pay. You're under my protection."

I sighed deeply. I definitely didn't seem to be explaining things well, but I pressed on, needing to get this out before I lost my nerve completely. "It's *my* fault. The Rogue was here because he was drawn to me, just as Isaac was drawn to me on the night of the train crash. And there'll be others. It puts all of you at risk, and I don't want that."

Caleb ignored my worries about his coven family being at risk. As always, he had complete faith in their unit, faith that they'd be fine. But he focused in on the one thing that most frightened me. "Why does Isaac want you? It isn't simply because he desires you, is it?"

"Honestly Caleb, I don't know. But he scares me so much. The night of the crash—when I thought he'd leave with me— all I could think about was how I'd rather die by his fangs than go with him." Even as I said "I don't know," I *did* know that a part of my secret was still unrevealed and needed to be exposed, now, but a sudden movement on his part distracted me.

Caleb pulled me to his chest, his lips planting several frantic kisses atop my head as his hands stroked my hair. "Don't ever say that. You're the most precious thing in my life. Never think that death is a better choice. You must always fight."

"Oh, Caleb," I whispered into his shoulder, my resolve softened by his statement of love. "My fears of him are still so real. When I had that nightmare last night, it was just as if I could feel him touching the back of my neck again."

Caleb jerked back, his face twisting with self-scolding. "I'm sorry, I didn't know," he began. "When you were sleeping . . . I was the one touching the back of your neck. When Jax was examining you he noticed a tattoo on the spot I was touching. I was just looking at it for myself. That's why your nightmare felt so real."

I was stunned. "I have a tattoo on my neck?"

"Yes. You don't know about it? It's under your hairline, hard to see. It looks like some sort of symbol or family crest."

"That makes more sense," I whispered.

"What does? Did Isaac say something to you?"

I thought back to the frightening scene at the site of the

crash.

His heightened concern momentarily outweighing his need to comfort me, he asked, "Olivia, what did he say to you?"

"He said, 'There you are. Davin's been looking for you.'"

Frustration filled Caleb's expression as he scraped his hand through his hair, exclaiming, "I wish you would have told me this sooner!"

"I wasn't trying to keep it from you," I defended. "I just sort of blocked it . . . I didn't really remember it until now."

He relented a bit at my words and explained the reason for his reaction. "From what you just told me, not only had Isaac been looking for you, but he knew how to identify you from this mark on your neck. It means something specific to him. Do you have any idea what that is?"

A deep gulp caught in the back of my throat as I replayed Isaac's words in my mind. Now maybe it all made sense.

Caleb watched me carefully, waiting for the rest of my story. But suddenly there was a single knock on the bedroom door and Jax's muffled voice came through.

"Caleb, we have a problem."

Chapter Twenty-One

"There are several men coming up the mountain, headed straight for the house. It may be nothing, but after last night I am not taking any chances." Jax sounded deeply concerned.

Caleb paused for a moment, his eyes focusing elsewhere. "Yes, I can sense them. I'll be right there, Jax."

He pulled me forward, planting a quick kiss on my forehead, then began dressing, quickly but effortlessly. "Don't worry about a thing, my sweet. I want you to wait here for me. We'll continue this discussion."

Placing the bedcovers back over my naked upper torso, he dashed from the bed and out the door before I could get a word in otherwise. "Wait!" I cried after him, wrapping a sheet around me as I scrambled from the bed.

After rushing downstairs as fast as I could, being dressed in only a skirt and sheet, I caught up with Caleb and Jax just as they reached the glass doors. Caleb was surprised by my distressed state and lack of dress. "What is it, Olivia?"

I turned to Jax. "You said 'men.' How many?"

"Four," he responded, his tone guarded.

Four was not the answer I expected, but something in my gut told me it was Alec coming up the mountain. I had not returned as I had promised him. But how on earth had he found me so quickly? "Were they down by the cars before they started coming up?"

"Olivia, calm down," Caleb replied. "We'll check it out. I'm sure it's just some hikers. They'll stay on the trails and move right past us." But there was a flicker in Caleb's eyes that said he knew it was more than that. He was sensing something and not telling me. Damn my not knowing how to use my Dhampir gifts yet!

He and Jax turned to leave again, but now frantic, I grabbed

Caleb's arm while simultaneously grappling with the sheet. "Please, just answer the question. Did they see my car?"

Jax moved beside Caleb. "What is it, Olivia?"

I knew I was the cause of all of this, but Caleb still did not have all of my truth, and there just wasn't time to tell him now. All I could say was, "The Rogue last night—he was here for me. These men coming up the mountain are here for me, as well. You must take me with you so I can speak with them."

"You're not going anywhere," Caleb announced in an almost startled tone, making it clear the topic was not up for discussion.

Just then, Gemma appeared, asking, "Are these the men you were talking about with me, Olivia? The ones you said you're obligated to?"

Caleb's face instantly reflected a mix of anger and surprise. "*Obligated?*"

"Yes," I nodded.

Caleb glanced at Jax as if asking a silent question. "We will handle this your way," Jax replied to the younger vampire, obviously knowing his mind very well and trusting him.

Caleb then turned back to me, trying to control his anger as he asked, "Why are these men that you feel *obligated to . . .*"—his voice provided the emphasis and his face flashed his contempt at the word—"coming for you?"

"They want to take me back with them so I can be trained."

"Trained? Trained to do what?" he asked, his voice suddenly rising to a higher pitch.

Jax broke in. "We need to go, Caleb. If she is right, we cannot let them get too close to the house. There is a Dhampir with them."

Ah, so they were sensing more than what they were letting on.

Caleb nodded, never diverting his attention from me. "Do you want to go with these men, Olivia? Do you want to leave here?"

I stared at him dumbly. "No. I want to stay with you."

His expression remained calm, but relief flashed through his eyes just before he called out his next orders. "Good. Gem, I want you to stay here with her. She's not to leave this house.

Bring up the security right after we leave. Do you understand?"

Gemma's smile lit up the room. "Yep, got it."

"But Caleb—" I began to protest, but he didn't wait for me to finish, and in an instant he and Jax were gone, over the edge of the tree house entryway and into the threatening darkness beyond.

I panicked. Caleb and Jax didn't fully understand what they were walking into. Alec may be human, but he had been well trained by The Brethren, as I saw firsthand when he grabbed me. "Gemma, wait right here. Give me two minutes."

I raced back up to Caleb's study and threw on some jeans, the bra that was removed last night, and one of Caleb's white button-down shirts, since I had no time to search for clothes in Gemma's closet. Caleb's long shirt swallowed me to just above my knees, but his scent was all over it, which I loved. On my way back down the stairs I almost tripped trying to put on my canvas tennis shoes.

Gemma had already closed the glass doors.

"Gemma, wait," I cried, running to her side. As promised, she seemed almost fully recovered from her injuries, for which I was relieved. But right now I needed her to listen to me. "These men coming up the mountain are hunters. They seek and destroy vampires. If I don't go back with them, there could be more who return. Do you want Caleb and Jax to be hurt or killed because of me?"

The smile disappeared from her face, and I could tell that my question worried her. "Olivia, I can't take you down. Caleb has good instincts for these things. If he thinks it's better for you to stay here, then it is. Trust him!"

"I can't! I won't let him be hurt or killed over me."

I ran to the control switch and turned the lever to re-open the glass doors.

Gemma simply sighed. "Olivia, I'm not taking you down, so close the doors and bring up the security like Caleb asked."

My eyes flashed at the opening between the now open doors, and Gemma knew instantly what I was thinking. I was a Dhampir, same as her. If she could make the long jump from the tree house, then so could I. In one giant step I flung myself over the edge, hearing Gemma call my name as she followed behind.

Air pounded against my body and adrenaline raced through my blood as I tried to keep my flailing feet below me, which wasn't exactly working. Gemma's arm stretched to grab hold of my waist and pull me upright while I focused on the fast approaching ground, hoping I was not about to shatter both of my legs in the process.

I had wondered how it would feel to fly, but I wasn't quite sure I was ready for this.

As we landed, Gemma's arm managed to break my fall, but I tumbled down onto the thick grass, rolling several times before I finally stopped. When I looked up, her currently not-so-angelic face was right above me, and she was more than a bit angry. "Are you crazy?"

"Yes," I replied, coming to my feet. "Now we have to go."

"*Freeze!*" she warned, immobilizing me instantly. "That was an incredibly stupid thing to do. You could've been killed, even if you are a Dhampir!"

Jax had evidently told her about his and Caleb's suspicions.

I couldn't restrain a long sigh. "Gemma, I just jumped thirty feet out a window. So I think I've proved I'm going to do this with or without your help . . . although I'd prefer *with.*"

She seemed to take a moment to think about that. "Are they really in danger?" she asked, now convinced that if I would go to such lengths, there must be something very wrong.

"Not if we can stop it. Can you lead the way?"

Gemma gave me a taunting smirk. "Can your new legs keep up?"

I nodded. "You betcha. Don't worry about me," I answered, having no clue if I could keep up, but now was not the time to fall behind.

Racing between a blanket of gray skies above and rough terrain under foot, I was surprised at how fast and sure my steps were as we sped down the mountain. The landscape was blurring past us, and my long strides kept me within ten yards of Gemma—and I wasn't tiring at all. Within minutes we reached the grassy, alpine meadow where the blue-eyed warriors were already confronting Alec and three other men—Brethren Guardians, I presumed—at a distance of about twenty feet

It was obvious that the Guardians had been surprised to see the vampires standing before them in the middle of the day. I was surprised, given all their obsessed interest, that The Brethren didn't act like they were aware of Daywalkers, but they were prepared with lethal weapons just the same. I panicked when I saw Alec's crossbow, loaded with a silver-tipped arrow, aiming with precision at Caleb's chest. Caleb stood straight in front of it as if he had no fear. Then he glanced back over his shoulder at Gemma and me, his sapphire eyes, so cold and bright, flashed in fury and he turned his attention back to Alec.

"No, Alec. Stop!" I cried, racing over to use my body as a shield in front of Caleb, which seemed a bit ridiculous, since he was much bigger than me, but I knew Alec would never release that arrow while I was standing there.

But before I could place myself fully in front of him, Caleb blocked me with his arm, his body not even registering the jolt when I crashed against it. And his eyes never left Alec or the crossbow that now I, too, was in the line of fire.

More than a little irritated with me at that moment, Caleb's strong arm forced me backwards until his body became a shield in front of me. "So help me, Olivia, if you move from that spot . . ." he warned in a voice that was out of range of human ears. His tone was angry—but also fiercely protective.

"Sorry, Caleb," Gemma murmured, but the vampire never turned his eyes away from Alec, "she jumped."

A low, incensed growl rumbled from Caleb's throat. "Olivia!" he growled, and I knew he was incredibly angry at me. I curled my hand around his arm, my head hidden just behind his shoulder.

He couldn't be too disturbed, I thought, because he didn't shake off my possessive hold on his arm.

Alec seemed relieved to see that I was all right, but his expression tightened as he appraised the oversized man's shirt I was wearing while clinging to the vampire's arm. His focused stare on Caleb hardened, but as I had expected, he lowered his crossbow.

Alec called out to the blond Guardian directly beside him, a man who looked as if he could be Alec's older brother. He had a similar build—with short, spiky hair and light brown eyes—but his features were rougher, projecting a feeling of steel resolve, and he had a long scar running from his right temple to his cheek. "Lucas, don't aim your bow at her. She's not to be harmed. Understood?"

Lucas lowered his bow but growled, "Women."

The third Guardian, who was smaller and appeared a bit younger, still had his crossbow fixed on Gemma. And the fourth man, a rather striking addition to the male gender, gifted with extraordinary blue-gray eyes that stood out from his light chocolate skin, was locked on Jax. But instead of carrying a crossbow like the others, he held a long, silver-tipped lance that appeared to have sharp blades at both ends. He weaved the weapon confidently through his fingers and it was clear this man was somehow different from the others. I suspected he was the Dhampir Jax was referring to, which was confirmed by the flash of acknowledgement in Jax's eyes, as if he sensed the man was, at least in part, a worthy adversary.

For a moment, Alec turned his attention from me to Gemma. His gaze swept over her as if he was intrigued, and I doubted he missed her obvious speed and lack of fear, qualities Alec would admire. He then alternated his gaze between me and Gemma, and I could tell that he had already guessed that she was a Dhampir. A wry smile crossed his lips as he continued to watch her.

Gemma noted Alec's intense stare, and she did not back down an inch. Quite the opposite, in fact. She took a couple of steps towards him, flashing a wicked smile, as if daring him to try something. Alec responded by widening his grin, his gaze just as challenging.

The Guardian whose bow was aimed at Gemma raised it, warning her to not step any closer, but Alec waved his hand as if telling the man to stand down. It was clear Alec was the leader of this group, which didn't surprise me. He had that quality about him.

"Gemma!" Jax barked, nodding to the spot behind him, his hands balled into fists at his sides. She immediately did as he asked and moved into place. Alec's eyes followed her the whole way, continuing to indicate wordlessly to the Guardian aiming his bow at her that he should let her pass.

I liked Alec, but I didn't like the way he was staring at Gemma. The Brethren seemed to feel some weird, proprietary ownership over Dhampirs, and there was no way I wanted them to get any ideas about Gemma. I moved to step toward Alec, but the strong hand attached to the arm I was holding tapped against my abdomen, reminding me that I was to stay put. "Don't even think about it," Caleb warned.

"I worried when you didn't return as you promised, Olivia" Alec began, his voice sounding relaxed, almost playful, even though I knew this situation had to make him very tense. "The Brethren thought it wise to send reinforcements." He nodded toward the men standing at each side of him.

"I've been fine, Alec. I just needed more time before I could give you my answer." At my words, Caleb shifted his stance, the movement small but noticeable—and telling for a man who could otherwise be so still.

"Really, Olivia? Because you don't seem fine. Staying with vampires is hardly the path The Brethren—or your mother—had intended for you."

Caleb growled, shifting his stance ever so slightly once again, his hand pushing harder against my abdomen to force me farther behind him. It was taking every ounce of restraint in him to keep his warrior temper under control.

"The Brethren?" Gemma questioned.

"Yes," Jax began, his voice filled with contempt. "The Brethren is a secret society that likes to war with vampires. They were formed two centuries ago when a nobleman's wife became impregnated by a vampire and died giving birth to the child."

Of course, Jax would know some of the history of The Brethren, since he had been alive when they were formed. I found it interesting, though, that Gideon and Alec had never mentioned the woman's pregnancy when they told me the story.

"The nobleman, a man named Seamus Davin, was a descendant of a Duke of the Irish peerage and held some wealth and power of his own," Jax continued. "He took in the abandoned child and raised him as his own. Then he used the boy as a sort of call to arms to form his aristocratic little club—one whose mission was to hunt and destroy all vampires."

My grip tightened around Caleb's arm as Jax mentioned Davin's name. Alec glared at me, noticing the obvious closeness between Caleb and me, and it was clear he didn't like it.

I was now even more confused as to why a descendent of The Brethren would be looking for me on his own. Caleb had not said a word, standing in front of the small army as if confident he could take them all by himself, and that terrified me. He listened, surveyed the men while studying their weapons, and I knew he believed there would be a fight. There was no way I would let that happen. I refused to let one scratch land on him because of me.

"Where's the descendent of Seamus now?" Caleb asked.

"You should know," Lucas replied with contempt in his voice. "Luther Davin was killed by vampires here in Seattle several months ago when he came to make contact with Olivia. I suspect your coven might know something about that?"

"Killed?" Caleb laughed humorlessly. He understood now just as I did, that Davin was not dead but instead had been turned into a vampire by Isaac's coven. Things were starting to make more sense.

"What do your Brethren want with Olivia?" Caleb demanded.

Alec didn't look at him but focused his attention on me. "He doesn't know who you are, does he?"

Shaking my head, I pleaded, "Alec, no." As I tried to take a step forward again, Caleb held me back. I didn't want him to find out this way. Not this way.

Why had I not gotten the words out sooner?

Alec's crooked smile returned. His hatefully bright eyes filled with vengeful amusement as he looked at Caleb. He saw an opportunity to drive a wedge between me and the vampire I was clinging to, and he was about to take full advantage.

As he said the words I closed my eyes and braced myself. "She's a Charmer, and she belongs with The Brethren. Your coven is interfering in our business."

"She belongs to no one!" Caleb hissed through his sharp fangs.

Opening my eyes again, I stared up at Caleb's face. He was still focused like a laser on Alec, his own eyes now glaring with hate for the young Guardian.

"What?" Jax questioned. "Rumors of Charmers were nothing more than fable and myth for your drunken aristocrats in back room parlor discussions."

"Are you sure about that?" Alec taunted, while his gaze remained on Caleb. "It looks like she has your entire coven wrapped around her special little touch."

"Jax, what's a Charmer?" Gemma asked, fear weighing her voice, as somehow she sensed things were about to change.

Jax was shaking his head, clearly trying to deny it was possible. "There has only ever been one real Charmer. Her name was Eve, and she was with The Brethren for many years. She was a Dhampir who had the ability to charm vampires, trapping their minds with just her touch . . . rendering them incapable of killing her."

Gemma gasped, understanding that what Alec was saying about me was true. She had seen my gifts in action the night before with the Rogue. Caleb did not respond but shifted his stance again. My worry now started to grow; I began to feel the world crumbling around me.

"Vampires were inescapably drawn to Eve," Jax continued, " . . . attracted to her scent, beauty, and ethereal nature. But that was all part of the illusion. Once Eve disabled her prey, they were unable to focus or defend themselves. Then The Brethren's minions would finish them off. She was as powerful to them as any weapon."

The way he talked about my mother was as if he had known her.

"Actually, it works more like a mirror," Alec corrected. "While she has you in her touch—if she focuses—she reflects back the true nature of the vampire. And when that happens, vampires don't much like what they see. In the supernatural world, it's the closest thing to facing judgment day."

Alec waited to see Caleb's face as the realization dawned— that he had been deceived by someone he trusted. But Caleb's face remained frozen, displaying only pure neutrality on the outside. Inside, though, I was sure it was another matter.

Listening to Jax and Alec explain what I was made me feel disgusted and ashamed. My stomach twisted into hard knots and I thought I was going to be sick.

"You say that Olivia is this 'Charmer,'" Caleb began carefully. "I've touched her skin. She hasn't had that effect on me."

Alec grimaced at Caleb's claim that he had touched me. "That's because she doesn't yet understand how to use her gift —how to target her energy, her focus. She must be trained."

"She's not a dog!" Caleb growled back.

I wrapped my hand more tightly around his arm, trying desperately to hold on to the one person I most feared losing in this world.

"It does not matter, Caleb," Jax tried to assure the younger vampire, as if confident this was some kind of game being played by The Brethren. "Eve was the only Charmer, and her abilities died with her over twenty years ago . . . so . . ."

Jax's voice trailed off in mid-sentence as the truth dawned on him, and he turned toward me, stunned. I didn't know if I looked like my real mother, but given the look of absolute shock on his face, I was now guessing that I did. Jax looked as if someone had just staked him in the heart. "You are Eve's daughter?" he whispered, struggling to disbelieve what he could not.

Caleb stood rigid as Jax stared at his coven brother with sadness and complete understanding of what this would mean for the younger vampire.

Meanwhile, Alec's eyes twinkled as if he had just been given an early Christmas present. "Yes, she is. And you know why The Brethren kept her existence a secret. She's too important. We believe her gifts are even more powerful than her mother's."

Alec's unrelenting stare at Caleb made me want to scream at him, but it was too late, the damage was done. "Whatever you think you feel for her vampire, it's not real. You're trapped in—"

"An illusion," Caleb finished, his somber tone signaling the end was here.

I moved around his arm, and this time he did not stop me. Looking into his blank face, I watched the light leave his sapphire eyes as he met my gaze.

"Yes," Alec replied, "she's pretty good isn't she?" His mouth slowly curved into an evil smirk of delight at the wedge he hammered between us.

"Alec, stop this! Please!" I cried, my voice starting to break.

"It is real for her!" Jax bit out in fury. Of all of the members of the Walker coven, Jax seemed to have the most empathy towards me, even though I didn't deserve it. He returned a disbelieving stare that locked onto my eyes, his expression revealing that his mind was racing with a thousand different thoughts. "Your Brethren are nothing but a bunch of spineless cowards!" he snapped at Alec, "taking ownership of an innocent young girl and using her as bait to fight their war. It is sick!"

"Oh, I don't know if he would agree with you right now that she's so innocent," Lucas smiled, nodding in Caleb's direction.

Once again, low growls of fury rumbled inside my Caleb. A battle was going to erupt any second, and I couldn't let that happen, not over me. It was time for me to stop being selfish and try somehow to repair the damage I had caused.

What I had feared most was now real. Caleb knew the truth, and because of the sins of my mother and the gifts I inherited from her I was about to lose the only man I had ever truly loved. I released my hand from his arm, in essence letting him know I was releasing him, and walked several steps forward. Caleb did not try to stop me. The space between us now was destined to become only wider.

I turned to Caleb one last time, trying to penetrate his hard, angry expression, and I could see there was enormous pain underneath. I had hurt him more than I thought I could ever hurt anyone. "I'm sorry I deceived you." I whispered so Alec would not hear. "I came back to tell you the truth . . . but I didn't know how." Barely holding back tears, I whispered with frustration, "I am in love with you! But I also know that our love was real only for me. And on my part, that is the worst kind of selfishness. I will make this right."

I turned to face Alec, finding strength in my tone from the insidious confusion, frustration and anger building inside me. I was quite sure I would never speak to my pigheaded Guardian again after this. I locked my gaze on Alec's and spat out, "If I go back with you, you must promise me that none of you will return to this place. You'll leave this coven alone."

Alec just scowled at me. "Olivia, you aren't really in a position to make these kinds of demands. I don't think they'd take you back, anyway—now that they know who you are."

"She can stay," Jax replied without hesitation. "She would be safer with us protecting her than being bait for you and your Brethren."

I was grateful that Jax had offered, but I knew he didn't really mean it. He was protecting his coven, his family, and if Alec believed Jax would let me come back, then I might have something to bargain with.

"She might be protected by you, but she'll never be safe. She's a lure, a magnet for vampires. They can't help but be drawn to her, want to possess her, just as you all were. If she stayed with you she would bring a constant stream of unwanted guests. I know you vampires like to stay within your particular covens. You don't mix well with others."

I was grateful that my back was turned to the family I loved. I didn't want them to see how hard I was working to fight off tears. I knew that I couldn't afford to break down now. It would just be handing the victory to Alec.

"She must train," the Brethren leader continued, "learn how to defend herself—to use her extraordinary gifts. That's the only way she'll *ever* be safe. So, very well, Olivia, I accept your terms on behalf of The Brethren. Come with me now and we won't ever return to this place."

I nodded and began walking forward, not even remotely able to look again at the faces of the family I would miss so much.

Then I heard my true love's deep, heavenly voice behind me for the last time. "You don't have to do this," he said, speaking to me through his agony. "Your life is your own. It doesn't belong to this Brethren."

I stopped but didn't look back, whispering my words again, knowing he could hear me. "Yes I do. It's the only way to set things right for your family. I must return it to the way it was before that night when you saved my life." I then marched forward quickly, brushing past Alec without even acknowledging him as I continued down the hill, away from my home.

Anger and rage now welled in the empty space left by the heart that had just been ripped from my chest. I had left my heart, my whole heart, behind me in the meadow—at Caleb's feet.

I had no further use for it.

Chapter Twenty-Two

The drive back to the city seemed to take forever. I occupied my mind by watching through the back seat window of Alec's SUV as trees flew by almost as though we were standing still and they were moving. This sort of off-the-wall head tripping was the only way I could come up with to block the unyielding emotional pain I was feeling. Years ago, when both of my parents had died in an instant, I thought that was it—the biggest loss I'd ever feel. But the unrelenting heartbreak of loving Caleb as much as I did yet knowing that I could never be with him, believing to the depths of my being that simply because of who I was his feelings for me could never be real—felt as if I had been condemned to pay for some atrocious sin in my life.

At this point, I couldn't understand why The Brethren would even want me. I didn't really care whether I lived or died, and that hardly seemed useful in a war against vampires.

To make matters worse, Alec constantly glanced back at me through the rear view mirror, and that was beginning to annoy me. He had been waiting for me to say something since we left the meadow, but I refused to, choosing instead to sit where I was and stare out the window.

By the time we had hiked down to the vehicles and during the hour or so of our long drive thus far, the sun had already set, and the oncoming darkness further darkened my mood. I wasn't quite sure if I could make it all the way back to Seattle without saying something snarly to him.

"I know you're angry with me, Olivia" he finally said. "Why don't you just get it out?"

"I don't care about you enough to be angry with you!"

And there it was. Totally snarly.

"Ouch. That's a pretty good shot," Alec replied in a

surprisingly light voice that indicated he wasn't too worried about my temper, and that just ticked me off even more.

"I'm glad you're so amused," I replied, averting his mirrored eyes by going back to staring out the window.

"Oh come on, Olivia. You need to look at this from my perspective. My job is to protect you from vampires, and less than four days after we meet I find you living with an entire coven of them? What am I supposed to do? Just leave you there and say, 'hey, no problem, I'll check back in a couple of weeks to see if you're still alive' . . . ?"

"Stop the car!"

"No."

Reaching for the door handle this time, I yelled again, "Stop the car!" But it wouldn't open. My eyes now threw darts as I glared back at the rear view mirror.

Alec had been glancing through the mirror at me every few moments, but this time he beamed a rather satisfied smile at me. "Child locks," he said. "They're for when someone is behaving as if she were ten!"

Oh, I wanted to scream at him! He was being completely unreasonable. He had no idea what he had just done to me up there on the mountain. And he was supposed to protect me? He was breaking me.

I unfastened my seat belt and bolted for the open sun roof above me. Standing on the seat, my upper body was being pummeled by the speeding force of the wind while I tried to climb out and onto the roof.

"Damnit, Olivia! Are you crazy?" Steering the car to the side of the road, Alec eased the vehicle to a slow stop, avoiding slamming the breaks (which I did appreciate), so I wasn't chucked over the front of the SUV. But as the car was slowing I crawled out onto the roof and jumped to the road below at the moment it came to a stop. As I began my stormy march towards Seattle, sure that I could get there sometime before tomorrow, it occurred to me that perhaps I *was* being childish and unreasonable, but I would rather walk than have to ride with the arrogant jerk.

The other two SUVs had screeched to a halt, one stopping behind us while the other pulled in ahead. *Hadn't any of them ever heard of carpooling?* I glanced quickly over my shoulder to check them out. Lucas was in the front car, and the other two men, whom I now knew were named Phin and Ryan, were at the rear. Phin was, indeed, a Dhampir and a Vampire Hunter for The Brethren. His acute vampire senses were probably how Alec had been able to track me. So I pretty much hated him, too, right now.

"Christ, Alec, what's going on?" Lucas scowled, which seemed to be the only expression the man had—but it didn't seem to bother Alec. "Can you not control the woman?"

"Just hold on," Alec called back calmly, and I could hear the running footfalls that told me he was right on my heels.

He reached for my arm and whirled me around. Oh, yeah, despite the even tone of his voice, he was pissed. "What the hell are you doing? Do you want to get yourself killed? It's not safe for you to be out in the open like this. It's nearly dark."

Glancing over Alec's shoulder in the growing darkness, I could still see the other three men standing in the headlight beams of their vehicles and seeming to look bored, as if they were waiting for Alec to get my tantrum under control. With all these stupid, black SUV's I felt like I was being guarded by the Secret Service.

I pushed myself away from Alec by throwing my arms upward toward the sky. "I don't care! Let 'em come get me. Do you hear that? Come and get me!"

Alec stared at me in complete disbelief, his mind finally comprehending just how much pain I was in—how, in this moment, I could place so little value on my own life. I lowered my head and covered my face with my hands so he wouldn't see the agony that must be showing up there, but I was caught off guard when he drew me against him. I fought him, pounding my fists into his chest. He showed no signs that I was even hurting him. He simply grabbed my wrists and brought them down behind my back, holding me to him as I crumbled in tears against his shoulder.

Without saying a word, he let me cry and patiently waited for me to calm down. "Olivia," he began, his voice gentle but troubled, " . . . you didn't answer my question. As your protector, what would you have me do? I can't guard you against vampires when you're living with them."

I raised my eyes to him, my voice emerging as only a whisper because he was so close, his breath brushing over my cheek. "You're supposed to trust me . . . to know that I would've returned as I promised. You're supposed to trust that I wouldn't endanger my life with a coven of evil vampires. Their coven is good. They value human life, they don't take it."

Alec's eyes swept the now dark area around us. "Here," he began, taking my arm, "let's finish this discussion inside the vehicle. You can't be out here like this. It's too dangerous."

I supposed he was right, even though I really wanted to keep marching back to Seattle on my own. Alec led me back towards the SUV, and as we passed Lucas, the man's brows slashed over his scowl, an expression that certainly wasn't a stretch for him. It was obvious he'd had enough of this dramatic scene and was letting Alec know it.

Alec simply met his intense glare and said, "Stay alert."

"Of course," Lucas responded.

Alec helped me into the back seat, then scooted in beside me. He reached for my hands, but I snapped them back. Lacking appreciation for my tough stand on the issue of pissing me off, he rolled his eyes heavenward and sighed. "So, what was the plan, Olivia? To live happily ever after with a coven of vampires? To have them fight off constant threats to your life by their own kind? By them?"

When he put it that way it did seem a bit ridiculous, but it didn't lessen the absolute devastation to my heart.

"I know you don't want to hear this, but the vampires cared for you because they were drawn to you. It wasn't real."

My heart cracked all over again. I didn't want to believe that the kindness shown to me by Caleb and his coven was nothing more than an illusion. I didn't want to believe that they couldn't see even just a little part of me, the woman underneath.

"It's impossible for anyone to be around you for any length of time and not be drawn to you, and that includes me," Alec continued.

I blinked at him, never considering how my gifts might be influencing him. "My gifts affect you, too?"

He nodded. "Your gifts do affect humans, just not as intensely as vampires. Their senses are so powerful that your affect is much faster and much more painful to them. But humans can be drawn to you, too. Humans, though, must be closer, and they must touch your skin over a longer period of time. You'll probably notice it more in human men—boyfriends. Over time, they'll most likely become possessive, just as a vampire would."

I sat there for a moment in stunned silence, recalling how my past boyfriends had all been controlling and possessive. And now to realize that it wasn't *them* at all—it was *me*—was quite a shock. Yes, I had caused those feelings in each of them, the very same feelings I had blamed them for. "Will women react in the same way?"

"Some. Both men and women will be naturally drawn to you, but unless she's touching your skin a lot, your pull won't be as strong on a female. Women may feel jealousy towards you because the men around you won't be focused on them, but that can happen to any woman," he laughed lightly.

My lips pursed, trying to hide the smile I really wanted to respond with. He seemed pleased that my anger towards him was easing. "What's the difference, then? Why are you touching me now if I can hurt you in the same way?"

"You're not hurting me," he assured, pulling his hand back from mine almost as if he hadn't realized it was there. "I know the truth. I've been trained on what to expect. I know when I'm drawn to you, as I am right now—but I also know that it's not real. So I've no expectations of you other than that you'll let me do my job." He paused for a long moment before adding, "You had to leave him, Olivia."

Though it pained me to admit it, he was right. I had lied to Caleb, betrayed his trust—betrayed all of them. There would be nothing I could do to make up for that, and there would have been no way for me to stay.

"I'm sorry I hurt you today," Alec offered sincerely. "I'll keep my promise to you and not go back. But you must start accepting your future before you're hurt or killed."

There he went again, giving me the simple truth and holding nothing back. That was something I really appreciated about

Alec. Maybe the truth would be exactly what I'd need to start me down the path I'd choose for myself.

His hand stroked over my hair, his need to touch me making me wonder if he had as much control over the illusion as he believed. "What's bothering you?" he asked.

"You'll think it's stupid."

"Try me," he said, wiping the last of the tears from my cheek.

"It's just that . . . how will I . . . how *can* I . . . ever know true love in my life? You know, the kind where the other person is as in love with you as you are with them? If everyone around me is just responding to some illusion I'm projecting, how will someone ever truly love me? And how will I ever know it?"

I glanced up to see a warm smile on his face. "You'll know true love," he replied. "You just have to know what to look for. This energy you have fades as you're no longer around the person. With true love, his feelings will never fade, even when you're away from him. He'll not try to possess you like an object. He'll put your needs equal to—or ahead of—his own."

Alec then lifted my chin very gently, bringing my eyes back to his. "He'll let you be free, Olivia. That kind of love will be more powerful than your gifts. Your touch won't affect him."

"Free? I guess we're not talking about anyone from The Brethren, then," I joked. Alec ignored my attempt at humor, perhaps taking personal offense, so I changed the subject. "Caleb will stop loving me, then, after I'm gone?"

Alec rolled his eyes. "So, Caleb's the vampire's name? Yes, trust me, he'll eventually return to the dark life he was leading before you met him. He'll be fine."

If anything good was to come from this miserable day, it was that only one of us would have to carry the burden of a shattered heart. I would accept that pain as the way in which I'd have to repay the horrible mess I had caused, if only I knew for certain that Caleb would return to his happy life with Gemma and Jax.

"Let's get you home," he smiled.

"No, not home . . . the church. Caleb can't sense me there. It'll help him get over me faster."

Alec paused, appearing to consider that for a moment. "That is, if Father Karras will let us?"

Shaking his head, he said, "It should be fine. We'll only be here a few more days. I'm hoping you'll agree to leave here soon and start your training."

"Alec!" a frustrated Lucas barked from outside the car. "For fuck sake man! What's going on? Are you negotiating a peace treaty in there?"

I gasped in outright shock. Why were these Guardians so handicapped in making a first impression? "Olivia, don't—" Alec interrupted. But I was determined to give his friend a piece of my mind.

I lowered the window beside me and stuck my head out. "Are you ever nice?" I snapped at him. Lucas responded by muttering more curses under his breath while Ryan, the youngest of the four men, stifled a laugh and succeeded only in snorting in amusement.

I was about to add to my previous comment when Alec stopped me by placing his hand on my arm. "Believe it or not, he's just concerned because it's dark. He knows we need to get you out of here. He's a good man, just takes a bit of getting used to."

Alec then closed the sun roof to the cooler night air. "Wait here in the car. I need to let Lucas and Ryan know what's going on." He reached into the front seat to grab a bottle of water, and grinned. "Phin already knows. Lock the door behind me."

He joined Lucas and Ryan at the front car. I watched as they engaged in a low but intense exchange of words after Lucas asked Alec, "How the hell do you explain vampires being outside during the day?"

Interesting. So The Brethren didn't know about Daywalkers.

Taking a slow sip from the water bottle Alec left, I felt it. That familiar pull over my chest that had been absent since I left the mountain. Hesitating for a moment, I scanned the distance through the window beside me, trying to figure out the warning inside my chest. I wondered if Jax was nearby and I just didn't recognize his energy. But as the feeling began to suffocate my heart, I realized there was nothing familiar about it.

I could hardly breathe!

"Alec!" Phin called in warning. "We've got company."

I turned to see the Hunter grabbing several weapons from the back of the vehicle, racing them to the other Guardians in seconds. Alec's head snapped up as his wide eyes found mine just before he turned towards the darkness. Following his eyes over my left shoulder, I saw an object torpedoing towards me through the night air. My breath caught as two bloodshot eyes pierced the darkness, and I saw two arms outstretched in front of them. I had just enough time to begin a scream before the SUV was pounded with shattering force, sending it rolling over the roadside embankment.

Metal scraped and glass shattered as the car flipped several times down the twenty-foot embankment. I felt like clothing being tossed around inside of a dryer.

When the rollover finally stopped I was able to take a few seconds to try and comprehend what had just happened before the door above me was ripped from its hinges and tossed like a Frisbee into the air. I screamed when those long, hideous arms snatched me from the wreckage and hauled me into the night. Long, pale fingers and sharp nails bit into my shirt as I was held in the crushing grip of the dark shadow behind me. I glanced in horror up the embankment to find Alec and the others already battling for their lives with at least a half dozen other vampires. "Oh, God."

Suddenly, my captor roughly lifted up the hair at the back of my neck and I felt ice-cold fingers rubbing over the tattoo at the base of my skull. A low, harsh laugh crackled from the vampire's throat as he spun me around to face his gaunt features. My entire body froze as I recognized Isaac glowering down at me with that icy-pale stare of his, the stink of his awful breath nearly choking me.

"Oh, my . . . You're even prettier than I remember," he said, his tongue licking over his bottom lip as bile rose up in my throat. "Guess you're all mine now that you're no longer under his protection." He flipped me back against him, his aroused body pressing against me as his rough hands pried between my thighs. "Oh, we're going to have fun," he rasped in my ear. "I'd fuck you right here, but alas, there's no time."

Oh, God. Please, no!

I caught site of Alec, battling with fierce force against his attacker. After he drove a silver-tipped arrow into the vampire's heart, instantly immobilizing him, he turned to find me.

"Alec!" I cried to him.

He barreled down the embankment towards me with steely determination in his eyes, but just before he could reach us, Isaac bounded high into the trees above, stealing me away into the night.

"Olivia!" he called, just as another vampire descended on top of him.

"No, Alec!" Soon I could no longer see him through the darkness as Isaac dragged me farther into the forest. I prayed that he and the others would be OK even as dizziness came over me from the almost weightless feeling of springing blindly from tree to tree through the pitch black of night. Isaac held me like a rag doll, my arms trapped at my sides by one of his arms while he grabbed for outstretched limbs with the other.

"You fool!" a harsh voice snapped when Isaac finally came to a stop. "Use the chloroform. She needs to be unconscious or she'll be easy for him to track."

Him? He couldn't mean Alec. Alec would never be able to—

My heart stopped. He meant Caleb. Caleb would be able to feel my panic. I didn't know if he would even help me after what I had done to him today, but he was the best chance I had right now.

I had to fight!

I struggled against Isaac's unrelenting hold on me, kicking him as hard as I could while he was trying to bring the toxic rag over my mouth. In my mind I screamed for Caleb, hoping he would somehow hear my plea and still want to help. Isaac's hold around my waist loosened as he tried to maintain his agile balance on the tree limb.

Then, suddenly, another hand grabbed the rag from Isaac and slammed it over my mouth, jerking it back hard against my lips. The sweet-smelling cloth was choking me, and I feared the force being used would soon have me swallowing the rag.

Continuing to fight, I begged for fresh oxygen, but as the noxious gas filled my lungs, I began to lose strength until my limbs fell weightless. Then the blackness came.

***

When I regained consciousness I was being jolted, upward then downward. I was closely contained in a dark, cramped space. Every few seconds, the rushing sound of waves crashing against whatever I was traveling in told me that I was in a speedboat that was slicing through water. The vampires were taking me off the mainland. Remembering the situation just before I was knocked out, I immediately worried that the more distance between myself and Caleb and Alec, the less chance there would be that they'd be able to find me . . . if they were trying at all.

Alec might very well be dead because of me, and I feared that Caleb hated me. I couldn't forget the numb expression of disappointment and sadness on Caleb's face as he learned I had deceived him. It was etched into my memory forever.

My head throbbed, and my tongue was coated with the medicinal taste of the chloroform fumes. I knew I had to focus on my surroundings so I could determine where I had been taken. I was stretched out flat on some sort of cushion, able to see nothing, capable only of listening to the sounds in the darkness. The air I was breathing was stagnant and thin. My hands examined the four padded walls snug around me and I began to panic.

It felt like I was in a coffin.

I didn't have long to adjust to the idea, because a panel swung open above me to expose Isaac's snarl staring down at me. "Hello there, beauty. Did you have a nice sleep?"

"Don't—" I started just before he pinned me down inside the storage hold and jammed the rag back over my mouth, the sweet smelling liquid once again filling my head as I screamed for Caleb in my mind.

Then there was nothing.

The second time I woke, my skin was freezing, as if I were wrapped in dry ice. Cold winds blew over me so fast that my teeth actually chattered. At least I wasn't in that coffin thing, I thought, so I risked opening my eyes, and the first thing I saw was a blurred landscape racing by at a speed that made me dizzy. I was lying on ice-cold, ribbed metal and heard the sound of wheels scraping along steel tracks, telling me that I was on train. But I could see the sky above. I was, literally, on the *roof* of a speeding train car!

I turned my head and saw Isaac, in his human form, a man just as distasteful as the vampire Isaac, with his bony nose and sharply jutting chin, gaunt complexion, and lifeless dark eyes. He saw I was awake and reached into his pocket to retrieve a small glass bottle and rag. I cringed at the thought of any more of the sweet-smelling liquid being shoved against my face. My head was aching at my temples—a result, I was sure, of the toxic anesthetic.

After pouring the liquid onto the rag, he was atop my body in an instant, trapping my limbs to the cold metal beneath. But this time, fear was not my primary emotion—anger was. I was tired of being schlepped around like a piece of meat, my mouth stuffed with a toxic vapor that was making me sick and my body so cold in the night air that I thought I was developing frostbite on my hands and feet.

I despised Isaac with every ounce of my being, and it would be a chilly day in hell before I let him touch me, lick me, or fuck me, as he threatened. Now straddled over my waist, he prepared to stuff the choking rag back into my mouth. I used all the strength I had to pull my arm out from between his legs, swinging so hard against his arm that the bottle of chloroform and rag dislodged from his grip, forcing him to juggle to hold onto it and thus shifting his focus to the items instead of paying attention to me.

While he was off balance in this way I kneed him in the groin, the force of it doubling him over, groaning, and then I delivered an immediate second blow, my free foot smashing into his chest, which sent him over the side of the car. Knowing he would return soon, I crawled as fast as I could toward the nearest ladder that would take me down to a platform between the cars, hoping that once inside with other people, the vampires would not want to be discovered.

The scenery around me was unfamiliar, rugged, and lush, like a temperate rainforest. Farther off in the distance were the moonlit waters of the Pacific. I understood I was somewhere near the coast . . . but the coast of where?

The ladder's side rails were in my grasp and I was climbing down toward the platform vestibule when I noticed the train's emblem on the side of the car. The decorative script read *Vancouver Island Railway.* They had taken me across the water to the enormous island off the coast of Canada. I didn't know if it was even possible for Caleb or Alec to find me over such a long distance and separated by such a large body of water, so I needed to get inside this car.

My hands gripped at the frigid railing as I tried pulling myself through the force of the wind and onto the train itself. But I had no time to get my bearings or to prepare my body for any sort of normal movement. A sound, a gnarling growl like that of an angry wolf, erupted from behind me as my feet hit the floor. I swung around just before Isaac's hands latched around my ankles, yanking my legs out from under me. I fell hard onto the steel roof and almost instantly was trapped beneath his thighs again. He no longer had the chloroform or the rag, so I knew that when he had fallen from the train, he must have realized that he needed to get back to where he could control me rather than to retrieve the tools he had used to incapacitate me. Now his face was full of fury, and I detected yet another figure moving behind him. I couldn't see who it was, but I caught a glimpse as Isaac leaned forward to comply with the order from the other man.

"Get it done. Don't let her touch your skin," the sharp voice snapped, his long, blanched fingers clutching the hood of his cloak to keep it from blowing back from the force of the wind and revealing his face.

The deep cuts from Isaac's fall from the speeding train had caused severe damage to his face and limbs. Though he was already grotesque, I took some satisfaction in knowing I had made him more so and hurt him some in the process, even as I could see that his wounds were already healing themselves. But the violent seething contained in his words was the last thing I remembered.

"You bitch!" he snapped, curling his gloved hand back and blasting it hard across my cheek.

Chapter Twenty-Three

When I regained consciousness all I could feel was the pounding in my cheek from the force of Isaac's blow just before I blacked out. Gingerly touching my hand to the swollen skin, one thing was clear . . . the foul-breathed vampire had a brutal backhand.

I wasn't quite sure I wanted to open my eyes this time, fearing that Isaac might be standing right there above me, ready to strike again. But wherever I was, it was eerily quiet, as though no one was there but me, even though I still felt the tightness over my heart that meant Isaac was close by.

Carefully sliding my eyelids open, I watched the dim room come into focus. Crumbling stone walls and floors, rough and uneven, were the nicest thing about the drafty room. Moonlight beamed down on my small, metal cot through a steel-barred opening high in the ceiling above me. I was lying on a lumpy mattress, the musty infusion of dirt and mold overwhelming every other scent in the room.

As I sat up slowly and finally rose to my feet, I felt more than a little unsteady. The chloroform, freezing cold winds, and the mighty backhand across my cheek had all taken their toll, and I just wished I could go home.

"Sorry about the accommodations," intoned a rough, masculine voice.

Startled, I swung on my heels to face a man old enough to be my grandfather. He was moving towards me in eerie silence and with effortless strides, almost as if he were floating across the room. When he reached me, his head tilted up and back with an arrogance that fit more with the aristocracy than with vampires, gazing on me with arched, gray brows and a disapproving purse to his lips. He was pale and a bit heavy, the passing of his previous human life wrinkling his skin and silvering the little hair he had left. In spite of his proud carriage and large size, he appeared frailer than his bloodthirsty counterparts, but his eyes were far from frail. Cold, they were, and black as coal; there was absolutely no warmth in them. Yes, these were the eyes of pure evil.

"Where am I, and why have you taken me?" I demanded.

I had no idea where all this bravado was coming from; my hands were trembling at my sides.

The vampire continued to sweep around me, seemingly without moving his feet, those black eyes of his never leaving me. "So many questions for someone with so little life experience. If I were you, I would give more consideration to the tone with which you ask them."

OK, so he was letting me know that this situation was completely in his control, which I really couldn't argue with.

"This used to be an old prison, about a hundred and fifty years ago. It's boarded up and unused now except for the occasional vampire accommodations in a pinch." Spreading his arms to indicate the space around us, he added, "As for why we brought you here, I assure you, Olivia, this wasn't my first choice. Even a bloodthirsty vampire has to have standards."

Great. A vampire who thought he had a sense of humor.

"Don't get me wrong, I applaud your tenacity. Just as we found you, you managed to get yourself tangled up with a very protective and irritatingly persistent vampire. He's been making my efforts to acquire you most difficult, ever since he interfered with that train crash. We put a lot of effort into finding you on that train."

I didn't like at all how familiar he seemed to be with Caleb, nor did I like the fact that he was confirming the suspicions about the train crash that Caleb already had. "You crashed an entire train, killed all of those innocent people, just to get to me? Why? Why didn't you just take *me?*"

"Yes, that would've been a better plan. But you see, Olivia, I knew I was looking for you, I just couldn't recognize you—except, of course, for your tattoo. I mean, since Isaac and his coven had to check the back of every passenger's neck for a tattoo, they might as well get a little something for their efforts, don't you think?"

Two things were just made clear to me: one, this man was sick; and two, I was responsible for the fate of all of those passengers. If only I had never gotten on the train that night! But then I would have never known Caleb, and this man would have eventually found me, either way. Who knew if, when he did, he might have ended up having killed even more people?

"When my second attempt to acquire you failed, after your vampire finally left your side, I didn't think I would get another opportunity so soon."

"The Rogue," I whispered. "You sent him to attack us?"

"Well, no, his task was merely to bring you to me, but I hadn't counted on the fact that you seem to be growing into your gifts rather quickly. That is actually fine, though—fits with my plans quite nicely. Then, to add to my good fortune, you yourself opened the door for me today when you left the vampire's protection and went with The Brethren Guardians and Hunter. I know well the strength and weaknesses of each."

At the mention of the Guardians I thought about Alec. I didn't even know whether he or his team had survived the vampire attack. They were completely outnumbered, and it was all because of my tantrum. If anything happened to them because of me, I would never forgive myself.

"Once I had you, I needed to get you far enough away from the vampire so he wouldn't sense you. Caleb is his name, right? A little too cocky for his own good, I think, but we'll take care of that."

Another shiver ran down my spine just then. I was so glad Caleb wouldn't come. I didn't want him anywhere near this despicable man. "He won't come for me."

"Ah, yes, that whole messy Charmer business. Well, if he's too short-sighted to see the potential benefits of having a Charmer at his side, then good for you for getting rid of him—though it's certainly no secret that he can feel you quite strongly. I'll be disappointed, in fact, if he doesn't show up. I was rather looking forward to killing him for all of the trouble he has caused . . . but not before I let him know that you'll be under *my* protection from now on."

"He won't come for me!" I snapped, my heart pounding so hard I could hear it beating in my ears. Relax, Olivia, he doesn't even know where you are. He won't come.

"Listen to your heart pound, child. You really do care for the vampire, don't you?"

Desperate to get off this subject, I snapped, "What do you want with me?"

His black eyes seemed to come to life, as if he were playing a game. "We're going to run some experiments. Should be great fun."

"Experiments?"

"Yes. I knew your mother well. She was a special creature. But you, Olivia . . . I believe are even more special. I saw it in you from when you were a very young girl. You were my special project, so to speak. After your mother died, I fostered your development myself—before you were entrusted to those silly fools, the Hendrickses."

I blinked at him. "You're Luther Davin."

"Of course, child," he drawled, "and it's time you show me just how gifted you really are."

Comprehending the seriousness of my situation, I focused only on finding a way out of this horrible place and away from this vile man. I was trapped on an unfamiliar island with two malicious vampires, one of whom wanted to run experiments on me like a lab rat, while the other wanted me as a mate. As the knot began to ball up ever more tightly in my stomach I tried to tell myself that I couldn't give up. For all of my threats to Alec to just let them come and do what they wanted with me, I didn't really mean it. I didn't mean it!

"There's a water basin over there with clean rags, and you'll find a fresh set of clothes on the chair. Use them and get the scent of that vampire off of you. But keep your feet bare, no shoes. You'll need to have your skin exposed if you're to survive the evening."

"No!" I shot back in defiance, trying not to focus on his last words . . . 'if you are to survive.'

His slick smile only widened; he seemed to enjoy my act of rebellion. "Such spirit. Good. Of course, it's your choice, child. Either you can do it or I can send Isaac in here to do it for you. My guess is, though, that he'd prefer to *lick* you clean instead of wash you."

I struggled to swallow, revolted at the thought. "I'll do it!" I said with a hard breath, trying to sound strong but falling far short.

"Wise choice. You've one hour."

Once he left the room, I fell to my knees on the grimy floor, hugging my arms around my shoulders as if they would somehow sustain me through the night. I didn't know how I got here, and I was scared out of my mind. Kneeling there, I realized there was no hope for help. I didn't know if Alec and the others had survived the vampire attack, and Caleb wouldn't be able to find me in time—if he was even looking for me at all. I was fine with that, though. My life would be over, anyway, if anything happened to him because of me.

Pull it together, Olivia! He wouldn't want you to give up. You must fight to live. Fight!

Just then, I realized that I wouldn't have wanted to fight six weeks ago. My more conciliatory nature would've surrendered in hopelessness. The warrior had changed me. After knowing such joy with him—knowing it was possible to love so deeply in this life—made me want to survive. Even if I had little chance to live and would never see him again, the warrior would always fight.

And so would I.

Inhaling deeply, I moved to the water basin, quickly removing my clothing but spending precious time to fold the shirt I had grabbed from Caleb's closet. I pressed the soft cotton to my nose and inhaled his scent—sage, fir and man.

My heart felt as if it were drowning in pain. Why couldn't I just keep this one thing? This one piece of him?

I washed with the fresh rags and water from the basin. It did feel good to clean myself after being dragged around by Isaac, but no amount of soap and water would be able to scrub away his stench.

Grabbing the clothes from the chair, I unfolded a simple, full-length, white linen dress. Loose-fitted below the hip, a deep v-line cut dropped over the chest and plunged to the stomach. Long-sleeved arms draped wide at the wrist, while the dress itself cinched at the waist.

I rolled my eyes at Davin's flare for the dramatic. This dress seemed ridiculous, considering the situation. But I wasn't about to challenge him by wearing my old clothes and having him send Isaac in to change me. I left my feet bare, as he had instructed, but they were already cold against the rough stone floor.

Because I had worked so quickly I still had about twenty-five minutes before the one-hour deadline was up. I started looking for a way out, and it didn't take me long to zoom in on the barred window high above me. The opening between the bars was small, but I thought I could fit if I could somehow climb the fifteen feet to the ceiling.

I fixed on the opening, realizing I had never tested my jumping abilities to this height, at least not going up. But if Gemma could make that tall leap up to the glass doors of the tree house, then I should be able to at least do this.

Concentrating, I squatted low on my knees and then sprung upward with all the strength I could muster, swinging my arms high, feeling the lift in my muscles as I pushed off from the ground. Stretching for the window bars above, my arms found unexpected strength as they gripped the bars and pulled my body towards the moonlight. The frigid air hit my face, signaling freedom—just before rough arms grabbed me from below, wrapping tightly around my waist and causing me to lose my grip. Amazingly, I didn't drop to the floor below. My captor—whom I instantly identified as Isaac by the putrid smell of his breath—simply floated us down. And while that was happening, I felt my arms being forced to my sides and pinned there with amazing strength. Before I knew it, my bare feet again made contact with the cold floor. I didn't have to see Isaac's face to know how much hatred he possessed for me.

What I did see, directly in front of me, was Davin, his black eyes now assessing the clothing he had provided as it draped my cold body. "Yes, that will do nicely. Isaac?"

His grip loosened, and I swung on him, just in time to see his fist coming at my face before the world went black again.

When I returned to consciousness, I found myself lying down, shackled in iron chains to a cement block in an open, grassy field, my limbs numb in the bitter, evening cold. There was a bright full moon above me. I rolled onto my side, pulling the chains with me, until the thick shackles tautened and tore at my wrists. The grassy field sat high atop a rocky cliff, and the soaring Pacific Ocean stretched far beyond, with no land in sight. I guessed we must be somewhere on the western side of Vancouver Island, which meant I couldn't be any further west without swimming

Slowly rising to my feet, I looked around and noticed another figure chained to a second platform about fifteen yards in front of me. The man was on his knees, his head and shoulders slumped forward as if he didn't have an ounce of energy, and his arms were extended, held by chains similar to mine.

Davin was there, too, between me and the other captive, looking extraordinarily pleased with himself. "Perfect timing," he said. "Things are just about to start."

"Why are you doing this?" I pleaded. "If you cared at all about my mother or me as a child, how can you do this?"

"You were like a daughter to me, Olivia . . . a very special girl. But the other Elders believed your charm over me was affecting my judgment, so they placed you in the care of foster parents who were trained to handle your gifts. Stupid decision on their part."

"But why are you doing this?"

"It's simple really . . . survival. Now that I'm part of this world, I must survive. In the short time I've lived among the vampires, I've managed to unite three covens."

It didn't make any sense. Why would the vampires unite under a man who clearly was not as powerful or strong?

As if he could read my mind, his lips curved into a knowing smile. "Becoming a vampire has its advantages. I seem to have acquired the ability to persuade others to come around to my way of thinking. It's proven useful in getting them to follow me. And in exchange for being their leader, I've promised to deliver the ultimate weapon against the vampire's worst enemy—the Lycanthrope."

I blinked at him, not sure I had heard him correctly.

"Lycanthrope?" he repeated. "Just think of it as a stronger, smarter werewolf."

He couldn't be serious!

"You see, child, it's a win-win. The three covens get their weapon to fight against the Lycans—namely you. And I get back my birthright to rule. Not over The Brethren, but over the largest, most powerful coven in this part of the planet. And as I keep building it—with your help, of course—eventually I will rule the world."

"You're insane!" I said with a shocked gasp. "You can't do this. I'm chained! I've no way to defend myself."

"Oh, but you do, I assure you. You have your touch. My, but you're a fetching girl. I've kept my distance, and yet I still feel completely drawn to you. Your poor vampire must be turned inside out over you. And just look at what you've done to Isaac, here. Why, he's no better than a dog, really, who wants to lick a juicy bone."

Before I took even two seconds to think better of it, I spit at him, hitting him squarely on his left cheek. He had to have been caught off guard, but he didn't show it. His hand moved slowly to wipe the saliva from his skin, a low, incensed growl emanating from deep inside himself as Isaac came forward—but Davin stopped him, raising his palm into the air. "Careful, child."

In the end, my small show of defiance wouldn't matter, because his next words absolutely froze me in place. "There's been a Lycan hunting in these woods for the past several weeks. His appetite seems to be insatiable right now. And, if I'm right, he'll be drawn to you like a magnet. But I believe your gifts may be powerful enough to sway the creature from tearing you apart. Of course, if I'm wrong . . . well. . . ."

His words absolutely paralyzed me. Horrific images of what I was about to face started flashing in my mind. Now I had multiple knots tightening in my stomach, feeling as if they were being pulled from two opposing sides deep inside myself.

Oh, God, why didn't I listen to Alec and stay in the car!

Just then, the slumped figure chained to the other platform raised his head. It was the Rogue who attacked Gemma and me at the tree house. He had survived the glass through his heart and the long fall to the ground below, but now he seemed doomed to share the same inescapable fate as mine. Several long, silver chains were hanging from his neck, glistening against the moonlight and burning like sun into his skin. The silver was making him weak and unable to break free of his chains, which normally he would be easily capable of doing.

"He's here to test which one of you the Lycan goes for first. It's his penance for doing such an inept job of trying to bring you to me the first time. And for letting his thirst get the better of him."

"How can you do this to your own kind?"

Davin didn't get a chance to answer the question because a sudden, high-pitched howl sounded just beyond the tree line. The beast they had been waiting for was here.

"Time to go, child. Don't disappoint me," he said as he and Isaac bounded high into the safety of the trees to observe, the menacing howl of the Lycan sounding again.

Only this time, much closer.

Chapter Twenty-Four

So this was it. This was to be my fate—one I could never have imagined. As my bare feet rattled against the frigid concrete, I raised my chin, deciding I was going to face this with as much strength as I possibly could. Yet all it took was another shrill howl from the approaching beast to weaken my newfound steel resolve. The Lycan was almost on top of us, our bodies' scents drawing him straight to us.

Beyond terrified, I tried so hard to wrench my hands through the heavy shackles that both of them began to bleed. Reaching for one of the chains and grasping it with both hands, I dug my heels into the platform, using my arms to try and break free, but their retaining bolts still did not budge, and every link remained unbroken.

Irrationally, I was angry at Alec and almost cursed his name. How dare he let me believe I have strength when I can't even manage to get out of a simple set of iron chains when I need to!

Then, out of the tree-line darkness, the Lycan appeared. The beast's body was enormous, resembling a large, walking wolf. His hindquarters were thin at the hips and waist, but his front limbs and shoulders were massive, like those of a grizzly bear. The force and power of this creature centered there, as well as in his front claws and elongated snout, which, gaping open as he bellowed in rage, displayed several rows of serrated, canine-like teeth. My eyes widened in total disbelief and awe, and I tried to force my gaze to look away—but I couldn't. The enormous creature continued to pound forward, zeroing in on his target, and I could have sworn that my heart stopped beating. I continued to fight wildly against the chains, desperate to somehow pull myself to freedom, but the metal cuffs only cut deeper into my skin.

It was no use; I wasn't strong enough.

The Lycan's angry glare fixed on the defenseless vampire still slumped under the weight of all that silver. The Rogue raised his head, his barely-there, icy-blue eyes glaring at the creature in warning as he drew closer. Snarling rage erupted from the vampire's throat as he presented his sharp fangs, but he had very little strength and was already using what was left to try and rip the silver from his neck. His hands burned visibly as he touched the scalding metal, and his snarl turned into a whine of anguish from the pain.

Rising up in a victorious stance over his prey, the Lycan stretched to its full height, easily reaching eight feet, dwarfing the weakened vampire beneath him. He snapped open his thick snout even wider now and saliva began to drool from the rim of his gums.

I turned my head away, closing my eyes, unwilling to witness the savage attack that was about to take place. The ferocious noises of war broke out in front of me, sounding like the crunch of a shark's jaws thrashing into a seal. My arms and legs were shaking so much that I even began to lose my ability to stand up. I raised my head toward the heavens, letting the tears roll from my eyes and down my face, and prepared myself for the end, praying for the strength to meet my fate with as much courage as I could. And I was surprised at the place to which my mind retreated as I tried to escape that paralyzing fear.

I had always imagined that in the moments just before my death I would flash on all the significant memories of my life, but that was not what happened. Instead, an image appeared in my head, the vision so vivid, so real, I could feel the tiniest sensations moving within it.

***

I was free!

Under the starry skies of blue night, I raced along the forest floor, flying past rugged landscape and thick trees, the full moon lighting a path ahead of me. My feet skimmed the earth as if it had never known the pull of gravity, allowing me to push my newly discovered Dhampir body to its absolute limits. Unlike the first time I ran like this, on the long climb up the mountain to the tree house, the heavy underbrush and fallen logs were of no concern. My easy breathing and sure steps came so naturally that it was as if I'd known this part of myself my entire life.

Crisp, night air pressed against my cheeks and I knew, 'this is what it feels like to fly.'

***

I wanted to hold on to this image, sink into its power, and feel its gentle caress of my soul. The peace and serenity of this moment was something to be grateful for—just one thing. But the Lycan's piercing howl snapped me back from my reverie. Finished with its attack on the lifeless vampire, it now made his way toward me, the rage inside the jaundice-like, orange-yellow coloring of his eyes radiating just as fiercely as it had with the Rogue.

I snapped my eyes closed, trying to find comfort in the image once again.

***

This time, the wet, rain forest terrain surrounding me was familiar, and the full moon hanging overhead had the same spectacular white glow as the one above me now. It was all the same! My breath caught in my throat as gripping pressure constricted my chest, but this specific signal to my heart was one that my mind easily recognized. Pulling back inside the image, I now understood it wasn't me flying across the forest. The tall, hard figure continuing to push the muscles of his body to the brink could only be one.

Hope lifted my soul, and my heart pounded in my ears like the increasing, rhythmic beats of a drum. Just as on the night of the attack by the Rogue, I could see him—somehow I could feel him. The vampire's long arms swung his powerful frame forward under even breaths. His gray eyes were focused ahead of him, fixed with determination, resolve, and unrelenting purpose.

He was coming. Caleb was coming.

No, Caleb! It's too late for me. Go back.

Another shrill howl jarred me out of my connection. The

Lycan's enormous form loomed just over me, his vicious snout sniffing at my face as saliva dropped onto my collarbone. The shaking in my limbs and the hammering in my heart were now out of control. I feared that any second he would tear me apart in his jaws.

"*Caleb*," I whispered, because I wanted it to be the last word I spoke, but the Lycan seemed to hesitate just then. His hot breath all but scorched my throat as the coarse hairs around his snout poked at my skin. The creature appeared stalled, guarded, even confused as he continued to sniff over my skin.

Concentrating again on the figure tearing through the moonlight towards me, I could see Caleb clearly now. He was driving his body harder, as if he just expected it to respond. His clothes, the dark jeans and long navy shirt, were unchanged from when we were last safe together on the mattress. It was as if his body had not stopped since I had left him standing there in the mountain meadow.

I was stunned. Even after everything I had done to him—the lies, the deceit—the warrior was still coming for me. Still chasing some kind of redemption, I guessed.

Feeling the steady rhythm of his heavy breathing as if they were my own breaths, I matched mine to his, wanting to be one with him in these final moments. But sharp anger slashed over his brows as his lips moved for the first time. I couldn't hear him, but I could read the single, tense word on his lips —"Olivia." It was as if he was ordering me not to give up, to keep fighting, to know that he would be there soon—and I found strength through him.

If he wasn't giving up on me, then I wouldn't give up on myself. "I'll find a way."

Then his powerful body leaped forward onto a steep, mountainous incline, his feet not missing a single step as he tore up the angled terrain. If possible, his strides were even longer as the muscles flexed in his thighs, adjusting to the vertical climb. He crested the hill, where the ground leveled off and became a flat, grassy plain with the ocean cliffs just beyond. My breath caught as the change in his eyes occurred— the soulful gray of the man replaced by the warrior's brilliant, sapphire-blue.

The fierce creature from the night of the train crash was close—and he was ready for battle.

***

The Lycan's deep growl brought me back to the reality of the moment. If I wanted to survive this, I had to stall him, at least long enough for Caleb to get here. My head had been forced back by the animal's sharp teeth right there at my throat, his sticky, odorous breath triggering nauseating bile to rise to the back of my mouth.

Slowly, I reached my hand up, extending my fingertips until the beast's brittle hairs were threaded between my fingers. Grazing my hand over his shoulder in gentle, soothing strokes, I watched as the Lycan's sounds seemed to calm with each pass. The beast appeared confused, as if he couldn't decide what to do with me.

My touch was working! I couldn't believe it. And when I stared more closely into the animal's eyes, I thought I could see traces of the man, the human beneath the beast's terrifying exterior. For a brief moment, unbelievably, the rage in his eyes was replaced with a flicker of . . . what was it? Pain?

"It's OK," I whispered, and the animal let out a moan that sounded almost like whimpering, not unlike that of a dog rolling over in its sleep.

I started to think that everything might be all right, but suddenly the Lycan pulled back and began tearing at my chains. It took me only a moment to realize that he was trying to free me so he could take me with him.

That hadn't been part of the plan at all!

Within a single heartbeat, the beast had ripped one of the chains from the concrete foundation and was reaching for the other one.

"No!" I cried, just before the Lycan's head snapped up and a thunderous howl left his throat.

My blue-eyed warrior slammed into him with such force, it drove them both into the ground with the impact of a Mack truck.

Caleb flew instantly back to his feet, focused, his attack stance fearless, the corded muscles in his shoulders flexing as he mirrored the movements of the beast. Absent was any doubt that he wouldn't defeat the terrifying creature now arising to tower over him. I remembered Gemma's words—that the warrior did not consider his own life when in battle.

"Oh, God," I cried, pulling with both hands on the remaining chain. "Caleb."

I was too weak to break through the thick metal. Angry, I whipped the chain down, cutting my skin more deeply at my wrist and stifling a cry of excruciating pain. Caleb's face flashed in fury between pounding blows as the scent of my fresh blood reached him. The Lycan took full advantage while Caleb was distracted, driving him backwards towards the ground, the animal's savage jaws snapping at him just before the warrior disappeared from my view behind the evil creature's giant body.

"No!" I cried, remembering the horrible sounds of the beast ripping into the Rogue, fearing that soon the animal would kill the one person who meant everything in the world to me. It felt like I had held my breath for the longest moment of my life when suddenly, Jax charged in, his big wall of a body pounding against the beast and forcing the Lycan's deadly snout away from Caleb.

"Jax! Thank, God," I whispered, relieved that Caleb would not be fighting alone.

The creature rose to its full height and released an ear-shattering roar as it turned toward Jax. Caleb, momentarily freed from the beast's grip, was quick to respond, knocking the monster backward with such force it swept all the breath out of my body. In that moment, Caleb was stronger than Jax, and he knew it, feeding the muscles that pushed him forward with fury.

Caleb avoided another loud snap of the Lycan's jaws and thrust an iron elbow at the creature's ribs, causing a loud cracking sound to whip through the night air.

My attention was ripped from the scene by a sudden blast of cool air against my body. A familiar, bright angel appeared in front of me, flashing a quick smile before reaching for the chains. "Let's get you out of here," she said.

"Gemma! I'm so glad to see you."

We barely had time to reach for the chains before a large force smashed against us, sweeping us both from our feet. Gemma crashed to the grass below, while I fell hard on my back against the concrete block. I cried out at the searing pain of the chain that was cutting into my wrist again. Caleb heard my cry and looked over with anguished fury in his eyes.

For a moment I thought he was going to leave Jax, but the beast was soon on him again.

Don't be distracted, Caleb.

Shaking away the dizziness, I swung around to see Isaac crouched over Gemma. He had her pinned to the ground with his long, strong arms, and his sharp fangs were moving for her neck. Without hesitation, I stretched my arm as far as the chain would allow, cutting deeper into my skin, but I gained the last couple of inches needed to kick my foot toward the jaw of the vampire. Got him! The contact with my skin stunned him. He staggered to his feet and backward, shaking his head, his baleful glare shooting fire like darts just before he lunged at me.

When his body slammed into mine I was crushed against the platform, the wind knocked out of me. Gasping, I managed to claw at his face, focusing as hard as I could. Got him again!

He staggered backward, allowing me a momentary reprieve.

"Olivia!" Gemma called out, bounding to her feet just before Isaac turned and lunged at her. She leapt into the air, floating light as a feather just out of his reach, daring Isaac with her eyes to challenge her.

"So, the Dhampir wants to play," Isaac snarled, hurling his body into the air, where they collided with shattering force before spiraling to the ground.

Gemma bounced back to her feet, but Isaac barreled at her again from his hands and knees, giving the small woman no chance to recover before smashing her brutally against the edge of the concrete slab. Blood started to pour from her scalp, and her unmoving figure now lay perfectly still beside me.

Isaac laughed wickedly. "Oh, don't tell me playtime's over, honey. I was just getting started."

Gemma!"

Isaac's dark eyes shifted to me. I was preparing for another hard blow when a lightning-fast arrow sank into his chest.

Isaac's rage bordered on madness as he cursed under his breath and pulled at the silver-tipped arrow. Stunned, I glanced over to see Alec look away from aiming his crossbow, just a trace of a satisfied smile spreading over his lips as he quickly reloaded. His concentrated gaze slid to me for a second before he shot a second arrow into the vampire's chest. The silver tip just missed Isaac's heart. Now I noticed that Lucas, Phin and Ryan were all standing behind Alec, preparing their weapons.

They were OK! They had survived!

I ripped a large piece of cloth from my dress and bunched it into a ball to press against Gemma's wound. "It's going to be OK, Gemma," I whispered as I swung back towards the battle with the Lycan. I feared The Brethren might attack Caleb or Jax instead of the Lycan, but my fears were erased once I saw Lucas aim his weapon at the beast. They appeared to be working together—vampire and Brethren—instead of battling each other.

Alec dropped to one knee beside me, while Ryan moved forward to challenge the wounded Isaac.

"Alec!" I cried, just as Jax glanced over to see Gemma lying—unmoving—on the hard slab. It was clear that he wanted to be at her side, but the Lycan was still battling strongly, even though it was now severely outnumbered.

"Are you OK?" Alec questioned, holding me at my shoulders with clear concern.

"Yes." I nodded, grateful to see him alive. "But please take Gemma out of here. Help her with this bleeding."

"I will. But I need to get you out of here first."

"No! Please, Alec," I begged, grabbing at his arm. "Help her first!"

From what I knew about Alec, he probably had no interest in helping a vampire coven in any way, but his soft gaze stared at the small Dhampir woman in front of him with startling feeling.

"Gemma, can you hear me?" he asked. "Gemma?"

He picked her up and, pressing the cloth to her head, he carried her a safe distance from the fighting, stopped near a grouping of trees and carefully set her on the grass and applied further pressure to her cut. Then he reached into one of the

satchels they had carried with them and pulled out supplies to
help her.

"Thank you, Alec," I whispered, but was startled by a loud
roar behind me. I swung around just in time to see Isaac's sharp
fangs sinking into Ryan's throat.

"Ryan," I gasped. "Oh, God, no . . ."

It happened so fast. Ryan slumped limply in Isaac's arms just
before the vampire tossed his lifeless body to the ground. There
was no time for me to even process the scene before Isaac
turned and trapped me in his gaze as though I was a deer in a
cage. He moved toward me and grasped me by both shoulders.

"No," was all I could get out before he smashed me against
the concrete, appearing almost crazed as he brought his horrid
face to within inches of mine.

"Nowhere to run, beauty." His ugly eyes shone in triumph.

Yanking me roughly onto my feet, he encircled my waist and
arms while ripping the remaining chain from the foundation
with one hand. "Now you're mine!" he croaked. Complete
revulsion filled me as he licked my cheek, his tongue snaking
out from between his deadly fangs. I tried to pull away but it
was useless. His hold was too strong. Glancing up, I saw
murderous rage in Caleb's eyes, his hand balling into a fist right
before the Lycan's sharp jaws lunged at him again.

Please don't get distracted, Caleb!

"Go!" Jax yelled, slamming forcefully into the Lycan's back.

In the next instant I watched Caleb straddle the Lycan's
body, pulling out one of the arrows lodged in the beast's
shoulder. That caused the vicious animal to swing up with a
howl, as Caleb became a blur and flew straight at us.

As fast as the wave of air hit my skin, Caleb had Isaac on his
back, the bloodied weapon in his hand taking aim at the
vampire's chest. His face was hideously livid—I'd never seen
this part of him before. "You'll never touch her again!" he
snarled, plunging the silver-tipped arrow into Isaac's heart,
freezing the vampire in place.

Then Jax was there, and I turned to see Alec take Jax's place,
along with his Brethren brothers, in fighting the Lycan. "This
one's mine!" Jax snarled, remembering how Isaac had thrown
Gemma against the concrete block.

Within moments, Caleb and Jax had gathered stray pieces of wood and piled them in the center of the field, setting fire to the dry sticks as Jax tossed Isaac's frozen body into the flames.

Caleb turned from the fire to me, his worried, sapphire gaze searching mine as I shakily stood erect once more. That's when I saw the one thing happen that would completely tear my world apart. Davin dropped from above, landing right behind Caleb. The warrior sensed the challenger and spun around quickly, but the devil was ready with a silver tipped arrow in hand and unhesitatingly drove it straight into Caleb's heart. I watched Caleb fall back, stiff, to the ground as the black-eyed vampire kneeled and bent over his fallen body like a conquering force .

"Nooooo!" I screamed.

Davin whispered something in Caleb's ear, and I suddenly remembered what my deplorable captor had promised: that he would taunt Caleb by letting him know, just before he killed him, that I would forever after be under his protection.

"Oh, God, *no!*"

Without thinking, I reached for an arrow from the crossbow Alec had left when he carried Gemma away, positioning it dead center over my heart. Both hands curled tight over the stem as I sank the knife-like tip into my chest.

"Davin!" I screamed.

The vampire turned to see blood rolling over my stomach, his eyes furious once he realized what I was doing.

"You can't have us both," I warned, gasping from the searing pain that only increased as I continued to push the silver tip into my chest, knowing that it would be bearable only if it saved Caleb's life. "You have a choice . . . him, or the weapon for your army."

He didn't hesitate for a second.

He made the right choice!

Davin was on me at the same moment Jax reached Caleb and begun pulling the arrow out of his chest. The young warrior quickly showed signs of life—and fight—but Jax held him against the ground. "Give yourself a moment."

Thank God!

"You stupid child!" Davin barked, distracting me while he

ripped the arrow out of my chest and hurled it away. "Your lack of strength disappoints me."

Suddenly he started to shake. The scent of my blood infusing his nostrils and stirring him into a frenzy of need! And that's what I wanted—a few seconds in which to use my own weapon.

"I don't need strength to hurt you," I screamed, throwing my hands up, the heavy chains following me as I clawed at Davin's temples. Focusing my mind, I let nothing distract me. He tried to push back, but I held on. "There's a reason you had Isaac do all of your dirty work, Davin. You're a *new* vampire. My gift should be even stronger on you."

In agonizing pain, Davin continued to back away, but I wouldn't let go, hanging on for dear life as he fell to the ground. My much smaller body fell on top of him, staying with him in relentless obsession.

"Get off me, you devil!" he shouted, his face twisting as if his mind was in a state of complete torment. I held on for a few moments longer, but somehow he found the strength to throw me off. I was flung high into the air and landed hard on my back almost ten feet away from him, the wind knocked out of me once again. Gasping, I rolled to my side and watched Davin stumble to his feet, still shaking his head and trying to think clearly, just as a silver tipped arrow pierced his chest, barely missing his heart.

"It's Judgment Day, Luther," Alec smiled wickedly, his voice full of loathing for the man who was once his Brethren leader.

Davin, realizing he was defeated, disappeared towards the forest. Alec rushed after him as Lucas and Phin joined the chase. The Lycan they had defeated was crumpled on the ground, lifeless, transformed back into his naked, human form.

The battle was finally over.

"Caleb," I groaned as I tried once again to stand, but I had no strength left and fell back to the ground, blood spilling from my wound as I collapsed on my side.

A rush of cold air blew above me as the sound of an angel called my name. "Olivia! Olivia!" I turned my face upward to see Caleb kneeling beside me, the cut over his heart looking horrid, indeed, but I could see that it was already beginning to heal.

He lifted my bleeding body over his knees, cradling me in his arms. "Dammit, Olivia. Why did you do this? Jax was coming. I would've been all right."

Even as he said the words I could see that something was very wrong. Caleb's powerful body began to shake violently; it appeared as if he was being torn in half. He was becoming frenzied and uncontrolled.

It was the blood—my blood!

Too much sweet wine was pouring from my cut. He couldn't control the overwhelming thirst consuming him. He dropped me out of his arms, sending me back to the ground as he forced himself to crawl away from the blood he so desperately wanted.

I reached for him.

"Olivia, stay back!" Jax ordered. "He is weak. He cannot control it." Jax was also unable to come near me for fear of losing his own control around so much blood, but I didn't listen. Every muscle in my body ached, and the pain in my cut was excruciating, but I could not sit by and watch him struggle like this.

I crawled to him.

"Olivia! Stay back!"

"No, Caleb. Let me help you."

Then, in an abrupt jolt, he snagged his arm around my waist and swung me in front of him, bringing his lethal fangs right to my throat with a fierce growl. I flashed on what he told me the day of our first kiss. He wouldn't be able to stop once he tasted me, but I remained still, unafraid, gazing at him with all the love in my heart, having absolute faith he wouldn't hurt me, that he would never hurt me.

And I was right.

Caleb paused over my throat, every muscle in his body shaking. His lids slammed closed as he raised his chin, the taut muscles of his neck and face straining to what seemed a breaking point. He was in agonizing pain but still trying to regain control as the blood continued to seep over my skin. Worried he wouldn't be able to hold on, I reached my hands up —blood on my fingertips—and pressed them against his temples. He let out a long, rolling growl, his breathing so labored that his chest swelled like a balloon.

"Don't pull away from me, Caleb," I pleaded. "This will help you control your thirst. Let me help you."

As I held on, I watched him struggle, knowing if he hurt me he would never again let himself know peace in his immortal life. So I continued to focus, to fight for him. All the love I had in my heart became vibrating energy through my fingertips, and he accepted my gift freely.

After a few moments his breathing finally began to calm and I found his still-blue eyes with mine. But now I could see something within him that had never been there before . . . a light, a measurable brightness coming from deep inside him. A light so beautiful that I wasn't quite sure it was real, that I could trust the truth it was trying to convey.

And then I knew—I knew everything I needed to know. "Do you see what's happening, Caleb? I am a mirror. I can only reflect your true nature." Happy tears began to fall over my cheeks. "And your reflection is beautiful." His features softened and his eyes reverted as I watched them change to the beautiful gray tones of Caleb, the man.

I could then see clearly that he, too, knew. Gray eyes were now looking back at me, into me, filled with love and wonder.

"Don't you see?" I continued. "You're in control . . . even though I'm bleeding. I can only calm you if your nature is good." I removed my fingers from his temples, smiling up at him through tears. "The warrior doesn't need to fight for redemption any longer, Caleb. Redemption has found you."

Everything he felt for me at that moment was brilliantly reflecting back to me in those two brilliant pools of gray. Though his love might still be trapped in an illusion, I would take it gladly, wanting to stay here with him for just a little while longer.

He curled his arms around me, protectively cradling me against his body. Ripping away his shirtsleeve, he balled up the fabric and pressed it over my cut.

Grimacing at the pain I tried to pull away from him, but he held me still, refusing to let go. "You can never hurt yourself like this again," he said. "Illusion or not, I cannot bear it."

"I'll be—"

"Don't say it," he interjected. "Please, I beg of you . . . do not say you'll be all right."

The heavy weight I had placed over his heart was there in his face as he reached for my hand and the shackle around my wrist, but I pulled the clamoring chains away.

His brows furrowed at me in confusion.

"I wanted to help you control your thirst, Caleb, but you can't keep touching my skin. It will only make it harder for you to stop loving me."

His expression was a mix of surprise and anger. "I won't leave you in chains, Olivia."

He reached for my hand again, bringing it towards him gently. In one swift motion, he broke the heavy shackle from my wrist. The air hit my swollen and bloodied skin, causing waves of pain. I hissed in response to the added pain as he removed the second shackle and the last of the horrid metal clinked to the ground below.

Shaking his head, he said, "This can't be what you want for your life—to be used as bait like an animal. I don't want this for you."

I stared up at him sadly. "What I wanted for my life isn't possible for me anymore."

He slid his eyes away, looking as if he was considering something, then returned his gaze to me. "I love you, Olivia. I want you to know that. I want to be the man to shelter you, protect you—love only you. But you deserve that love without doubt, without hesitation." His features twisted from the conflict raging inside him. "I can't give you that right now. I need time to know if this is—"

"Something real?" I finished for him. He stared at me and the entire world around us seemed to disappear. "I understand." My sad voice broke. "I don't want you to be trapped by my illusion. I'd rather you found real love with someone else."

"I don't want it with someone else," he growled. "I want love with you!"

Even though everything he said was perfect, I understood that it was not likely he would come back to me once the illusion wore off. But understanding it and accepting it were two completely different things.

"Olivia," his deep voice rasped. "I need you to make me a

promise. You must keep yourself safe. You must do whatever you have to. Do you understand me? Lock yourself in that damn church if it'll keep you safe. Please! Promise me!"

I touched my fingers over his jaw and smiled. "I will keep myself safe, Caleb."

Relief seemed to wash though him as I dared myself to ask the one question I wanted answered most. " . . . And if by some chance this is real?"

A small smile pursed his lips, his eyes glimmering with a calm resolve. "Then I'll be back for you, Olivia Ann Greyson. And nothing on this earth will ever keep me from your side again. You will choose the life you want. No being—no Brethren—will choose it for you."

My heart jumped at his declaration as Caleb's focus shifted above us. Footsteps approached, and I turned to see Alec staring down at me. Though weary, his stance was proud, his shoulders high as Lucas and Phin flanked him on each side. The battle was now over and The Brethren were back—for me.

Jax stood off in the distance with Gemma, who was now conscious and cradled easily in his large arms. Her head was wrapped tight, the bleeding slowed, and I knew the older vampire would never hurt her, no matter how much blood she spilled. They both stared at Caleb and me in utter amazement, witnesses to the blood thirst miracle that just happened on the field.

Caleb rose smoothly to his feet, with me in his arms, glaring at Alec as the flames engulfing Isaac's body cast a fired glow over the Daywalker's bewitching face.

While I continued to be lost in this man I loved, a long, warm coat was draped around my cold body. Alec tucked his arms under my back and legs, removing me from the comfortable arms I rested in, and brought me into his, but my gaze remained on Caleb.

"Davin?" Caleb questioned hard.

"We'll find him and take care of him," Alec replied.

Anxiety rose within me as I realized that the black-eyed demon was still out there somewhere. I understood that one day he would return for me, the need for his weapon too great.

"And if you don't, I will," Caleb assured, looking right at me.

Alec ignored him, then wiggled me in his arms a little bit, calling my attention back to him. "Are you OK, Olivia? We have supplies here to clean and stitch up your wound."

I frowned up at him with tired eyes. "I'll be all right."

Turning back to Caleb, I saw that he was shaking his head as if he was in on a private joke.

"Thank you for helping us get her back safe," Alec began. "But she's my responsibility now."

Caleb balled his hands into tight fist at his sides. "You *will* keep her safe this time," he warned, " . . . or you and your Brethren will answer to me."

Alec scowled. "I promised Olivia I wouldn't be back to bother your coven. Don't make me break that promise with idle threats, vampire."

The two warriors were now standing their ground, neither of them backing down even an inch.

"Please, don't," I pleaded, my higher-pitched voice matching my eyes . . . tired.

"Come, Caleb," Jax called to the rigid figure in front of him. "It is time for us to go." Then the coven leader looked at me for a moment before adding, " . . . for now."

"Thank you for coming for me," I whispered, my heart still trying to absorb the pain of losing what I had come to think of as my family.

Gemma's face went slack against Jax's shoulder. "I want her to stay, Jax," she whimpered; then she buried her head in his shirt and began to cry softly.

"I know, angel," his low voice soothed, "I know."

Caleb's pained eyes finally broke contact with mine as he turned and walked towards his coven family.

And just like that . . . I watched him walk away from me for the last time.

My heart once again left with him, hoping that some day he might bring it back to me.

Chapter Twenty-Five

Except for watching Caleb disappear into the forest with Jax and Gemma, I remember very little else about the day that followed. I suppose my last lucid moment was when I curled up into the warmth of the long coat Alec provided while he carried me, all the while thinking about the words Caleb had uttered that so stirred my heart.

"Then I'll be back for you . . ."

When I awoke I was back in the small room in the church, and the comforting scent of vanilla bean was rising from a flickering candle on the bedside table. My eyes began to focus, and I could see Alec leaning back in his chair, which he had placed against the door of the tiny room. He met my gaze with a faint smile, his prominent dimple firmly denting his chin.

I stirred restlessly beneath the covers, then tossed them aside.

The Guardian laughed. "So now you're too warm. Women. They can never make up their minds."

"Can I have some water?" I asked. My throat was painfully dry, making my voice scratchy.

He nodded. "On the table, there beside you."

I sat up on the cot and took a long sip. "How long have I been asleep?"

Alec rocked forward, rose to his feet and moved his chair beside the cot. Taking my hand in his, he squeezed, his features relaxed. "It took us the better part of a day to get you stitched up and back down to the vehicles. You were pretty much out of it most of the way. Since we brought you back here, you've been in and out of sleep for about a day. But you seem brighter and more awake now."

"I am."

His words, though, only made me think of one thing: that

Caleb had been unable to sense me for a day. Knowing that he still cared for me, at least for now, anyway, he would be worried when he couldn't sense me, and I wanted him to know that I was all right.

"Thank you for coming to get me, Alec. I know I didn't deserve it after the way I behaved."

He cocked his brow in surprise. "I'll always come for you. That's my job as your Guardian. I know you didn't mean to put yourself in danger . . ." He brushed his fingers lightly over my wrists where the metal shackle had cut me but were nearly healed. " . . . but I think that finally you understand the risks."

"I do. I hate to think what would've happened if you all hadn't shown up."

"Luckily, you don't have to. And as much as I hate to admit it, I know we wouldn't have succeeded without the help of the vampire."

My heart skipped several beats as I smiled to myself. "Yes, I was more than a little surprised to see you working together. How did that happen?"

"Yeah well, not long after our little confrontation in the meadow, Caleb evidently sensed that Isaac was near. And like a stubborn bull, he followed after us to demand that you be placed back under his protection. He, the other brooding vampire, and the Dhampir, Gemma, had tracked your scent and showed up at the roadside not long after Isaac and Davin took off with you. Together we fought off Davin's army, but we lost precious time in following after you."

I was grateful that Caleb, Jax and Gemma had not just left The Brethren men there to fight on their own. In fact, they had more than likely saved their lives, which made me smile. Of course, Caleb would save them. That's who he was.

"Caleb?" Alec paused, " . . . that's his name, right?"

I nodded.

"He put everything together with Davin. He was fuming mad that we had let this happen within hours of your leaving his protection . . . as he should've been. But he knew that together, with our knowledge of Davin and his ability to track you," he rolled his eyes at the thought, "we stood a better chance of getting to you before it was too late."

Alec shook his head with a snort. "He is an ill-tempered creature, though, Olivia. He did nothing but spout curse words and pound his fist through solid objects every time he felt Isaac choke you with the chloroform. And I thought we were going to have to stake him to get him to calm down after he felt the pain in your cheek. He just knew that Isaac had hit you, and he kept cursing the rest of the way over, growling like a lion that Isaac was his to take care of."

"Alec! You wouldn't really stake him, would you?"

"Maybe," he laughed, with a wink.

I could tell, though, that there was still no love lost between the two men, but they had seemed to find a common ground—me—even if it was only temporary.

Alec touched the cheek where Isaac had hit me, but I felt no pain. The bruised and swollen skin, like all my other injuries, was healed. "I'm sorry they hurt you. This is my fault. I need to do a better job of protecting you."

I squeezed his hand. "It's not your fault, Alec. It's mine. I'm the one who behaved like a child, throwing a tantrum and putting all of your lives at risk."

Just then my mind jumped back to the moment in the battle when Ryan realized that Isaac had him—the look of complete surprise on his face. In a way it was so different from Sarah, and yet just the same. "Ryan lost his life because I refused to listen. And now I'll never be able to repay that debt."

He pulled me into his shoulder and stroked my hair. "Ryan was a good man. But he knew the risk, and he believed in what he was doing. He wouldn't have changed that."

"I don't want anyone to die protecting me. I'm not worth it."

Alec pulled back from me, jarring me a bit with the quickness of it. His face was contorted into a deep frown that caught me off guard. "We're going to have to work on that."

"On what?"

"You—understanding your importance. You *are* worth it," he said with a sigh. "Look, Caleb and his entire coven found out the truth of your gifts, but still they came after you the second he sensed you were in the slightest danger. He tracked you over water. Quite honestly, I think he could track you over an entire ocean."

"You almost sound impressed."

"Don't get me wrong. I couldn't care less if I ever cross paths with that cranky vampire again. And I'm sure he will forget you as soon as your hold over him lessens, but I'm grateful to him for helping get you back."

My heart broke a little more as I once again became mired in the awful thought that every passing minute of my life was like the loud ticking of a clock. Each tick represented one moment closer to when Caleb's affection for me would disappear completely, and the thought of it hurt me beyond words.

"At least the vampire . . ." Alec started, then stopped as he saw my frown. "Caleb," he corrected . . ."At least Caleb kept his word and returned you to us."

"I know you don't want to hear this, Alec, but it's the truth. You're both very similar—warriors with honor."

That caused the Guardian to scowl even harder. "You're right. I didn't want to hear that."

"Where's Gideon?" I laughed, surprised he was not already here hovering over me.

"He, Phin and Lucas have returned to The Brethren. He's expecting me to follow in a couple of days—with you, of course."

Dread suddenly gripped the middle of my stomach. I couldn't put off my answer much longer.

"You need to come back with me, Olivia," he said, reading my thoughts perfectly. "It's time for you to begin your training. You must learn how to protect yourself."

I pushed back the covers, swinging my knees over the edge of the cot. "I don't want to be bait, Alec. And I'm not as strong as you think. I wasn't able to fight off Isaac. I couldn't escape the chains I was in. And even Davin cursed my lack of strength."

Alec seemed to be caught off guard, which, for a man trained to always be prepared, probably didn't happen that often. "We don't know what you're capable of yet. That's the whole point of training. So you can understand your abilities—learn to use them to your best advantage. It's not like there's some blueprint for Charmers. You're unique. But we can find the answers together."

There, he did it again. Alec never held anything back, just gave me the simple truth. I was starting to really trust him in that way.

I took another long drink of water and allowed my thoughts once again to return to Caleb. I wondered if his own wound had healed, if he was all right. I knew I couldn't see him, but I thought about how worried he'd been the last time he couldn't feel me, needing to know I was safe. And at that moment I made a decision. It was time to leave the security of sacred ground. "Alec, will you take me home?"

He seemed to mull the idea around in his head for a while before he answered, "You're not as safe there as you are here. But I understand . . . this isn't home for you."

"No, it's not," I replied with a half-hearted smile, but I realized something important just then. For the first time since my parents' death, I wanted to go to their home. No—to my home now. The condo no longer reminded me of their death; rather, it conjured up all the memories of their happy life together. It was an important step for me in truly beginning to heal.

About an hour later we were walking through the front door of the condo—my home. Alec, in true Guardian form, told me to wait in the kitchen while he checked all of the rooms for any signs of danger. I resigned myself to needing to get used to the overprotection and perched myself on a barstool, where he joined me a couple minutes later, sliding onto the other stool in a very comfortable way. "Everything's fine," he announced.

"I see," I replied, smiling as his gaze dropped to my fingers, which were tapping wildly over the island countertop. Immediately, I stopped and curled them into my hand.

"Are you sure you're going to be all right if I leave you here for a bit?" he asked.

"I'll be fine. But . . ." I was about to ask him something, but I hesitated, knowing already that he wasn't going to like it.

"What is it?"

"How long does it take for someone to move on from the illusion?"

Unexpectedly, his lips twitched in a half smile, half frown. "It depends on the amount of exposure, I guess. For example, with Caleb . . . who you've had a lot of exposure to . . ."—his words held no subtlety, letting me know I was not fooling him in the least as to why I was asking—"it might take a couple of weeks for the effects to burn off."

Startled, I blinked back at him and jumped from the stool. "Weeks?"

Alec sprung to his feet beside me, his face almost as alarmed as my own because he assumed he had just said something to upset me. But it was exactly the opposite.

"Alec, why didn't you tell me this before?"

His eyes widened, staring at me like a boy who was just caught with his hand in the cookie jar. "I told you that the effects would burn off quickly," he defended.

Two weeks! That meant when Caleb brought me back here the first time and I was away from him for a month, he should have been completely over me, but instead he was scouring the city trying to find me.

He loved me!

What he felt was real! And in an instant my heart began pounding so forcefully that I thought the world could hear it, beating so hard I didn't think I could contain it.

Someday Caleb Wolfe would realize it and be back for me, as he promised. I couldn't know how much time would be enough for him to be convinced that what he felt in his heart was real, but some day he would be back, and now I knew what I had to do. "This place you want to take me to train? Will I be safe there? Safe from Davin and his army?"

"Yes," he replied slowly, as if he were questioning whether it was the right answer. "It would actually be the safest place for you."

Literally, I could feel the huge smile that spread over my lips as I hugged him around his shoulders and then kissed him on his cheek. "Alec!" I cheered. "Yes, I'll leave with you to complete my training . . . tomorrow, if you'd like. The sooner the better."

Alec's bewildered expression seemed only to get more tangled up. "What just happened here?"

I laughed. "Never mind. The point is, I'm willing to train. I want to better understand who I am and what my capabilities are—learn how to defend myself. But I won't make The

Brethren any promises for the future. Is that understood?"

"Yes," he answered quickly, still stunned but not wanting to give me any time to change my mind. "I have to get a few things ready. I'll be back for you in the morning. Be packed and ready by eight."

"Ok," I nodded agreeably.

Alec was shaking his head, trying to escape his own befuddlement, as he headed for the door. Just shy of the threshold, he turned and said, "You're doing the right thing."

"I hope so."

He smiled. "Don't open this door to anyone until I return. Clear?"

I saluted him with a stiff hand. "Clear. Vampires must be invited in. Got it."

He was still shaking his head as he left. "Women," he muttered under his breath as the door closed behind him.

Now alone with my excitement, I threw my head back and flung my arms out, stretching them as far as I could. Taking a deep breath, I hoped Caleb could feel that I was no longer in pain, that there was joy once again in my heart. I didn't want him to worry about me while I was gone. Unfortunately, I could do nothing to help him with his own feelings until he realized he truly did love me. Maybe, somehow, if he knew I was all right, it would help him for now.

I jumped into the oversized lounge chair by the fireplace, kicked my feet over the rounded arm, and squealed with delight. To no one in particular, but loudly, I shouted, "He loves me!"

For that reason alone, I knew I had to go with Alec. Caleb had said that when he came back for me he would let me choose the life I wanted for myself, and without question I wanted to be with him—to live with him, Jax and Gemma in the tree house. But I didn't want to be a constant burden, always putting their immortal—but not impenetrable—lives at risk from other vampires who would be drawn to me. I needed to learn how to defend myself, or better yet, how to control my gifts. If I worked hard and increased my strength, learned how to use my gifts, then I could return to him.

Hopefully, he would still want me.

Just then, I noticed something unusual out of the corner of my eye. A piece of linen drapery floated on a breeze. One of the tall retracting doors to the patio was open a couple of inches, allowing cool air to come in from the outside. The draping ivory was sucked out of the small opening and into the night. Had Alec left the door open when he checked the area?

My heart sped up and my breath sort of stuck in my throat. Had we missed something? Was Davin closer than I thought? I didn't sense anything, and the pull inside my chest had been absent since we left the island.

Coming to my feet, I walked towards the door, seeing light filtering in through the drapes from outside. Opening the tall door, I gasped in stunned amazement as the patio widened in front of me. "Caleb!" I whispered in stunned amazement. The once empty outdoor space was now filled with a spectacular atrium, fully enclosed in glass. It was the very same atrium I had seen sketched on the wall in Caleb's study. Each of the tall, glass side panels was opened to a forty-five degree angle to welcome in the warm night air and twinkling city lights beyond.

The spectacular glass house was dressed at the corners in thick velvet drapes in a most luxurious and warm ivory color, adding softness to the hard, transparent walls. Hundreds of sparkling white lights were laced across the glass ceiling, reflecting on the shiny object centered in the space—a grand piano.

Only it wasn't just any grand, it was the Fazioli from the tree house. I crossed my hands over my heart when I saw the unrepaired scratches on the Plexiglas base. The gift was flawed but absolutely perfect. There would never be another piano in the world for me in my lifetime. This piano was where Caleb had first kissed me, then claimed my heart and soul, releasing a passion inside me I never knew existed.

"How did he do this?" I said to myself, out loud. Stepping through one of the open glass panels, I ran my fingers over the smooth piano case, reflections of the small lights from above sparkling from its glossy, black surface. Then I recalled the two days when he and Jax were gone from the Tree House. This was his project—the work that I resented because it took him away from me. It was all for me!

Scanning the view from the new reincarnation of my parents' favorite terrace, I remembered what Caleb had said the first time I played for him. "You should play somewhere that the whole city of Seattle can hear you."

He wanted me to play for the city, and right now I couldn't think of anything I wanted to do more. I sat down purposefully on the bench. Then I noticed the single, long-stemmed, white rose he had left for me on the keyboard. I picked up the fragile, freshly-cut flower, smelling the sweet fragrance from the just-opened bloom.

He had just been here. I just knew it!

I made another quick visual sweep of my patio itself and the nearby buildings, but didn't see him. Setting the flower in my lap, I poised my fingers over the keys and began playing an improvised andante movement with supreme confidence.

I had no sheet music. Instead, I had begun playing a composition that had been rolling around inside my head over the last couple of months. In these precious moments I would deliver it to the world through the tips of my fingers. Closing my eyes, I listened to the melody and harmonies as they vibrated from the Fazioli's wonderful strings—the sounds so clear, so vivid, it seemed I was hearing my own playing for the very first time. The high, bright chords emanating from the piano but coming from within my heart, resonating for him— only him—had been created in lovely little pieces over the time I had been with him, awakening my soul to real love.

There was absolutely no hesitation in my fingers as the variations on my theme grew in strength and increased in complexity, changing their rhythms to match my soaring heart's journey. I could see the music, feel it flowing effortlessly from my heart to my mind to my fingers, then to the keys, and finally expressed in lovely, harmonies by the strings—and it was perfect. Then, in the midst of a seriously slow largo passage that was literally writing itself as I played, note after note parading in the air high above the city, the tranquility of it all was interrupted by a familiar, pulling sensation over my heart. My breath caught and I smiled as I continued to play, feverishly now, as though projecting the triumphal sound to wake the rest of the sleeping city. He was here! Caleb was here!

Then, just as in the forest when he came to save me, I could see him clearly in my mind when I closed my eyes. He kept his distance on a nearby rooftop, gazing down at me as I played. The light of the almost-full moon washed over his relaxed face as his deep, strong breathing rose and fell in his chest with ease. He was feeling the music, inhaling it, and it was giving him pleasure.

And it should, because this was all for him.

This moment was for him.

I continued to let the joyful noise pour from deep within my soul, wanting to give him more . . . as much as I could. Then it hit me like a giant wave as tears of joy began to fall over my cheeks.

This was something real!

The music that I loved was a vital part of me that I could give freely to him, and it had nothing to do with my calling, The Brethren, or my mother's gifts that might well be meant to trap him. It was a real part of the woman underneath that he could see—that he believed in—and so it had been since the beginning.

As the melody moved into and through his powerful body, peace and contentment filled his beautiful shades of gray. I understood now that no one could ever take this moment away from us, and I pushed myself even harder. My gift had returned to me, granting me freedom, a complete absence of fear and hesitation, a self-contained power that was totally liberating, and it was possible only because of the vampire who never lost his faith that I would find mine again—and I had!

Beneath the blanket of the starry skies and the diffuse light of the moon, I continued to play for him, every note reminding the man, the vampire, and the warrior how much I truly, deeply, loved him, and letting him know that I would continue to live in the complete faith that some day he would find his way back to me.

But tonight I would play.

Acknowledgments

A huge, heartfelt thanks to my editor, Paul, who slipped into my second voice so effortlessly and guided me through every step of the process.

And for Samantha, who designed a cover that matched the vision that inspired the book.

About the Author

The Charmed is Christine's debut novel and every page is a true labor of love, reflecting the literary daydreamer she has become. She lives in the scenic Pacific Northwest, where she enjoys hiking, camping, and photographing many of the wonderful places that served as inspiration for her *Charmed* Trilogy . . . especially on a cold, rainy day.

3452966R00165

Made in the USA
San Bernardino, CA
02 August 2013